The Little Lame Prince

How terribly sad life must have been for the little lame prince confined high up in a lonely tower on a barren plain with only a nurse to take care of him!

When his father and mother, the King and Queen, died, a wicked uncle who wanted the throne for himself banished the young prince from the kingdom. For many years, Prince Dolor's only occupations were books and toys.

But one day, when it seemed that the prince no longer could bear his solitude, his kind and gentle fairy godmother appeared, bringing him a magical traveling cloak. With the aid of this miraculous gift, Prince Dolor floated through the air at will, and saw much of the world to both gladden and sadden him.

This classic tale of the lonely little boy who found happiness and became the wise and beloved king of Nomansland is touching and unforgettable.

BY DINAH MARIA MULOCK CRAIK

The Little Lame Prince

ILLUSTRATIONS BY
EARL MAYAN

Companion Library
Grosset & Dunlap

PUBLISHERS NEW YORK

Author's Note

If any reader, big or little, should wonder whether there is a meaning in this story deeper than that of an ordinary fairy tale, I will own that there is. But I have hidden it so carefully that the smaller people, and many larger folk, will never find it out, and meantime the book may be read straight on . . . for whatever interest or what amusement it may bring.

ILLUSTRATIONS

The Little Lame Prince

CHAPTER 1

~~~~~~
~~~~~~

YES, HE WAS the most beautiful Prince that ever was born.

Of course, being a prince, people said this; but it was true besides. When he looked at the candle, his eyes had an expression of earnest inquiry quite startling in a newborn baby. His nose—there was not much of it certainly, but what there was seemed an aquiline shape. His complexion was a charming, healthy purple. He was round and fat, straight-limbed and long—in fact, a splendid baby. Everybody was exceedingly proud of him, especially his father and mother, the King and Queen of Nomansland, who had waited for him during their happy reign of ten years—now made happier than ever to themselves and their subjects, by the appearance of a son and heir.

He was the most beautiful prince ever born

The Little Lame Prince

The only person who was not quite happy was the King's brother, the heir presumptive, who would have been king one day had the baby not been born. But as his Majesty was very kind to him, and even rather sorry for him—insomuch that at the Queen's request he gave him a dukedom almost as big as a county—the Crown Prince, as he was called, tried to seem pleased also; and let us hope he succeeded.

The Prince's christening was to be a grand affair. According to the custom of the country, there were chosen for him four-and-twenty godfathers and godmothers, who each had to give him a name, and promise to do their utmost for him. When he came of age, he himself had to choose the name—and the godfather or godmother—that he liked the best, for the rest of his days.

Meantime all was rejoicing. Subscriptions were made among the rich to give pleasure to the poor; dinners in town halls for the working-men; tea parties in the streets for their wives; and milk-and-bun feasts for the children in the schoolrooms. For Nomansland, though I cannot point it out on any map or read of it in any history, was, I believe, much like our own or many another country.

As for the palace—which was no different

from other palaces—it was clean "turned out of the windows," as people say, with the preparations going on. The only quiet place in it was the room which, though the Prince was six weeks old, his mother the Queen had never quitted. Nobody said she was ill, however—it would have been so inconvenient. And as she said nothing about it herself, but lay pale and placid, giving no trouble to anybody, nobody thought much about her. All the world was absorbed in admiring the baby.

The christening day came at last, and it was as lovely as the Prince himself. All the people in the palace were lovely too—or thought themselves so—in the elegant new clothes which the Queen, who thought of everybody, had taken care to give them, from the ladies-in-waiting down to the poor little kitchenmaid, who looked at herself in her pink cotton gown and thought, doubtless, that there never was such a pretty girl as she.

By six in the morning all the royal household had dressed itself in its very best. And then the little Prince was dressed in his best—his magnificent christening robe; which proceeding his Royal Highness did not like at all, but kicked and screamed like any common baby. When he had calmed down a little, they carried him to be

looked at by the Queen his mother, who, though her royal robes had been brought and laid upon the bed, was, as everybody well knew, quite unable to rise and put them on.

She admired her baby very much; kissed and blessed him, and lay looking at him, as she did for hours sometimes, when he was placed beside her fast asleep. Then she gave him up with a gentle smile, and, saying she hoped he would be very good, that it would be a very nice christening, and all the guests would enjoy themselves, turned peacefully over on her bed, saying nothing more to anybody. She was a very uncomplaining person, the Queen—and her name was Dolorez.

Everything went on exactly as if she had been present. All, even the King himself, had grown used to her absence; for she was not strong, and for years had not joined in any gaieties. She always did her royal duties, but as to pleasures, they could go on quite well without her, or it seemed so. The company arrived: great and notable persons in this and neighboring countries; also the four-and-twenty godfathers and godmothers, who had been chosen with care, as the people who would be most useful to his Royal Highness should he ever want friends, which did not seem likely. What such want

could possibly happen to the heir of the powerful monarch of Nomansland?

They came, walking two and two, with their coronets on their heads—being dukes and duchesses, princes and princesses, or the like. They all kissed the child and pronounced the name each had given him. Then the four-and-twenty names were shouted out with great energy by

six heralds, one after the other, and afterward written down, to be preserved in the state records, in readiness for the next time they were wanted, which would be either on his Royal Highness's coronation or his funeral.

Soon the ceremony was over, and everybody satisfied; except, perhaps, the little Prince him-

self, who moaned faintly under his christening robes, which nearly smothered him.

In truth, though very few knew, the Prince in coming to the chapel had met with a slight disaster. His nurse—not his ordinary one, but the state nursemaid—an elegant and fashionable young lady of rank, whose duty it was to carry him to and from the chapel, had been so occupied in arranging her train with one hand, while she held the baby with the other, that she stumbled and let him fall, just at the foot of the marble staircase.

To be sure, she contrived to pick him up again the next minute; and the accident was so slight it seemed hardly worth speaking of. Consequently nobody did speak of it. The baby had turned deadly pale but did not cry, so no person a step or two behind could discover anything wrong. Afterward, even if he had moaned, the silver trumpets were loud enough to drown his voice. It would have been a pity to let anything trouble such a day of felicity.

So, after a minute's pause, the procession had moved on. Such a procession! Heralds in blue and silver; pages in crimson and gold; and a troop of little girls in dazzling white, carrying baskets of flowers, which they strewed all the way before the nurse and child. Finally the

four-and-twenty godfathers and godmothers, as proud as possible, and so splendid to look at that they would have quite extinguished their small godson—merely a heap of lace and muslin with a baby face inside—had it not been for a canopy of white satin and ostrich feathers which was held over him wherever he was carried.

Thus, with the sun shining on them through the painted windows, they stood; the King and his train on one side, the Prince and his attendants on the other, as pretty a sight as ever was seen out of fairyland.

"It's just like fairyland," whispered the eldest little girl to the next eldest, as she shook the last rose out of her basket; "and I think the only thing the Prince wants now is a fairy godmother."

"Does he?" said a shrill but soft and not unpleasant voice behind; and there was seen among the group of children somebody—not a child, yet no bigger than a child—somebody whom nobody had seen before, and who certainly had not been invited, for she had no christening clothes on.

She was a little old woman dressed all in gray: gray gown; gray hooded cloak, of a material excessively fine, and a tint that seemed perpetually changing, like the gray of an evening sky.

Her hair was gray, and her eyes also—even her complexion had a soft gray shadow over it. But there was nothing unpleasantly old about her, and her smile was as sweet and childlike as the Prince's own, which stole over his pale little face the instant she came near enough to touch him.

"Take care! Don't let the baby fall again."

The grand young lady nurse started, flushing angrily.

"Who spoke to me? How did anybody know?—I mean, what business has anybody—" Then, frightened, but still speaking in a much sharper tone than I hope young ladies of rank are in the habit of speaking—"Old woman, you will be kind enough not to say 'the baby,' but 'the Prince.' Keep away; his Royal Highness is just going to sleep."

"Nevertheless I must kiss him. I am his god-mother."

"You!" cried the elegant lady nurse.

"You!" repeated all the gentlemen- and ladies-in-waiting.

"You!!!" echoed the heralds and pages—and they began to blow the silver trumpets in order to stop all further conversation.

The Prince's procession formed itself for returning—the King and his train having already moved off toward the palace—but on the top-

most step of the marble stairs stood, right in front of all, the little old woman clothed in gray.

She stretched herself on tiptoe by the help of her stick, and gave the little Prince three kisses.

"This is intolerable!" cried the young lady nurse, wiping the kisses off rapidly with her lace handkerchief. "Such an insult to his Royal Highness! Take yourself out of the way, old woman, or the King shall be informed immediately."

"The King knows nothing of me, more's the pity," replied the old woman, with an indifferent air, as if she thought the loss was more on his Majesty's side than hers. "My friend in the palace is the King's wife."

"Kings have not wives, but queens," said the lady nurse, with a contemptuous air.

"You are right," replied the old woman. "Nevertheless, I know her Majesty well, and I love her and her child. And—since you dropped him on the marble stairs (this she said in a mysterious whisper, which made the young lady tremble in spite of her anger) —I choose to take him for my own, and be his godmother, ready to help him whenever he wants me."

"You help him!" cried all the group, breaking into shouts of laughter, to which the little

The Little Lame Prince

old woman paid not the slightest attention. Her soft gray eyes were fixed on the Prince, who seemed to answer to the look, smiling again and again in the causeless, aimless fashion that babies do smile.

"His Majesty must hear of this," said a gentleman-in-waiting.

"His Majesty will hear quite enough news in a minute or two," said the old woman sadly. And again stretching up to the little Prince, she kissed him on the forehead solemnly.

"Be called by a new name which nobody has ever thought of. Be Prince Dolor, in memory of your mother Dolorez."

"In memory of!" Everybody started at the ominous phrase, and also at a most terrible breach of etiquette which the old woman had committed. In Nomansland, neither the King nor the Queen was supposed to have any Christian name at all. They dropped it on their coronation day, and it never was mentioned again till it was engraved on their coffins when they died.

"Old woman, you are exceedingly ill-bred," cried the eldest lady-in-waiting, much horrified. "How you could know the fact passes my comprehension. But even if you did know it, how

[22]

dared you presume to hint that her most gracious Majesty is called Dolorez?"

"*Was* called Dolorez," said the old woman, with a tender solemnity.

The first gentleman, called the Gold-stick-in-waiting, raised it to strike her, and all the rest stretched out their hands to seize her; but the gray mantle melted from between their fingers like air. And, before anybody had time to do anything more, there came a heavy, muffled, startling sound.

The great bell of the palace—the bell which was heard only on the death of someone of the royal family, and for as many times as he or she was years old—began to toll. They listened, mute and horror-stricken. Someone counted: one—two—three—four—on up to nine-and-twenty—just the Queen's age.

It was, indeed, the Queen. Her Majesty was dead! In the midst of the festivities she had slipped away out of her new happiness and her old sufferings, not few nor small. Sending away all her women to see the grand sight—at least they said afterward, in excuse, that she had done so, and it was very like her to do it—she had turned with her face to the window, whence one could just see the tops of the distant moun-

tains—the Beautiful Mountains, as they were called—where she was born. So gazing, she had quietly passed away.

When the little Prince was carried back to his mother's room, there was no mother to kiss him. And, though he did not know it, there would be for him no mother's kiss any more.

As for his godmother—the little old woman in gray who called herself so—whether she melted into air, like her gown when they touched it, or whether she flew out the chapel window, or slipped through the doorway among the bewildered crowd, nobody knew—nobody ever thought about her.

Only the nurse, the ordinary homely one, coming out of the Prince's nursery in the middle of the night in search of a cordial to quiet his continual moans, saw, sitting in the doorway, something which she would have thought a mere shadow had she not seen shining out of it two eyes, gray and soft and sweet. She put her hands before her own, screaming loudly. When she took them away the old woman was gone.

CHAPTER 2

EVERYBODY WAS VERY KIND to the poor little
Prince. I think people generally are kind
to motherless children, whether princes or peasants. He had a magnificent nursery and a regular suite of attendants, and was treated with the
greatest respect and state. Nobody was allowed
to talk to him in silly baby language, or dandle
him, or above all to kiss him, though perhaps
some people did it surreptitiously, for he was
such a sweet baby that it was difficult to help it.

It could not be said that the Prince missed his
mother—children of his age cannot do that; but
somehow after she died everything seemed to go
wrong with him. From a beautiful baby he
became sickly and pale, seeming to have almost
ceased growing, especially in his legs, which had
been so fat and strong.

But after the day of his christening they with-
ered and shrank. He no longer kicked them

out in either passion or play, and when, as he got to be nearly a year old, his nurse tried to make him stand upon them, he only tumbled down.

This happened so many times that at last people began to talk about it. A prince, and not able to stand on his own legs! What a dreadful thing! What a misfortune for the country!

Rather a misfortune to him also, poor little boy! but nobody seemed to think of that. And when, after a while, his health revived, and the old bright look came back to his sweet little face, and his body grew larger and stronger, though still his legs remained the same, people continued to speak of him in whispers, and with grave shakes of the head. Everybody knew, though nobody said it, that something, it was impossible to guess what, was not quite right with the poor little Prince.

Of course, nobody hinted this to the King his father. It does not do to tell great people anything unpleasant. And besides, his Majesty took very little notice of his son, or of his other affairs, beyond the necessary duties of his kingdom.

People had said he would not miss the Queen at all, she having been so long an invalid, but he did. After her death he never was quite the

same. He established himself in her empty rooms, the only rooms in the palace whence one could see the Beautiful Mountains, and was often observed looking at them as if he thought she had flown away thither, and that his longing could bring her back again. And by a curious coincidence, which nobody dared inquire into, he desired that the Prince might be called, not by any of the four-and-twenty grand names given him by his godfathers and godmothers, but by the identical name mentioned by the little old woman in gray—Dolor, after his mother Dolorez.

Once a week, according to established state custom, the Prince, dressed in his very best, was brought to the King his father for half an hour, but his Majesty was generally too ill and too melancholy to pay much heed to the child.

Only once, when he and the Crown Prince, who was exceedingly attentive to his royal brother, were sitting together, with Prince Dolor playing in a corner of the room, dragging himself about with his arms rather than his legs, and sometimes trying feebly to crawl from one chair to another, it seemed to strike the father that all was not right with his son.

"How old is his Royal Highness?" said he suddenly to the nurse.

"Two years, three months, and five days, please your Majesty."

"It does not please me," said the King, with a sigh. "He ought to be far more forward than he is now—ought he not, brother? You, who have so many children, must know. Is there not something wrong about him?"

"Oh, no," said the Crown Prince, exchanging meaning looks with the nurse, who did not understand at all, but stood frightened and trembling with the tears in her eyes. "Nothing to make your Majesty at all uneasy. No doubt his Royal Highness will outgrow it in time."

"Outgrow—what?"

"A slight delicacy—ahem!—in the spine; something inherited, perhaps, from his dear mother."

"Ah, she was always delicate; but she was the sweetest woman that ever lived. Come here, my little son."

And as the Prince turned round upon his father a small, sweet, grave face—so like his mother's—his Majesty the King smiled and held out his arms. But when the boy came to him, not running like a boy, but wriggling awkwardly along the floor, the royal countenance clouded over.

"I ought to have been told of this. It is ter-

rible—terrible! And for a prince too. Send for all the doctors in my kingdom immediately."

They came, and each gave a different opinion and ordered a different mode of treatment. The only thing they agreed in was what had been pretty well known before, that the Prince must have been hurt when he was an infant—let fall, perhaps, so as to injure his spine and lower limbs. Did nobody remember?

No, nobody. Indignantly, all the nurses denied that any such accident had happened, was possible to have happened, until the faithful country nurse recollected that it really had happened on the day of the christening. For which unluckily good memory all the others scolded her so severely that she had no peace of her life, and soon after, by the influence of the young lady nurse who had carried the baby that fatal day, and who was a sort of connection of the Crown Prince—being his wife's second cousin once removed—the poor woman was pensioned off and sent to the Beautiful Mountains from whence she came, with orders to remain there for the rest of her days.

But of all this the King knew nothing, for, indeed, after the first shock of finding out that his son could not walk, and seemed never likely

to walk, he interfered very little concerning him. The whole thing was too painful, and his Majesty never liked painful things. Sometimes he inquired after Prince Dolor, and they told him his Royal Highness was going on as well as could be expected, which really was the case. For, after worrying the poor child and perplexing themselves with one remedy after another, the Crown Prince, not wishing to offend any of the differing doctors, had proposed leaving him to Nature; and Nature, the safest doctor of all, had come to his help and done her best.

He could not walk, it is true. His limbs were mere useless appendages to his body; but the body itself was strong and sound. And his face was the same as ever—just his mother's face, one of the sweetest in the world.

Even the King, indifferent as he was, sometimes looked at the little fellow with sad tenderness, noticing how cleverly he learned to crawl and swing himself about by his arms, so that in his own awkward way he was as active in motion as most children of his age.

"Poor little man! he does his best, and he is not unhappy—not half so unhappy as I, brother," addressing the Crown Prince, who was more constant than ever in his attendance upon the sick monarch. "If anything should

befall me, I have appointed you Regent. In case of my death, you will take care of my poor little boy?"

"Certainly, certainly; but do not let us imagine any such misfortune. I assure your Majesty—everybody will assure you—that it is not in the least likely."

He knew, however, and everybody knew, that it was likely, and soon after it actually did happen. The King died as suddenly and quietly as the Queen had done—indeed, in her very room and bed; and Prince Dolor was left without either father or mother—as sad a thing as could happen, even to a prince.

He was more than that now, though. He was a king. In Nomansland, as in other countries, the people were struck with grief one day and revived the next. "The King is dead—long live the King!" was the cry that rang through the nation, and almost before his late Majesty had been laid beside the Queen in their splendid mausoleum, crowds came thronging from all parts to the royal palace, eager to see the new monarch.

They did see him—the Prince Regent took care they should—sitting on the floor of the council chamber, sucking his thumb! And when one of the gentlemen-in-waiting lifted

him up and carried him—fancy carrying a king!—to the chair of state, and put the crown on his head, he shook it off again, it was so heavy and uncomfortable. Sliding down to the foot of the throne he began playing with the golden lions that supported it, stroking their paws and putting his tiny fingers into their eyes, and laughing—laughing as if he had at last found something to amuse him.

"There's a fine king for you!" said the first lord-in-waiting, a friend of the Prince Regent's (the Crown Prince that used to be, who, in the deepest mourning, stood silently beside the throne of his young nephew; he was a handsome man, very grand and clever-looking). "What a king! who can never stand to receive his subjects, never walk in processions, who to the last day of his life will have to be carried about like a baby. Very unfortunate!"

"Exceedingly unfortunate," repeated the second lord. "It is always bad for a nation when its king is a child; but such a child—a permanent cripple, if not worse."

"Let us hope not worse," said the first lord in a very hopeless tone, and looking toward the Regent, who stood erect and pretended to hear nothing. "I have heard that these children with very large heads, and great broad foreheads

and staring eyes, are—well, well, let us hope for the best and be prepared for the worst. In the meantime—"

"I swear," said the Crown Prince, coming forward and kissing the hilt of his sword—"I swear to perform my duties as Regent, to take all care of his Royal Highness—his Majesty, I mean," with a grand bow to the little child, who laughed innocently back again. "And I will do my humble best to govern the country. Still, if the country has the slightest objection—"

But the Crown Prince being generalissimo, having the whole army at his beck and call, so that he could have begun a civil war in no time, the country had, of course, not the slightest objection.

So the King and Queen slept in their tomb in peace, and Prince Dolor reigned over the land—that is, his uncle did; and everybody said what a fortunate thing it was for the poor little Prince to have such a clever uncle to take care of him.

All things went on as usual. Indeed, after the Regent had brought his wife and her seven sons, and established them in the palace, they went on rather better than usual. For they gave such splendid entertainments and made the capital so lively that trade revived, and the

country was said to be more flourishing than it had been for a century.

Whenever the Regent and his sons appeared, they were received with shouts: "Long live the Crown Prince!" "Long live the royal family!" And, in truth, they were very fine children, the whole seven of them, and made a great show when they rode out together on seven beautiful horses, one height above another, down to the youngest, on his tiny black pony, no bigger than a large dog.

As for the other child, his Royal Highness Prince Dolor—for somehow people soon ceased to call him his Majesty, which seemed such a ridiculous title for a poor little fellow, a helpless cripple—with only head and trunk, and no legs to speak of—he was seen very seldom by anybody.

Sometimes people daring enough to peer over the high wall of the palace garden noticed there, carried in a footman's arms, or drawn in a chair, or left to play on the grass, often with nobody to mind him, a pretty little boy, with a bright, intelligent face and large, melancholy eyes—no, not exactly melancholy, for they were his mother's, and she was by no means sad-minded, but thoughtful and dreamy. They rather perplexed people, those childish eyes; they were so

exceedingly innocent and yet so penetrating. If anybody did a wrong thing—told a lie, for instance—they would turn round with such a grave, silent surprise—the child never talked much—that every naughty person in the palace was rather afraid of Prince Dolor.

He could not help it, and perhaps he did not even know it, being no better a child than many other children, but there was something about him which made bad people sorry, and grumbling people ashamed of themselves, and ill-natured people gentle and kind.

I suppose because they were touched to see a poor little fellow who did not in the least know what had befallen him or what lay before him, living his baby life as happily as the day is long. Thus, whether or not he was good himself, the sight of him and his affliction made other people good, and, above all, made everybody love him—so much so that his uncle the Regent began to feel a little uncomfortable.

Now, I have nothing to say against uncles in general. They are usually very excellent people, and very convenient to little boys and girls. Even the "cruel uncle" of the *Babes in the Wood* I believe to be quite an exceptional character. And this "cruel uncle" of whom I am telling was, I hope, an exception, too.

He did not mean to be cruel. If anybody had called him so, he would have resented it extremely. He would have said that what he did was done entirely for the good of the country. But he was a man who had always been accustomed to consider himself first and foremost, believing that whatever he wanted was sure to be right, and therefore he ought to have it. So he tried to get it, and got it too, as people like him very often do. Whether they enjoy it when they have it is another question.

Therefore he went one day to the council chamber, determined on making a speech, and informing the ministers and the country at large that the young King was in failing health, and that it would be advisable to send him for a time to the Beautiful Mountains. Whether he really meant to do this, or whether it occurred to him afterward that there would be an easier way of attaining his great desire, the crown of Nomansland, is a point which I cannot decide.

But soon after, when he had obtained an order in council to send the King away—which was done in great state, with a guard of honor composed of two whole regiments of soldiers— the nation learned, without much surprise, that the poor little Prince—nobody ever called him

king now—had gone on a much longer journey than to the Beautiful Mountains.

He had fallen ill on the road and died within a few hours; at least so declared the physician in attendance and the nurse who had been sent to take care of him. They brought his coffin back in great state, and buried it in the mausoleum with his parents.

So Prince Dolor was seen no more. The country went into deep mourning for him, and then forgot him, and his uncle reigned in his stead. That illustrious personage accepted his crown with great decorum, and wore it with great dignity to the last. But whether he enjoyed it or not there is no evidence to show.

CHAPTER 3

~~~~~~

A ND WHAT of the lame Prince, whom everybody seemed so easily to have forgotten?
Not everybody. There were a few kind souls,
mothers of families, who had heard his sad story,
and some servants about the palace, who had
been familiar with his sweet ways—these many
a time sighed and said, "Poor Prince Dolor!"
Or, looking at the Beautiful Mountains, which
were visible all over Nomansland, though few
people ever visited them, "Well, perhaps his
Royal Highness is better where he is than even
there."

They did not know—indeed, hardly anybody
did know—that beyond the mountains, between them and the sea, lay a tract of country,
barren, level, bare, except for short, stunted

grass, and here and there a patch of tiny flowers. Not a bush—not a tree—not a resting place for bird or beast was in that dreary plain. In summer the sunshine fell upon it hour after hour with a blinding glare. In winter the winds and rains swept over it unhindered, and the snow came down steadily, noiselessly, covering it from end to end in one great white sheet, which lay for days and weeks unmarked by a single footprint.

Not a pleasant place to live in—and nobody did live there, apparently. The only sign that human creatures had ever been near the spot was one large round tower which rose up in the center of the plain, and might be seen from every part of it—if there had been anybody to see, which there never was. Rose right up out of the ground, as if it had grown of itself, like a mushroom. But it was not at all mushroom-like; on the contrary, it was very solidly built. In form it resembled the Irish round towers, which have puzzled people for so long, nobody being able to find out when, or by whom, or for what purpose they were made; seemingly for no use at all, like this tower. It was circular, of very firm brickwork, with neither doors nor windows, until near the top, when you could perceive some slits in the wall through which

one might possibly creep in or look out. Its height was nearly a hundred feet, and it had a battlemented parapet showing sharp against the sky.

As the plain was quite desolate—almost like a desert, only without sand, and led to nowhere except the still more desolate seacoast—nobody ever crossed it. Whatever mystery there was about the tower, it and the sky and the plain kept their secret to themselves.

It was a very great secret indeed—a state secret—which none but so clever a man as the present King of Nomansland would ever have thought of. How he carried it out, undiscovered, I cannot tell. People said, long afterward, that it was by means of a gang of condemned criminals, who were set to work, and executed immediately after they had finished, so that nobody knew anything, or in the least suspected the real fact.

And what was the fact? Why, that this tower, which seemed a mere mass of masonry, utterly forsaken and uninhabited, was not so at all. Within twenty feet of the top some ingenious architect had planned a perfect little house, divided into four rooms—as by drawing a cross within a circle you will see might easily be done.

By making skylights, and a few slits in the walls for windows, and raising a peaked roof which was hidden by the parapet, here was a dwelling complete, eighty feet from the ground, and as inaccessible as a rook's nest on the top of a tree.

A charming place to live in! If you once got up there—and never wanted to come down again.

Inside—though nobody could have looked inside except a bird, and hardly even a bird flew past that lonely tower—inside it was furnished with all the comfort and elegance imaginable; with lots of books and toys, and everything that the heart of a child could desire. For its only inhabitant, except a nurse of course, was a poor solitary child.

One winter's night, when all the plain was white with moonlight, there was seen crossing it a great tall black horse, ridden by a man also big and equally black, carrying before him on the saddle a woman and a child. The woman—she had a sad, fierce look, and no wonder, for she was a criminal under sentence of death, but her sentence had been changed to almost as severe a punishment. She was to inhabit the lonely tower with the child, and was allowed to live as long as the child lived—no longer. This in

order that she might take the utmost care of him; for those who put him there were equally afraid of his dying and of his living.

Yet he was only a little gentle boy with a sweet, sleepy smile—he had been very tired from his long journey—and with clinging arms, which held tight to the man's neck, for he was rather frightened, and the face, stern as it was, looked kindly at him. And he was very helpless, with his poor, small, shriveled legs, which

could neither stand nor run away—for the little forlorn boy was Prince Dolor.

He had not been dead at all—or buried either. His grand funeral had been a mere pretense: a wax figure having been put in his place, while he himself was spirited away under charge of these two, the condemned woman and the black man. The latter was deaf and dumb, so could neither tell nor repeat anything.

When they reached the foot of the tower,

there was light enough to see a huge chain dangling from the parapet, but dangling only half-way. The deaf-mute took from his saddle wallet a sort of ladder, arranged in pieces like a puzzle, fitted it together, and lifted it up to meet the chain. Then he mounted to the top of the tower, and slung from it a sort of chair, in which the woman and the child placed themselves and were drawn up, never to come down again as long as they lived. Leaving them there, the man descended the ladder, took it to pieces again and packed it in his pack, mounted the horse and disappeared across the plain.

Every month they used to watch for him, appearing like a speck in the distance. He fastened his horse to the foot of the tower, and climbed it, as before, laden with provisions and many other things. He always saw the Prince, so as to make sure that the child was alive and well, and then went away until the following month.

While his first childhood lasted, Prince Dolor was happy enough. He had every luxury that even a prince could need, and the one thing wanting—love—never having known, he did not miss. His nurse was very kind to him, though she was a wicked woman. But either she had not been quite so wicked as people said,

or she grew better through being shut up continually with a little innocent child who was dependent upon her for every comfort and pleasure of his life.

It was not an unhappy life. There was nobody to tease or ill-use him, and he was never ill. He played about from room to room—there were four rooms, parlor, kitchen, his nurse's bedroom, and his own; learned to crawl like a fly, and to jump like a frog, and to run about on all fours almost as fast as a puppy. In fact, he was very much like a puppy or a kitten, as thoughtless and as merry—scarcely ever cross, though sometimes a little weary.

As he grew older, he occasionally liked to be quiet for a while, and then he would sit at the slits of windows—which were, however, much bigger than they looked from the bottom of the tower—and watch the sky above and the ground below, with the storms sweeping over and the sunshine coming and going, and the shadows of the clouds running races across the blank plain.

By and by he began to learn lessons—not that his nurse had been ordered to teach him, but she did it partly to amuse herself. She was not a stupid woman, and Prince Dolor was by no means a stupid boy; so they got on very well, and his continual entreaty, "What can I do?

what can you find me to do?" was stopped, at least for an hour or two in the day.

It was a dull life, but he had never known any other; anyhow, he remembered no other, and he did not pity himself at all. Not for a long time, till he grew quite a big little boy, and could read quite easily. Then he suddenly took to books, which the deaf-mute brought him from time to time—books which, not being acquainted with the literature of Nomansland, I cannot describe, but no doubt they were very interesting; and they informed him of everything in the outside world, and filled him with an intense longing to see it.

From this time a change came over the boy. He began to look sad and thin, and to shut himself up for hours without speaking. For his nurse hardly spoke, and whatever questions he asked beyond their ordinary daily life she never answered. She had, indeed, been forbidden, on pain of death, to tell him anything about himself, who he was, or what he might have been.

He knew he was Prince Dolor, because she always addressed him as "my Prince" and "your Royal Highness," but what a prince was he had not the least idea. He had no idea of anything in the world, except what he found in his books.

He sat one day surrounded by them, having built them up round him like a little castle wall. He had been reading them half the day, but feeling all the while that to read about things which you never can see is like hearing about a beautiful dinner while you are starving. For almost the first time in his life he grew melancholy; his hands fell on his lap; he sat gazing out the window slit upon the view outside—the view he had looked at every day of his life, and might look at for endless days more.

Not a very cheerful view—just the plain and the sky—but he liked it. He used to think, if he could only fly out that window, up to the sky or down to the plain, how nice it would be! Perhaps when he died—his nurse had told him once in anger that he would never leave the tower till he died—he might be able to do this. Not that he understood much what dying meant, but it must be a change, and any change seemed to him a blessing.

"And I wish I had somebody to tell me all about it—about that and many other things; somebody that would be fond of me, like my poor white kitten."

Here the tears came into his eyes, for the boy's one friend, the one interest of his life, had been a little white kitten, which the deaf-mute,

kindly smiling, once took out of his pocket and gave him—the only living creature Prince Dolor had ever seen.

For four weeks it was his constant plaything and companion, till one moonlight night it took a fancy for wandering, climbed onto the parapet of the tower, dropped over and disappeared. It was not killed, he hoped, for cats have nine lives; indeed, he almost fancied he saw it pick itself up and scamper away; but he never caught sight of it again.

"Yes, I wish I had something better than a kitten—a person, a real live person, who would be fond of me and kind to me. Oh, I want somebody—dreadfully, dreadfully!"

As he spoke, there sounded behind him a slight tap-tap-tap, as of a stick or a cane, and twisting himself round, he saw—what do you think he saw?

Nothing either frightening or ugly, but still exceedingly curious. A little woman, no bigger than he might himself have been had his legs grown like those of other children; but she was not a child—she was an old woman. Her hair was gray, and her dress was gray, and there was a gray shadow over her wherever she moved. But she had the sweetest smile, the prettiest hands,

and when she spoke it was in the softest voice imaginable.

"My dear little boy"—and dropping her cane, the only bright and rich thing about her, she laid those two tiny hands on his shoulders—"my own little boy, I could not come to you until you had said you wanted me; but now you do want me, here I am."

"And you are very welcome, madam," replied the Prince, trying to speak politely, as princes always did in books; "and I am exceedingly obliged to you. May I ask who you are? Perhaps my mother?" For he knew that little boys usually had a mother, and had occasionally wondered what had become of his own.

"No," said the visitor, with a tender, half-sad smile, putting back the hair from his forehead, and looking right into his eyes—"no, I am not your mother, though she was a dear friend of mine; and you are as like her as you can be."

"Will you tell her to come and see me, then?"

"She cannot; but I dare say she knows all about you. And she loves you very much—and so do I; and I want to help you all I can, my poor little boy."

"Why do you call me poor?" asked Prince Dolor, in surprise.

The little old woman laughed like a chime of silver bells

The little old woman glanced down on his legs and feet, which he did not know were different from those of other children, and then at his sweet, bright face, which, though he knew not that either, was exceedingly different from many children's faces, which are often so fretful, cross, sullen. Looking at him, instead of sighing, she smiled. "I beg your pardon, my Prince," said she.

"Yes, I am a prince, and my name is Dolor; will you tell me yours, madam?"

The little old woman laughed like a chime of silver bells.

"I have not got a name—or, rather, I have so many names that I don't know which to choose. However, it was I who gave you yours, and you will belong to me all your days. I am your godmother."

"Hurrah!" cried the little Prince; "I am glad I belong to you, for I like you very much. Will you come and play with me?"

So they sat down together and played. By and by they began to talk.

"Are you very dull here?" asked the little old woman.

"Not particularly, thank you, godmother. I have plenty to eat and drink, and my lessons to do, and my books to read—lots of books."

"And you want nothing?"

"Nothing. Yes—perhaps— If you please, godmother, could you bring me just one more thing?"

"What sort of thing?"

"A little boy to play with."

The old woman looked very sad. "Just the thing, alas! which I cannot give you. My child, I cannot alter your lot in any way, but I can help you to bear it."

"Thank you. But why do you talk of bearing it? I have nothing to bear."

"My poor little man!" said the old woman in the very tenderest tone of her tender voice. "Kiss me!"

"What is kissing?" asked the wondering child.

His godmother took him in her arms and embraced him many times. By and by he kissed her back again—at first awkwardly and shyly, then with all the strength of his warm little heart.

"You are better to cuddle than even my white kitten, I think. Promise me that you will never go away."

"I must; but I will leave a present behind me—something as good as myself to amuse you—something that will take you wherever

you want to go, and show you all that you wish to see."

"What is it?"

"A traveling cloak."

The Prince's countenance fell. "I don't want a cloak, for I never go out. Sometimes nurse hoists me onto the roof, and carries me round by the parapet; but that is all. I can't walk, you know, as she does."

"The more reason why you should ride; and besides, this traveling cloak—"

"Hush!—she's coming."

There sounded outside the room door a heavy step and a grumpy voice, and a rattle of plates and dishes.

"It's my nurse, and she is bringing my dinner; but I don't want dinner at all—I only want you. Will her coming drive you away, godmother?"

"Perhaps; but only for a little while. Never mind; all the bolts and bars in the world couldn't keep me out. I'd fly in at the window, or down through the chimney. Only wish for me, and I come."

"Thank you," said Prince Dolor, but almost in a whisper, for he was very uneasy at what might happen next. His nurse and his godmother—what would they say to one another?

how would they look at one another?—two such different faces: one harsh-lined, sullen, cross, and sad; the other sweet and bright and calm as a summer evening before the dark begins.

When the door was flung open, Prince Dolor shut his eyes, trembling all over. Opening them again, he saw he need fear nothing—his lovely old godmother had melted away just like the rainbow out of the sky, as he had watched it many a time. Nobody but his nurse was in the room.

"What a muddle your Royal Highness is sitting in," said she sharply. "Such a heap of untidy books; and what's this rubbish?" knocking a little bundle that lay beside them.

"Oh, nothing, nothing—give it me!" cried the Prince, and, darting after it, he hid it under his pinafore, and then pushed it quickly into his pocket. Rubbish as it was, it was left in the place where she sat, and might be something belonging to her—his dear, kind godmother, whom already he loved with all his lonely, tender, passionate heart.

It was, though he did not know this, his wonderful traveling cloak.

CHAPTER 4

~~~~~~

A ND WHAT of the traveling cloak? What sort of cloak was it, and what good did it do the Prince?

Stay, and I'll tell you all about it.

Outside it was the commonest-looking bundle imaginable—shabby and small; and the instant Prince Dolor touched it, it grew smaller still, dwindling down till he could put it in his trousers pocket, like a handkerchief rolled up in a ball. He did this at once, for fear his nurse should see it, and kept it there all day—all night, too. Till after his next morning's lessons he had no opportunity of examining his treasure.

When he did, it seemed no treasure at all; but a mere piece of cloth—circular in form, dark

green in color—that is, if it had any color at all, being so worn and shabby, though not dirty. It had a split cut to the center, forming a round hole for the neck—and that was all its shape; the shape, in fact, of those cloaks which in South America are called ponchos—very simple, but most graceful and convenient.

Prince Dolor had never seen anything like it. In spite of his disappointment, he examined it curiously. He spread it out on the floor, then arranged it on his shoulders. It felt very warm and comfortable; but it was so exceedingly shabby—the only shabby thing that the Prince had ever seen in his life.

"And what use will it be to me?" said he sadly. "I have no need of outdoor clothes, as I never go out. Why was this given me? I wonder. And what in the world am I to do with it? She must be a rather funny person, this dear godmother of mine."

Nevertheless, because she was his godmother, and had given him the cloak, he folded it carefully and put it away, poor and shabby as it was, hiding it in a safe corner of his top cupboard, which his nurse never meddled with. He did not want her to find it, or to laugh at it or at his godmother—as he felt sure she would, if she knew all.

There it lay, and by and by he forgot all about it. Nay, I am sorry to say that, being but a child, and not seeing her again, he almost forgot his sweet old godmother, or thought of her only as he did of the angels or fairies that he read of in his books, and of her visit as if it had been a mere dream of the night.

There were times, certainly, when he recalled her: of early mornings, like that morning when she appeared beside him, and late evenings, when the gray twilight reminded him of the color of her hair and her pretty soft garments; above all, when, waking in the middle of the night, with the stars peering in at his window, or the moonlight shining across his little bed, he would not have been surprised to see her standing beside it, looking at him with those beautiful tender eyes, which seemed to have a pleasantness and comfort in them different from anything he had ever known.

But she never came, and gradually she slipped out of his memory—only a boy's memory, after all; until something happened which made him remember her and want her as he had never wanted anything before.

Prince Dolor fell ill. He caught—his nurse could not tell how—a complaint common to the people of Nomansland, called the doldrums, as

unpleasant as measles or any other of our complaints; and it made him restless, cross, and disagreeable. Even when a little better, he was too weak to enjoy anything, but lay all day long on his sofa, fidgeting his nurse extremely—while, in her intense terror lest he might die, she fidgeted him still more. At last, seeing he really was getting well, she left him to himself—which he was most glad of, in spite of his dullness and dreariness. There he lay, alone, quite alone.

Now and then an irritable fit came over him, in which he longed to get up and do something, or to go somewhere. He would have liked to imitate his white kitten—jump down from the

tower and run away, taking the chance of whatever might happen.

Only one thing, alas! was likely to happen; for the kitten, he remembered, had four active legs, while he—

"I wonder what my godmother meant when she looked at my legs and sighed so bitterly? I wonder why I can't walk straight and steady like my nurse—only I wouldn't like to have her great, noisy, clumping shoes. Still it would be very nice to move about quickly—perhaps to fly, like a bird, like that string of birds I saw the other day skimming across the sky, one after the other."

These were the passage birds—the only living creatures that ever crossed the lonely plain; and he had been much interested in them, wondering whence they came and whither they were going.

"How nice it must be to be a bird! If legs are no good, why cannot one have wings? People have wings when they die—perhaps. I wish I were dead, that I do. I am so tired, so tired; and nobody cares for me. Nobody ever did care for me, except perhaps my godmother. Godmother, dear, have you quite forsaken me?"

He stretched himself wearily, gathered himself up, and dropped his head upon his hands; as

he did so, he felt somebody kiss him at the back of his neck, and, turning, found that he was resting, not on the sofa pillows, but on a warm shoulder—that of the little old woman clothed in gray.

How glad he was to see her! How he looked into her kind eyes and felt her hands, to see if she were all real and alive! Then he put both his arms round her neck, and kissed her as if he would never have done kissing.

"Stop, stop!" cried she, pretending to be smothered. "I see you have not forgotten my teachings. Kissing is a good thing—in moderation. Only just let me have breath to speak one word."

"A dozen!" he said.

"Well, then, tell me all that has happened to you since I saw you—or, rather, since you saw me, which is quite a different thing."

"Nothing has happened—nothing ever does happen to me," answered the Prince dolefully.

"And are you very dull, my boy?"

"So dull that I was just thinking whether I could not jump down to the bottom of the tower, like my white kitten."

"Don't do that, not being a white kitten."

"I wish I were—I wish I were anything but what I am."

"And you can't make yourself any different, nor can I do it either. You must be content to stay just what you are."

The little old woman said this—very firmly, but gently, too—with her arms round his neck and her lips on his forehead. It was the first time the boy had ever heard anyone talk like this, and he looked up in surprise—but not in pain, for her sweet manner softened the hardness of her words.

"Now, my Prince—for you are a prince, and must behave as such—let us see what we can do; how much I can do for you, or show you how to do for yourself. Where is your traveling cloak?"

Prince Dolor blushed extremely. "I—I put it away in the cupboard. I suppose it is there still."

"You have never used it; you dislike it?"

He hesitated, not wishing to be impolite. "Don't you think it's—just a little old and shabby for a prince?"

The old woman laughed—long and loud, though very sweetly.

"Prince, indeed! Why, if all the princes in the world craved for it, they couldn't get it, unless I gave it them. Old and shabby! It's the most valuable thing imaginable! Very few

ever have it; but I thought I would give it to you, because—because you are different from other people."

"Am I?" said the Prince, and looked first with curiosity, then with a sort of anxiety, into his godmother's face, which was sad and grave, with slow tears beginning to steal down.

She touched his poor little legs. "These are not like those of other little boys."

"Indeed!—my nurse never told me that."

"Very likely not. But it is time you were told; and I tell you, because I love you."

"Tell me what, dear godmother?"

"That you will never be able to walk or run or jump or play—that your life will be quite different from most people's lives; but it may be a very happy life for all that. Do not be afraid."

"I am not afraid," said the boy. But he turned very pale, and his lips began to quiver, though he did not actually cry—he was too old for that, and, perhaps, too proud.

Though not wholly comprehending, he began dimly to guess what his godmother meant. He had never seen any real live boys, but he had seen pictures of them running and jumping; which he had admired and tried hard to imitate, but always failed. Now he began to understand

why he failed, and that he always should fail—that, in fact, he was not like other little boys; and it was of no use his wishing to do as they did, and play as they played, even if he had had them to play with. His was a separate life, in which he must find out new work and new pleasures for himself.

The sense of *the inevitable,* as grown-up people call it—that we cannot have things as we want them to be, but as they are, and that we must learn to bear them and make the best of them—this lesson, which everybody has to learn soon or late—came, alas! sadly soon to the poor boy. He fought against it for a while, and then, quite overcome, turned and sobbed bitterly in his godmother's arms.

She comforted him—I do not know how, except that love always comforts. And then she whispered to him, in her sweet, strong, cheerful voice: "Never mind!"

"No, I don't think I do mind—that is, I *won't* mind," replied he, catching the courage of her tone and speaking like a man, though he was still such a mere boy.

"That is right, my Prince!—that is being like a prince. Now we know exactly where we are; let us put our shoulders to the wheel and—"

"We are in Hopeless Tower [this was its

*She comforted him—I do not know how,
except that love always comforts*

name, if it had a name], and there is no wheel to put our shoulders to," said the child sadly.

"You little matter-of-fact goose! Well for you that you have a godmother called—"

"What?" he eagerly asked.

"Stuff-and-nonsense."

"Stuff-and-nonsense! What a funny name!"

"Some people give it me, but they are not my most intimate friends. These call me—never mind what," added the old woman, with a soft twinkle in her eyes. "So as you know me, and know me well, you may give me any name you please; it doesn't matter. But I am your godmother, child. I have few godchildren. Those I have love me dearly, and find me the greatest blessing in all the world."

"I can well believe it," cried the little lame Prince, and forgot his troubles in looking at her—as her figure dilated, her eyes grew lustrous as stars, her very raiment brightened, and the whole room seemed filled with her beautiful and beneficent presence like light.

He could have looked at her forever—half in love, half in awe; but she suddenly dwindled down into the little old woman all in gray, and, with a malicious twinkle in her eyes, asked for the traveling cloak.

"Bring it out of the rubbish cupboard, and

shake the dust off it, quick!" said she to Prince
Dolor, who hung his head, rather ashamed.
"Spread it out on the floor, and wait till the split
closes and the edges turn up like a rim all
round. Then go and open the skylight—mind,
I say *open the skylight*—set yourself down in
the middle of it, like a frog on a water-lily leaf;
say, 'Abracadabra, dum dum dum,' and—see
what will happen!"

The Prince burst into a fit of laughing. It all
seemed so exceedingly silly; he wondered that a
wise old woman like his godmother should talk
such nonsense.

"Stuff-and-nonsense, you mean," said she, answering, to his great alarm, his unspoken
thoughts. "Did I not tell you some people
called me by that name? Never mind; it
doesn't harm me."

And she laughed—her merry laugh—as
childlike as if she were the Prince's age instead
of her own, whatever that might be. She certainly was a most extraordinary old woman.

"Believe me or not, it doesn't matter," said
she. "Here is the cloak. When you want to go
traveling on it, say, 'Abracadabra, dum dum
dum'; when you want to come back again, say,
'Abracadabra, tum tum ti.' That's all; good-
by."

A puff of most pleasant air passing by him, making him feel for the moment quite strong and well, was all the Prince was conscious of. His most extraordinary godmother was gone.

"Really now, how rosy your Royal Highness's cheeks have grown! You seem to have got well already," said the nurse, entering the room.

"I think I have," replied the Prince very gently—he felt gentle and kind even to his grim nurse. "And now let me have my dinner, and go you to your sewing as usual."

The instant she was gone, however, taking with her the plates and dishes, which for the first time since his illness he had satisfactorily cleared, Prince Dolor hopped down from his sofa, and with one or two of his froglike jumps reached the cupboard where he kept his toys, and looked everywhere for his wonderful traveling cloak.

Alas! it was not there.

While he was ill of the doldrums, his nurse, thinking it a good opportunity for putting things to rights, had made a grand clearance of all his "rubbish"—as she considered it. His beloved headless horses, broken carts, sheep without feet, and birds without wings—all the treasures of his baby days, which he could not bear to part with, were gone. Though he sel-

dom played with them now, he liked just to feel they were there.

They were all gone and with them the traveling cloak. He sat down on the floor, looking at the empty shelves, so beautifully clean and tidy, then burst out sobbing as if his heart would break.

But quietly—always quietly. He never let his nurse hear him cry. She only laughed at him, as he felt she would laugh now.

"And it is all my own fault!" he cried. "I ought to have taken better care of my godmother's gift. Oh, godmother, forgive me! I'll never be so careless again. I don't know what the cloak is exactly, but I am sure it is something precious. Help me to find it again. Oh, don't let it be stolen from me—don't, please!"

"Ha, ha, ha!" laughed a silvery voice. "Why, that traveling cloak is the one thing in the world which nobody can steal. It is of no use to anybody except the owner. Open your eyes, my Prince, and see what you shall see."

His dear old godmother, he thought, and turned eagerly round. But no; he beheld, lying in a corner of the room, all dust and cobwebs, his precious traveling cloak.

Prince Dolor darted toward it, tumbling sev-

eral times on the way, as he often did tumble, poor boy! and pick himself up again, never complaining. Snatching it to his breast, he hugged and kissed it, cobwebs and all, as if it had been something alive. Then he began unrolling it, wondering each minute what would happen. What did happen was so curious that I must leave it for another chapter.

CHAPTER 5

~~~~~~

IF ANY READER, big or little, should wonder whether there is a meaning in this story deeper than that of an ordinary fairy tale, I will own that there is. But I have hidden it so carefully that the smaller people, and many larger folk, will never find it out, and meantime the book may be read straight on, like *Cinderella,* or *Bluebeard,* or *Hop-o'-My-Thumb,* for what interest it has or what amusement it may bring.

Having said this, I return to Prince Dolor, that little lame boy whom many may think so exceedingly to be pitied. But if you had seen him as he sat patiently untying his wonderful cloak, which was done up in a very tight and perplexing parcel, using skillfully his deft little

hands, and knitting his brows with firm deter-
mination, while his eyes glistened with pleasure
and energy and eager anticipation—if you had
beheld him thus, you might have changed your
opinion.

When we see people suffering or unfortunate,
we feel very sorry for them. But when we see
them bravely bearing their sufferings and making the best of their misfortunes, it is quite a
different feeling. We respect, we admire them.
One can respect and admire even a little child.

When Prince Dolor had patiently untied all
the knots, a remarkable thing happened. The
cloak began to undo itself. Slowly unfolding, it
laid itself down on the carpet, as flat as if it had
been ironed. The split joined with a little
sharp crick-crack, and the rim turned up all
round till it was breast-high. Meantime the
cloak had grown and grown, and become quite
large enough for one person to sit in it as comfortably as if in a boat.

The Prince watched it rather anxiously; it
was such an extraordinary, not to say a frightening, thing. However, he was no coward, but a
thorough boy, who, if he had been like other
boys, would doubtless have grown up daring
and adventurous—a soldier, a sailor, or the like.
As it was, he could only show his courage mor-

ally, not physically, by being afraid of nothing, and by doing boldly all that it was in his narrow powers to do. And I am not sure but that in this way he showed more real valor than if he had had six pairs of proper legs.

He said to himself: "What a goose I am! As if my dear godmother would ever have given me anything to hurt me. Here goes!"

So, with one of his active leaps, he sprang right into the middle of the cloak, where he squatted down, wrapping his arms tight round his knees, for they shook a little and his heart beat fast. But there he sat, steady and silent, waiting for what might happen next.

Nothing did happen, and he began to think nothing would, and to feel rather disappointed, when he recollected the words he had been told to repeat—"Abracadabra, dum dum dum!"

He repeated them, laughing all the while, they seemed such nonsense. And then—and then—

Now I don't expect anybody to believe what I am going to relate, though a good many wise people have believed a good many sillier things. And as seeing's believing, and I never saw it, I cannot be expected implicitly to believe it myself, except in a sort of way. And yet there is truth in it—for some people.

The cloak rose, slowly and steadily, at first only a few inches, then gradually higher and higher, till it nearly touched the skylight. Prince Dolor's head actually bumped against the glass, or would have done so had he not crouched down, crying, "Oh, please don't hurt me!" in a most melancholy voice.

Then he suddenly remembered his godmother's express command—"Open the skylight!"

Regaining his courage at once, without a moment's delay he lifted up his head and began searching for the bolt—the cloak meanwhile remaining perfectly still, balanced in the air. But the minute the window was opened, out it sailed—right out into the clear, fresh air, with nothing between it and the cloudless blue.

Prince Dolor had never felt any such delicious sensation before. I can understand it. Cannot you? Did you never think, in watching the rooks going home singly or in pairs, soaring their way across the calm evening sky till they vanish like black dots in the misty gray, how pleasant it must feel to be up there, quite out of the noise and din of the world, able to hear and see everything down below, yet troubled by nothing and teased by no one—all alone, but perfectly content?

Something like this was the happiness of the little lame Prince when he got out of Hopeless Tower, and found himself for the first time in the pure open air, with the sky above him and the earth below.

True, there was nothing but earth and sky; no houses, no trees, no rivers, mountains, seas—not a beast on the ground or a bird in the air. But to him even the level plain looked beautiful. And then there was the glorious arch of the sky, with a little young moon sitting in the west like a baby queen. And the evening breeze was so sweet and fresh—it kissed him like his godmother's kisses. And by and by a few stars came out—first two or three, and then quantities—quantities! so that when he began to count them he was utterly bewildered.

By this time, however, the cool breeze had become cold. The mist gathered; and as he had, as he said, no outdoor clothes, poor Prince Dolor was not very comfortable. The dews fell damp on his curls. He began to shiver.

"Perhaps I had better go home," thought he.

But how? For in his excitement the other words which his godmother had told him to use had slipped his memory. They were only a little different from the first, but in that slight difference all the importance lay. As he

repeated his "Abracadabra," trying ever so many other syllables after it, the cloak only went faster and faster, skimming on through the dusky, empty air.

The poor little Prince began to feel frightened. What if his wonderful traveling cloak should keep on thus traveling, perhaps to the world's end, carrying with it a poor, tired, hungry boy, who, after all, was beginning to think there was something very pleasant in supper and bed!

"Dear godmother," he cried pitifully, "do help me! Tell me just this once and I'll never forget again."

Instantly the words came rushing into his head—"Abracadabra, tum tum ti!" Was that it? Ah! yes—for the cloak began to turn slowly. He repeated the charm again, more distinctly and firmly, when it gave a gentle dip, like a nod of satisfaction, and immediately started back, as fast as ever, in the direction of the tower.

He reached the skylight, which he found exactly as he had left it, and slipped in, cloak and all, as easily as he had got out. He had scarcely reached the floor, and was still sitting in the middle of his traveling cloak—like a frog on a water-lily leaf, as his godmother had expressed

it—when he heard his nurse's voice outside.

"Bless us! What has become of your Royal Highness all this time? To sit stupidly here at the window till it is quite dark, and leave the skylight open, too. Prince! What can you be thinking of? You are the silliest boy I ever knew."

"Am I?" said he absently, and never heeding her crossness; for his only anxiety was lest she might find out what he had been doing.

She would have been a very clever person to have done so. The instant Prince Dolor got off it, the cloak folded itself up into the tiniest possible parcel, tied all its own knots, and rolled itself of its own accord into the farthest and darkest corner of the room. If the nurse had seen it, which she didn't, she would have taken it for a mere bundle of rubbish not worth noticing.

Shutting the skylight with an angry bang, she brought in the supper and lit the candles with her usual unhappy expression of countenance. But Prince Dolor hardly saw it. He saw only, hid in the corner where nobody else would see it, his wonderful traveling cloak. And though his supper was not particularly nice, he ate it heartily, scarcely hearing a word of his nurse's

grumbling, which tonight seemed to have taken the place of her sullen silence.

"Poor woman!" he thought, when he paused a minute to listen and look at her with those quiet, happy eyes, so like his mother's. "Poor woman! She hasn't got a traveling cloak!"

And when he was left alone at last, and crept into his little bed, where he lay awake a good while, watching what he called his "sky-garden," all planted with stars, like flowers, his chief thought was—"I must be up very early tomorrow morning, and get my lessons done, and then I'll go traveling all over the world on my beautiful cloak."

So next day he opened his eyes with the sun, and went with a good heart to his lessons. They had hitherto been the chief amusement of his dull life. Now, I am afraid, he found them also a little dull. But he tried to be good—I don't say Prince Dolor always was good, but he generally tried to be—and when his mind went wandering after the dark, dusty corner where lay his precious treasure, he resolutely called it back again.

"For," he said, "how ashamed my godmother would be of me if I grew up a stupid boy!"

But the instant lessons were done, and he was

alone in the empty room, he crept across the floor, undid the shabby little bundle, his fingers trembling with eagerness, climbed on the chair, and thence to the table, so as to unbar the skylight—he forgot nothing now—said his magic charm, and was away out the window, as children say, "in a few minutes less than no time."

Nobody missed him. He was accustomed to sit so quietly always that his nurse, though only in the next room, perceived no difference. And besides, she might have gone in and out a dozen times, and it would have been just the same; she never could have found out his absence.

For what do you think the clever godmother did? She took a quantity of moonshine, or some equally convenient material, and made an image, which she set on the window sill reading, or by the table drawing, where it looked so like Prince Dolor that any common observer would never have guessed the deception. And even the boy would have been puzzled to know which was the image and which was himself.

And all this while the happy little fellow was away, floating in the air on his magic cloak, and seeing all sorts of wonderful things—or they seemed wonderful to him, who had hitherto seen nothing at all.

First, there were the flowers that grew on the

plain, which, whenever the cloak came near enough, he strained his eyes to look at. They were very tiny, but very beautiful—white saxifrage, and yellow lotus, and ground thistles, purple and bright, with many others the names of which I do not know. No more did Prince Dolor, though he tried to find them out by recalling any pictures he had seen of them. But he was too far off; and though it was pleasant enough to admire them as brilliant patches of color, still he would have liked to examine them all. He was, as a little girl I know once said of a playfellow, "a very examining boy."

"I wonder," he thought, "whether I could see better through a pair of glasses like those my nurse reads with, and takes such care of. How I would take care of them, too, if I only had a pair!"

Immediately he felt something queer and hard fixing itself to the bridge of his nose. It was a pair of the prettiest gold spectacles ever seen. Looking downward, he found that, though ever so high above the ground, he could see every minute blade of grass, every tiny bud and flower—nay, even the insects that walked over them.

"Thank you, thank you!" he cried, in a gush of gratitude—to anybody or everybody, but especially to his dear godmother, who he felt sure had given him this new present. He amused himself with it for ever so long, with his chin pressed on the rim of the cloak, gazing down upon the grass, every square foot of which was a mine of wonders.

Then, just to rest his eyes, he turned them up to the sky—the blue, bright, empty sky, which he had looked at so often and seen nothing.

Now surely there was something. A long, black, wavy line, moving on in the distance, not by chance, as the clouds move apparently, but deliberately, as if it were alive. He might have

seen it before—he almost thought he had; but then he could not tell what it was. Looking at it through his spectacles, he discovered that it really was alive; being a long string of birds, flying one after the other, their wings moving steadily and their heads pointed in one direction, as steadily as if each were a little ship, guided invisibly by an unerring helm.

"They must be the passage birds flying seaward!" cried the boy, who had read a little about them, and had a great talent for putting two and two together and finding out all he could. "Oh, how I should like to see them quite close, and to know where they come from and whither they are going! How I wish I knew everything in all the world!"

A silly speech for even an "examining" little boy to make; because, as we grow older, the more we know the more we find out there is to know. And Prince Dolor blushed when he had said it, and hoped nobody had heard him.

Apparently somebody had, however. For the cloak gave a sudden bound forward, and presently he found himself high in the air, in the very middle of that band of aerial travelers, who had no magic cloak to travel on—nothing except their wings. Yet there they were, making their fearless way through the sky.

Prince Dolor looked at them as one after the other they glided past him; and they looked at him—those pretty swallows with their changing necks and bright eyes—as if wondering to meet in mid-air such an extraordinary sort of bird.

"Oh, I wish I were going with you, you lovely creatures! I'm getting so tired of this dull plain, and the dreary and lonely tower. I do so want to see the world! Pretty swallows, dear swallows! tell me what it looks like—the beautiful, wonderful world!"

But the swallows flew past him—steadily,

slowly pursuing their course as if inside each little head had been a mariner's compass, to guide him safe over land and sea, direct to the place where he wished to go.

The boy looked after them with envy. For a long time he followed with his eyes the faint, wavy black line as it floated away, sometimes changing its curves a little, but never deviating from its settled course, till it vanished entirely out of sight.

Then he settled himself down in the center of the cloak, feeling quite sad and lonely.

"I think I'll go home," said he, and repeated his "Abracadabra, tum tum ti!" with a rather heavy heart. The more he had, the more he wanted. It is not always one can have everything one wants—at least, at the exact minute one craves for it; not even though one is a prince, and has a powerful and beneficent godmother.

He did not like to vex her by calling for her and telling her how unhappy he was, in spite of all her goodness. So he just kept his trouble to himself, went back to his lonely tower, and spent three days in silent melancholy, without even attempting another journey on his traveling cloak.

CHAPTER 6

~~~~~~
~~~~~~

THE FOURTH DAY it happened that the deaf-mute paid his accustomed visit, after which Prince Dolor's spirits rose. They always did when he got the new books which, just to relieve his conscience, the King of Nomansland regularly sent to his nephew; with many new toys also, though the latter were disregarded now.

"Toys, indeed! when I'm a big boy," said the Prince, with disdain, and would scarcely condescend to mount a rocking horse which had come, somehow or other—I can't be expected to explain things very exactly—packed on the back of the other, the great black horse, which stood and fed contentedly at the bottom of the tower.

Prince Dolor leaned over and looked at it, and thought how grand it must be to get upon its back—this grand live steed—and ride away, like the pictures of knights.

"Suppose I were a knight," he said to himself; "then I should be obliged to ride out and see the world."

But he kept all these thoughts to himself, and just sat still, devouring his new books till he had come to the end of them all. It was a repast not unlike the Barmecide feast which you read of in the *Arabian Nights,* which consisted of very elegant but empty dishes, or that supper of Sancho Panza in *Don Quixote,* where, the minute the smoking dishes came on the table, the physician waved his hand and they were all taken away.

Thus almost all the ordinary delights of boy life had been taken away from, or rather never given to, this poor little prince.

"I wonder," he would sometimes think—"I wonder what it feels like to be on the back of a horse, galloping away, or holding the reins in a carriage, and tearing across the country, or jumping a ditch, or running a race, such as I read of or see in pictures. What a lot of things there are that I should like to do! But first I should like to go and see the world. I'll try."

Apparently it was his godmother's plan al-

*"Suppose I were a knight; then I should be
obliged to ride out and see the world"*

ways to let him try, and try hard, before he gained anything. This day the knots that tied up his traveling cloak were more than usually troublesome, and he was a full half hour before he got out into the open air, and found himself floating merrily over the top of the tower.

Hitherto, in all his journeys, he had never let himself go out of sight of home, for the dreary building, after all, was home—he remembered no other. But now he felt sick of the very look of his tower, with its round smooth walls and level battlements.

"Off we go!" cried he, when the cloak stirred itself with a slight, slow motion, as if awaiting his orders. "Anywhere—anywhere, so that I am away from here, and out into the world."

As he spoke, the cloak, as if seized suddenly with a new idea, bounded forward and went skimming through the air, faster than the very fastest railway train.

"Gee-up! gee-up!" cried Prince Dolor in great excitement. "This is as good as riding a race."

And he patted the cloak as if it had been a horse—that is, in the way he supposed horses ought to be patted—and tossed his head back to meet the fresh breeze, and pulled his coat collar up and his hat down as he felt the wind grow

keener and colder—colder than anything he had ever known.

"What does it matter, though?" said he. "I'm a boy, and boys ought not to mind anything."

Still, for all his good will, by and by, he began to shiver exceedingly. Also, he had come away without his dinner, and he grew frightfully hungry. And to add to everything, the sunshiny day changed into rain, and being high up, in the very midst of the clouds, he got soaked through and through in a very few minutes.

"Shall I turn back?" meditated he. "Suppose I say 'Abracadabra'?"

Here he stopped, for already the cloak gave an obedient lurch, as if it were expecting to be sent home immediately.

"No—I can't—I can't go back! I must go forward and see the world. But oh! if I had but the shabbiest old rug to shelter me from the rain, or the driest morsel of bread and cheese, just to keep me from starving! Still, I don't much mind. I'm a prince, and ought to be able to stand anything. Hold on, cloak, we'll make the best of it."

It was a most curious circumstance, but no sooner had he said this than he felt stealing over his knees something warm and soft; in fact, a

most beautiful bearskin, which folded itself round him quite naturally, and cuddled him up as closely as if he had been the cub of the kind old mother bear that once owned it. Then feeling in his pocket, which suddenly stuck out in a marvelous way, he found, not exactly bread and cheese, nor even sandwiches, but a packet of the most delicious food he had ever tasted. It was not meat, nor pudding, but a combination of both, and it served him excellently for both. He ate his dinner with the greatest gusto imaginable, till he grew so thirsty he did not know what to do.

"Couldn't I have just one drop of water, if it didn't trouble you too much, kindest of godmothers?"

For he really thought this want was beyond her power to supply. All the water which supplied Hopeless Tower was pumped up with difficulty from a deep artesian well—there were such things known in Nomansland—which had been drilled at the foot of it. But around, for miles upon miles, the desolate plain was perfectly dry. And above it, high in the air, how could he expect to find a well, or to get even a drop of water?

He forgot one thing—the rain. While he spoke, it came on in another wild burst, as if the

clouds had poured themselves out in a passion of crying, wetting him certainly, but leaving behind, in a large glass vessel which he had never noticed before, enough water to quench the thirst of two or three boys at least. And it was so fresh, so pure—as water from the clouds always is when it does not catch the soot from city chimneys and other defilements—that he drank it, every drop, with the greatest delight and content.

Also, as soon as it was empty the rain filled it again, so that he was able to wash his face and hands and refresh himself exceedingly. Then the sun came out and dried him in no time. After that he curled himself up under the bearskin rug, and though he determined to be the most wide-awake boy imaginable, being so snug and warm and comfortable, Prince Dolor condescended to shut his eyes just for one minute. The next minute he was sound asleep.

When he awoke, he found himself floating over a country quite unlike anything he had ever seen before.

Yet it was nothing but what most of you children see every day and never notice it—a pretty country landscape, like England, Scotland, America, or any other land you choose to name. It had no particular features—nothing in it was

grand or lovely. It was simply pretty, nothing more. Yet to Prince Dolor, who had never gone beyond his lonely tower and level plain, it appeared the most charming sight imaginable.

First, there was a river. It came tumbling down the hillside, frothing and foaming, playing at hide-and-seek among the rocks, then bursting out in noisy fun like a child, to bury itself in deep, still pools. Afterward it went steadily on for a while, like a good grown-up person, till it came to another big rock, where it misbehaved itself extremely. It turned into a cataract, and went tumbling over and over, after a fashion that made the Prince—who had never seen water before, except in his bath or his drinking cup—clap his hands with delight.

"It is so active, so alive! I like things active and alive!" cried he, and watched it shimmering and dancing, whirling and leaping, till, after a few windings and vagaries, it settled into a respectable stream. After that it went along, deep and quiet, but flowing steadily on, till it reached a large lake, into which it slipped and so ended its course.

All this the boy saw, either with his own naked eyes or through his gold spectacles. He saw also as in a picture, beautiful but silent,

many other things which struck him with wonder, especially a grove of trees.

Only think, to have lived to his age (which he himself did not know, as he did not know his own birthday) and never to have seen trees! As he floated over these oaks, they seemed to him—trunk, branches, and leaves—the most curious sight imaginable.

"If I could only get nearer, so as to touch them," said he, and immediately the obedient cloak ducked down. Prince Dolor made a snatch at the topmost twig of the tallest tree, and caught a bunch of leaves in his hand.

Just a bunch of green leaves—such as we see in myriads; watching them bud, grow, fall, and then kicking them along on the ground as if they were worth nothing. Yet how wonderful they are—every one of them a little different. I don't suppose you could ever find two leaves exactly alike in form, color, and size—no more than you could find two faces alike, or two characters exactly the same. The plan of this world is infinite similarity and yet infinite variety.

Prince Dolor examined his leaves with the greatest curiosity—and also a little caterpillar that he found walking over one of them. He coaxed it to take an additional walk over his

finger, which it did with the greatest dignity
and decorum, as if it, Mr. Caterpillar, were the
most important individual in existence. It
amused him for a long time; and when a sudden
gust of wind blew it overboard, leaves and all,
he felt quite disconsolate.

"Still there must be many live creatures in
the world besides caterpillars. I should like to
see a few of them."

The cloak gave a little dip down, as if to say
"All right, my Prince," and bore him across the
oak forest to a long fertile valley—called in Scotland a strath and in England a weald, but what
they call it in the tongue of Nomansland I do
not know. It was made up of cornfields, pas-
turefields, lanes, hedges, brooks, and ponds.
Also, in it were what the Prince desired to see—
a quantity of living creatures, wild and tame.
Cows and horses, lambs and sheep fed in the
meadows; pigs and fowls walked about the farm-
yards; and in lonelier places hares scudded, rab-
bits burrowed, and pheasants and partridges,
with many other smaller birds, inhabited the
fields and woods.

Through his wonderful spectacles the Prince
could see everything. But, as I said, it was a
silent picture; he was too high up to catch any-

thing except a faint murmur, which only aroused his anxiety to hear more.

"I have as good as two pairs of eyes," he thought. "I wonder if my godmother would give me a second pair of ears."

Scarcely had he spoken than he found lying on his lap the most curious little parcel, all done up in silvery paper. And it contained—what do you think? Actually a pair of silver ears, which, when he tried them on, fitted so exactly over his own that he hardly felt them, except for the difference they made in his hearing.

There is something which we listen to daily and never notice. I mean the sounds of the visible world, animate and inaminate. Winds blowing, waters flowing, trees stirring, insects whirring (dear me! I am quite unconsciously writing rhyme), with the various cries of birds and beasts—lowing cattle, bleating sheep, grunting pigs, and cackling hens—all the infinite discords that somehow or other make a beautiful harmony.

We hear this, and are so accustomed to it that we think nothing of it. But Prince Dolor, who had lived all his days in the dead silence of Hopeless Tower, heard it for the first time. And oh! if you had seen his face.

He listened, listened, as if he could never have done listening. And he looked and looked, as if he could not gaze enough. Above all, the motion of the animals delighted him: cows walking, horses galloping, little lambs and calves running races across the meadows, were such a treat for him to watch—he that was always so quiet. But, these creatures having four legs, and he only two, the difference did not strike him painfully.

Still, by and by, after the fashion of children—and, I fear, of many big people too—he began to want something more than he had, something fresh and new.

"Godmother," he said, having now begun to believe that, whether he saw her or not, he could always speak to her with full confidence that she would hear him—"godmother, all these creatures I like exceedingly; but I should like better to see a creature like myself. Couldn't you show me just one little boy?"

There was a sigh behind him—it might have been only the wind—and the cloak remained so long balanced motionless in air that he was half afraid his godmother had forgotten him, or was offended with him for asking too much. Suddenly a shrill whistle startled him, even through his silver ears, and looking downward, he saw

start up from behind a bush on a common, something—

Neither a sheep nor a horse nor a cow—nothing upon four legs. This creature had only two; but they were long, straight, and strong.

And it had a lithe, active body, and a curly head of black hair set upon its shoulders. It was a boy, a shepherd boy, about the Prince's own age—but, oh! so different.

[97]

Not that he was an ugly boy—though his face was almost as red as his hands, and his shaggy hair matted like the backs of his own sheep. He was rather a nice-looking lad; and seemed so bright and healthy and good-tempered—"jolly" would be the word, only I am not sure if they have such a one in the elegant language of Nomansland—that the little Prince watched him with great admiration.

"Might he come and play with me? I would drop down to the ground to him, or fetch him up to me here. Oh, how nice it would be if I only had a little boy to play with me."

But the cloak, usually so obedient to his wishes, disobeyed him now. There were evidently some things which his godmother either could not or would not give. The cloak hung stationary, high in air, never attempting to descend. The shepherd lad evidently took it for a large bird, and, shading his eyes, looked up at it, making the Prince's heart beat fast.

However, nothing ensued. The boy turned round, with a long, loud whistle—seemingly his usual and only way of expressing his feelings. He could not make the thing out exactly—it was a rather mysterious affair, but it did not trouble him much—he was not an "examining" boy.

Then, stretching himself, for he had been evidently half asleep, he began flopping his shoulders with his arms to wake and warm himself; while his dog, a rough collie, who had been guarding the sheep meanwhile, began to jump upon him, barking with delight.

"Down, Snap, down! Stop that, or I'll thrash you," the Prince heard him say; though with such a rough, hard voice and queer pronunciation that it was difficult to make the words out. "Hollo! Let's warm ourselves by a race."

They started off together, boy and dog— barking and shouting, till it was doubtful which made the more noise or ran the faster. A regular steeplechase it was: first across the level common, greatly disturbing the quiet sheep; and then tearing away across country, scrambling through hedges and leaping ditches, and tumbling up and down over plowed fields. They did not seem to have anything to run for—but they ran as if they did it, both of them, for the mere pleasure of motion.

And what a pleasure that seemed! To the dog of course, but scarcely less so to the boy. How he skimmed along over the ground—his cheeks glowing, and his hair flying, and his legs—oh, what a pair of legs he had!

Prince Dolor watched him with great intentness, and in a state of excitement almost equal to that of the runner himself—for a while. Then the sweet, pale face grew a trifle paler, the lips began to quiver, and the eyes to fill.

"How nice it must be to run like that!" he said softly, thinking that never—no, never in this world—would he be able to do the same.

Now he understood what his godmother had meant when she gave him his traveling cloak, and why he had heard that sigh—he was sure it was hers—when he had asked to see "just one little boy."

"I think I had rather not look at him again," said the poor little Prince, drawing himself back into the center of his cloak, and resuming his favorite posture, sitting like a Turk, with his arms wrapped round his feeble, useless legs.

"You're no good to me," he said, patting them mournfully. "You never will be any good to me. I wonder why I had you at all. I wonder why I was born at all, since I was not to grow up like other boys. Why not?"

A question so strange, so sad, yet so often occurring in some form or other in this world— as you will find, my children, when you are older—that even if he had put it to his mother she could only have answered it, as we have to

answer many as difficult things, by simply saying, "I don't know." There is much that we do not know and cannot understand—we big folks any more than you little ones. We have to accept it all just as you have to accept anything which your parents may tell you, even though you don't as yet see the reason of it. You may sometimes, if you do exactly as they tell you, and are content to wait.

Prince Dolor sat a good while thus, or it appeared to him a good while, so many thoughts came and went through his poor young mind— thoughts of great bitterness, which, little though he was, seemed to make him grow years older in a few minutes.

Then he fancied the cloak began to rock gently to and fro, with a soothing kind of motion, as if he were in somebody's arms, somebody who did not speak, but loved him and comforted him without need of words. Not by deceiving him with false encouragement or hope, but by making him see the plain, hard truth in all its hardness, and thus letting him quietly face it, till it became softened, and did not seem nearly so dreadful after all.

Through the dreary silence and blankness, for he had placed himself so that he could see nothing but the sky, and had taken off his silver

ears as well as his gold spectacles—what was the use of either when he had no legs with which to walk or run?—up from below there rose a delicious sound.

You have heard it hundreds of times, my children, and so have I. When I was a child I thought there was nothing so sweet; and I think so still. It was just the song of a skylark, mounting higher and higher from the ground, till it

came so close that Prince Dolor could distinguish its quivering wings and tiny body, almost too tiny to contain such a gush of music.

"Oh, you beautiful, beautiful bird!" cried he; "I should dearly like to take you in and cuddle you. That is, if I could—if I dared."

But he hesitated. The little brown creature with its loud heavenly voice almost made him afraid. Nevertheless, it also made him happy.

And he watched and listened—so absorbed that he forgot all regret and pain, forgot everything in the world except the little lark.

It soared and soared, and he was just wondering if it would soar out of sight, and what in the world he should do when it was gone, when it suddenly closed its wings, as larks do when they mean to drop to the ground. But, instead of dropping to the ground, it dropped right into the little boy's breast.

What felicity! If it would only stay! A tiny, soft thing to fondle and kiss, to sing to him all day long, and be his playfellow and companion, tame and tender, while to the rest of the world it was a wild bird of the air. What a pride, what a delight! To have something that nobody else had—something all his own. As the traveling cloak traveled on, he little heeded where, and the lark still stayed, nestled down in his bosom, hopped from his hand to his shoulder, and kissed him with its dainty beak, as if it loved him. Prince Dolor forgot all his grief, and was entirely happy.

But when he got in sight of Hopeless Tower a painful thought struck him.

"My pretty bird, what am I to do with you? If I take you into my room and shut you up there, you, a wild skylark of the air, what will

become of you? I am used to this, but you are not. You will be so miserable. And suppose my nurse should find you—she who can't bear the sound of singing? Besides, I remember her once telling me that the nicest thing she ever ate in her life was lark pie!"

The little boy shivered all over at the thought. And, though the merry lark immediately broke into the loudest carol, as if saying derisively that he defied anybody to eat him, still Prince Dolor was very uneasy. In another minute he had made up his mind.

"No, my bird, nothing so dreadful shall happen to you if I can help it. I would rather do without you altogether. Yes, I'll try. Fly away, my darling, my beautiful! Good-by, my merry, merry bird."

Opening his two caressing hands in which, as if for protection, he had folded it, he let the lark go. It lingered a minute, perching on the rim of the cloak, and looking at him with eyes of almost human tenderness. Then away it flew, far up into the blue sky. It was only a bird.

But some time afterward, when Prince Dolor had eaten his supper—somewhat drearily, except for the thought that he could not possibly sup off lark pie now—and gone quietly to bed, the old familiar little bed, where he was accus-

The Little Lame Prince

tomed to sleep, or lie awake contentedly thinking—suddenly he heard outside the window a little faint carol—faint but cheerful—cheerful even though it was the middle of the night.

The dear little lark! it had not flown away, after all. And it was truly the most extraordinary bird, for, unlike ordinary larks, it kept hovering about the tower in the silence and darkness of the night, outside the window or over the roof. Whenever he listened for a moment, he heard it singing still.

He went to sleep as happy as a king.

CHAPTER 7

~~~~~~

H APPY AS A KING." How far kings are happy
I cannot say, no more than could Prince
Dolor, though he had once been a king himself.
But he remembered nothing about it, and there
was nobody to tell him, except his nurse, who
had been forbidden upon pain of death to let
him know anything about his dead parents, or
the King his uncle, or indeed any part of his
own history.

Sometimes he speculated about himself,
whether he had had a father and mother as
other little boys had, what they had been like,
and why he had never seen them. But, knowing nothing about them, he did not miss
them—only once or twice, reading pretty stories
about little children and their mothers, who

helped them when they were in difficulty and comforted them when they were sick, he, feeling ill and dull and lonely, wondered what had become of his mother and why she never came to see him.

Then, in his history lessons, of course, he read about kings and princes, and the governments of different countries, and the events that happened there. And though he but faintly took in all this, still he did take it in a little, and worried his young brain about it, and perplexed his nurse with questions, to which she returned sharp and mysterious answers, which only set him thinking the more.

He had plenty of time for thinking. After his last journey in the traveling cloak, the journey which had given him so much pain, his desire to see the world somehow faded away. He contented himself with reading his books, and looking out the tower windows, and listening to his beloved little lark, which had come home with him that day, and had never left him again.

True, it kept out of the way; and though his nurse sometimes dimly heard it, and said, "What is that horrid noise outside?" she never got the faintest chance of making it into a lark pie. Prince Dolor had his pet all to himself,

and though he seldom saw it, he knew it was near him, and he caught continually, at odd hours of the day, and even in the night, fragments of its delicious song.

All during the winter—so far as there ever was any difference between summer and winter in Hopeless Tower—the little bird cheered and amused him. He scarcely needed anything more—not even his traveling cloak, which lay bundled up unnoticed in a corner, tied up in its innumerable knots.

Nor did his godmother come near him. It seemed as if she had given these treasures and left him alone—to use them or lose them, apply them or misapply them, according to his own choice. That is all we can do with children when they grow into big children old enough to distinguish between right and wrong, and too old to be forced to do either.

Prince Dolor was now quite a big boy. Not tall—alas! he never could be that, with his poor little shrunken legs, which were of no use, only an encumbrance. But he was stout and strong, with great sturdy shoulders, and muscular arms, upon which he could swing himself about almost like a monkey. As if in compensation for his useless lower limbs, Nature had given to these extra strength and activity. His face, too,

was very handsome. It was thinner, firmer, more manly; but still the sweet face of his childhood—his mother's own face.

How his mother would have liked to look at him! Perhaps she did—who knows?

The boy was not a stupid boy either. He could learn almost anything he chose—and he did choose, which was more than half the battle. He never gave up his lessons till he had learned them all—never thought it a punishment that he had to work at them, and that they cost him a deal of trouble sometimes.

"But," thought he, "men work, and it must be so grand to be a man—a prince too; and I fancy princes work harder than anybody—except kings. The princes I read about generally turn into kings. I wonder—" the boy was always wondering. "Nurse"—and one day he startled her with a sudden question—"tell me —shall I ever be a king?"

The woman stood, perplexed beyond expression. So long a time had passed by since her crime—if it were a crime—and her sentence that she now seldom thought of either. Even her punishment—to be shut up for life in Hopeless Tower—she had gradually got used to. Used also to the little lame Prince, her charge—whom at first she had hated,

though she carefully did everything to keep him alive, since upon him her own life hung.

But latterly she had ceased to hate him, and, in a sort of way, almost loved him—at least, enough to be sorry for him—an innocent child, imprisoned here till he grew into an old man, and became a dull, worn-out creature like herself. Sometimes, watching him, she felt more sorry for him than even for herself; and then, seeing she looked a less miserable and ugly woman, he did not shrink from her as usual.

He did not now. "Nurse—dear nurse," said he, "I don't mean to vex you, but tell me—what is a king? Shall I ever be one?"

When she began to think less of herself and more of the child, the woman's courage increased. The idea came to her—what harm would it be, even if he did know his own history? Perhaps he ought to know it—for there had been various ups and downs, usurpations, revolutions, and restorations in Nomansland, as in most other countries. Something might happen—who could tell? Changes might occur. Possibly a crown would even yet be set upon those pretty, fair curls—which she began to think prettier than ever when she saw the imaginary coronet upon them.

She sat down, considering whether her oath,

never to "say a word" to Prince Dolor about himself, would be broken if she were to take a pencil and write what was to be told. A mere quibble—a mean, miserable quibble. But then she was a miserable woman, more to be pitied than scorned.

After long doubt, and with great trepidation, she put her fingers to her lips, and taking the Prince's slate—with the sponge tied to it, ready to rub out the writing in a minute—she wrote:

"You are a king."

Prince Dolor started. His face grew pale, and then flushed all over; he held himself erect. Lame as he was, anybody could see he was born to be a king.

"Hush!" said the nurse, as he was beginning to speak. And then, terribly frightened all the while—people who have done wrong always are frightened—she wrote down in a few hurried sentences his history. How his parents had died—his uncle had usurped his throne, and sent him to end his days in this lonely tower.

"I, too," added she, bursting into tears. "Unless, indeed, you could get out into the world, and fight for your rights like a man. And fight for me also, my Prince, that I may not die in this desolate place."

"Poor old nurse!" said the boy compassion-

ately. For somehow, boy as he was, when he heard he was born to be a king, he felt like a man—like a king—who could afford to be tender because he was strong.

He scarcely slept that night, and even though he heard his little lark singing in the sunrise, he barely listened to it. Things more serious and important had taken possession of his mind.

"Suppose," thought he, "I were to do as she says, and go out in the world, no matter how it hurts me—the world of people, active people, as active as that boy I saw. They might only laugh at me—poor helpless creature that I am. But still I might show them I could do something. At any rate, I might go and see if there were anything for me to do. Godmother, help me!"

It was so long since he had asked her help that he was hardly surprised when he got no

answer—only the little lark outside the window sang louder and louder, and the sun rose, flooding the room with light.

Prince Dolor sprang out of bed, and began dressing himself, which was hard work, for he was not used to it—he had always been accustomed to depend upon his nurse for everything.

"But I must now learn to be independent," thought he. "Fancy a king being dressed like a baby!"

So he did the best he could—awkwardly but cheerily—and then he leaped to the corner where lay his traveling cloak, untied it as before, and watched it unrolling itself—which it did rapidly, with a hearty good will, as if quite tired of idleness. So was Prince Dolor—or felt as if he were. He jumped into the middle of it, said his charm, and was out through the skylight immediately.

"Good-by, pretty lark!" he shouted, as he passed it on the wing, still warbling its carol to the newly risen sun. "You have been my pleasure, my delight; now I must go and work. Sing to old nurse till I come back again. Perhaps she'll hear you—perhaps she won't—but it will do her good all the same. Good-by!"

But, as the cloak hung irresolute in air, he

suddenly remembered that he had not determined where to go—indeed, he did not know, and there was nobody to tell him.

"Godmother," he cried, in much perplexity, "you know what I want—at least, I hope you do, for I hardly do myself—take me where I ought to go. Show me whatever I ought to see—never mind what I like to see," as a sudden idea came into his mind that he might see many painful and disagreeable things. But this journey was not for pleasure—as before. He was not a baby now, to do nothing but play—big boys do not always play. Nor men neither—they work. Thus much Prince Dolor knew—though very little more.

As the cloak started off, traveling faster than he had ever known it to do—through sky-land and cloud-land, over freezing mountaintops, and desolate stretches of forest, and smiling cultivated plains, and great lakes that seemed to him almost as shoreless as the sea—he was often rather frightened. But he crouched down, silent and quiet; what was the use of making a fuss? And, wrapping himself up in his bearskin, he waited for what was to happen.

After some time he heard a murmur in the distance, increasing more and more till it grew like the hum of a gigantic hive of bees. And,

stretching his chin over the rim of his cloak, Prince Dolor saw—far, far below him, yet, with his gold spectacles and silver ears on, he could distinctly hear and see—what?

Most of us have some time or other visited a great metropolis—have wandered through its network of streets—lost ourselves in its crowds of people—looked up at its tall rows of houses, its grand public buildings, churches, and squares. Also, perhaps, we have peeped into its miserable little back alleys, where dirty children play in gutters all day and half the night—even young boys go about picking pockets, with nobody to tell them it is wrong except the policeman, and he simply takes them off to prison. And all this wretchedness is close behind the grandeur—like the two sides of the leaf of a book.

An awful sight is a large city, seen anyhow from anywhere. But, suppose you were to see it from the upper air, where, with your eyes and ears open, you could take in everything at once? What would it look like? How would you feel about it? I hardly know myself. Do you?

Prince Dolor had need to be a king—that is, a boy with a kingly nature—to be able to stand such a sight without being utterly overcome. But he was very much bewildered—as bewil-

dered as a blind person who is suddenly made to see.

He gazed down on the city below him, and then put his hand over his eyes.

"I can't bear to look at it, it is so beautiful— so dreadful. And I don't understand it—not one bit. There is nobody to tell me about it. I wish I had somebody to speak to."

"Do you? Then pray speak to me. I was always considered good at conversation."

The voice that squeaked out this reply was an excellent imitation of the human one, though it came only from a bird. No lark this time, however, but a great black and white creature that flew into the cloak, and began walking round and round on the edge of it with a dignified stride, one foot before the other, like any unfeathered biped you could name.

"I haven't the honor of your acquaintance, sir," said the boy politely.

"Ma'am, if you please. I am a mother bird, and my name is Mag, and I shall be happy to tell you everything you want to know. For I know a great deal; and I enjoy talking. My family is of great antiquity. We have built in this palace for hundreds—that is to say, dozens of years. I am intimately acquainted with the King, the Queen, and the little Princes and Princesses—

*"I am a magpie. You will find me a most
respectable bird"*

also the maids of honor, and all the inhabitants of the city. I talk a good deal, but I always talk sense, and I dare say I should be exceedingly useful to a poor little ignorant boy like you."

"I am a prince," said the other gently.

"All right. And I am a magpie. You will find me a most respectable bird."

"I have no doubt of it," was the polite answer—though he thought in his own mind that Mag must have a very good opinion of herself. But she was a lady and a stranger, so of course he was civil to her.

She settled herself at his elbow, and began to chatter away, pointing out with one skinny claw, while she balanced herself on the other, every object of interest, evidently believing, as no doubt all its inhabitants did, that there was no capital in the world like the great metropolis of Nomansland.

I have not seen it, and therefore cannot describe it, so we will just take it upon trust, and suppose it to be, like every other fine city, the finest city that ever was built. Mag said so— and of course she knew.

Nevertheless, there were a few things in it which surprised Prince Dolor—and, as he had said, he could not understand them at all. One half the people seemed so happy and busy—

hurrying up and down the full streets, or driving lazily along the parks in their grand carriages, while the other half were so wretched and miserable.

"Can't the world be made a little more equal? I would try to do it if I were a king."

"But you're not the King: only a little goose of a boy," returned the magpie loftily. "And I'm here not to explain things, only to show them. Shall I show you the royal palace?"

It was a very magnificent palace. It had terraces and gardens, battlements and towers. It extended over acres of ground, and had in it rooms enough to accommodate half the city. Its windows looked in all directions, but none of them had any particular view—except a small one, high up toward the roof, which looked out on the Beautiful Mountains. But since the Queen died there it had been closed, boarded up, indeed, the magpie said. It was so little and inconvenient that nobody cared to live in it. Besides, the lower apartments, which had no view, were magnificent—worthy of being inhabited by the King.

"I should like to see the King," said Prince Dolor.

CHAPTER 8

~~~~~~
~~~~~~

WHAT, I WONDER, would be most people's idea of a king? What was Prince Dolor's? Perhaps a very splendid personage, with a crown on his head and a scepter in his hand, sitting on a throne and judging the people. Always doing right, and never wrong—"The king can do no wrong" was a law laid down in olden times. Never cross, or tired, or sick, or suffering; perfectly handsome and well dressed, calm and good-tempered, ready to see and hear everybody, and discourteous to nobody; all things always going well with him, and nothing unpleasant ever happening.

This, probably, was what Prince Dolor expected to see. And what did he see? But I must tell you how he saw it.

The King

What was he like, this great, bad, clever man?

"Ah," said the magpie, "no levee today. The King is ill, though his Majesty does not wish it to be generally known—it would be so very inconvenient. He can't see you, but perhaps you might like to go and take a look at him in a way I often do? It is so very amusing."

Amusing, indeed!

The Prince was just now too much excited to talk much. Was he not going to see the King his uncle, who had succeeded his father and dethroned himself; had stepped into all the pleasant things that he, Prince Dolor, ought to have had, and shut him up in a desolate tower? What was he like, this great, bad, clever man? Had he got all the things he wanted, which another ought to have had? And did he enjoy them?

"Nobody knows," answered the magpie, just as if she had been sitting inside the Prince's heart, instead of on the top of his shoulder. "He is a king, and that's enough. For the rest nobody knows."

As she spoke, Mag flew down onto the palace roof, where the cloak had rested, settling down between the great stacks of chimneys as comfortably as if on the ground. She pecked at the tiles with her beak—truly she was a wonderful

bird—and immediately a little hole opened, a sort of door, through which could be seen distinctly the chamber below.

"Now look in, my Prince. Make haste, for I must soon shut it up again."

But the boy hesitated. "Isn't it rude?—won't they think us intruding?"

"Oh, dear, no! There's a hole like this in every palace; dozens of holes, indeed. Everybody knows it, but nobody speaks of it. Intrusion! Why, though the royal family are supposed to live shut up behind stone walls ever so thick, all the world knows that they live in a glass house where everybody can see them and throw a stone at them. Now pop down on your knees, and take a peep at his Majesty!"

His Majesty!

The Prince gazed eagerly down into a large room, the largest room he had ever beheld, with furniture and hangings grander than anything he could have ever imagined. A stray sunbeam, coming through a crevice of the darkened windows, struck across the carpet, and it was the loveliest carpet ever woven—just like a bed of flowers to walk over; only nobody walked over it, the room being perfectly empty and silent.

"Where is the King?" asked the puzzled boy.

[*123*]

"There," said Mag, pointing with one wrinkled claw to a magnificent bed, large enough to contain six people. In the center of it, just visible under the silken counterpane—quite straight and still—with its head on the lace pillow, lay a small figure, something like waxwork, fast asleep—very fast asleep! There were a number of sparkling rings on the tiny yellow hands, that were curled a little, helplessly, like a baby's, outside the coverlet. The eyes were shut, the nose looked sharp and thin, and the long gray beard hid the mouth and lay over the breast. A sight not ugly nor frightening, only solemn and quiet. And so very silent—two little flies buzzing about the curtains of the bed being the only audible sound.

"Is that the King?" whispered Prince Dolor.

"Yes," replied the bird.

He had been angry—furiously angry—ever since he knew how his uncle had taken the crown, and sent him, a poor little helpless child, to be shut up for life, just as if he had been dead. Many times the boy had felt as if, king as he was, he should like to strike him, this great, strong, wicked man.

Why, you might as well have struck a baby! How helpless he lay, with his eyes shut, and his

The Prince gazed eagerly down into a large room

idle hands folded. They had no more work to do, bad or good.

"What is the matter with him?" asked the Prince.

"He is dead," said the magpie, with a croak.

No, there was not the least use in being angry with him now. On the contrary, the Prince felt almost sorry for him, except that he looked so peaceful with all his cares at rest. And this was being dead? So even kings died?

"Well, well, he hadn't an easy life, folk say, for all his grandeur. Perhaps he is glad it is over. Good-by, your Majesty."

With another cheerful tap of her beak, Mistress Mag shut down the little door in the tiles, and Prince Dolor's first and last sight of his uncle was ended.

He sat in the center of his traveling cloak, silent and thoughtful.

"What shall we do now?" said the magpie. "There's nothing much more to be done with his Majesty, except a fine funeral, which I shall certainly go and see. All the world will. He interested the world exceedingly when he was alive, and he ought to do it now he's dead—just once more. And since he can't hear me, I may as well say that, on the whole, his Majesty is

much better dead than alive—if we can only get somebody in his place. There'll be such a row in the city presently. Suppose we float up again and see it all—at a safe distance, though. It will be such fun!"

"What will be fun?"

"A revolution."

Whether anybody except a magpie would have called it "fun" I don't know, but it certainly was a remarkable scene.

As soon as the cathedral bell began to toll and the minute guns to fire, announcing to the kingdom that it was without a king, the people gathered in crowds, stopping at street corners to talk together. The murmur now and then rose into a shout, and the shout into a roar. When Prince Dolor, quietly floating in upper air, caught the sound of their different and opposite cries, it seemed to him as if the whole city had gone mad together.

"Long live the King!" "The King is dead— down with the King!" "Down with the crown, and the King too!" "Hurrah for the republic!"

"Hurrah for no government at all!"

Such were the shouts which traveled up to the traveling cloak. And then began—oh, what a scene!

When you children are grown men and women—or before—you will hear and read in books about what are called revolutions—earnestly I trust that neither I nor you may ever see one. But they have happened, and may happen again, in other countries besides Nomansland, when wicked kings have helped to make their people wicked too, or out of an unrighteous nation have sprung rulers equally bad; or, without either of these causes, when a restless country has fancied any change better than no change at all.

For me, I don't like changes, unless I am pretty sure that they are for good. And how good can come out of absolute evil—the horrible evil that went on this night under Prince Dolor's very eyes—soldiers shooting down people by hundreds in the streets, scaffolds erected, and heads dropping off—houses burned, and women and children murdered—this is more than I can understand.

But all these things you will find in history, my children, and must by and by judge for yourselves the right and wrong of them, as far as anybody ever can judge.

Prince Dolor saw it all. Things happened so fast one after another that they quite confused his faculties.

"Oh, let me go home," he cried at last, stopping his ears and shutting his eyes; "only let me go home!" For even his lonely tower seemed home, and its dreariness and silence absolute paradise after all this.

"Good-by, then," said the magpie, flapping her wings. She had been chatting incessantly all day and all night, for it was actually thus long that Prince Dolor had been hovering over the city, neither eating nor sleeping, with all these terrible things happening under his very eyes. "You've had enough, I suppose, of seeing the world?"

"Oh, I have—I have!" cried the Prince, with a shudder.

"That is, till next time. All right, your Royal Highness. You don't know me, but I know you. We may meet again sometime."

She looked at him with her clear, piercing eyes, sharp enough to see through everything, and it seemed as if they changed from bird's eyes to human eyes—the very eyes of his godmother, whom he had not seen for ever so long. But the minute afterward she became only a bird, and with a screech and a chatter, spread her wings and flew away.

Prince Dolor fell into a kind of swoon of utter misery, bewilderment, and exhaustion, and

when he awoke he found himself in his own room—alone and quiet—with the dawn just breaking, and the long rim of yellow light in the horizon glimmering through the windowpanes.

CHAPTER 9

~~~~~~

WHEN PRINCE DOLOR SAT UP in bed, trying to remember where he was, whither he had been, and what he had seen the day before, he perceived that his room was empty.

Generally his nurse rather worried him by breaking his slumbers, coming in and "setting things to rights," as she called it. Now the dust lay thick upon chairs and tables. There was no harsh voice heard to scold him for not getting up immediately, which, I am sorry to say, this boy did not always do. For he so enjoyed lying still, and thinking lazily about everything or nothing, that, if he had not tried hard to avoid it, he would certainly have become like those celebrated

Two little men
Who lay in their bed till the clock struck ten.

It was striking ten now, and still no nurse was to be seen. He was rather relieved at first, for he felt so tired. And besides, when he stretched out his arm, he found to his dismay that he had gone to bed in his clothes.

Very uncomfortable he felt, of course; and just a little frightened. Especially when he began to call and call again, but nobody answered. Often he used to think how nice it would be to get rid of his nurse and live in this tower all by himself—like a sort of monarch, able to do everything he liked, and leave undone all that he did not want to do. But now that this seemed really to have happened, he did not like it at all.

"Nurse—dear nurse—please come back!" he called out. "Come back, and I will be the best boy in all the land."

And when she did not come back, and nothing but silence answered his lamentable call, he very nearly began to cry.

"This won't do," he said at last, dashing the tears from his eyes. "It's just like a baby, and I'm a big boy—shall be a man someday. What has happened? I wonder. I'll go and see."

He sprang out of bed—not to his feet, alas! but to his poor little weak knees, and crawled on them from room to room. All the four cham-

bers were deserted—not forlorn or untidy, for everything seemed to have been done for his comfort—the breakfast and dinner things were laid, the food spread in order. He might live "like a prince," as the proverb is, for several days. But the place was entirely forsaken— there was evidently not a creature but himself in the solitary tower.

A great fear came over the poor boy. Lonely as his life had been, he had never known what it was to be absolutely alone. A kind of despair seized him—no violent anger or terror, but a sort of patient desolation.

"What in the world am I to do?" thought he, and sat down in the middle of the floor, half inclined to believe that it would be better to give up entirely, lay himself down, and die.

This feeling, however, did not last long, for he was young and strong, and, I said before, by nature a very courageous boy. There came into his head, somehow or other, a proverb that his nurse had taught him—the people of Nomans-land were very fond of proverbs—

> *For every evil under the sun*
> *There is a remedy, or there's none;*
> *If there is one, try to find it—*
> *If there isn't, never mind it.*

"I wonder is there a remedy now, and could I find it?" cried the Prince, jumping up and looking out the window.

No help there. He saw only the broad, bleak, sunshiny plain—that is, at first. But by and by, in the circle of mud that surrounded the base of the tower, he perceived distinctly the marks of a horse's feet, and just in the spot where the deaf-mute was accustomed to tie up his great black charger, while he himself ascended, there lay the remains of a bundle of hay and a feed of corn.

"Yes, that's it. He has come and gone, taking nurse away with him. Poor nurse! How glad she would be to go!"

That was Prince Dolor's first thought. His second—wasn't it natural?—was a passionate indignation at her cruelty—at the cruelty of all the world toward him, a poor little helpless boy. Then he determined, forsaken as he was, to try and hold on to the last, and not to die as long as he could possibly help it.

Anyhow, it would be easier to die here than out in the world, among the terrible doings which he had just beheld—from the midst of which, it suddenly struck him, the deaf-mute had come, contriving somehow to make the

nurse understand that the King was dead, and she need have no fear in going back to the capital, where there was a grand revolution, and everything turned upside down. So, of course, she had gone. "I hope she'll enjoy it, miserable woman—if they don't cut off her head, too."

And then a kind of remorse smote him for feeling so bitterly toward her, after all the years she had taken care of him—grudgingly, perhaps, and coldly; still she had taken care of him, and that even to the last. For, as I have said, all his four rooms were as tidy as possible, and his meals laid out, that he might have no more trouble than could be helped.

"Possibly she did not mean to be cruel. I won't judge her," said he. And afterward he was very glad that he had so determined.

For the second time he tried to dress himself, and then to do everything he could for himself—even to sweeping up the hearth and putting on more coals. "It's a funny thing for a prince to have to do," said he, laughing. "But my godmother once said princes need never mind doing anything."

And then he thought a little of his godmother. Not of summoning her, or asking her to help him—she had evidently left him to help

himself, and he was determined to try his best to
do it, being a very proud and independent
boy—but he remembered her tenderly and re-
gretfully, as if even she had been a little hard
upon him—poor, forlorn boy that he was. But
he seemed to have seen and learned so much
within the last few days that he scarcely felt like
a boy, but a man—until he went to bed at
night.

When I was a child, I used often to think how
nice it would be to live in a little house all by my
own self—a house built high up in a tree, or far
away in a forest, or halfway up a hillside—so
deliciously alone and independent. Not a lesson to learn—but no! I always liked learning
my lessons. Anyhow, to choose the lessons I
liked best, to have as many books to read and
dolls to play with as ever I wanted: above all, to
be free and at rest, with nobody to tease or
trouble or scold me, would be charming. For I
was a lonely little thing, who liked quietness—
as many children do; which other children, and
sometimes grown-up people even, cannot understand. And so I can understand Prince Dolor.

After his first despair, he was not merely comfortable, but actually happy in his solitude,
doing everything for himself, and enjoying

everything by himself—until bedtime. Then he did not like it at all. No more, I suppose, than other children would have liked my imaginary house in a tree when they had had sufficient of their own company.

But the Prince had to bear it—and he did bear it, like a prince—for fully five days. All that time he got up in the morning and went to bed at night without having spoken to a creature, or, indeed, having heard a single sound. For even his little lark was silent. And as for his traveling cloak, either he never thought about it, or else it had been spirited away—for he made no use of it, nor attempted to do so.

A very strange existence it was, those five lonely days. He never entirely forgot it. It threw him back upon himself, and into himself—in a way that all of us have to learn when we grow up, and are the better for it; but it is somewhat hard learning.

On the sixth day Prince Dolor had a strange composure in his look, but he was very grave and thin and white. He had nearly come to the end of his provisions—and what was to happen next? Get out of the tower he could not. The ladder the deaf-mute used was always carried away again; and if it had not been, how could the poor boy have used it? And even if he slung

or flung himself down, and by miraculous chance came alive to the foot of the tower, how could he run away?

Fate had been very hard on him, or so it seemed.

He made up his mind to die. Not that he wished to die. On the contrary, there was a great deal that he wished to live to do; but if he must die, he must. Dying did not seem so very dreadful; not even to lie quiet like his uncle, whom he had entirely forgiven now, and never be miserable or naughty any more, and escape all those horrible things that he had seen going on outside the palace, in that awful place which was called "the world."

"It's a great deal nicer here," said the poor little Prince, and collected all his pretty things round him: his favorite pictures, which he thought he should like to have near him when he died; his books and toys—no, he had ceased to care for toys now; he only liked them because he had done so as a child. And there he sat very calm and patient, like a king in his castle, waiting for the end.

"Still, I wish I had done something first— something worth doing, that somebody might remember me by," thought he. "Suppose I had grown a man, and had had work to do, and

people to care for, and was so useful and busy
that they liked me, and perhaps even forgot I
was lame? Then it would have been nice to
live, I think."

A tear came into the little fellow's eyes, and
he listened intently through the dead silence for
some hopeful sound.

Was there one?—was it his little lark, whom
he had almost forgotten? No, nothing half so
sweet. But it really was something—something
which came nearer and nearer, so that there was
no mistaking it. It was the sound of a trumpet,
one of the great silver trumpets so admired in
Nomansland. Not pleasant music, but very
bold, grand, and inspiring.

As he listened to it the boy seemed to recall
many things which had slipped his memory for
years, and to nerve himself for whatever might
be going to happen.

What had happened was this.

The poor condemned woman had not been
such a wicked woman after all. Perhaps her
courage was not wholly disinterested, but she
had done a very heroic thing. As soon as she
heard of the death and burial of the King and of
the changes that were taking place in the country, a daring idea came into her head—to set
upon the throne of Nomansland its rightful

heir. Thereupon she persuaded the deaf-mute to take her away with him, and they galloped like the wind from city to city, spreading everywhere the news that Prince Dolor's death and burial had been an invention concocted by his wicked uncle—that he was alive and well, and the noblest young Prince that ever was born.

It was a bold stroke, but it succeeded. The country, weary perhaps of the late King's harsh rule, and yet glad to save itself from the horrors of the last few days, and the still further horrors of no rule at all, and having no particular interest in the other young Princes, jumped at the idea of this Prince, who was the son of their late good King and the beloved Queen Dolorez.

"Hurrah for Prince Dolor! Let Prince Dolor be our sovereign!" rang from end to end of the kingdom. Everybody tried to remember what a dear baby he once was—how like his mother, who had been so sweet and kind, and his father, the finest-looking king that ever reigned. Nobody remembered his lameness—or, if they did, they passed it over as a matter of no consequence. They were determined to have him reign over them, boy as he was—perhaps just because he was a boy, since in that case the great nobles thought they should be able to do as they liked with the country.

Accordingly, with a fickleness not confined to the people of Nomansland, no sooner was the late King laid in his grave than they pronounced him to have been a usurper; turned all his family out of the palace, and left it empty for the reception of the new sovereign, whom they went to fetch with great rejoicing, a select body of lords, gentlemen, and soldiers traveling night and day in solemn procession through the country until they reached Hopeless Tower.

There they found the Prince, sitting calmly on the floor—deadly pale, indeed, for he expected a quite different end from this, and was resolved, if he had to die, to die courageously, like a prince and a king.

But when they hailed him as Prince and King, and explained to him how matters stood, and went down on their knees before him, offering the crown (on a velvet cushion, with four golden tassels, each nearly as big as his head) — small though he was and lame, which lameness the courtiers pretended not to notice—there came such a glow into his face, such a dignity into his demeanor, that he became beautiful, kinglike.

"Yes," he said, "if you desire it, I will be your king. And I will do my best to make my people happy."

Then there arose, from inside and outside the tower, such a shout as never yet was heard across the lonely plain.

Prince Dolor shrank a little from the deafening sound. "How shall I be able to rule all this great people? You forget, my lords, that I am only a little boy still."

"Not so very little," was the respectful answer. "We have searched in the records, and found that your Royal Highness—your Majesty, I mean—is fifteen years old."

"Am I?" said Prince Dolor; and his first thought was a thoroughly childish pleasure that he should now have a birthday, with a whole nation to keep it. Then he remembered that his childish days were done. He was a monarch now. Even his nurse, to whom, the moment he saw her, he had held out his hand, kissed it reverently, and called him ceremoniously "his Majesty the King."

"A king must be always a king, I suppose," said he half sadly, when, the ceremonies over, he had been left to himself for just ten minutes, to put off his boy's clothes and be reattired in magnificent robes, before he was conveyed away from his tower to the royal palace.

He could take nothing with him; indeed, he soon saw that, however politely they spoke, they

would not allow him to take anything. If he was to be their king, he must give up his old life forever. So he looked with tender farewell on his old books, old toys, the furniture he knew so well, and the familiar plain in all its levelness— ugly yet pleasant, simply because it was familiar.

"It will be a new life in a new world," said he to himself; "but I'll remember the old things still. And, oh! if before I go I could but once see my dear old godmother."

While he spoke he had laid himself down on the bed for a minute or two, rather tired with his grandeur, and confused by the noise of the trumpets which kept playing incessantly down below. He gazed, half sadly, up to the skylight, whence there came pouring a stream of sun rays, with innumerable motes floating there, like a bridge thrown between heaven and earth. Sliding down it, as if she had been made of air, came the little old woman in gray.

So beautiful looked she—old as she was—that Prince Dolor was at first quite startled by the apparition. Then he held out his arms in eager delight.

"Oh, godmother, you have not forsaken me!"

"Not at all, my son. You may not have seen

me, but I have seen you many, many times."

"How?"

"Oh, never mind. I can turn into anything I please, you know. And I have been a bearskin rug, and a crystal goblet—and sometimes I have changed from inanimate to animate nature, put on feathers, and made myself very comfortable as a bird."

"Ha!" laughed the Prince, a new light breaking in upon him as he caught the infection of her tone, lively and mischievous. "Ha! ha! a lark, for instance?"

"Or a magpie," answered she, with a capital imitation of Mistress Mag's croaky voice. "Do you suppose I am always sentimental, and never funny? If anything makes you happy, gay, or grave, don't you think it is more than likely to come through your old godmother?"

"I believe that," said the boy tenderly, holding out his arms. They clasped one another in a close embrace.

Suddenly Prince Dolor looked very anxious. "You will not leave me now that I am a king? Otherwise I had rather not be a king at all. Promise never to forsake me!"

The little old woman laughed gaily. "Forsake you? that is impossible. But it is just possible you may forsake me. Not probable

though. Your mother never did, and she was a queen. The sweetest queen in all the world was the Lady Dolorez."

"Tell me about her," said the boy eagerly. "As I get older I think I can understand more. Do tell me."

"Not now. You couldn't hear me for the trumpets and the shouting. But when you are come to the palace, ask for a long-closed upper room, which looks out upon the Beautiful Mountains. Open it and take it for your own. Whenever you go there you will always find me, and we will talk together about all sorts of things."

"And about my mother?"

The little old woman nodded—and kept nodding and smiling to herself many times, as the boy repeated over and over again the sweet words he had never known or understood—"my mother—my mother."

"Now I must go," said she, as the trumpets blared louder and louder, and the shouts of the people showed that they would not endure any delay. "Good-by, good-by! Open the window and out I fly."

Prince Dolor repeated gaily the musical rhyme—but all the while tried to hold his godmother fast.

Vain, vain! for the moment that a knocking was heard at his door the sun went behind a cloud, the bright stream of dancing motes vanished, and the little old woman with them—he knew not where.

So Prince Dolor quitted his tower—which he had entered so mournfully and ignominiously as a little helpless baby carried in the deafmute's arms—quitted it as the great King of Nomansland.

The only thing he took away with him was something so insignificant that none of the lords, gentlemen, and soldiers who escorted him with such triumphant splendor could possibly notice it—a tiny bundle, which he had found lying on the floor just where the bridge of sunbeams had rested. At once he had pounced upon it, and thrust it secretly into his bosom, where it dwindled into such small proportions that it might have been taken for a mere chest comforter, a bit of flannel, or an old pocket handkerchief.

It was his traveling cloak!

CHAPTER 10

DID PRINCE DOLOR BECOME a great king? Was he, though little more than a boy, "the father of his people," as all kings ought to be? Did his reign last long—long and happy? And what were the principal events of it, as chronicled in the history of Nomansland?

Why, if I were to answer all these questions I should have to write another book. And I'm tired, children; tired—as grown-up people sometimes are, though not always with play. (Besides, I have a small person belonging to me, who, though she likes extremely to listen to the word-of-mouth story of this book, grumbles much at the writing of it, and has run about the house clapping her hands with joy when mamma told her that it was nearly finished. But that is neither here nor there.)

I have related as well as I could the history of Prince Dolor, but with the history of Nomansland I am as yet unacquainted. If anybody knows it, perhaps he or she will kindly write it all down in another book. But mine is done.

However, of this I am sure, that Prince Dolor made an excellent king. Nobody ever does anything less well, not even the commonest duty of

common daily life, for having such a godmother as the little old woman clothed in gray, whose name is—well, I leave you to guess. Nor, I think, is anybody less good, less capable of both work and enjoyment in afterlife, for having been a little unhappy in his youth, as the Prince had been.

I cannot take upon myself to say that he was

always happy now—who is?—or that he had no
cares; just show me the person who is quite free
from them! But whenever people worried and
bothered him—as they did sometimes, with
state etiquette, state squabbles, and the like,
setting up themselves and pulling down their
neighbors—he would take refuge in that upper
room which looked out on the Beautiful Mountains, and, laying his head on his godmother's
shoulder, become calmed and at rest.

Also, she helped him out of any difficulty
which now and then occurred—for there never
was such a wise old woman. When the people
of Nomansland raised the alarm—as sometimes
they did—for what people can exist without a
little fault-finding?—and began to cry out, "Unhappy is the nation whose king is a child," she
would say to him gently, "You are a child. Accept the fact. Be humble—be teachable. Lean
upon the wisdom of others till you have gained
your own."

He did so. He learned how to take advice
before attempting to give it, to obey before he
could righteously command. He assembled
round him all the good and wise of his kingdom—laid all its affairs before them, and was
guided by their opinions until he had maturely
formed his own.

This he did sooner than anybody would have imagined who did not know of his godmother and his traveling cloak—two secret blessings, which, though many guessed at, nobody quite understood. Nor did they understand why he loved so the little upper room, except that it had been his mother's room, in the window of which, as people remembered now, she had used to sit for hours watching the Beautiful Mountains.

Out that window he used to fly—not very often. As he grew older, the labors of state prevented the frequent use of his traveling cloak; still he did use it sometimes. Only now it was less for his own pleasure and amusement than to see something or investigate something for the good of the country. But he prized his godmother's gift as dearly as ever. It was a comfort to him in all his vexations, an enhancement of all his joys. It made him almost forget his lameness—which was never cured.

However, the cruel things which had been once foreboded of him did not happen. His misfortune was not such a heavy one, after all. It proved to be of much less inconvenience, even to himself, than had been feared. A council of eminent surgeons and mechanicians invented for him a wonderful pair of crutches,

with the help of which, though he never walked easily or gracefully, he did manage to walk so as to be quite independent. And such was the love his people bore him that they never heard the sound of his crutches on the marble palace floors without a leap of the heart, for they knew that good was coming to them whenever he approached.

Thus, though he never walked in processions, never reviewed his troops mounted on a magnificent charger, nor did any of the things which make a show monarch so much appreciated, he was able to perform all the duties and to enjoy a great many of the pleasures of his rank. When he held his levees, not standing, but seated on a throne ingeniously contrived to hide his infirmity, the people thronged to greet him. When he drove out through the city streets, shouts followed him wherever he went—every countenance brightened as he passed, and his own, perhaps, was the brightest of all.

First, because, accepting his affliction as inevitable, he took it patiently; second, because, being a brave man, he bore it bravely, trying to forget himself, and live out of himself, and in and for other people. Therefore other people grew to love him so well that I think hundreds of his subjects might have been found who were

almost ready to die for their poor lame king.

He never gave them a queen. When they implored him to choose one, he replied that his country was his bride, and he desired no other. But perhaps the real reason was that he shrank from any change; and that no wife in all the world would have been found so perfect, so lovable, so tender to him in all his weaknesses as his beautiful old godmother.

His twenty-four other godfathers and godmothers, or as many of them as were still alive, crowded round him as soon as he ascended the throne. He was very civil to them all, but adopted none of the names they had given him, keeping to the one by which he had been always known, though it had now almost lost its meaning; for King Dolor was one of the happiest and cheerfulest men alive.

He did a good many things, however, unlike most men and most kings, which a little astonished his subjects. First, he pardoned the condemned woman who had been his nurse, and ordained that from henceforth there should be no such thing as the punishment of death in Nomansland. All capital criminals were to be sent to perpetual imprisonment in Hopeless Tower and the plain round about it, where they could do no harm to anybody, and might in

time do a little good, as the woman had done.

Another surprise he shortly afterward gave the nation. He recalled his uncle's family, who had fled away in terror to another country, and restored them to all their honors. By and by he chose the eldest son of his eldest cousin (who had been dead a year) , and had him educated in the royal palace, as the heir to the throne. This little prince was a quiet, unobtrusive boy, so that everybody wondered at the King's choosing him when there were so many more. But as he grew into a fine young fellow, good and brave, they agreed that the King had judged more wisely than they.

"Not a lame prince, either," his Majesty observed one day, watching him affectionately. For he was the best runner, the highest leaper, the keenest and most active sportsman in the country. "One cannot make one's self, but one can sometimes help a little in the making of somebody else. It is well."

This was said, not to any of his great lords and ladies, but to a good old woman—his first homely nurse—whom he had sought for far and wide, and at last had found in her cottage among the Beautiful Mountains. He sent for her to visit him once a year, and treated her with great honor until she died. He was

equally kind, though somewhat less tender, to his other nurse, who, after receiving her pardon, returned to her native town and grew into a great lady, and I hope a good one. But as she was so grand a personage now, any little faults she had did not show.

Thus King Dolor's reign passed year after year, long and prosperous. Whether he was happy—"as happy as a king"—is a question no human being can decide. But I think he was, because he had the power of making everybody

about him happy, and did it too; also because he was his godmother's godson, and could shut himself up with her whenever he liked, in that quiet little room in view of the Beautiful Mountains, which nobody else ever saw or cared to see. They were too far off, and the city lay so low. But there they were, all the time. No change ever came to them; and I think, at any day throughout his long reign, the King would sooner have lost his crown than have lost sight of the Beautiful Mountains.

In course of time, when the little Prince his cousin was grown into a tall young man, capable of all the duties of a man, his Majesty did one of the most extraordinary acts ever known in a sovereign beloved by his people and prosperous in his reign. He announced that he wished to invest his heir with the royal purple—at any rate, for a time—while he himself went away on a distant journey, whither he had long desired to go.

Everybody marveled, but nobody opposed him. Who could oppose the good King, who was not a young king now? And besides, the nation had a great admiration for the young Regent—and possibly a lurking pleasure in change.

So there was a fixed day when all the people

whom it would hold assembled in the great square of the capital, to see the young Prince installed solemnly in his new duties, and undertaking his new vows. He was a very fine young fellow; tall and straight as a poplar tree, with a frank, handsome face—a great deal handsomer than the King's, some people said, but others thought differently. However, as his Majesty sat on his throne, with his gray hair falling from underneath his crown, and a few wrinkles showing in spite of his smile, there was something about his countenance which made his people, even while they shouted, regard him with a tenderness mixed with awe.

He lifted up his thin, slender hand, and there came a silence over the vast crowd immediately. Then he spoke, in his own accustomed way, using no grand words, but saying what he had to say in the simplest fashion, though with a clearness that struck their ears like the first song of a bird in the dusk of the morning.

"My people, I am tired; I want to rest. I have had a long reign, and done much work—at least, as much as I was able to do. Many might have done it better than I—but none with a better will. Now I leave it to others; I am tired, very tired. Let me go home."

There arose a murmur—of content or discon-

tent none could well tell; then it died down again, and the assembly listened silently once more.

"I am not anxious about you, my people—my children," continued the King. "You are prosperous and at peace. I leave you in good hands. The Prince Regent will be a fitter king for you than I."

"No, no, no!" rose the universal shout—and those who had sometimes found fault with him shouted louder than anybody. But he seemed as if he heard them not.

"Yes, yes," said he, as soon as the tumult had a little subsided; and his voice sounded firm and clear. Some very old people, who boasted of having seen him as a child, declared that his face took a sudden change, and grew as young and sweet as that of the little Prince Dolor. "Yes, I must go. It is time for me to go. Remember me sometimes, my people, for I have loved you well. And I am going a long way, and I do not think I shall come back any more."

He drew a little bundle out of his breast pocket—a bundle that nobody had ever seen before. It was small and shabby-looking, and tied up with many knots, which untied themselves in an instant. With a joyful countenance, he muttered over it a few half-

intelligible words. Then, so suddenly that even those nearest to his Majesty could not tell how it came about, the King was away—away—floating right up in the air—upon something, they knew not what, except that it appeared to be as safe and pleasant as the wings of a bird.

And after him sprang a bird—a dear little lark, rising from whence no one could say, since larks do not usually build their nests on the pavement of city squares. But there it was, a real lark, singing far over their heads, louder and clearer and more joyful as it vanished farther into the blue sky.

Shading their eyes, and straining their ears, the astonished people stood until the whole vision disappeared like a speck in the clouds—the rosy clouds that overhung the Beautiful Mountains.

King Dolor was never again beheld or heard of in his own country. But the good he had done there lasted for years and years. He was long missed and deeply mourned—at least, so far as anybody could mourn one who was gone on such a happy journey.

Whither he went, or who went with him, it is impossible to say. But I myself believe that his godmother took him on his traveling cloak to

the Beautiful Mountains. What he did there, or where he is now, who can tell? I cannot. But one thing I am quite sure of, that, wherever he is, he is perfectly happy.

And so, when I think of him, am I.

THE MERRY ADVENTURES OF

Robin Hood

Gallant Robin Hood and his merry band of outlaws live on in Howard Pyle's classic tale of the gay young leader and his stout Saxon yeomen—Little John, Friar Tuck, Allan a Dale and all the others—and of the carefree life they lead in the cool green of Sherwood Forest, sharing with the poor the rich spoils plundered from greedy Norman barons—and sometimes just barely avoiding capture by the determined Sheriff of Nottingham.

The story of Robin Hood, one of the most beloved heroes of early England, is a sheer delight to the reader besides being a fascinating picture of England after the Norman Conquest.

The soldiers, all unknowing, passed beneath.

THE MERRY ADVENTURES

OF Robin Hood

BY HOWARD PYLE

ILLUSTRATIONS BY JO POLSENO

Companion Library

GROSSET & DUNLAP

PUBLISHERS

NEW YORK

Preface

YOU WHO SO PLOD amid serious things that you feel it shame to give yourself up even for a few short moments to mirth and joyousness in the land of Fancy; you who think that life hath nought to do with innocent laughter that can harm no one; these pages are not for you. Clap to the leaves and go no farther than this, for I tell you plainly that if you go farther you will be scandalized by seeing good, sober folks of real history so frisk and caper in gay colors and motley that you would not know them but for the names tagged to them. Here is a stout, lusty fellow with a quick temper, yet none so ill for all that, who goes by the name of Henry II. Here is a fair, gentle lady before whom all the others bow and call her Queen Eleanor. Here is a fat rogue of a fellow, dressed up in rich robes of a clerical kind, that all the good folk call my Lord Bishop of Hereford. Here is a certain fellow with a sour temper and a grim look—the worshipful, the Sheriff of Nottingham. And here, above all, is a great, tall, merry fellow that roams the greenwood and joins in homely sports, and sits beside the Sheriff at merry feast, which same beareth the name of the proudest of the Plantagenets—Richard of the Lion's Heart. Besides

these are a whole host of knights, priests, nobles, burghers, yeomen, pages, ladies, lasses, landlords, beggars, peddlers, and what not, all living the merriest of merry lives, and all bound by nothing but a few odd strands of certain old ballads (snipped and clipped and tied together again in a score of knots) which draw these jocund fellows here and there, singing as they go.

Here you will find a hundred dull, sober, jogging places, all tricked out with flowers and what not, till no one would know them in their fanciful dress. And here is a country bearing a well-known name, wherein no chill mists press upon our spirits, and no rain falls but what rolls off our backs like April showers off the backs of sleek drakes; where flowers bloom forever and birds are always singing; where every fellow hath a merry catch as he travels the roads, and ale and beer and wine (such as muddle no wits) flow like water in a brook.

This country is not Fairyland. What is it? 'Tis the land of Fancy, and is of that pleasant kind that, when you tire of it—whisk!—you clap the leaves of this book together and 'tis gone, and you are ready for everyday life, with no harm done.

And now I lift the curtain that hangs between here and No-man's-land. Will you come with me, sweet reader? I thank you. Give me your hand.

Contents

CONTENTS

THE MERRY ADVENTURES OF
Robin Hood

How Robin Hood
Came to Be an Outlaw

In MERRY ENGLAND in the time of old, when good King Henry the Second ruled the land, there lived within the green glades of Sherwood Forest, near Nottingham Town, a famous outlaw whose name was Robin Hood. No archer ever lived that could speed a gray goose shaft with such skill and cunning as his, nor were there ever such yeomen as the sevenscore merry men that roamed with him through the greenwood shades. Right merrily they dwelled within the depths of Sherwood Forest, suffering neither care nor want, but passing the time in merry games of archery or bouts of cudgel play, living upon the King's venison, washed down with draughts of ale of October brewing.

Not only Robin himself but all the band were outlaws and dwelled apart from other men, yet they were beloved by the country people round about, for no one ever came to jolly Robin for help in time of need and went away again with an empty fist.

And now I will tell how it came about that Robin Hood fell afoul of the law.

When Robin was a youth of eighteen, stout of sinew and bold of heart, the Sheriff of Nottingham proclaimed a

shooting match and offered a prize of a butt of ale to whosoever should shoot the best shaft in Nottingham-shire. "Now," quoth Robin, "will I go too, for fain would I draw a string for the bright eyes of my lass and a butt of good October brewing." So up he got and took his good stout yew bow and a score or more of broad clothyard arrows, and started off from Locksley Town through Sherwood Forest to Nottingham.

It was at the dawn of day in the merry Maytime, when hedgerows are green and flowers bedeck the meadows, daisies pied and yellow cuckoo buds and fair primroses all along the briery hedges; when apple buds blossom and sweet birds sing, the lark at dawn of day, the throstle cock and cuckoo; when lads and lasses look upon each other with sweet thoughts; when busy housewives spread their linen to bleach upon the bright green grass. Sweet was the greenwood as he walked along its paths, and bright the green and rustling leaves, amid which the little birds sang with might and main: and blithely Robin whistled as he trudged along, thinking of Maid Marian and her bright eyes, for at such times a youth's thoughts are wont to turn pleasantly upon the lass that he loves the best.

As thus he walked along with a brisk step and a merry whistle, he came suddenly upon some foresters seated beneath a great oak tree. Fifteen there were in all, mak-ing themselves merry with feasting and drinking as they sat around a huge pasty, to which each man helped him-self, thrusting his hands into the pie, and washing down that which they ate with great horns of ale which they drew all foaming from a barrel that stood nigh. Each man was clad in Lincoln green, and a fine show they made, seated upon the sward beneath that fair, spreading tree. Then one of them, with his mouth full, called out to Robin, "Hulloa, where goest thou, little lad, with thy one-penny bow and thy farthing shafts?"

Then Robin grew angry, for no stripling likes to be taunted with his green years.

"Now," quoth he, "my bow and eke mine arrows are as good as thine; and moreover, I go to the shooting match at Nottingham Town, which same has been proclaimed by our good Sheriff of Nottinghamshire; there I will shoot with other stout yeomen, for a prize has been offered of a fine butt of ale."

Then one who held a horn of ale in his hand said, "Ho! listen to the lad! Why, boy, thy mother's milk is yet scarce dry upon thy lips, and yet thou pratest of standing up with good stout men at Nottingham butts, thou who art scarce able to draw one string of a two-stone bow."

"I'll hold the best of you twenty marks," quoth bold Robin, "that I hit the clout at threescore rods, by the good help of Our Lady fair."

At this all laughed aloud, and one said, "Well boasted, thou fair infant, well boasted! And well thou knowest that no target is nigh to make good thy wager."

And another cried, "He will be taking ale with his milk next."

At this Robin grew right mad. "Hark ye," said he, "yonder, at the glade's end, I see a herd of deer, even more than threescore rods distant. I'll hold you twenty marks that, by leave of Our Lady, I cause the best hart among them to die."

"Now done!" cried he who had spoken first. "And here are twenty marks. I wager that thou causest no beast to die, with or without the aid of Our Lady."

Then Robin took his good yew bow in his hand, and placing the tip at his instep, he strung it right deftly; then he nocked a broad clothyard arrow and, raising the bow, drew the gray goose feather to his ear; the next moment the bowstring rang and the arrow sped down the glade as a sparrowhawk skims in a northern wind. High leaped

the noblest hart of all the herd, only to fall dead, reddening the green path with his heart's blood.

"Ha!" cried Robin, "how likest thou that shot, good fellow? I wot the wager were mine, an it were three hundred pounds."

Then all the foresters were filled with rage, and he who had spoken the first and had lost the wager was more angry than all.

"Nay," cried he, "the wager is none of thine, and get thee gone, straightway, or, by all the saints of heaven, I'll baste thy sides until thou wilt ne'er be able to walk again."

"Knowest thou not," said another, "that thou hast killed the King's deer, and, by the laws of our gracious lord and sovereign King Harry, thine ears should be shaven close to thy head?"

"Catch him!" cried a third.

"Nay," said a fourth, "let him e'en go because of his tender years."

Never a word said Robin Hood, but he looked at the foresters with a grim face; then, turning on his heel, strode away from them down the forest glade. But his heart was bitterly angry, for his blood was hot and youthful and prone to boil.

Now, well would it have been for him who had first spoken had he left Robin Hood alone; but his anger was hot, both because the youth had gotten the better of him and because of the deep draughts of ale that he had been quaffing. So, of a sudden, without any warning, he sprang to his feet, and seized upon his bow and fitted it to a shaft.

"Ay," cried he, "and I'll hurry thee anon." And he sent the arrow whistling after Robin.

It was well for Robin Hood that that same forester's head was spinning with ale, or else he would never have taken another step. As it was, the arrow whistled within three inches of his head. Then he turned around and

quickly drew his own bow, and sent an arrow back in return.

"Ye said I was no archer," cried he aloud, "but say so now again!"

The shaft flew straight; the archer fell forward with a cry, and lay on his face upon the ground, his arrows rattling about him from out of his quiver, the gray goose shaft wet with his heart's blood. Then, before the others could gather their wits about them, Robin Hood was gone into the depths of the greenwood. Some started after him, but not with much heart, for each feared to suffer the death of his fellow; so presently they all came and lifted the dead man up and bore him away to Nottingham Town.

Meanwhile Robin Hood ran through the greenwood. Gone was all the joy and brightness from everything, for his heart was sick within him, and it was borne in upon his soul that he had slain a man.

"Alas!" cried he, "thou hast found me an archer that will make thy wife to wring! I would that thou hadst ne'er said one word to me, or that I had never passed thy way, or e'en that my right forefinger had been stricken off ere that this had happened! In haste I smote, but grieve I sore at leisure!" And then, even in his trouble, he remembered the old saw that "What is done is done; and the egg cracked cannot be cured."

And so he came to dwell in the greenwood that was to be his home for many a year to come, never again to see the happy days with the lads and lasses of sweet Locksley Town; for he was outlawed, not only because he had killed a man, but also because he had poached upon the King's deer, and two hundred pounds were set upon his head, as a reward for whoever would bring him to the court of the King.

Now the Sheriff of Nottingham swore that he himself would bring this knave Robin Hood to justice, and for

two reasons: first, because he wanted the two hundred pounds, and next, because the forester that Robin Hood had killed was of kin to him.

But Robin Hood lay hidden in Sherwood Forest for one year, and in that time there gathered around him many others like himself, cast out from other folk for this cause and for that. Some had shot deer in hungry wintertime, when they could get no other food, and had been seen in the act by the foresters, but had escaped, thus saving their ears; some had been turned out of their inheritance, that their farms might be added to the King's lands in Sherwood Forest; some had been despoiled by a great baron or a rich abbot or a powerful esquire—all, for one cause or another, had come to Sherwood to escape wrong and oppression.

So, in all that year, fivescore or more good stout yeomen gathered about Robin Hood, and chose him to be their leader and chief. Then they vowed that even as they themselves had been despoiled they would despoil their oppressors, whether baron, abbot, knight, or squire, and that from each they would take that which had been wrung from the poor by unjust taxes, or land rents, or in wrongful fines. But to the poor folk they would give a helping hand in need and trouble, and would return to them that which had been unjustly taken from them. Besides this, they swore never to harm a child nor to wrong a woman, be she maid, wife, or widow; so that, after a while, when the people began to find that no harm was meant to them, but that money or food came in time of want to many a poor family, they came to praise Robin and his merry men, and to tell many tales of him and of his doings in Sherwood Forest, for they felt him to be one of themselves.

Up rose Robin Hood one merry morn when all the birds were singing blithely among the leaves, and up rose

all his merry men, each fellow washing his head and hands in the cold brown brook that leaped laughing from stone to stone. Then said Robin, "For fourteen days have we seen no sport, so now I will go abroad to seek adventures forthwith. But tarry ye, my merry men all, here in the greenwood; only see that ye mind well my call. Three blasts upon the bugle horn I will blow in my hour of need; then come quickly, for I shall want your aid."

So saying, he strode away through the leafy forest glades until he had come to the verge of Sherwood. There he wandered for a long time, through highway and byway, through dingly dell and forest skirts. Now he met a fair buxom lass in a shady lane, and each gave the other a merry word and passed their way; now he saw a fair lady upon an ambling pad, to whom he doffed his cap, and who bowed sedately in return to the fairy youth; now he saw a fat monk on a pannier-laden ass; now a gallant knight, with spear and shield and armor that flashed brightly in the sunlight; now a page clad in crimson; and now a stout burgher from good Nottingham Town, pacing along with serious footsteps; all these sights he saw, but adventure found he none. At last he took a road by the forest skirts, a bypath that dipped toward a broad, pebbly stream spanned by a narrow bridge made of a log of wood. As he drew nigh this bridge he saw a tall stranger coming from the other side. Thereupon Robin quickened his pace, as did the stranger likewise, each thinking to cross first.

"Now stand thou back," quoth Robin, "and let the better man cross first."

"Nay," answered the stranger, "then stand back thine own self, for the better man, I wot, am I."

"That will we presently see," quoth Robin, "and meanwhile stand thou where thou art, or else, by the bright brow of Saint Ælfrida, I will show thee right good Nottingham play with a clothyard shaft betwixt thy ribs."

"Now," quoth the stranger, "I will tan thy hide till it be as many colors as a beggar's cloak, if thou darest so much as touch a string of that same bow that thou holdest in thy hands."

"Thou pratest like an ass," said Robin, "for I could send this shaft clean through thy proud heart before a curtal friar could say grace over a roast goose at Michaelmastide."

"And thou pratest like a coward," answered the stranger, "for thou standest there with a good yew bow to shoot at my heart, while I have nought in my hand but a plain blackthorn staff wherewith to meet thee."

"Now," quoth Robin, "by the faith of my heart, never have I had a coward's name in all my life before. I will lay by my trusty bow and eke my arrows, and if thou darest abide my coming, I will go and cut a cudgel to test thy manhood withal."

"Ay, marry, that will I abide thy coming, and joyously, too," quoth the stranger; whereupon he leaned sturdily upon his staff to await Robin.

Then Robin Hood stepped quickly to the coverside and cut a good staff of ground oak, straight, without flaw, and six feet in length, and came back trimming away the tender stems from it, while the stranger waited for him, leaning upon his staff, and whistling as he gazed round about. Robin observed him furtively as he trimmed his staff, measuring him from top to toe from out the corner of his eye, and thought that he had never seen a lustier or a stouter man. Tall was Robin, but taller was the stranger by a head and a neck, for he was seven feet in height. Broad was Robin across the shoulders, but broader was the stranger by twice the breadth of a palm, while he measured at least an ell around the waist.

"Nevertheless," said Robin to himself, "I will baste thy hide right merrily, my good fellow"; then, aloud, "Lo, here is my good staff, lusty and tough. Now wait my

coming, an thou darest, and meet me an thou fearest not. Then we will fight until one or the other of us tumble into the stream of dint of blows."

"Marry, that meeteth my whole heart!" cried the stranger, twirling his staff above his head, betwixt his fingers and thumb, until it whistled again.

Never did the Knights of Arthur's Round Table meet in a stouter fight than did these two. In a moment Robin stepped quickly upon the bridge where the stranger stood; first he made a feint, and then delivered a blow at the stranger's head that, had it met its mark, would have tumbled him speedily into the water. But the stranger turned the blow right deftly and in return gave one as stout, which Robin also turned as the stranger had done. So they stood, each in his place, neither moving a finger's-breadth back, for one good hour, and many blows were given and received by each in that time, till here and there were sore bones and bumps, yet neither thought of crying "Enough," nor seemed likely to fall from off the bridge. Now and then they stopped to rest, and each thought that he never had seen in all his life before such a hand at quarterstaff. At last Robin gave the stranger a blow upon the ribs that made his jacket smoke like a damp straw thatch in the sun. So shrewd was the stroke that the stranger came within a hair's-breadth of falling off the bridge; but he regained himself right quickly and, by a dexterous blow, gave Robin a crack on the crown that caused the blood to flow. Then Robin grew mad with anger and smote with all his might at the other. But the stranger warded the blow and once again thwacked Robin, and this time so fairly that he fell heels over head into the water, as the queen pin falls in a game of bowls.

"And where art thou now, my good lad?" shouted the stranger, roaring with laughter.

"Oh, in the flood and floating adown with the tide," cried Robin, nor could he forbear laughing himself at his

The stranger turned the blow right deftly
and in return gave one as stout.

sorry plight. Then, gaining his feet, he waded to the bank, the little fish speeding hither and thither, all frightened at his splashing.

"Give me thy hand," cried he, when he had reached the bank. "I must needs own thou art a brave and a sturdy soul and, withal, a good stout stroke with the cudgels. By this and by that, my head hummeth like to a hive of bees on a hot June day."

Then he clapped his horn to his lips and winded a blast that went echoing sweetly down the forest paths. "Ay, marry," quoth he again, "thou art a tall lad, and eke a brave one, for ne'er, I trow, is there a man betwixt here and Canterbury Town could do the like to me that thou hast done."

"And thou," quoth the stranger, laughing, "takest thy cudgeling like a brave heart and a stout yeoman."

But now the distant twigs and branches rustled with the coming of men, and suddenly a score or two of good stout yeomen, all clad in Lincoln green, burst from out the covert, with merry Will Stutely at their head.

"Good master," cried Will, "how is this? Truly thou art all wet from head to foot, and that to the very skin."

"Why, marry," answered jolly Robin, "yon stout fellow hath tumbled me neck and crop into the water and hath given me a drubbing beside."

"Then shall he not go without a ducking and eke a drubbing himself!" cried Will Stutely. "Have at him, lads!"

Then Will and a score of yeomen leaped upon the stranger, but though they sprang quickly they found him ready and felt him strike right and left with his stout staff, so that, though he went down with press of numbers, some of them rubbed cracked crowns before he was overcome.

"Nay, forbear!" cried Robin, laughing until his sore sides ached again. "He is a right good man and true, and

no harm shall befall him. Now hark ye, good youth, wilt thou stay with me and be one of my band? Three suits of Lincoln green shalt thou have each year, beside forty marks in fee, and share with us whatsoever good shall befall us. Thou shalt eat sweet venison and quaff the stoutest ale, and mine own good right-hand man shalt thou be, for never did I see such a cudgel player in all my life before. Speak! Wilt thou be one of my good merry men?"

"That know I not," quoth the stranger surlily, for he was angry at being so tumbled about. "If ye handle yew bow and apple shaft no better than ye do oaken cudgel, I wot ye are not fit to be called yeomen in my country; but if there be any man here that can shoot a better shaft than I, then will I bethink me of joining with you."

"Now by my faith," said Robin, "thou art a right saucy varlet, sirrah; yet I will stoop to thee as I never stooped to man before. Good Stutely, cut thou a fair white piece of bark four fingers in breadth, and set it fourscore yards distant on yonder oak. Now, stranger, hit that fairly with a gray goose shaft and call thyself an archer."

"Ay, marry, that will I," answered he. "Give me a good stout bow and a fair broad arrow, and if I hit it not, strip me and beat me blue with bowstrings."

Then he chose the stoutest bow among them all, next to Robin's own, and a straight gray goose shaft, well-feathered and smooth, and stepping to the mark—while all the band, sitting or lying upon the greensward, watched to see him shoot—he drew the arrow to his cheek and loosed the shaft right deftly, sending it so straight down the path that it clove the mark in the very center. "Aha!" cried he, "mend thou that if thou canst"; while even the yeomen clapped their hands at so fair a shot.

"That is a keen shot indeed," quoth Robin. "Mend it I cannot, but mar it I may, perhaps."

Then taking up his own good stout bow and nocking an arrow with care, he shot with his very greatest skill. Straight flew the arrow, and so true that it lit fairly upon the stranger's shaft and split it into splinters. Then all the yeomen leaped to their feet and shouted for joy that their master had shot so well.

"Now by the lusty yew bow of good Saint Withold," cried the stranger, "that is a shot indeed, and never saw I the like in all my life before! Now truly will I be thy man henceforth and for aye. Good Adam Bell * was a fair shot, but never shot he so!"

"Then have I gained a right good man this day," quoth jolly Robin. "What name goest thou by, good fellow?"

"Men call me John Little whence I came," answered the stranger.

Then Will Stutely, who loved a good jest, spoke up. "Nay, fair little stranger," said he, "I like not thy name and fain would I have it otherwise. Little art thou indeed, and small of bone and sinew, therefore shalt thou be christened Little John, and I will be thy godfather."

Then Robin Hood and all his band laughed aloud until the stranger began to grow angry.

"An thou make a jest of me," quoth he to Will Stutely, "thou wilt have sore bones and little pay, and that in short season."

"Nay, good friend," said Robin Hood, "bottle thine anger, for the name fitteth thee well. Little John shall thou be called henceforth, and Little John shall it be. So come, my merry men, we will prepare a christening feast for this fair infant."

So turning their backs upon the stream, they plunged into the forest once more, through which they traced their steps till they reached the spot where they dwelled in the

* Adam Bell, Clym o' the Clough, and William of Cloudesly were three noted north-country bowmen whose names have been celebrated in many ballads of the olden time.

depths of the woodland. There had they built huts of bark and branches of trees, and made couches of sweet rushes spread over with skins of fallow deer. Here stood a great oak tree with branches spreading broadly around, beneath which was a seat of green moss where Robin Hood was wont to sit at feast and at merrymaking with his stout men about him. Here they found the rest of the band, some of whom had come in with a brace of fat does. Then they all built great fires and after a time roasted the does and broached a barrel of humming ale. Then when the feast was ready they all sat down, but Robin placed Little John at his right hand, for he was henceforth to be the second in the band.

Then when the feast was done Will Stutely spoke up. "It is now time, I ween, to christen our bonny babe, is it not so, merry boys?" And "Aye! Aye!" cried all, laughing till the woods echoed with their mirth.

"Then seven sponsors shall we have," quoth Will Stutely, and hunting among all the band, he chose the seven stoutest men of them all.

"Now by Saint Dunstan," cried Little John, springing to his feet, "more than one of you shall rue it an you lay finger upon me."

But without a word they all ran upon him at once, seizing him by his legs and arms and holding him tightly in spite of his struggles, and they bore him forth while all stood around to see the sport. Then one came forward who had been chosen to play the priest because he had a bald crown, and in his hand he carried a brimming pot of ale. "Now, who bringeth this babe?" asked he right soberly.

"That do I," answered Will Stutely.

"And what name callest thou him?"

"Little John call I him."

"Now Little John," quoth the mock priest, "thou hast not lived heretofore, but only got thee along through the

world, but henceforth thou wilt live indeed. When thou livedst not thou wast called John Little, but now that thou dost live indeed, Little John shalt thou be called, so christen I thee." And at these last words he emptied the pot of ale upon Little John's head.

Then all shouted with laughter as they saw the good brown ale stream over Little John's beard and trickle from his nose and chin, while his eyes blinked with the smart of it. At first he was of a mind to be angry but found he could not, because the others were so merry; so he, too, laughed with the rest. Then Robin took this sweet, pretty babe, clothed him all anew from top to toe in Lincoln green, and gave him a good stout bow, and so made him a member of the merry band.

Robin Hood and the Tinker

Now it was told before how two hundred pounds were set upon Robin Hood's head, and how the Sheriff of Nottingham swore that he himself would seize Robin, both because he would fain have the two hundred pounds and because the slain man was a kinsman of his own. Now the Sheriff did not yet know what a force Robin had about him in Sherwood, but thought that he might serve a warrant for his arrest as he could upon any other man that had broken the laws; therefore he offered fourscore golden angels to anyone who would serve this warrant. But men of Nottingham Town knew more of Robin Hood and his doings than the Sheriff did, and many laughed to think of serving a warrant upon the bold outlaw, knowing well that all they would get for such service would be cracked crowns; so that no one came forward to take the matter in hand. Thus a fortnight passed, in which time none came forward to do the Sheriff's business. Then said he, "A right good reward have I offered to whosoever would serve my warrant upon Robin Hood, and I marvel that no one has come to undertake the task."

Then one of his men who was near him said, "Good master, thou wottest not the force that Robin Hood has about him and how little he cares for warrant of king or sheriff. Truly, no one likes to go on this service, for fear of cracked crowns and broken bones."

"Then I hold all Nottingham men to be cowards," said the Sheriff. "And let me see the man in all Nottingham-shire that dare disobey the warrant of our sovereign lord King Harry, for, by the shrine of Saint Edmund, I will hang him forty cubits high! But if no man in Nottingham dare win fourscore angels, I will send elsewhere, for there should be men of mettle somewhere in this land."

Then he called up a messenger in whom he placed great trust, and bade him saddle his horse and make ready to go to Lincoln Town to see whether he could find anyone there that would do his bidding and win the reward. So that same morning the messenger started forth upon his errand.

Bright shone the sun upon the dusty highway that led from Nottingham to Lincoln, stretching away all white over hill and dale. Dusty was the highway and dusty the throat of the messenger, so that his heart was glad when he saw before him the Sign of the Blue Boar Inn, when somewhat more than half his journey was done. The inn looked fair to his eyes, and the shade of the oak trees that stood around it seemed cool and pleasant, so he alighted from his horse to rest himself for a time, calling for a pot of ale to refresh his thirsty throat.

There he saw a party of right jovial fellows seated beneath the spreading oak that shaded the greensward in front of the door. There was a tinker, two barefoot friars, and a party of six of the King's foresters all clad in Lincoln green, and all of them were quaffing humming ale and singing merry ballads of the good old times. Loud laughed the foresters, as jests were bandied about between the singing, and louder laughed the friars, for they

were lusty men with beards that curled like the wool of black rams; but loudest of all laughed the Tinker, and he sang more sweetly than any of the rest. His bag and his hammer hung upon a twig of the oak tree, and near by leaned his good stout cudgel, as thick as his wrist and knotted at the end.

"Come," cried one of the foresters to the tired messenger, "come join us for this shot. Ho, landlord! Bring a fresh pot of ale for each man."

The messenger was glad enough to sit down along with the others who were there, for his limbs were weary and the ale was good.

"Now what news bearest thou so fast?" quoth one, "and whither ridest thou today?"

The messenger was a chatty soul and loved a bit of gossip dearly; besides, the pot of ale warmed his heart; so that, settling himself in an easy corner of the inn bench, while the host leaned upon the doorway and the hostess stood with her hands beneath her apron, he unfolded his budget of news with great comfort. He told all from the very first: how Robin Hood had slain the forester, and how he had hidden in the greenwood to escape the law; how that he lived therein, all against the law, God wot, slaying His Majesty's deer and levying toll on fat abbot, knight, and esquire, so that none dare travel even on broad Watling Street or the Fosse Way for fear of him; how that the Sheriff had a mind to serve the King's warrant upon this same rogue, though little would he mind warrant of either king or sheriff, for he was far from being a law-abiding man. Then he told how none could be found in all Nottingham Town to serve this warrant, for fear of cracked pates and broken bones, and how that he, the messenger, was now upon his way to Lincoln Town to find of what mettle the Lincoln men might be.

"Now come I, forsooth, from good Banbury Town," said the jolly Tinker, "and no one nigh Nottingham—nor

Sherwood either, an that be the mark—can hold cudgel with my grip. Why, lads, did I not meet that mad wag Simon of Ely, even at the famous fair at Hertford Town, and beat him in the ring at that place before Sir Robert of Leslie and his lady? This same Robin Hood, of whom, I wot, I never heard before, is a right merry blade, but gin he be strong, am not I stronger? And gin he be sly, am not I slyer? Now by the bright eyes of Nan o' the Mill, and by mine own name and that's Wat o' the Crabstaff, and by mine own mother's son, and that's myself, will I, even I, Wat o' the Crabstaff, meet this same sturdy rogue, and gin he mind not the seal of our glorious sovereign King Harry, and the warrant of the good Sheriff of Nottinghamshire, I will so bruise, beat, and bemaul his pate that he shall never move finger or toe again! Hear ye that, bully boys?"

"Now art thou the man for my farthing," cried the messenger. "And back thou goest with me to Nottingham Town."

"Nay," quoth the Tinker, shaking his head slowly from side to side. "Go I with no man gin it be not with mine own free will."

"Nay, nay," said the messenger, "no man is there in Nottinghamshire could make thee go against thy will, thou brave fellow."

"Ay, that be I brave," said the Tinker.

"Ay, marry," said the messenger, "thou art a brave lad; but our good Sheriff hath offered fourscore angels of bright gold to whosoever shall serve the warrant upon Robin Hood; though little good will it do."

"Then I will go with thee, lad. Do but wait till I get my bag and hammer, and my cudgel. Ay, let me but meet this same Robin Hood, and let me see whether he will not mind the King's warrant." So, after having paid their score, the messenger, with the Tinker striding beside his nag, started back to Nottingham again.

One bright morning soon after this time, Robin Hood started off to Nottingham Town to find what was a-doing there, walking merrily along the roadside where the grass was sweet with daisies, his eyes wandering and his thoughts also. His bugle horn hung at his hip and his bow and arrows at his back, while in his hand he bore a good stout oaken staff, which he twirled with his fingers as he strolled along.

As thus he walked down a shady lane he saw a tinker coming, trolling a merry song as he drew nigh. On his back hung his bag and his hammer, and in his hand he carried a right stout crabstaff full six feet long, and thus sang he:

> *"In peascod time, when hound to horn*
> *Gives ear till buck be killed,*
> *And little lads with pipes of corn*
> *Sit keeping beasts afield—"*

"Halloa, good friend!" cried Robin.

> *"I went to gather strawberries—"*

"Halloa!" cried Robin again.

> *"By woods and groves full fair—"*

"Halloa! Art thou deaf, man? Good friend, say I!"

"And who art thou dost so boldly check a fair song?" quoth the Tinker, stopping in his singing. "Halloa, thine own self, whether thou be good friend or no. But let me tell thee, thou stout fellow, gin thou be a good friend it were well for us both; but gin thou be no good friend it were ill for thee."

"And whence comest thou, my lusty blade?" quoth Robin.

"I come from Banbury," answered the Tinker.

"Alas!" quoth Robin, "I hear there is sad news this merry morn."

"Ha! Is it indeed so?" cried the Tinker eagerly. "Prythee tell it speedily, for I am a tinker by trade, as thou seest, and as I am in my trade I am greedy for news, even as a priest is greedy for farthings."

"Well then," quoth Robin, "list thou and I will tell, but bear thyself up bravely, for the news is sad, I wot. Thus it is: I hear that two tinkers are in the stocks for drinking ale and beer!"

"Now a murrain seize thee and thy news, thou scurvy dog," quoth the Tinker, "for thou speakest but ill of good men. But sad news it is indeed, gin there be two stout fellows in the stocks."

"Nay," said Robin, "thou hast missed the mark and dost but weep for the wrong sow. The sadness of the news lieth in that there be but two in the stocks, for the others do roam the country at large."

"Now by the pewter platter of Saint Dunstan," cried the Tinker, "I have a good part of a mind to baste thy hide for thine ill jest. But gin men be put in the stocks for drinking ale and beer, I trow thou wouldst not lose thy part."

Loud laughed Robin and cried, "Now well taken, Tinker, well taken! Why, thy wits are like beer, and do froth up most when they grow sour! But right art thou, man, for I love ale and beer right well. Therefore come straightway with me hard by to the Sign of the Blue Boar, and if thou drinkest as thou appearest—and I wot thou wilt not belie thy looks—I will drench thy throat with as good homebrewed as ever was tapped in all broad Nottinghamshire."

"Now by my faith," said the Tinker, "thou art a right good fellow in spite of thy scurvy jests. I love thee, my sweet chuck, and gin I go not with thee to that same Blue Boar thou mayst call me a heathen."

"Tell me thy news, good friend, I prythee," quoth Robin as they trudged along together, "for tinkers, I

ween, are all as full of news as an egg of meat."

"Now I love thee as my brother, my bully blade," said the Tinker, "else I would not tell thee my news; for sly am I, man, and I have in hand a grave undertaking that doth call for all my wits, for I come to seek a bold outlaw that men, hereabouts, call Robin Hood. Within my pouch I have a warrant, all fairly written out on parchment, forsooth, with a great red seal for to make it lawful. Could I but meet this same Robin Hood I would serve it upon his dainty body, and if he minded it not I would beat him till every one of his ribs would cry Amen. But thou livest hereabouts, mayhap thou knowest Robin Hood thyself, good fellow."

"Ay, marry, that I do somewhat," quoth Robin, "and I have seen him this very morn. But, Tinker, men say that he is but a sad, sly thief. Thou hadst better watch thy warrant, man, or else he may steal it out of thy very pouch."

"Let him but try!" cried the Tinker. "Sly may he be, but sly am I, too. I would I had him here now, man to man!" And he made his heavy cudgel to spin again. "But what manner of man is he, lad?"

"Much like myself," said Robin, laughing, "and in height and build and age nigh the same; and he hath blue eyes, too."

"Nay," quoth the Tinker, "thou art but a green youth. I thought him to be a great bearded man. Nottingham men feared him so."

"Truly, he is not so old nor so stout as thou art," said Robin. "But men do call him a right deft hand at quarterstaff."

"That may be," said the Tinker right sturdily, "but I am more deft than he, for did I not overcome Simon of Ely in a fair bout in the ring at Hertford Town? But if thou knowest him, my jolly blade, wilt thou go with me and bring me to him? Fourscore bright angels hath the

Sheriff promised me if I serve the warrant upon the knave's body, and ten of them will I give to thee if thou showest me him."

"Ay, that will I," quoth Robin, "but show me thy warrant, man, until I see whether it be good or no."

"That will I not do, even to mine own brother," answered the Tinker. "No man shall see my warrant till I serve it upon yon fellow's own body."

"So be it," quoth Robin. "And thou show it not to me I know not to whom thou wilt show it. But here we are at the Sign of the Blue Boar, so let us in and taste his brown October."

No sweeter inn could be found in all Nottinghamshire than that of the Blue Boar. None had such lovely trees standing around, or was so covered with trailing clematis and sweet woodbine; none had such good beer and such humming ale; nor, in wintertime, when the north wind howled and snow drifted around the hedges, was there to be found, elsewhere, such a roaring fire as blazed upon the hearth of the Blue Boar. At such times might be found a goodly company of yeomen or country folk seated around the blazing hearth, bandying merry jests, while roasted crabs * bobbed in bowls of ale upon the hearthstone. Well known was the inn to Robin Hood and his band, for there had he and such merry companions as Little John or Will Stutely or young David of Doncaster often gathered when all the forest was filled with snow. As for mine host, he knew how to keep a still tongue in his head, and to swallow his words before they passed his teeth, for he knew very well which side of his bread was spread with butter, for Robin and his band were the best of customers and paid their scores without having them chalked up behind the door. So now, when Robin Hood and the Tinker came thereto and called aloud for two great pots of ale, none would have known

* Small sour apples.

from look or speech that the host had ever set eyes upon the outlaw before.

"Bide thou here," quoth Robin to the Tinker, "while I go and see that mine host draweth ale from the right butt, for he hath good October, I know, and that brewed by Withold of Tamworth." So saying, he went within and whispered to the host to add a measure of Flemish strong waters to the good English ale; which the latter did and brought it to them.

"By Our Lady," said the Tinker, after a long draught of the ale, "yon same Withold of Tamworth—a right good Saxon name, too, I would have thee know—breweth the most humming ale that e'er passed the lips of Wat o' the Crabstaff."

"Drink, man, drink," cried Robin, only wetting his own lips meanwhile. "Ho, landlord! Bring my friend another pot of the same. And now for a song, my jolly blade."

"Ay, that will I give thee a song, my lovely fellow," quoth the Tinker, "for I never tasted such ale in all my days before. By'r Lady, it doth make my head hum even now! Hey, Dame Hostess, come listen, an thou wouldst hear a song; and thou too, thou bonny lass, for never sing I so well as when bright eyes do look upon me the while."

Then he sang an ancient ballad of the time of good King Arthur, called "The Marriage of Sir Gawaine," which you may some time read yourself, in stout English of early times; and as he sang, all listened to that noble tale of noble knight and his sacrifice to his king. But long before the Tinker came to the last verse his tongue began to trip and his head to spin, because of the strong waters mixed with the ale. First his tongue tripped, then it grew thick of sound; then his head wagged from side to side, until at last he fell asleep as though he never would waken again.

Then Robin Hood laughed aloud and quickly took the

warrant from out the Tinker's pouch with his deft fingers. "Sly art thou, Tinker," quoth he, "but not yet, I trow, art thou as sly as that same sly thief Robin Hood."

Then he called the host to him and said, "Here, good man, are ten broad shillings for the entertainment thou hast given us this day. See that thou takest good care of thy fair guest there, and when he wakes thou mayst again charge him ten shillings also, and if he hath it not, thou mayst take his bag and hammer, and even his coat, in payment. Thus do I punish those that come into the greenwood to deal dole to me. As for thine own self, never knew I landlord yet that would not charge twice an he could."

At this the host smiled slyly, as though he were saying to himself the rustic saw, "Teach a magpie to suck eggs."

The Tinker slept until the afternoon drew to a close and the shadows grew long beside the woodland edge, then he awoke. First he looked up, then he looked down, then he looked east, then he looked west, for he was gathering his wits together, like barley straws blown apart by the wind. First he thought of his merry companion, but he was gone. Then he thought of his stout crabstaff, and that he had within his hand. Then of his warrant, and of the fourscore angels he was to gain for serving it upon Robin Hood. He thrust his hand into his pouch, but not a scrap nor a farthing was there. Then he sprang to his feet in a rage.

"Ho, landlord!" cried he, "whither hath that knave gone that was with me but now?"

"What knave meaneth your Worship?" quoth the landlord, calling the Tinker Worship to soothe him, as a man would pour oil upon angry water. "I saw no knave with Your Worship, for I swear no man would dare call that man knave so nigh to Sherwood Forest. A right stout yeoman I saw with Your Worship, but I thought

that Your Worship knew him, for few there be about here that pass him by and know him not."

"Now, how should I, that ne'er have squealed in your sty, know all the swine therein? Who was he, then, an thou knowest him so well?"

"Why, yon same is a right stout fellow whom men hereabouts do call Robin Hood, which same—"

"Now, by'r Lady!" cried the Tinker hastily, and in a deep voice like an angry bull, "thou didst see me come into thine inn, I, a staunch, honest craftsman, and never told me who my company was, well knowing thine own self who he was. Now, I have a right round piece of a mind to crack thy knave's pate for thee!" Then he took up his cudgel and looked at the landlord as though he would smite him where he stood.

"Nay," cried the host, throwing up his elbow, for he feared the blow, "how knew I that thou knewest him not?"

"Well and truly thankful mayst thou be," quoth the Tinker, "that I be a patient man and so do spare thy bald crown, else wouldst thou ne'er cheat customer again. But as for this same knave Robin Hood, I go straightway to seek him, and if I do not score his knave's pate, cut my staff into fagots and call me woman." So saying, he gathered himself together to depart.

"Nay," quoth the landlord, standing in front of him and holding out his arms like a gooseherd driving his flock, for money made him bold, "thou goest not till thou hast paid me my score."

"But did not he pay thee?"

"Not so much as one farthing; and ten good shillings' worth of ale have ye drunk this day. Nay, I say, thou goest not away without paying me, else shall our good Sheriff know of it."

"But nought have I to pay thee with, good fellow," quoth the Tinker.

" 'Good fellow' not me," said the landlord. "Good fellow am I not when it cometh to lose ten shillings! Pay me that thou owest me in broad money, or else leave thy coat and bag and hammer; yet, I wot they are not worth ten shillings, and I shall lose thereby. Nay, an thou stirrest, I have a great dog within and I will loose him upon thee. Maken, open thou the door and let forth Brian if this fellow stirs one step."

"Nay," quoth the Tinker—for, by roaming the country, he had learned what dogs were—"take thou what thou wilt have, and let me depart in peace, and may a murrain go with thee. But oh, landlord! An I catch yon scurvy varlet, I swear he shall pay full with usury for that he hath had!"

So saying, he strode away toward the forest, talking to himself, while the landlord and his worthy dame and Maken stood looking after him, and laughed when he had fairly gone.

"Robin and I stripped yon ass of his pack main neatly," quoth the landlord.

Now it happened about this time that Robin Hood was going through the forest to Fosse Way, to see what was to be seen there, for the moon was full and the night gave promise of being bright. In his hand he carried his stout oaken staff, and at his side hung his bugle horn. As thus he walked up a forest path, whistling, down another path came the Tinker, muttering to himself and shaking his head like an angry bull; and so, at a sudden bend, they met sharply face to face. Each stood still for a time, and then Robin spoke:

"Halloa, my sweet bird," said he, laughing merrily, "how likest thou thine ale? Wilt not sing to me another song?"

The Tinker said nothing at first but stood looking at Robin with a grim face. "Now," quoth he at last, "I am right glad I have met thee, and if I do not rattle thy bones

within thy hide this day, I give thee leave to put thy foot upon my neck."

"With all my heart," cried merry Robin. "Rattle my bones, an thou canst." So saying, he gripped his staff and threw himself upon his guard. Then the Tinker spat upon his hands and, grasping his staff, came straight at the other. He struck two or three blows, but soon found that he had met his match, for Robin warded and parried all of them, and, before the Tinker thought, he gave him a rap upon the ribs in return. At this Robin laughed aloud, and the Tinker grew more angry than ever, and smote again with all his might and main. Again Robin warded two of the strokes, but at the third, his staff broke beneath the mighty blows of the Tinker. "Now, ill betide thee, traitor staff," cried Robin, as it fell from his hands; "a foul stick art thou to serve me thus in mine hour of need."

"Now yield thee," quoth the Tinker, "for thou art my captive; and if thou do not, I will beat thy pate to a pudding."

To this Robin Hood made no answer, but, clapping his horn to his lips, he blew three blasts, loud and clear.

"Ay," quoth the Tinker, "blow thou mayest, but go thou must with me to Nottingham Town, for the Sheriff would fain see thee there. Now wilt thou yield thee, or shall I have to break thy pretty head?"

"An I must drink sour ale, I must," quoth Robin, "but never have I yielded me to man before, and that without wound or mark upon my body. Nor, when I bethink me, will I yield now. Ho, my merry men! Come quickly!"

Then from out the forest leaped Little John and six stout yeomen clad in Lincon green.

"How now, good master," cried Little John, "what need hast thou that thou dost wind thy horn so loudly?"

"There stands a tinker," quoth Robin, "that would fain take me to Nottingham, there to hang upon the gallows tree."

"Then shall he himself hang forthwith," cried Little John, and he and the others made at the Tinker, to seize him.

"Nay, touch him not," said Robin, "for a right stout man is he. A metal man he is by trade, and a mettled man by nature; moreover, he doth sing a lovely ballad. Say, good fellow, wilt thou join my merry men all? Three suits of Lincoln green shalt thou have a year, besides forty marks in fee; thou shalt share all with us and lead a right merry life in the greenwood; for cares have we not, and misfortune cometh not upon us within the sweet shades of Sherwood, where we shoot the dun deer and feed upon venison and sweet oaten cakes, and curds and honey. Wilt thou come with me?"

"Ay, marry, will I join with you all," quoth the Tinker, "for I love a merry life, and I love thee, good master, though thou didst thwack my ribs and cheat me into the bargain. Fain am I to own thou art both a stouter and a slyer man than I; so I will obey thee and be thine own true servant."

So all turned their steps to the forest depths, where the Tinker was to live henceforth. For many a day he sang ballads to the band, until the famous Allan a Dale joined them, before whose sweet voice all others seemed as harsh as a raven's; but of him we will learn hereafter.

The Shooting Match at Nottingham Town

HEN THE SHERIFF was very wroth because of this failure to take jolly Robin, for it came to his ears, as ill news always does, that the people laughed at him and made a jest of his thinking to serve a warrant upon such a one as the bold outlaw. And a man hates nothing so much as being made a jest of; so he said: "Our gracious lord and sovereign King himself shall know of this, and how his laws are perverted and despised by this band of rebel outlaws. As for yon traitor Tinker, him will I hang, if I catch him, upon the very highest gallows tree in all Nottinghamshire."

Then he bade all his servants and retainers to make ready to go to London Town, to see and speak with the King.

At this there was bustling at the Sheriff's castle, and men ran hither and thither upon this business and upon that, while the forge fires of Nottingham glowed red far into the night like twinkling stars, for all the smiths of the town were busy making or mending armor for the Sheriff's troop of escort. For two days this labor lasted, then, on the third, all was ready for the journey. So forth

they started in the bright sunlight, from Nottingham Town to Fosse Way and thence to Watling Street; and so they journeyed for two days, until they saw at last the spires and towers of great London Town; and many folks stopped, as they journeyed along, and gazed at the show they made riding along the highways with their flashing armor and gay plumes and trappings.

In London King Henry and his fair Queen Eleanor held their court, gay with ladies in silks and satins and velvets and cloth of gold, and also brave knights and gallant courtiers.

Thither came the Sheriff and was shown into the King's presence.

"A boon, a boon," quoth he, as he knelt upon the ground.

"Now what wouldst thou have?" said the King. "Let us hear what may be thy desires."

"O good my Lord and Sovereign," spake the Sheriff, "in Sherwood Forest in our own good shire of Nottingham, liveth a bold outlaw whose name is Robin Hood."

"In good sooth," said the King, "his doings have reached even our own royal ears. He is a saucy, rebellious varlet, yet, I am fain to own, a right merry soul withal."

"But hearken, O my most gracious Sovereign," said the Sheriff. "I sent a warrant to him with thine own royal seal attached, by a right lusty knave, but he beat the messenger and stole the warrant. And he killeth thy deer and robbeth thine own liege subjects even upon the great highways."

"Why, how now," quoth the King wrathfully. "What wouldst thou have me do? Comest thou not to me with a great array of men-at-arms and retainers, and yet art not able to take a single band of lusty knaves without armor on breast, in thine own county! What wouldst thou have me do? Art thou not my Sheriff? Are not my laws in

force in Nottinghamshire? Canst thou not take thine own course against those that break the laws or do any injury to thee or thine? Go, get thee gone, and think well; devise some plan of thine own, but trouble me no further. But look well to it, Master Sheriff, for I will have my laws obeyed by all men within my kingdom, and if thou art not able to enforce them thou art no sheriff for me. So look well to thyself, I say, or ill may befall thee as well as all the thieving knaves in Nottinghamshire. When the flood cometh it sweepeth away grain as well as chaff."

Then the Sheriff turned away with a sore and troubled heart, and sadly he rued his fine show of retainers, for he saw that the King was angry because he had so many men about him and yet could not enforce the laws. So, as they all rode slowly back to Nottingham, the Sheriff was thoughtful and full of care. Not a word did he speak to anyone, and no one of his men spoke to him, but all the time he was busy devising some plan to take Robin Hood.

"Aha!" cried he suddenly, smiting his hand upon his thigh, "I have it now! Ride on, my merry men all, and let us get back to Nottingham Town as speedily as we may. And mark well my words: before a fortnight is passed, that evil knave Robin Hood will be safely clapped into Nottingham gaol."

But what was the Sheriff's plan?

As a usurer takes each one of a bag of silver angels, feeling each coin to find whether it be clipped or not, so the Sheriff, as all rode slowly and sadly back toward Nottingham, took up thought after thought in turn, feeling around the edges of each but finding in every one some flaw. At last he thought of the daring soul of jolly Robin and how, as he the Sheriff knew, he often came even within the walls of Nottingham.

"Now," thought the Sheriff, "could I but persuade

Robin nigh to Nottingham Town so that I could find him, I warrant I would lay hands upon him so stoutly that he would never get away again." Then of a sudden it came to him like a flash that were he to proclaim a great shooting match and offer some grand prize, Robin Hood might be overpersuaded by his spirit to come to the butts; and it was this thought which caused him to cry "Aha!" and smite his palm upon his thigh.

So, as soon as he had returned safely to Nottingham, he sent messengers north and south, and east and west, to proclaim through town, hamlet, and countryside, this grand shooting match, and everyone was bidden that could draw a longbow, and the prize was to be an arrow of pure beaten gold.

When Robin Hood first heard the news of this he was in Lincoln Town, and hastening back to Sherwood Forest he soon called all his merry men about him and spoke to them thus:

"Now hearken, my merry men all, to the news that I have brought from Lincoln Town today. Our friend the Sheriff of Nottingham hath proclaimed a shooting match, and hath sent messengers to tell of it through all the countryside, and the prize is to be a bright golden arrow. Now I fain would have one of us win it, both because of the fairness of the prize and because our sweet friend the Sheriff hath offered it. So we will take our bows and shafts and go there to shoot, for I know right well that merriment will be a-going. What say ye, lads?"

Then young David of Doncaster spoke up and said, "Now listen, I pray thee, good master, unto what I say. I have come straight from our friend Eadom o' the Blue Boar, and there I heard the full news of this same match. But, master, I know from him, and he got it from the Sheriff's man Ralph o' the Scar, that this same knavish Sheriff hath but laid a trap for thee in this shooting match and wishes nothing so much as to see thee there. So go

not, good master, for I know right well he doth seek to beguile thee, but stay within the greenwood lest we all meet dole and woe."

"Now," quoth Robin, "thou art a wise lad and keepest thine ears open and thy mouth shut, as becometh a wise and crafty woodsman. But shall we let it be said that the Sheriff of Nottingham did cow bold Robin Hood and sevenscore as fair archers as are in all merry England? Nay, good David, what thou tellest me maketh me to desire the prize even more than I else should do. But what sayeth our good gossip Swanthold? Is it not 'A hasty man burneth his mouth, and the fool that keepeth his eyes shut falleth into the pit'? Thus he says, truly, therefore we must meet guile with guile. Now some of you clothe yourselves as curtal friars, and some as rustic peasants, and some as tinkers, or as beggars, but see that each man taketh a good bow or broadsword, in case need should arise. As for myself, I will shoot for this same golden arrow, and should I win it, we will hang it to the branches of our good greenwood tree for the joy of all the band. How like you the plan, my merry men all?"

Then "Good, good!" cried all the band right heartily.

A fair sight was Nottingham Town on the day of the shooting match. All along upon the green meadow beneath the town wall stretched a row of benches, one above the other, which were for knight and lady, squire and dame, and rich burghers and their wives; for none but those of rank and quality were to sit there. At the end of the range, near the target, was a raised seat bedecked with ribbons and scarfs and garlands of flowers, for the Sheriff of Nottingham and his dame. The range was twoscore paces broad. At one end stood the target, at the other a tent of striped canvas, from the pole of which fluttered many-colored flags and streamers. In this booth were casks of ale, free to be broached by any of the archers who might wish to quench their thirst.

Across the range from where the seats for the better folk were raised was a railing to keep the poorer people from crowding in front of the target. Already, while it was early, the benches were beginning to fill with people of quality, who kept constantly arriving in little carts or upon palfreys that curveted gaily to the merry tinkle of silver bells at bridle reins. With these came also the poorer folk, who sat or lay upon the green grass near the railing that kept them from off the range. In the great tent the archers were gathering by twos and threes; some talking loudly of the fair shots each man had made in his day; some looking well to their bows, drawing a string betwixt the fingers to see that there was no fray upon it, or inspecting arrows, shutting one eye and peering down a shaft to see that it was not warped, but straight and true, for neither bow nor shaft should fail at such a time and for such a prize. And never was such a company of yeomen as were gathered at Nottingham Town that day, for the very best archers of merry England had come to this shooting match. There was Gill o' the Red Cap, the Sheriff's own head archer, and Diccon Cruikshank of Lincoln Town, and Adam o' the Dell, a man of Tamworth, of threescore years and more, yet hale and lusty still, who in his time had shot in the famous match at Woodstock, and had there beaten that renowned archer, Clym o' the Clough. And many more famous men of the longbow were there, whose names have been handed down to us in goodly ballads of the olden time.

But now all the benches were filled with guests, lord and lady, burgher and dame, when at last the Sheriff himself came with his lady, he riding with stately mien upon his milk-white horse and she upon her brown filly. Upon his head he wore a purple velvet cap, and purple velvet was his robe, all trimmed about with rich ermine; his jerkin and hose were of sea-green silk, and his shoes of black velvet, the pointed toes fastened to his garters with

golden chains. A golden chain hung about his neck, and at his collar was a great carbuncle set in red gold. His lady was dressed in blue velvet, all trimmed with swan's down. So they made a gallant sight as they rode along side by side, and all the people shouted from where they crowded across the space from the gentlefolk; so the Sheriff and his lady came to their place, where men-at-arms, with hauberk and spear, stood about, waiting for them.

Then when the Sheriff and his dame had sat down, he bade his herald wind upon his silver horn; who thereupon sounded three blasts that came echoing cheerily back from the gray walls of Nottingham. Then the archers stepped forth to their places, while all the folks shouted with a mighty voice, each man calling upon his favorite yeoman. "Red Cap!" cried some; "Cruikshank!" cried others; "Hey for William o' Leslie!" shouted others yet again; while ladies waved silken scarfs to urge each yeoman to do his best.

Then the herald stood forth and loudly proclaimed the rules of the game as follows:

"Shoot each man from yon mark, which is sevenscore yards and ten from the target. One arrow shooteth each man first, and from all the archers shall the ten that shooteth the fairest shafts be chosen for to shoot again. Two arrows shooteth each man of these ten, then shall the three that shoot the fairest shafts be chosen for to shoot again. Three arrows shooteth each man of those three, and to him that shooteth the fairest shafts shall the prize be given."

Then the Sheriff leaned forward, looking keenly among the press of archers to find whether Robin Hood was among them; but no one was there clad in Lincoln green, such as was worn by Robin and his band. "Nevertheless," said the Sheriff to himself, "he may still be there, and I miss him among the crowd of other men. But let

me see when but ten men shoot, for I wot he will be among the ten, or I know him not."

And now the archers shot, each man in turn, and the good folk never saw such archery as was done that day. Six arrows were within the clout, four within the black, and only two smote the outer ring; so that when the last arrow sped and struck the target, all the people shouted aloud, for it was noble shooting.

And now but ten men were left of all those that had shot before, and of these ten, six were famous throughout the land, and most of the folk gathered there knew them. These six men were Gilbert o' the Red Cap, Adam o' the Dell, Diccon Cruikshank, William o' Leslie, Hubert o' Cloud, and Swithin o' Hertford. Two others were yeomen of merry Yorkshire, another was a tall stranger in blue, who said he came from London Town, and the last was a tattered stranger in scarlet, who wore a patch over one eye.

"Now," quoth the Sheriff to a man-at-arms who stood near him, "seest thou Robin Hood among those ten?"

"Nay, that do I not, Your Worship," answered the man. "Six of them I know right well. Of those Yorkshire yeomen, one is too tall and the other too short for that bold knave. Robin's beard is as yellow as gold, while yon tattered beggar in scarlet hath a beard of brown, besides being blind of one eye. As for the stranger in blue, Robin's shoulders, I ween, are three inches broader than his."

"Then," quoth the Sheriff, smiting his thigh angrily, "yon knave is a coward as well as a rogue, and dares not show his face among good men and true."

Then, after they had rested a short time, those ten stout men stepped forth to shoot again. Each man shot two arrows, and as they shot, not a word was spoken, but all the crowd watched with scarce a breath of sound; but when the last had shot his arrow another great shout

arose, while many cast their caps aloft for joy of such marvelous shooting.

"Now by our gracious Lady fair," quoth old Sir Amyas o' the Dell, who, bowed with fourscore years and more, sat near the Sheriff, "ne'er saw I such archery in all my life before, yet have I seen the best hands at the longbow for threescore years and more."

And now but three men were left of all those that had shot before. One was Gill o' the Red Cap, one the tattered stranger in scarlet, and one Adam o' the Dell of Tamworth Town. Then all the people called aloud, some crying, "Ho for Gilbert o' the Red Cap!" and some, "Hey for stout Adam o' Tamworth!" But not a single man in the crowd called upon the stranger in scarlet.

"Now, shoot thou well, Gilbert," cried the Sheriff, "and if thine be the best shaft, fivescore broad silver pennies will I give to thee beside the prize."

"Truly I will do my best," quoth Gilbert right sturdily. "A man cannot do aught but his best, but that will I strive to do this day." So saying, he drew forth a fair smooth arrow with a broad feather and fitted it deftly to the string, then drawing his bow with care he sped the shaft. Straight flew the arrow and lit fairly in the clout, a finger's-breadth from the center. "A Gilbert, a Gilbert!" shouted all the crowd; and, "Now, by my faith," cried the Sheriff, smiting his hands together, "that is a shrewd shot."

Then the tattered stranger stepped forth, and all the people laughed as they saw a yellow patch that showed beneath his arm when he raised his elbow to shoot, and also to see him aim with but one eye. He drew the good yew bow quickly, and quickly loosed a shaft; so short was the time that no man could draw a breath betwixt the drawing and the shooting; yet his arrow lodged nearer the center than the other by twice the length of a barleycorn.

"Now by all the saints in Paradise!" cried the Sheriff, "that is a lovely shaft in very truth!"

Then Adam o' the Dell shot, carefully and cautiously, and his arrow lodged close beside the stranger's. Then after a short space they all three shot again, and once more each arrow lodged within the clout, but this time Adam o' the Dell's was farthest from the center, and again the tattered stranger's shot was the best. Then, after another time of rest, they all shot for the third time. This time Gilbert took great heed to his aim, keenly measuring the distance and shooting with shrewdest care. Straight flew the arrow, and all shouted till the very flags that waved in the breeze shook with the sound, and the rooks and daws flew clamoring about the roofs of the old gray tower, for the shaft had lodged close beside the spot that marked the very center.

"Well done, Gilbert!" cried the Sheriff right joyously. "Fain am I to believe the prize is thine, and right fairly won. Now, thou ragged knave, let me see thee shoot a better shaft than that."

Nought spake the stranger but took his place, while all was hushed, and no one spoke or even seemed to breathe, so great was the silence for wonder what he would do. Meanwhile, also, quite still stood the stranger, holding his bow in his hand, while one could count five; then he drew his trusty yew, holding it drawn but a moment, then loosed the string. Straight flew the arrow, and so true that it smote a gray goose feather from off Gilbert's shaft, which fell fluttering through the sunlit air as the stranger's arrow lodged close beside his of the Red Cap, and in the very center. No one spoke a word for a while and no one shouted, but each man looked into his neighbor's face amazedly.

"Nay," quoth old Adam o' the Dell presently, drawing a long breath and shaking his head as he spoke, "twoscore years and more have I shot shaft, and maybe not all times bad, but I shoot no more this day, for no man can match with yon stranger, whosoe'er he may be." Then he thrust

his shaft into his quiver, rattling, and unstrung his bow without another word.

Then the Sheriff came down from his dais and drew near, in all his silks and velvets, to where the tattered stranger stood leaning upon his stout bow, while the good folk crowded around to see the man who shot so wondrously well. "Here, good fellow," quoth the Sheriff, "take thou the prize, and well and fairly hast thou won it, I trow. What may be thy name, and whence comest thou?"

"Men do call me Jock o' Teviotdale, and thence am I come," said the stranger.

"Then, by Our Lady, Jock, thou art the fairest archer that e'er mine eyes beheld, and if thou wilt join my service I will clothe thee with a better coat than that thou hast upon thy back; thou shalt eat and drink of the best, and at every Christmastide fourscore marks shall be thy wage. I trow thou drawest better bow than that same coward knave Robin Hood, that dared not show his face here this day. Say, good fellow, wilt thou join my service?"

"Nay, that will I not," quoth the stranger roughly. "I will be mine own, and no man in all merry England shall be my master."

"Then get thee gone, and a murrain seize thee!" cried the Sheriff, and his voice trembled with anger. "And by my faith and troth, I have a good part of a mind to have thee beaten for thine insolence!" Then he turned upon his heel and strode away.

It was a right motley company that gathered about the noble greenwood tree in Sherwood's depths that same day. A score and more of barefoot friars were there, and some that looked like tinkers, and some that seemed to be sturdy beggars and rustic hinds; and seated upon a mossy couch was one all clad in tattered scarlet, with a patch over one eye; and in his hand he held the golden arrow that was the prize of the great shooting match. Then,

*"I will be mine own, and no man in all merry England
shall be my master!"*

amidst a noise of talking and laughter, he took the patch from off his eye and stripped away the scarlet rags from off his body and showed himself all clothed in fair Lincoln green; and quoth he, "Easy come these things away, but walnut stain cometh not so speedily from yellow hair." Then all laughed louder than before, for it was Robin Hood himself that had won the prize from the Sheriff's very hands.

Then all sat down to the woodland feast and talked among themselves of the merry jest that had been played upon the Sheriff, and of the adventures that had befallen each member of the band in his disguise. But when the feast was done, Robin Hood took Little John apart and said, "Truly am I vexed in my blood, for I heard the Sheriff say today, 'Thou shootest better than that coward knave Robin Hood, that dared not show his face here this day.' I would fain let him know who it was who won the golden arrow from out his hand, and also that I am no coward such as he takes me to be."

Then Little John said, "Good master, take thou me and Will Stutely, and we will send yon fat Sheriff news of all this by a messenger such as he doth not expect."

That day the Sheriff sat at meat in the great hall of his house at Nottingham Town. Long tables stood down the hall, at which sat men-at-arms and household servants and good stout villains,* in all fourscore and more. There they talked of the day's shooting as they ate their meat and quaffed their ale. The Sheriff sat at the head of the table upon a raised seat under a canopy, and beside him sat his dame.

"By my troth," said he, "I did reckon full roundly that that knave Robin Hood would be at the game today. I did not think that he was such a coward. But who could that saucy knave be who answered me to my beard so bravely? I wonder that I did not have him beaten; but

* Bond-servants.

there was something about him that spoke of other things than rags and tatters."

Then, even as he finished speaking, something fell rattling among the dishes on the table, while those that sat near started up wondering what it might be. After a while one of the men-at-arms gathered courage enough to pick it up and bring it to the Sheriff. Then everyone saw that it was a blunted gray goose shaft, with a fine scroll, about the thickness of a goose quill, tied near to its head. The Sheriff opened the scroll and glanced at it, while the veins upon his forehead swelled and his cheeks grew ruddy with rage as he read, for this was what he saw:

> *"Now Heaven bless Thy Grace this day,*
> *Say all in sweet Sherwood,*
> *For thou didst give the prize away*
> *To merry Robin Hood."*

"Whence came this?" cried the Sheriff in a mighty voice.

"Even through the window, Your Worship," quoth the man who had handed the shaft to him.

Will Stutely Rescued by His Companions

ᴺow when the sheriff found that neither law nor guile could overcome Robin Hood, he was much perplexed, and said to himself, "Fool that I am! Had I not told our King of Robin Hood, I would not have gotten myself into such a coil; but now I must either take him captive or have wrath visited upon my head from his most gracious Majesty. I have tried law, and I have tried guile, and I have failed in both; so I will try what may be done with might."

Thus communing within himself, he called his constables together and told them what was in his mind. "Now take ye each four men, all armed in proof," said he, "and get ye gone to the forest, at different points, and lie in wait for this same Robin Hood. But if any constable finds too many men against him, let him sound a horn, and then let each band within hearing come with all speed and join the party that calls them. Thus, I think, shall we take this green-clad knave. Furthermore, to him that first meeteth with Robin Hood shall one hundred pounds of silver money be given, if he be brought to me dead or alive; and to him that meeteth with any of his band shall

twoscore pounds be given, if such be brought to me dead or alive. So, be ye bold and be ye crafty."

So thus they went in threescore companies of five to Sherwood Forest, to take Robin Hood, each constable wishing that he might be the one to find the bold outlaw, or at least one of his band. For seven days and nights they hunted through the forest glades, but never saw so much as a single man in Lincoln green; for tidings of all this had been brought to Robin Hood by trusty Eadom o' the Blue Boar.

When he first heard the news, Robin said, "If the Sheriff dare send force to meet force, woe will it be for him and many a better man besides, for blood will flow and there will be great trouble for all. But fain would I shun blood and battle, and fain would I not deal sorrow to womenfolk and wives because good stout yeomen lose their lives. Once I slew a man, and never do I wish to slay a man again, for it is bitter for the soul to think thereon. So now we will abide silently in Sherwood Forest, so that it may be well for all; but should we be forced to defend ourselves, or any of our band, then let each man draw bow and brand with might and main."

At this speech many of the band shook their heads, and said to themselves, "Now the Sheriff will think that we are cowards, and folk will scoff throughout the countryside, saying that we fear to meet these men." But they said nothing aloud, swallowing their words and doing as Robin bade them.

Thus they hid in the depths of Sherwood Forest for seven days and seven nights and never showed their faces abroad in all that time; but early in the morning of the eighth day Robin Hood called the band together and said, "Now who will go and find what the Sheriff's men are at by this time? For I know right well they will not bide forever within Sherwood shades."

At this a great shout arose, and each man waved his

bow aloft and cried that he might be the one to go. Then Robin Hood's heart was proud when he looked around on his stout, brave fellows, and he said, "Brave and true are ye all, my merry men, and a right stout band of good fellows are ye; but ye cannot all go, so I will choose one from among you, and it shall be good Will Stutely, for he is as sly as e'er an old dog fox in Sherwood Forest."

Then Will Stutely leaped high aloft and laughed loudly, clapping his hands for pure joy that he should have been chosen from among them all. "Now thanks, good master," quoth he, "and if I bring not news of those knaves to thee, call me no more thy sly Will Stutely."

Then he clad himself in a friar's gown, and underneath the robe he hung a good broadsword in such a place that he could easily lay hands upon it. Thus clad, he set forth upon his quest, until he came to the verge of the forest, and so to the highway. He saw two bands of the Sheriff's men, yet he turned neither to the right nor the left, but only drew his cowl the closer over his face, folding his hands as if in meditation. So at last he came to the Sign of the Blue Boar. "For," quoth he to himself, "our good friend Eadom will tell me all the news."

At the Sign of the Blue Boar he found a band of the Sheriff's men drinking right lustily; so, without speaking to anyone, he sat down upon a distant bench, his staff in his hand, and his head bowed forward as though he were meditating. Thus he sat waiting until he might see the landlord apart, and Eadom did not know him, but thought him to be some poor tired friar, so he let him sit without saying a word to him or molesting him, though he liked not the cloth. "For," said he to himself, "it is a hard heart that kicks the lame dog from off the sill." As Stutely sat thus, there came a great house cat and rubbed against his knee, raising his robe a palm's-breadth high. Stutely pushed his robe quickly down again, but the constable who commanded the Sheriff's men saw what had

passed, and saw also fair Lincoln green beneath the friar's robe. He said nothing at the time, but communed within himself in this wise: "Yon is no friar of orders gray, and also, I wot, no honest yeoman goeth about in priest's garb, nor doth a thief go so for nought. Now I think in good sooth that is one of Robin Hood's own men." So, presently, he said aloud, "O holy father, wilt thou not take a good pot of March beer to slake thy thirsty soul withal?"

But Stutely shook his head silently, for he said to himself, "Maybe there be those here who know my voice."

Then the constable said again, "Whither goest thou, holy friar, upon this hot summer's day?"

"I go a pilgrim to Canterbury Town," answered Will Stutely, speaking gruffly, so that none might know his voice.

Then the constable said, for the third time, "Now tell me, holy father, do pilgrims to Canterbury wear good Lincoln green beneath their robes? Ha! By my faith, I take thee to be some lusty thief, and perhaps one of Robin Hood's own band! Now, by Our Lady's grace, if thou movest hand or foot, I will run thee through the body with my sword!"

Then he flashed forth his bright sword and leaped upon Will Stutely, thinking he would take him unaware; but Stutely had his own sword tightly held in his hand, beneath his robe, so he drew it forth before the constable came upon him. Then the stout constable struck a mighty blow; but he struck no more in all that fight, for Stutely, parrying the blow right deftly, smote the constable back again with all his might. Then he would have escaped, but could not, for the other, all dizzy with the wound and with the flowing blood, seized him by the knees with his arms even as he reeled and fell. Then the others rushed upon him, and Stutely struck again at

another of the Sheriff's men, but the steel cap glanced the blow, and though the blade bit deep, it did not kill. Meanwhile, the constable, fainting as he was, drew Stutely downward, and the others, seeing the yeoman hampered so, rushed upon him again, and one smote him a blow upon the crown so that the blood ran down his face and blinded him. Then, staggering, he fell, and all sprang upon him, though he struggled so manfully that they could hardly hold him fast. Then they bound him with stout hempen cords so that he could not move either hand or foot, and thus they overcame him.

Robin Hood stood under the greenwood tree, thinking of Will Stutely and how he might be faring, when suddenly he saw two of his stout yeomen come running down the forest path, and betwixt them ran buxom Maken of the Blue Boar. Then Robin's heart fell, for he knew they were the bearers of ill tidings.

"Will Stutely hath been taken," cried they, when they had come to where he stood.

"And is it thou that hast brought such doleful news?" said Robin to the lass.

"Ay, marry, for I saw it all," cried she, panting as the hare pants when it has escaped the hounds, "and I fear he is wounded sore, for one smote him main shrewdly i' the crown. They have bound him and taken him to Nottingham Town, and ere I left the Blue Boar I heard that he should be hanged tomorrow day."

"He shall not be hanged tomorrow day," cried Robin; "or, if he be, full many a one shall gnaw the sod, and many shall have cause to cry Alack-a-day!"

Then he clapped his horn to his lips and blew three blasts right loudly, and presently his good yeomen came running through the greenwood until sevenscore bold blades were gathered around him.

"Now hark you all!" cried Robin. "Our dear companion Will Stutely hath been taken by that vile Sheriff's

men, therefore doth it behoove us to take bow and brand in hand to bring him off again; for I wot that we ought to risk life and limb for him, as he hath risked life and limb for us. Is it not so, my merry men all?" Then all cried, "Ay!" with a great voice.

So the next day they all wended their way from Sherwood Forest, but by different paths, for it behooved them to be very crafty; so the band separated into parties of twos and threes, which were all to meet again in a tangled dell that lay near to Nottingham Town. Then, when they had all gathered together at the place of meeting, Robin spoke to them thus:

"Now we will lie here in ambush until we can get news, for it doth behoove us to be cunning and wary if we would bring our friend Will Stutely off from the Sheriff's clutches."

So they lay hidden a long time, until the sun stood high in the sky. The day was warm and the dusty road was bare of travelers, except an aged palmer who walked slowly along the highroad that led close beside the gray castle wall of Nottingham Town. When Robin saw that no other wayfarer was within sight, he called young David of Doncaster, who was a shrewd man for his years, and said to him, "Now get thee forth, young David, and speak to yonder palmer that walks beside the town wall, for he hath come but now from Nottingham Town, and may tell thee news of good Stutely, perchance."

So David strode forth, and when he came up to the pilgrim, he saluted him and said, "Good morrow, holy father, and canst thou tell me when Will Stutely will be hanged upon the gallows tree? I fain would not miss the sight, for I have come from afar to see so sturdy a rogue hanged."

"Now, out upon thee, young man," cried the Palmer, "that thou shouldst speak so when a good stout man is to be hanged for nothing but guarding his own life!" And

he struck his staff upon the ground in anger. "Alas, say I, that this thing should be! For even this day, toward evening, when the sun falleth low, he shall be hanged, fourscore rods from the great town gate of Nottingham, where three roads meet; for there the Sheriff sweareth he shall die as a warning to all outlaws in Nottinghamshire. But yet, I say again, Alas! For, though Robin Hood and his band may be outlaws, yet he taketh only from the rich and the strong and the dishonest man, while there is not a poor widow nor a peasant with many children, nigh to Sherwood, but has barley flour enough all the year long through him. It grieves my heart to see one as gallant as this Stutely die, for I have been a good Saxon yeoman in my day, ere I turned palmer, and well I know a stout hand and one that smiteth shrewdly at a cruel Norman or a proud abbot with fat moneybags. Had good Stutely's master but known how his man was compassed about with perils, perchance he might send succor to bring him out of the hand of his enemies."

"Ay, marry, that is true," cried the young man. "If Robin and his men be nigh this place, I wot right well they will strive to bring him forth from his peril. But fare thee well, thou good old man, and believe me, if Will Stutely die, he shall be right well avenged."

Then he turned and strode rapidly away; but the Palmer looked after him, muttering, "I wot that youth is no country hind that hath come to see a good man die. Well, well, perchance Robin Hood is not so far away but that there will be stout doings this day." So he went upon his way, muttering to himself.

When David of Doncaster told Robin Hood what the Palmer had said to him, Robin called the band around him and spoke to them thus:

"Now let us get straightway into Nottingham Town and mix ourselves with the people there; but keep ye one another in sight, pressing as near the prisoner and his

guards as ye can, when they come outside the walls. Strike no man without need, for I would fain avoid bloodshed, but if ye do strike, strike hard, and see that there be no need to strike again. Then keep all together until we come again to Sherwood, and let no man leave his fellows."

The sun was low in the western sky when a bugle note sounded from the castle wall. Then all was bustle in Nottingham Town and crowds filled the streets, for all knew that the famous Will Stutely was to be hanged that day. Presently the castle gates opened wide and a great array of men-at-arms came forth with noise and clatter, the Sheriff, all clad in shining mail of linked chain, riding at their head. In the midst of all the guard, in a cart, with a halter about his neck, rode Will Stutely. His face was pale with his wound and with loss of blood, like the moon in broad daylight, and his fair hair was clotted in points upon his forehead, where the blood had hardened. When he came forth from the castle he looked up and he looked down, but though he saw some faces that showed pity and some that showed friendliness, he saw none that he knew. Then his heart sank within him like a plummet of lead, but nevertheless he spoke up boldly.

"Give a sword into my hand, Sir Sheriff," said he, "and wounded man though I be, I will fight thee and all thy men till life and strength be gone."

"Nay, thou naughty varlet," quoth the Sheriff, turning his head and looking right grimly upon Will Stutely, "thou shalt have no sword but shall die a mean death, as beseemeth a vile thief like thee."

"Then do but untie my hands and I will fight thee and thy men with no weapon but only my naked fists. I crave no weapon, but let me not be meanly hanged this day."

Then the Sheriff laughed aloud. "Why, how now," quoth he, "is thy proud stomach quailing? Shrive thyself, thou vile knave, for I mean that thou shalt hang this

day, and that where three roads meet, so that all men shall see thee hang, for carrion crows and daws to peck at."

"O thou dastard heart!" cried Will Stutely, gnashing his teeth at the Sheriff. "Thou coward hind! If ever my good master meet thee thou shalt pay dearly for this day's work! He doth scorn thee, and so do all brave hearts. Knowest thou not that thou and thy name are jests upon the lips of every brave yeoman? Such a one as thou art, thou wretched craven, will never be able to subdue bold Robin Hood."

"Ha!" cried the Sheriff in a rage, "is it even so? Am I a jest with thy master, as thou callest him? Now I will make a jest of thee and a sorry jest withal, for I will quarter thee limb from limb, after thou art hanged." Then he spurred his horse forward and said no more to Stutely.

At last they came to the great town gate, through which Stutely saw the fair country beyond, with hills and dales all clothed in verdure, and far away the dusky line of Sherwood's skirts. Then when he saw the slanting sunlight lying on field and fallow, shining redly here and there on cot and farmhouse, and when he heard the sweet birds singing their vespers, and the sheep bleating upon the hillside, and beheld the swallows flying in the bright air, there came a great fullness to his heart so that all things blurred to his sight through salt tears, and he bowed his head lest the folk should think him unmanly when they saw the tears in his eyes. Thus he kept his head bowed till they had passed through the gate and were outside the walls of the town. But when he looked up again he felt his heart leap within him and then stand still for pure joy, for he saw the face of one of his own dear companions of merry Sherwood; then glancing quickly around he saw well-known faces upon all sides of him, crowding closely upon the men-at-arms who were guarding him. Then of a sudden the blood sprang to his

cheeks, for he saw for a moment his own good master in the press and, seeing him, knew that Robin Hood and all his band were there. Yet betwixt him and them was a line of men-at-arms.

"Now, stand back!" cried the Sheriff in a mighty voice, for the crowd pressed around on all sides. "What mean ye, varlets, that ye push upon us so? Stand back, I say!"

Then came a bustle and a noise, and one strove to push between the men-at-arms so as to reach the cart, and Stutely saw that it was Little John that made all that stir.

"Now stand thou back!" cried one of the men-at-arms whom Little John pushed with his elbows.

"Now stand thou back thine own self," quoth Little John, and straightway smote the man a buffet beside his head that felled him as a butcher fells an ox, and then he leaped to the cart where Stutely sat.

"I pray thee take leave of thy friends ere thou diest, Will," quoth he, "or maybe I will die with thee if thou must die, for I could never have better company." Then with one stroke he cut the bonds that bound the other's arms and legs, and Stutely leaped straightway from the cart.

"Now as I live," cried the Sheriff, "yon varlet I know right well is a sturdy rebel! Take him, I bid you all, and let him not go!"

So saying, he spurred his horse upon Little John, and rising in his stirrups smote with might and main, but Little John ducked quickly underneath the horse's belly and the blow whistled harmlessly over his head.

"Nay, good Sir Sheriff," cried he, leaping up again when the blow had passed, "I must e'en borrow thy most worshipful sword." Thereupon he twitched the weapon deftly from out the Sheriff's hand. "Here, Stutely," he cried, "the Sheriff hath lent thee his sword! Back to back

with me, man, and defend thyself, for help is nigh!"

"Down with them!" bellowed the Sheriff in a voice like an angry bull; and he spurred his horse upon the two who now stood back to back, forgetting in his rage that he had no weapon with which to defend himself.

"Stand back, Sheriff!" cried Little John; and even as he spoke, a bugle horn sounded shrilly and a clothyard shaft whistled within an inch of the Sheriff's head. Then came a swaying hither and thither, and oaths, cries, and groans, and clashing of steel, and swords flashed in the setting sun, and a score of arrows whistled through the air. And some cried, "Help, help!" and some, "A rescue, a rescue!"

"Treason!" cried the Sheriff in a loud voice. "Bear back! Bear back! Else we be all dead men!" Thereupon he reined his horse backward through the thickest of the crowd.

Now Robin Hood and his band might have slain half of the Sheriff's men had they desired to do so, but they let them push out of the press and get them gone, only sending a bunch of arrows after them to hurry them in their flight.

"Oh stay!" shouted Will Stutely after the Sheriff. "Thou wilt never catch bold Robin Hood if thou dost not stand to meet him face to face." But the Sheriff, bowing along his horse's back, made no answer but only spurred the faster.

Then Will Stutely turned to Little John and looked him in the face till the tears ran down from his eyes and he wept aloud; and kissing his friend's cheeks, "O Little John!" quoth he, "mine own true friend, and he that I love better than man or woman in all the world beside! Little did I reckon to see thy face this day, or to meet thee this side Paradise." Little John could make no answer, but wept also.

Then Robin Hood gathered his band together in a

close rank, with Will Stutely in the midst, and thus they moved slowly away toward Sherwood, and were gone, as a storm cloud moves away from the spot where a tempest has swept the land.   But they left ten of the Sheriff's men lying along the ground wounded—some more, some less —yet no one knew who smote them down.

Thus the Sheriff of Nottingham tried thrice to take Robin Hood and failed each time; and the last time he was frightened, for he felt how near he had come to losing his life; so he said, "These men fear neither God nor man, nor king nor king's officers.   I would sooner lose mine office than my life, so I will trouble them no more."   So he kept close within his castle for many a day and dared not show his face outside of his own household, and all the time he was gloomy and would speak to no one, for he was ashamed of what had happened that day.

Robin Hood Turns Butcher

$\mathcal{N}$OW AFTER all these things had happened, and it became known to Robin Hood how the Sheriff had tried three times to make him captive, he said to himself, "If I have the chance, I will make our worshipful Sheriff pay right well for that which he hath done to me. Maybe I may bring him some time into Sherwood Forest and have him to a right merry feast with us." For when Robin Hood caught a baron or a squire, or a fat abbot or bishop, he brought them to the greenwood tree and feasted them before he lightened their purses.

But in the meantime Robin Hood and his band lived quietly in Sherwood Forest, without showing their faces abroad, for Robin knew that it would not be wise for him to be seen in the neighborhood of Nottingham, those in authority being very wroth with him. But though they did not go abroad, they lived a merry life within the woodlands, spending the days in shooting at garlands hung upon a willow wand at the end of the glade, the leafy aisles ringing with merry jests and laughter: for whoever missed the garland was given a sound buffet, which, if delivered

by Little John, never failed to topple over the unfortunate yeoman. Then they had bouts of wrestling and of cudgel play, so that every day they gained in skill and strength.

Thus they dwelled for nearly a year, and in that time Robin Hood often turned over in his mind many means of making an even score with the Sheriff. At last he began to fret at his confinement; so one day he took up his stout cudgel and set forth to seek adventure, strolling blithely along until he came to the edge of Sherwood. There, as he rambled along the sunlit road, he met a lusty young butcher driving a fine mare and riding in a stout new cart, all hung about with meat. Merrily whistled the Butcher as he jogged along, for he was going to the market, and the day was fresh and sweet, making his heart blithe within him.

"Good morrow to thee, jolly fellow," quoth Robin, "thou seemest happy this merry morn."

"Ay, that am I," quoth the jolly Butcher, "and why should I not be so? Am I not hale in wind and limb? Have I not the bonniest lass in all Nottinghamshire? And lastly, am I not to be married to her on Thursday next in sweet Locksley Town?"

"Ha," said Robin, "comest thou from Locksley Town? Well do I know that fair place for miles about, and well do I know each hedgerow and gentle pebbly stream, and even all the bright little fishes therein, for there I was born and bred. Now, where goest thou with thy meat, my fair friend?"

"I go to the market at Nottingham Town to sell my beef and my mutton," answered the Butcher. "But who art thou that comest from Locksley Town?"

"A yeoman am I, and men do call me Robin Hood."

"Now, by Our Lady's grace," cried the Butcher, "well do I know thy name, and many a time have I heard thy deeds both sung and spoken of. But Heaven forbid that thou shouldst take aught of me! An honest man am I,

and have wronged neither man nor maid; so trouble me not, good master, as I have never troubled thee."

"Nay, Heaven forbid, indeed," quoth Robin, "that I should take from such as thee, jolly fellow! Not so much as one farthing would I take from thee, for I love a fair Saxon face like thine right well—more especially when it cometh from Locksley Town, and most especially when the man that owneth it is to marry a bonny lass on Thursday next. But come, tell me for what price thou wilt sell me all of thy meat and thy horse and cart."

"At four marks do I value meat, cart, and mare," quoth the Butcher, "but if I do not sell all my meat I will not have four marks in value."

Then Robin Hood plucked the purse from his girdle, and quoth he, "Here in this purse are six marks. Now, I would fain be a butcher for the day and sell my meat in Nottingham Town. Wilt thou close a bargain with me and take six marks for thine outfit?"

"Now may the blessings of all the saints fall on thine honest head!" cried the Butcher right joyfully, as he leaped down from his cart and took the purse that Robin held out to him.

"Nay," quoth Robin, laughing loudly, "many do like me and wish me well, but few call me honest. Now get thee gone back to thy lass, and give her a sweet kiss from me." So saying, he donned the Butcher's apron, and, climbing into the cart, he took the reins in his hand and drove off through the forest to Nottingham Town.

When he came to Nottingham, he entered that part of the market where butchers stood, and took up his inn * in the best place he could find. Next, he opened his stall and spread his meat upon the bench, then, taking his cleaver and steel and clattering them together, he trolled aloud in merry tones:

* Stand for selling.

"Now come, ye lasses, and eke ye dames,
And buy your meat from me;
For three pennyworths of meat I sell
For the charge of one penny.

"Lamb have I that hath fed upon nought
But the dainty daisies pied,
And the violet sweet, and the daffodil
That grow fair streams beside.

"And beef have I from the heathery wolds,
And mutton from dales all green,
And veal as white as a maiden's brow,
With its mother's milk, I ween.

"Then come, ye lasses, and eke ye dames,
Come, buy your meat from me;
For three pennyworths of meat I sell
For the charge of one penny."

Thus he sang blithely, while all who stood near listened amazedly. Then, when he had finished, he clattered the steel and cleaver still more loudly, shouting lustily, "Now, who'll buy? Who'll buy? Four fixed prices have I. Three pennyworths of meat I sell to a fat friar or priest for sixpence, for I want not their custom; stout aldermen I charge threepence, for it doth not matter to me whether they buy or not; to buxom dames I sell three pennyworths of meat for one penny, for I like their custom well; but to the bonny lass that hath a liking for a good tight butcher I charge nought but one fair kiss, for I like her custom the best of all."

Then all began to stare and wonder and crowd around, laughing, for never was such selling heard of in all Nottingham Town; but when they came to buy they found it as he had said, for he gave goodwife or dame as much meat for one penny as they could buy elsewhere for three,

and when a widow or a poor woman came to him, he gave
her flesh for nothing; but when a merry lass came and
gave him a kiss, he charged not one penny for his meat;
and many such came to his stall, for his eyes were as blue
as the skies of June, and he laughed merrily, giving to
each full measure. Thus he sold his meat so fast that no
butcher that stood near him could sell anything.

Then they began to talk among themselves, and some
said, "This must be some thief who has stolen cart, horse,
and meat"; but others said, "Nay, when did ye ever see a
thief who parted with his goods so freely and merrily?
This must be some prodigal who hath sold his father's
land, and would fain live merrily while the money lasts."
And these latter being the greater number, the others
came round, one by one, to their way of thinking.

Then some of the butchers came to him to make his
acquaintance. "Come, brother," quoth one who was the
head of them all, "we be all of one trade, so wilt thou go
dine with us? For this day the Sheriff hath asked all the
Butcher Guild to feast with him at the Guild Hall. There
will be stout fare and much to drink, and that thou likest,
or I much mistake thee."

"Now, beshrew his heart," quoth jolly Robin, "that
would deny a butcher. And, moreover, I will go dine
with you all, my sweet lads, and that as fast as I can hie."
Whereupon, having sold all his meat, he closed his stall
and went with them to the great Guild Hall.

There the Sheriff had already come in state, and with
him many butchers. When Robin and those that were
with him came in, all laughing at some merry jest he had
been telling them, those that were near the Sheriff whispered to him, "Yon is a right mad blade, for he hath sold
more meat for one penny this day than we could sell for
three, and to whatsoever merry lass gave him a kiss he
gave meat for nought." And others said, "He is some

prodigal that hath sold his land for silver and gold, and meaneth to spend all right merrily."

Then the Sheriff called Robin to him, not knowing him in his butcher's dress, and made him sit close to him on his right hand; for he loved a rich young prodigal—especially when he thought that he might lighten that prodigal's pockets into his own most worshipful purse. So he made much of Robin, and laughed and talked with him more than with any of the others.

At last the dinner was ready to be served and the Sheriff bade Robin say grace, so Robin stood up and said, "Now Heaven bless us all and eke good meat and good sack within this house, and may all butchers be and remain as honest men as I am."

At this all laughed, the Sheriff loudest of all, for he said to himself, "Surely this is indeed some prodigal, and perchance I may empty his purse of some of the money that the fool throweth about so freely." Then he spake aloud to Robin, saying, "Thou art a jolly young blade, and I love thee mightily"; and he smote Robin upon the shoulder.

Then Robin laughed loudly too. "Yea," quoth he, "I know thou dost love a jolly blade, for didst thou not have jolly Robin Hood at thy shooting match and didst thou not gladly give him a bright golden arrow for his own?"

At this the Sheriff looked grave and all the guild of butchers too, so that none laughed but Robin, only some winked slyly at each other.

"Come, fill us some sack!" cried Robin. "Let us e'er be merry while we may, for man is but dust, and he hath but a span to live here till the worm getteth him, as our good gossip Swanthold sayeth; so let life be merry while it lasts, say I. Nay, never look down i' the mouth, Sir Sheriff. Who knowest but that thou mayest catch Robin Hood yet, if thou drinkest less good sack and Malmsey,

and bringest down the fat about thy paunch and the dust from out thy brain. Be merry, man."

Then the Sheriff laughed again, but not as though he liked the jest, while the butchers said, one to another, "Before Heaven, never have we seen such a mad rollicking blade. Mayhap, though, he will make the Sheriff mad."

"How now, brothers," cried Robin, "be merry! nay, never count over your farthings, for by this and by that I will pay this shot myself, e'en though it cost two hundred pounds. So let no man draw up his lip, nor thrust his forefinger into his purse, for I swear that neither butcher nor Sheriff shall pay one penny for this feast."

"Now thou art a right merry soul," quoth the Sheriff, "and I wot thou must have many a head of horned beasts and many an acre of land, that thou dost spend thy money so freely."

"Ay, that have I," quoth Robin, laughing loudly again, "five hundred and more horned beasts have I and my brothers, and none of them have we been able to sell, else I might not have turned butcher. As for my land, I have never asked my steward how many acres I have."

At this the Sheriff's eyes twinkled, and he chuckled to himself. "Nay, good youth," quoth he, "if thou canst not sell thy cattle, it may be I will find a man that will lift them from thy hands; perhaps that man may be myself, for I love a merry youth and would help such a one along the path of life. Now how much dost thou want for thy horned cattle?"

"Well," quoth Robin, "they are worth at least five hundred pounds."

"Nay," answered the Sheriff slowly, and as if he were thinking within himself, "well do I love thee, and fain would I help thee along, but five hundred pounds in money is a good round sum; besides I have it not by me.

Yet I will give thee three hundred pounds for them all, and that in good hard silver and gold."

"Now thou old miser!" quoth Robin, "well thou knowest that so many horned cattle are worth seven hundred pounds and more, and even that is but small for them, and yet thou, with thy gray hairs and one foot in the grave, wouldst trade upon the folly of a wild youth."

At this the Sheriff looked grimly at Robin. "Nay," quoth Robin, "look not on me as though thou hadst sour beer in thy mouth, man. I will take thine offer, for I and my brothers do need the money. We lead a merry life, and no one leads a merry life for a farthing, so I will close the bargain with thee. But mind that thou bringest a good three hundred pounds with thee, for I trust not one that driveth so shrewd a bargain."

"I will bring the money," said the Sheriff. "But what is thy name, good youth?"

"Men call me Robert o' Locksley," quoth bold Robin.

"Then, good Robert o' Locksley," quoth the Sheriff, "I will come this day to see thy horned beasts. But first my clerk shall draw up a paper in which thou shalt be bound to the sale, for thou gettest not my money without I get thy beasts in return."

Then Robin Hood laughed again. "So be it," he said, smiting his palm upon the Sheriff's hand. "Truly my brothers will be thankful to thee for thy money."

Thus the bargain was closed, but many of the butchers talked among themselves of the Sheriff, saying that it was but a scurvy trick to beguile a poor spendthrift youth in this way.

The afternoon had come when the Sheriff mounted his horse and joined Robin Hood, who stood outside the gateway of the paved court waiting for him, for he had sold his horse and cart to a trader for two marks. Then they set forth upon their way, the Sheriff riding upon his

horse and Robin running beside him.   Thus they left Nottingham Town and traveled forward along the dusty highway, laughing and jesting together as though they had been old friends.   But all the time the Sheriff said within himself, "Thy jest to me of Robin Hood shall cost thee dear, good fellow, even four hundred pounds, thou fool."   For he thought he would make at least that much by his bargain.

So they journeyed onward till they came within the verge of Sherwood Forest, when presently the Sheriff looked up and down and to the right and to the left of him, and then grew quiet and ceased his laughter. "Now," quoth he, "may Heaven and its saints preserve us this day from a rogue men call Robin Hood."

Then Robin laughed aloud.   "Nay," said he, "thou mayst set thy mind at rest, for well do I know Robin Hood and well do I know that thou art in no more danger from him this day than thou art from me."

At this the Sheriff looked askance at Robin, saying to himself, "I like not that thou seemest so well acquainted with this bold outlaw, and I wish that I were well out of Sherwood Forest."

But still they traveled deeper into the forest shades, and the deeper they went, the more quiet grew the Sheriff.   At last they came to where the road took a sudden bend, and before them a herd of dun deer went tripping across the path.   Then Robin Hood came close to the Sheriff and pointing his finger, he said, "These are my horned beasts, good Master Sheriff.   How dost thou like them?   Are they not fat and fair to see?"

At this the Sheriff drew rein quickly.   "Now fellow," quoth he, "I would I were well out of this forest, for I like not thy company.   Go thou thine own path, good friend, and let me but go mine."

But Robin only laughed and caught the Sheriff's bridle rein.   "Nay," cried he, "stay awhile, for I would thou

"These are my horned beasts, good Master Sheriff.
How dost thou like them?"

shouldst see my brothers, who own these fair horned beasts with me." So saying, he clapped his bugle to his mouth and winded three merry notes, and presently up the path came leaping fivescore good stout yeomen with Little John at their head.

"What wouldst thou have, good master?" quoth Little John.

"Why," answered Robin, "dost thou not see that I have brought goodly company to feast with us today? Fye, for shame! Do you not see our good and worshipful master, the Sheriff of Nottingham? Take thou his bridle, Little John, for he has honored us today by coming to feast with us."

Then all doffed their hats humbly, without smiling or seeming to be in jest, while Little John took the bridle rein and led the palfrey still deeper into the forest, all marching in order, with Robin Hood walking beside the Sheriff, hat in hand.

All this time the Sheriff said never a word but only looked about him like one suddenly awakened from sleep; but when he found himself going within the very depths of Sherwood his heart sank within him, for he thought, "Surely my three hundred pounds will be taken from me, even if they take not my life itself, for I have plotted against their lives more than once." But all seemed humble and meek and not a word was said of danger, either to life or money.

So at last they came to that part of Sherwood Forest where a noble oak spread its branches wide, and beneath it was a seat all made of moss, on which Robin sat down, placing the Sheriff at his right hand. "Now busk ye, my merry men all," quoth he, "and bring forth the best we have, both of meat and wine, for his worship the Sheriff hath feasted me in Nottingham Guild Hall today, and I would not have him go back empty."

All this time nothing had been said of the Sheriff's

money, so presently he began to pluck up heart. "For," said he to himself, "maybe Robin Hood hath forgotten all about it."

Then, while beyond in the forest bright fires crackled and savory smells of sweetly roasting venison and fat capons filled the glade, and brown pasties warmed beside the blaze, did Robin Hood entertain the Sheriff right royally. First, several couples stood forth at quarterstaff, and so shrewd were they at the game, and so quickly did they give stroke and parry, that the Sheriff, who loved to watch all lusty sports of the kind, clapped his hands, forgetting where he was, and crying aloud, "Well struck! Well struck, thou fellow with the black beard!" little knowing that the man he called upon was the Tinker that tried to serve his warrant upon Robin Hood.

Then several yeomen came forward and spread cloths upon the green grass, and placed a royal feast; while others still broached barrels of sack and Malmsey and good stout ale, and set them in jars upon the cloth, with drinking horns about them. Then all sat down and feasted and drank merrily together until the sun was low and the half-moon glimmered with a pale light betwixt the leaves of the trees overhead.

Then the Sheriff arose and said, "I thank you all, good yeomen, for the merry entertainment ye have given me this day. Right courteously have ye used me, showing therein that ye have much respect for our glorious King and his deputy in brave Nottinghamshire. But the shadows grow long, and I must away before darkness comes, lest I lose myself within the forest."

Then Robin Hood and all his merry men arose also, and Robin said to the Sheriff, "If thou must go, worshipful sir, go thou must; but thou hast forgotten one thing."

"Nay, I forgot nought," said the Sheriff; yet all the same his heart sank within him.

"But I say thou hast forgot something," quoth Robin.

"We keep a merry inn here in the greenwood, but whoever becometh our guest must pay his reckoning."

Then the Sheriff laughed, but the laugh was hollow. "Well, jolly boys," quoth he, "we have had a merry time together today, and even if ye had not asked me, I would have given you a score of pounds for the sweet entertainment I have had."

"Nay," quoth Robin seriously, "it would ill beseem us to treat Your Worship so meanly. By my faith, Sir Sheriff, I would be ashamed to show my face if I did not reckon the King's deputy at three hundred pounds. Is it not so, my merry men all?"

Then "Ay!" cried all, in a loud voice.

"Three hundred devils!" roared the Sheriff. "Think ye that your beggarly feast was worth three pounds, let alone three hundred?"

"Nay," quoth Robin gravely. "Speak not so roundly, Your Worship. I do love thee for the sweet feast thou hast given me this day in merry Nottingham Town; but there be those here who love thee not so much. If thou wilt look down the cloth thou wilt see Will Stutely, in whose eyes thou hast no great favor; then two other stout fellows are there here that thou knowest not, that were wounded in a brawl nigh Nottingham Town, some time ago—thou wottest when; one of them was sore hurt in one arm, yet he hath got the use of it again. Good Sheriff, be advised by me; pay thy score without more ado, or maybe it may fare ill with thee."

As he spoke the Sheriff's ruddy cheeks grew pale, and he said nothing more but looked upon the ground and gnawed his nether lip. Then slowly he drew forth his fat purse and threw it upon the cloth in front of him.

"Now take the purse, Little John," quoth Robin Hood, "and see that the reckoning be right. We would not doubt our Sheriff, but he might not like it if he should find he had not paid his full score.

Then Little John counted the money and found that the bag held three hundred pounds in silver and gold. But to the Sheriff it seemed as if every clink of the bright money was a drop of blood from his veins. And when he saw it all counted out in a heap of silver and gold, filling a wooden platter, he turned away and silently mounted his horse.

"Never have we had so worshipful a guest before!" quoth Robin, "and, as the day waxeth late, I will send one of my young men to guide thee out of the forest depths."

"Nay, Heaven forbid!" cried the Sheriff hastily. "I can find mine own way, good man, without aid."

"Then I will put thee on the right track mine own self," quoth Robin, and, taking the Sheriff's horse by the bridle rein, he led him into the main forest path. Then, before he let him go, he said, "Now, fare thee well, good Sheriff, and when next thou thinkest to despoil some poor prodigal, remember thy feast in Sherwood Forest. 'Ne'er buy a horse, good friend, without first looking into its mouth,' as our good gaffer Swanthold says. And so, once more, fare thee well." Then he clapped his hand to the horse's back, and off went nag and Sheriff through the forest glades.

Then bitterly the Sheriff rued the day that first he meddled with Robin Hood, for all men laughed at him and many ballads were sung by folk throughout the country, of how the Sheriff went to shear and came home shorn to the very quick. For thus men sometimes overreach themselves through greed and guile.

Little John Goes to Nottingham Fair

SPRING HAD GONE since the Sheriff's feast in Sherwood, and summer also, and the mellow month of October had come. All the air was cool and fresh; the harvests were gathered home, the young birds were full fledged, the hops were plucked, and apples were ripe. But though time had so smoothed things over that men no longer talked of the horned beasts that the Sheriff wished to buy, he was still sore about the matter and could not bear to hear Robin Hood's name spoken in his presence.

With October had come the time for holding the great Fair which was celebrated every five years at Nottingham Town, to which folk came from far and near throughout the country. At such times archery was always the main sport of the day, for the Nottinghamshire yeomen were the best hand at the longbow in all merry England; but this year the Sheriff hesitated a long time before he issued proclamation of the Fair, fearing lest Robin Hood and his band might come to it. At first he had a great part of a mind not to proclaim the Fair, but second thought told him that men would laugh at him and say among themselves that he was afraid of Robin Hood, so he put that

thought by. At last he fixed in his mind that he would offer such a prize as they would not care to shoot for. At such times it had been the custom to offer a half score of marks or a tun of ale, so this year he proclaimed that a prize of two fat steers should be given to the best bowman.

When Robin Hood heard what had been proclaimed he was vexed, and said, "Now beshrew this Sheriff that he should offer such a prize that none but shepherd hinds will care to shoot for it! I would have loved nothing better than to have had another bout at merry Nottingham Town, but if I should win this prize nought would it pleasure or profit me."

Then up spoke Little John: "Nay, but hearken, good master," said he, "only today Will Stutely, young David of Doncaster, and I were at the Sign of the Blue Boar, and there we heard all the news of this merry Fair, and also that the Sheriff hath offered this prize, that we of Sherwood might not care to come to the Fair; so, good master, if thou wilt, I would fain go and strive to win even this poor thing among the stout yeomen who will shoot at Nottingham Town."

"Nay, Little John," quoth Robin, "thou art a sound stout fellow, yet thou lackest the cunning that good Stutely hath, and I would not have harm befall thee for all Nottinghamshire. Nevertheless, if thou wilt go, take some disguise lest there be those there who may know thee."

"So be it, good master," quoth Little John, "yet all the disguise that I wish is a good suit of scarlet instead of this of Lincoln green. I will draw the cowl of my jacket about my head so that it will hide my brown hair and beard, and then, I trust, no one will know me."

"It is much against my will," said Robin Hood, "ne'er-theless, if thou dost wish it, get thee gone, but bear thyself seemingly, Little John, for thou art mine own right-hand man and I could ill bear to have harm befall thee."

So Little John clad himself all in scarlet and started off to the Fair at Nottingham Town.

Right merry were these Fair days at Nottingham, when the green before the great town gate was dotted with booths standing in rows, with tents of many-colored canvas, hung about with streamers and garlands of flowers, and the folk came from all the countryside, both gentle and common. In some booths there was dancing to merry music, in others flowed ale and beer, and in others yet again sweet cakes and barley sugar were sold; and sport was going outside the booths also, where some minstrel sang ballads of the olden time, playing a second upon the harp, or where the wrestlers struggled with one another within the sawdust ring; but the people gathered most of all around a raised platform where stout fellows played at quarterstaff.

So Little John came to the Fair. All scarlet were his hose and jerkin, and scarlet was his cowled cap, with a scarlet feather stuck in the side of it. Over his shoulders was slung a stout bow of yew, and across his back hung a quiver of good round arrows. Many turned to look after such a stout, tall fellow, for his shoulders were broader by a palm's-breadth than any that were there, and he stood a head taller than all the other men. The lasses, also, looked at him askance, thinking they had never seen a lustier youth.

First of all he went to the booth where stout ale was sold, and, standing aloft on a bench, he called to all that were near to come and drink with him. "Hey, sweet lads!" cried he, "who will drink ale with a stout yeoman? Come, all! Come, all! Let us be merry, for the day is sweet and the ale is tingling. Come hither, good yeoman, and thou, and thou; for not a farthing shall one of you pay. Nay, turn hither, thou lusty beggar, and thou jolly tinker, for all shall be merry with me."

Thus he shouted, and all crowded around, laughing,

while the brown ale flowed; and they called Little John a brave fellow, each swearing that he loved him as his own brother; for when one has entertainment with nothing to pay, one loves the man that gives it to one.

Then he strolled to the platform where they were at cudgel play, for he loved a bout at quarterstaff as he loved meat and drink; and here befell an adventure that was sung in ballads throughout the mid-country for many a day.

One fellow there was that cracked crowns of everyone who threw cap into the ring. This was Eric o' Lincoln, of great renown, whose name had been sung in ballads throughout the countryside. When Little John reached the stand he found none fighting, but only bold Eric walking up and down the platform, swinging his staff and shouting lustily, "Now, who will come and strike a stroke for the lass he loves the best, with a good Lincolnshire yeoman? How now, lads? Step up! Step up! Or else the lasses' eyes are not bright hereabouts, or the blood of Nottingham youth is sluggish and cold. Lincoln against Nottingham, say I! For no one hath put foot upon the boards this day such as we of Lincoln call a cudgel player."

At this, one would nudge another with his elbow, saying, "Go thou, Ned!" or "Go thou, Thomas!" but no lad cared to gain a cracked crown for nothing.

Presently Eric saw where Little John stood among the others, a head and shoulders above them all, and he called to him loudly, "Halloa, thou long-legged fellow in scarlet! Broad are thy shoulders and thick thy head; is not thy lass fair enough for thee to take cudgel in hand for her sake? In truth, I believe that Nottingham men do turn to bone and sinew, for neither heart nor courage have they! Now, thou great lout, wilt thou not twirl staff for Nottingham?"

"Ay," quoth Little John, "had I but mine own good

staff here, it would pleasure me hugely to crack thy knave's pate, thou saucy braggart! I wot it would be well for thee an thy cock's comb were cut!" Thus he spoke, slowly at first, for he was slow to move; but his wrath gathered headway like a great stone rolling down a hill, so that at the end he was full of anger.

Then Eric o' Lincoln laughed aloud. "Well spoken for one who fears to meet me fairly, man to man," said he. "Saucy are thou thine own self, and if thou puttest foot upon these boards, I will make thy saucy tongue rattle within thy teeth!"

"Now," quoth Little John, "is there never a man here that will lend me a good stout staff till I try the mettle of yon fellow?" At this, half a score reached him their staves, and he took the stoutest and heaviest of them all. Then, looking up and down the cudgel, he said, "Now, I have in my hand but a splint of wood—a barley straw, as it were—yet I trow it will have to serve me, so here goeth." Thereupon he cast the cudgel upon the stand and, leaping lightly after it, snatched it up in his hand again.

Then each man stood in his place and measured the other with fell looks until he that directed the sport cried, "Play!" At this they stepped forth, each grasping his staff tightly in the middle. Then those that stood around saw the stoutest game of quarterstaff that e'er Nottingham Town beheld. At first Eric o' Lincoln thought that he would gain an easy advantage, so he came forth as if he would say, "Watch, good people, how that I carve you this cockerel right speedily"; but he presently found it to be no such speedy matter. Right deftly he struck, and with great skill of fence, but he had found his match in Little John. Once, twice, thrice, he struck, and three times Little John turned the blows to the left hand and to the right. Then quickly and with a dainty backhanded blow, he rapped Eric beneath his guard so shrewdly that

it made his head ring again. Then Eric stepped back to gather his wits, while a great shout went up and all were glad that Nottingham had cracked Lincoln's crown; and thus ended the first bout of the game.

Then presently the director of the sport cried, "Play!" and they came together again; but now Eric played warily, for he found his man was of right good mettle, and also he had no sweet memory of the blow that he had got; so this bout neither Little John nor the Lincoln man caught a stroke within his guard. Then, after a while, they parted again, and this made the second bout.

Then for the third time they came together, and at first Eric strove to be wary, as he had been before; but, growing mad at finding himself so foiled, he lost his wits and began to rain blows so fiercely and so fast that they rattled like hail on penthouse roof; but, in spite of all, he did not reach within Little John's guard. Then at last Little John saw his chance and seized it right cleverly. Once more, with a quick blow, he rapped Eric beside the head, and ere he could regain himself, Little John slipped his right hand down to his left and, with a swinging blow, smote the other so sorely upon the crown that down he fell as though he would never move again.

Then the people shouted so loud that folk came running from all about to see what was the ado; while Little John leaped down from the stand and gave the staff back to him that had lent it to him. And thus ended the famous bout between Little John and Eric o' Lincoln of great renown.

But now the time had come when those who were to shoot with the longbow were to take their places, so the people began flocking to the butts where the shooting was to be. Near the target, in a good place, sat the Sheriff upon a raised dais, with many gentlefolk around him. When the archers had taken their places, the herald came forward and proclaimed the rules of the game, and how

each should shoot three shots, and to him that should shoot the best the prize of two fat steers was to belong. A score of brave shots were gathered there, and among them some of the keenest hands at the longbow in Lincoln and Nottinghamshire; and among them Little John stood taller than all the rest. "Who is yon stranger clad all in scarlet?" said some, and others answered, "It is he that hath but now so soundly cracked the crown of Eric o' Lincoln." Thus the people talked among themselves, until at last it reached even the Sheriff's ears.

And now each man stepped forward and shot in turn; but though each shot well, Little John was the best of all, for three times he struck the clout, and once only the length of a barleycorn from the center. "Hey for the tall archer!" shouted the crowd, and some among them shouted, "Hey for Reynold Greenleaf!" for this was the name that Little John had called himself that day.

Then the Sheriff stepped down from the raised seat and came to where the archers stood, while all doffed their caps that saw him coming. He looked keenly at Little John but did not know him, though he said, after a while, "How now, good fellow, methinks there is that about thy face that I have seen erewhile."

"Mayhap it may be so," quoth Little John, "for often have I seen Your Worship." And, as he spoke, he looked steadily into the Sheriff's eyes so that the latter did not suspect who he was.

"A brave blade art thou, good friend," said the Sheriff, "and I hear that thou hast well upheld the skill of Nottinghamshire against that of Lincoln this day. What may be thy name, good fellow?"

"Men do call me Reynold Greenleaf, Your Worship," said Little John; and the old ballad that tells of this, adds, "So, in truth, was he a green leaf, but of what manner of tree the Sheriff wotted not."

"Now, Reynold Greenleaf," quoth the Sheriff, "thou

art the fairest hand at the longbow that mine eyes ever beheld, next to that false knave, Robin Hood, from whose wiles Heaven forfend me! Wilt thou join my service, good fellow? Thou shalt be paid right well, for three suits of clothes shalt thou have a year, with good food and as much ale as thou canst drink; and, besides this, I will pay thee forty marks each Michaelmastide."

"Then here stand I a free man, and right gladly will I enter thy household," said Little John, for he thought he might find some merry jest, should he enter the Sheriff's service.

"Fairly hast thou won the fat steers," said the Sheriff, "and thereunto I will add a butt of good March beer, for joy of having gotten such a man; for, I wot, thou shootest as fair a shaft as Robin Hood himself."

"Then," said Little John, "for joy of having gotten myself into thy service, I will give fat steers and brown ale to all these good folk, to make them merry withal." At this arose a great shout, many casting their caps aloft, for joy of the gift.

Then some built great fires and roasted the steers, and others broached the butt of ale, with which all made themselves merry. Then, when they had eaten and drunk as much as they could, and when the day faded and the great moon arose, all red and round, over the spires and towers of Nottingham Town, they joined hands and danced around the fires, to the music of bagpipes and harps. But long before this merrymaking had begun, the Sheriff and his new servant Reynold Greenleaf were in the Castle of Nottingham.

How Little John Lived at the Sheriff's

THUS LITTLE JOHN entered into the Sheriff's service and found the life he led there easy enough, for the Sheriff made him his right-hand man and held him in great favor. He sat nigh the Sheriff at meat, and he ran beside his horse when he went a-hunting; so that, what with hunting and hawking a little, and eating rich dishes and drinking good sack, and sleeping until late hours in the morning, he grew as fat as a stall-fed ox. Thus things floated easily along with the tide, until one day when the Sheriff went a-hunting, there happened that which broke the smooth surface of things.

This morning the Sheriff and many of his men set forth to meet certain lords, to go a-hunting. He looked all about him for his good man, Reynold Greenleaf, but, not finding him, was vexed, for he wished to show Little John's skill to his noble friends. As for Little John, he lay abed, snoring lustily, till the sun was high in the heavens. At last he opened his eyes and looked about him but did not move to arise. Brightly shone the sun in at the window, and all the air was sweet with the scent of

woodbine that hung in sprays about the wall without, for the cold winter was past and spring was come again, and Little John lay still, thinking how sweet was everything on this fair morn.   Just then he heard, faint and far away, a distant bugle note sounding thin and clear.   The sound was small, but, like a little pebble dropped into a glassy fountain, it broke all the smooth surface of his thoughts, until his whole soul was filled with disturbance.   His spirit seemed to awaken from its sluggishness, and his memory brought back to him all the merry greenwood life—how the birds were singing blithely there this bright morning, and how his loved companions and friends were feasting and making merry, or perhaps talking of him with sober speech; for when he first entered the Sheriff's service he did so in jest; but the hearthstone was warm during the winter, and the fare was full, and so he had abided, putting off from day to day his going back to Sherwood, until six long months had passed.   But now he thought of his good master and of Will Stutely, whom he loved better than anyone in all the world, and of young David of Doncaster, whom he had trained so well in all manly sports, till there came over his heart a great and bitter longing for them all, so that his eyes filled with tears.   Then he said aloud, "Here I grow fat like a stall-fed ox and all my manliness departeth from me while I become a sluggard and dolt.   But I will arouse me and go back to mine own dear friends once more, and never will I leave them again till life doth leave my lips."   So saying, he leaped from bed, for he hated his sluggishness now.

When he came downstairs he saw the Steward standing near the pantry door—a great, fat man, with a huge bundle of keys hanging to his girdle.   Then Little John said, "Ho, Master Steward, a hungry man am I, for nought have I had for all this blessed morn.   Therefore, give me to eat."

Then the Steward looked grimly at him and rattled the

keys in his girdle, for he hated Little John because he had found favor with the Sheriff. "So, Master Reynold Greenleaf, thou art anhungered, art thou?" quoth he. "But, fair youth, if thou livest long enough, thou wilt find that he who getteth overmuch sleep for an idle head goeth with an empty stomach. For what sayeth the old saw, Master Greenleaf? Is it not 'The late fowl findeth but ill faring'?"

"Now, thou great purse of fat!" cried Little John, "I ask thee not for fool's wisdom, but for bread and meat. Who art thou, that thou shouldst deny me to eat? By Saint Dunstan, thou hadst best tell me where my breakfast is, if thou wouldst save broken bones!"

"Thy breakfast, Master Fireblaze, is in the pantry," answered the Steward.

"Then fetch it hither!" cried Little John, who waxed angry by this time.

"Go thou and fetch it thine own self," quoth the Steward. "Am I thy slave, to fetch and carry for thee?"

"I say, go thou, bring it me!"

"I say, go thou, fetch it for thyself!"

"Ay, marry, that will I, right quickly!" quoth Little John in a rage. And, so saying, he strode to the pantry and tried to open the door but found it locked, whereat the Steward laughed and rattled his keys. Then the wrath of Little John boiled over, and, lifting his clenched fist, he smote the pantry door, bursting out three panels and making so large an opening that he could easily stoop and walk through it.

When the the Steward saw what was done, he waxed mad with rage; and, as Little John stooped to look within the pantry, he seized him from behind by the nape of the neck, pinching him sorely and smiting him over the head with his keys till the yeoman's ears rang again. At this Little John turned upon the Steward and smote him such a buffet that the fat man fell to the floor and lay there as

though he would never move again. "There," quoth
Little John, "think well of that stroke and never keep a
good breakfast from a hungry man again."

So saying, he crept into the pantry and looked about
him to see if he could find something to appease his
hunger. He saw a great venison pasty and two roasted
capons, beside which was a platter of plover's eggs; moreover, there was a flask of sack and one of canary—a sweet
sight to a hungry man. These he took down from the
shelves and placed upon a sideboard, and prepared to
make himself merry.

Now the Cook, in the kitchen across the courtyard,
heard the loud talking between Little John and the Steward, and also the blow that Little John struck the other,
so he came running across the court and up the stairway
to where the Steward's pantry was, bearing in his hands
the spit with the roast still upon it. Meanwhile the
Steward had gathered his wits about him and risen to his
feet, so that when the Cook came to the Steward's pantry
he saw him glowering through the broken door at Little
John, who was making ready for a good repast, as one
dog glowers at another that has a bone. When the
Steward saw the Cook, he came to him, and, putting one
arm over his shoulder, "Alas, sweet friend!" quoth he—
for the Cook was a tall, stout man—"seest thou what that
vile knave Reynold Greenleaf hath done? He hath
broken in upon our master's goods, and hath smitten me a
buffet upon the ear, so that I thought I was dead. Good
Cook, I love thee well, and thou shalt have a good pottle
of our master's best wine every day, for thou art an old
and faithful servant. Also, good Cook, I have ten shillings that I mean to give as a gift to thee. But hatest thou
not to see a vile upstart like this Reynold Greenleaf taking
it upon him so bravely?"

"Ay, marry, that do I," quoth the Cook boldly, for he
liked the Steward because of his talk of the wine and

of the ten shillings. "Get thee gone straightway to thy room, and I will bring out this knave by his ears." So saying, he laid aside his spit and drew the sword that hung by his side; whereupon the Steward left as quickly as he could, for he hated the sight of naked steel.

Then the Cook walked straightway to the broken pantry door, through which he saw Little John tucking a napkin beneath his chin and preparing to make himself merry.

"Why, how now, Reynold Greenleaf?" said the Cook, "thou art no better than a thief, I wot. Come thou straight forth, man, or I will carve thee as I would carve a sucking pig."

"Nay, good Cook, bear thou thyself more seemingly, or else I will come forth to thy dole. At most times I am as a yearling lamb, but when one cometh between me and my meat, I am a raging lion, as it were."

"Lion or no lion," quoth the valorous Cook, "come thou straight forth, else thou art a coward heart as well as a knavish thief."

"Ha!" cried Little John, "coward's name have I never had; so, look to thyself, good Cook, for I come forth straight, the roaring lion I did speak of but now."

Then he, too, drew his sword and came out of the pantry; then, putting themselves into position, they came slowly together, with grim and angry looks; but suddenly Little John lowered his point. "Hold, good Cook!" said he. "Now, I bethink me it were ill of us to fight with good victuals standing so nigh, and such a feast as would befit two stout fellows such as we are. Marry, good friend, I think we should enjoy this fair feast ere we fight. What sayest thou, jolly Cook?"

At this speech the Cook looked up and down, scratching his head in doubt, for he loved good feasting. At last he drew a long breath and said to Little John, "Well, good friend, I like thy plan right well; so, pretty boy, say I, let

*"Ha!" cried Little John, "coward's name
have I never had!"*

us feast, with all my heart, for one of us may sup in Paradise before nightfall."

So each thrust his sword back into the scabbard and entered the pantry. Then, after they had seated themselves, Little John drew his dagger and thrust it into the pie. "A hungry man must be fed," quoth he, "so, sweet chuck, I help myself without leave." But the Cook did not lag far behind, for straightway his hands also were deeply thrust within the goodly pasty. After this, neither of them spoke further, but used their teeth to better purpose. But though neither spoke, they looked at one another, each thinking within himself that he had never seen a more lusty fellow than the one across the board.

At last, after a long time had passed, the Cook drew a full, deep breath, as though of much regret, and wiped his hands upon the napkin, for he could eat no more. Little John, also, had enough, for he pushed the pasty aside, as though he would say, "I want thee by me no more, good friend." Then he took the pottle of sack, and said he, "Now, good fellow, I swear by all that is bright, that thou art the stoutest companion at eating that ever I had. Lo! I drink thy health." So saying, he clapped the flask to his lips and cast his eyes aloft, while the good wine flooded his throat. Then he passed the pottle to the Cook, who also said, "Lo, I drink thy health, sweet fellow!" Nor was he behind Little John in drinking any more than in eating.

"Now," quoth Little John, "thy voice is right round and sweet, jolly lad. I doubt not thou canst sing a ballad most blithely; canst thou not?"

"Truly, I have trolled one now and then," quoth the Cook, "yet I would not sing alone."

"Nay, truly," said Little John, "that were but ill courtesy. Strike up thy ditty, and I will afterward sing one to match it, if I can."

"So be it, pretty boy," quoth the Cook. "And hast

thou e're heard the song of the Deserted Shepherdess?"

"Truly, I know not," answered Little John, "but sing thou and let me hear."

Then the Cook took another draught from the pottle, and, clearing his throat, sang right sweetly:

THE SONG OF THE DESERTED SHEPHERDESS

"In Lententime, when leaves wax green,
And pretty birds begin to mate,
When lark doth sing, and thrush, I ween,
And stockdove cooeth soon and late,
Fair Phillis sat beside a stone,
And thus I heard her make her moan:
'O willow, willow, willow, willow!
I'll take me of thy branches fair
And twine a wreath to deck my hair.

" 'The thrush hath taken him a she,
The robin, too, and eke the dove;
My Robin hath deserted me,
And left me for another love.
So here, by brookside, all alone,
I sit me down and make my moan.
O willow, willow, willow, willow!
I'll take me of thy branches fair
And twine a wreath to deck my hair.'

"But ne'er came herring from the sea,
But good as he were in the tide;
Young Corydon came o'er the lea,
And sat him Phillis down beside.
So, presently, she changed her tone,
And 'gan to cease her from her moan,
'O willow, willow, willow, willow!
Thou mayst e'en keep thy garlands fair,
I want them not to deck my hair.' "

"Now, by my faith," cried Little John, "that same is a right good song, and hath truth in it, also."

"Glad am I thou likest it, sweet lad," said the Cook. "Now sing thou one also, for ne'er should a man be merry alone, or sing and list not."

"Then I will sing thee a song of a right good knight of Arthur's court, and how he cured his heart's wound without running upon the dart again, as did thy Phillis; for I wot she did but cure one smart by giving herself another. So, list thou while I sing:

THE GOOD KNIGHT AND HIS LOVE

"When Arthur, King, did rule this land,
A goodly king was he,
And had he of stout knights a band
Of merry company.

"Among them all, both great and small,
A good stout knight was there,
A lusty childe, and eke a tall,
That loved a lady fair.

"But nought would she to do with he,
But turned her face away;
So gat he gone to far countrye,
And left that lady gay.

"There all alone he made his moan,
And eke did sob and sigh,
And weep till it would move a stone,
And he was like to die.

"But still his heart did feel the smart,
And eke the dire distress,
And rather grew his pain more sharp
As grew his body less.

"Then gat he back where was good sack
And merry companye,
And soon did cease to cry 'Alack!'
When blithe and gay was he.

"From which I hold, and feel full bold
To say, and eke believe,
That gin the belly go not cold
The heart will cease to grieve."

"Now, by my faith," cried the Cook, as he rattled the pottle against the sideboard, "I like that same song hugely, and eke the motive of it, which lieth like a sweet kernel in a hazelnut."

"Now thou art a man of shrewd opinions," quoth Little John, "and I love thee truly as thou wert my brother."

"And I love thee, too. But the day draweth on, and I have my cooking to do ere our master cometh home; so let us e'en go and settle this brave fight we have in hand."

"Ay, marry," quoth Little John, "and that right speedily. Never have I been more laggard in fighting than in eating and drinking. So come thou straight forth into the passageway, where there is good room to swing a sword, and I will try to serve thee."

Then they both stepped forth into the broad passage that led to the Steward's pantry, where each man drew his sword again and without more ado fell upon the other as though he would hew his fellow limb from limb. Then their swords clashed upon one another with great din, and sparks flew from each blow in showers. So they fought up and down the hall for an hour and more, neither striking the other a blow, though they strove their best to do so; for both were skillful at the fence; so nothing came of all their labor. Ever and anon they rested, panting; then, after getting their wind, at it they would go again more fiercely than ever. At last Little John cried aloud, "Hold, good Cook!" whereupon each rested upon his sword, panting.

"Now will I make my vow," quoth Little John, "thou art the very best swordsman that ever mine eyes beheld. Truly, I had thought to carve thee ere now."

"And I had thought to do the same by thee," quoth the Cook, "but I have missed the mark somehow."

"Now I have been thinking within myself," quoth Little John, "what we are fighting for; but albeit I do not rightly know."

"Why, no more do I," said the Cook. "I bear no love for that pursy Steward, but I thought that we had engaged to fight with one another and that it must be done."

"Now," quoth Little John, "it doth seem to me that instead of striving to cut one another's throats, it were better for us to be boon companions. What sayst thou, jolly Cook, wilt thou go with me to Sherwood Forest and join with Robin Hood's band? Thou shalt live a merry life within the woodlands, and sevenscore good companions shalt thou have, one of whom is mine own self. Thou shalt have three suits of Lincoln green each year, and forty marks in pay."

"Now, thou art a man after mine own heart!" cried the Cook right heartily, "and, as thou speakest of it, that is the very service for me. I will go with thee, and that right gladly. Give me thy palm, sweet fellow, and I will be thine own companion from henceforth. What may be thy name, lad?"

"Men do call me Little John, good fellow."

"How? And art thou indeed Little John, and Robin Hood's own right-hand man? Many a time and oft I heard of thee, but never did I hope to set eyes upon thee. And thou art indeed the famous Little John!" And the Cook seemed lost in amazement, and looked upon his companion with open eyes.

"I am Little John, indeed, and I will bring to Robin Hood this day a right stout fellow to join his merry band. But ere we go, good friend, it seemeth to me to be a vast pity that, as we have had so much of the Sheriff's food, we should not also carry off some of his silver plate to Robin Hood, as a present from his worship."

"Ay, marry is it," said the Cook. And so they began hunting about, and took as much silver as they could lay

hands upon, clapping it into a bag, and when they had filled the sack they set forth to Sherwood Forest.

Plunging into the woods, they came at last to the greenwood tree, where they found Robin Hood and threescore of his merry men lying upon the fresh green grass. When Robin and his men saw who it was that came, they leaped to their feet. "Now welcome!" cried Robin Hood. "Now welcome, Little John! For long hath it been since we have heard from thee, though we all knew that thou hadst joined the Sheriff's service. And how hast thou fared all these long days?"

"Right merrily have I lived at the Lord Sheriff's," answered Little John, "and I have come straight thence. See, good master! I have brought thee his cook, and even his silver plate." Thereupon he told Robin Hood and his merry men that were there, all that had befallen him since he had left them to go to the Fair at Nottingham Town. Then all shouted with laughter, except Robin Hood; but he looked grave.

"Nay, Little John," said he, "thou art a brave blade and a trusty fellow. I am glad thou hast brought thyself back to us, and with such a good companion as the Cook, whom we all welcome to Sherwood. But I like not so well that thou hast stolen the Sheriff's plate like some paltry thief. The Sheriff hath been punished by us, and hath lost three hundred pounds, even as he sought to despoil another; but he hath done nought that we should steal his household plate from him."

Though Little John was vexed with this, he strove to pass it off with a jest. "Nay, good master," quoth he, "if thou thinkest the Sheriff gave us not the plate, I will fetch him, that he may tell us with his own lips he giveth it all to us." So saying, he leaped to his feet, and was gone before Robin could call him back.

Little John ran for full five miles till he came to where the Sheriff of Nottingham and a gay company were hunt-

ing near the forest. When Little John came to the Sheriff he doffed his cap and bent his knee. "God save thee, good master," quoth he.

"Why, Reynold Greenleaf!" cried the Sheriff, "whence comest thou and where hast thou been?"

"I have been in the forest," answered Little John, speaking amazedly, "and there I saw a sight such as ne'er before man's eyes beheld! Yonder I saw a young hart all in green from top to toe, and about him was a herd of threescore deer, and they, too, were all of green from head to foot. Yet I dared not shoot, good master, for fear lest they should slay me."

"Why, how now, Reynold Greenleaf," cried the Sheriff, "art thou dreaming or art thou mad, that thou dost bring me such a tale?"

"Nay, I am not dreaming nor am I mad," said Little John, "and if thou wilt come with me, I will show thee this fair sight, for I have seen it with mine own eyes. But thou must come alone, good master, lest the others frighten them and they get away."

So the party all rode forward, and Little John led them downward into the forest.

"Now, good master," quoth he at last, "we are nigh where I saw this herd."

Then the Sheriff descended from his horse and bade them wait for him until he should return; and Little John led him forward through a close copse until suddenly they came to a great open glade, at the end of which Robin Hood sat beneath the shade of the great oak tree, with his merry men all about him. "See, good Master Sheriff," quoth Little John, "yonder is the hart of which I spake to thee."

At this the Sheriff turned to Little John and said bitterly, "Long ago I thought I remembered thy face, but now I know thee. Woe betide thee, Little John, for thou hast betrayed me this day."

In the meantime Robin Hood had come to them. "Now welcome, Master Sheriff," said he. "Hast thou come today to take another feast with me?"

"Nay, Heaven forbid!" said the Sheriff in tones of deep earnest. "I care for no feast and have no hunger today."

"Nevertheless," quoth Robin, "if thou hast no hunger, maybe thou hast thirst, and well I know thou wilt take a cup of sack with me. But I am grieved that thou wilt not feast with me, for thou couldst have victuals to thy liking, for there stands thy Cook."

Then he led the Sheriff, willy-nilly, to the seat he knew so well beneath the greenwood tree.

"Ho, lads!" cried Robin, "fill our good friend the Sheriff a right brimming cup of sack and fetch it hither, for he is faint and weary."

Then one of the band brought the Sheriff a cup of sack, bowing low as he handed it to him; but the Sheriff could not touch the wine, for he saw it served in one of his own silver flagons, on one of his own silver plates.

"How now," quoth Robin, "dost thou not like our new silver service? We have gotten a bag of it this day." So saying, he held up the sack of silver that Little John and the Cook had brought with them.

Then the Sheriff's heart was bitter within him; but, not daring to say anything, he only gazed upon the ground. Robin looked keenly at him for a time before he spoke again. Then said he, "Now, Master Sheriff, the last time thou camest to Sherwood Forest thou didst come seeking to despoil a poor spendthrift, and thou wert despoiled thine own self; but now thou comest seeking to do no harm, nor do I know that thou hast despoiled any man. I take my tithes from fat priests and lordly squires, to help those that they despoil and to raise up those that they bow down; but I know not that thou hast tenants of thine own whom thou hast wronged in any way. Therefore, take thou thine own again, nor will I dispossess thee today of

so much as one farthing. Come with me, and I will lead thee from the forest back to thine own party again."

Then, slinging the bag upon his shoulder, he turned away, the Sheriff following him, all too perplexed in mind to speak. So they went forward until they came to within a furlong of the spot where the Sheriff's companions were waiting for him. Then Robin Hood gave the sack of silver back to the Sheriff. "Take thou thine own again," he said, "and hearken to me, good Sheriff, take thou a piece of advice with it. Try thy servants well ere thou dost engage them again so readily." Then, turning, he left the other standing bewildered, with the sack in his hands.

The company that waited for the Sheriff were all amazed to see him come out of the forest bearing a heavy sack upon his shoulders; but though they questioned him, he answered never a word, acting like one who walks in a dream. Without a word, he placed the bag across his nag's back and then, mounting, rode away, all following him; but all the time there was a great turmoil of thoughts within his head, tumbling one over the other. And thus ends the merry tale of Little John and how he entered the Sheriff's service.

Little John and the Tanner of Blyth

ONE FINE DAY, not long after Little John had left abiding with the Sheriff and had come back, with his worship's cook, to the merry greenwood, as has just been told, Robin Hood and a few chosen fellows of his band lay upon the soft sward beneath the greenwood tree where they dwelled. The day was warm and sultry, so that while most of the band were scattered through the forest upon this mission and upon that, these few stout fellows lay lazily beneath the shade of the tree, in the soft afternoon, passing jests among themselves and telling merry stories, with laughter and mirth.

All the air was laden with the bitter fragrance of the May, and all the bosky shades of the woodlands beyond rang with the sweet song of birds—the throstle cock, the cuckoo, and the wood pigeon—and with the song of birds mingled the cool sound of the gurgling brook that leaped out of the forest shades, and ran fretting amid its rough, gray stones across the sunlit open glade before the trysting tree. And a fair sight was that halfscore of tall, stout yeomen, all clad in Lincoln green, lying beneath the broad-spreading branches of the great oak tree, amid the quivering leaves of which the sunlight shivered and fell in dancing patches upon the grass.

Suddenly Robin Hood smote his knee.

"By Saint Dunstan," quoth he, "I had nigh forgot that quarter-day cometh on apace, and yet no cloth of Lincoln

green in all our store. It must be looked to, and that in quick season. Come, busk thee, Little John! Stir those lazy bones of thine, for thou must get thee straightway to our good gossip, the draper Hugh Longshanks of Ancaster. Bid him send us straightway twentyscore yards of fair cloth of Lincoln green; and mayhap the journey may take some of the fat from off thy bones, that thou hast gotten from lazy living at our dear Sheriff's.

"Nay," muttered Little John (for he had heard so much upon this score that he was sore upon the point), "nay, truly, mayhap I have more flesh upon my joints than I once had, yet, flesh or no flesh, I doubt not that I could still hold my place and footing upon a narrow bridge against e'er a yeoman in Sherwood, or Nottinghamshire, for the matter of that, even though he had no more fat about his bones than thou hast, good master."

At this reply a great shout of laughter went up, and all looked at Robin Hood, for each man knew that Little John spake of a certain fight that happened between their master and himself, through which they first became acquainted.

"Nay," quoth Robin Hood, laughing louder than all. "Heaven forbid that I should doubt thee, for I care for no taste of thy staff myself, Little John. I must needs own that there are those of my band can handle a seven-foot staff more deftly than I; yet no man in all Nottinghamshire can draw gray goose shaft with my fingers. Nevertheless, a journey to Ancaster may not be ill for thee; so go thou, as I bid, and thou hadst best go this very evening, for since thou hast abided at the Sheriff's many know thy face, and if thou goest in broad daylight, thou mayst get thyself into a coil with some of his worship's men-at-arms. Bide thou here till I bring thee money to pay our good Hugh. I warrant he hath no better customers in all Nottinghamshire than we." So saying, Robin left them and entered the forest.

Not far from the trysting tree was a great rock in which a chamber had been hewn, the entrance being barred by a massive oaken door two palms'-breadth in thickness, studded about with spikes, and fastened with a great padlock. This was the treasure house of the band, and thither Robin Hood went and, unlocking the door, entered the chamber, from which he brought forth a bag of gold which he gave to Little John, to pay Hugh Longshanks withal, for the cloth of Lincoln green.

Then up got Little John, and, taking the bag of gold, which he thrust into his bosom, he strapped a girdle about his loins, took a stout pikestaff full seven feet long in his hand, and set forth upon his journey.

So he strode whistling along the leafy forest path that led to Fosse Way, turning neither to the right hand nor the left, until at last he came to where the path branched, leading on the one hand onward to Fosse Way, and on the other, as well Little John knew, to the merry Blue Boar Inn. Here Little John suddenly ceased whistling and stopped in the middle of the path. First he looked up and then he looked down, and then, tilting his cap over one eye, he slowly scratched the back part of his head. For thus it was: at the sight of these two roads, two voices began to alarum within him, the one crying, "There lies the road to the Blue Boar Inn, a can of brown October, and a merry night with sweet companions such as thou mayst find there"; the other, "There lies the way to Ancaster and the duty thou art sent upon." Now the first of these two voices was far the louder, for Little John had grown passing fond of good living through abiding at the Sheriff's house; so, presently, looking up into the blue sky, across which bright clouds were sailing like silver boats, and swallows skimming in circling flight, quoth he, "I fear me it will rain this evening, so I'll e'en stop at the Blue Boar till it passes by, for I know my good master would not have me wet to the skin." So, without more ado, off

he strode down the path that lay the way of his likings.
Now there was no sign of any foul weather, but when one
wishes to do a thing, as Little John did, one finds no lack
of reasons for the doing.

Four merry wags were at the Blue Boar Inn; a butcher,
a beggar, and two barefoot friars. Little John heard
them singing from afar, as he walked through the hush of
the mellow twilight that was now falling over hill and
dale. Right glad were they to welcome such a merry
blade as Little John. Fresh cans of ale were brought, and
with jest and song and merry tales the hours slipped away
on fleeting wings. None thought of time or tide till the
night was so far gone that Little John put by the thought
of setting forth upon his journey again that night, and so
bided at the Blue Boar Inn until the morrow.

Now it was an ill piece of luck for Little John that he
left his duty for his pleasure, and he paid a great score for
it, as we are all apt to do in the same case, as you shall
see.

Up he rose at the dawn of the next day, and, taking his
stout pikestaff in his hand, he set forth upon his journey
once more, as though he would make up for lost time.

In the good town of Blyth there lived a stout tanner,
celebrated far and near for feats of strength and many
tough bouts at wrestling and the quarterstaff. For five
years he had held the mid-country champion belt for
wrestling, till the great Adam o' Lincoln cast him in the
ring and broke one of his ribs; but at quarterstaff he had
never yet met his match in all the country about. Besides
all this, he dearly loved the longbow, and a sly jaunt in the
forest when the moon was full and the dun deer in season; so that the King's rangers kept a shrewd eye upon
him and his doings, for Arthur a Bland's house was apt to
have aplenty of meat in it that was more like venison than
the law allowed.

Now Arthur had been to Nottingham Town the day

before Little John set forth on his errand, there to sell a halfscore of tanned cowhides. At the dawn of the same day that Little John left the inn, he started from Nottingham, homeward for Blyth. His way led, all in the dewy morn, past the verge of Sherwood Forest, where the birds were welcoming the lovely day with a great and merry jubilee. Across the Tanner's shoulders was slung his stout quarterstaff, ever near enough to him to be gripped quickly, and on his head was a cap of doubled cowhide, so tough that it could hardly be cloven even by a broadsword.

"Now," quoth Arthur a Bland to himself, when he had come to that part of the road that cut through a corner of the forest, "no doubt at this time of year the dun deer are coming from the forest depths nigher to the open meadow lands. Mayhap I may chance to catch a sight of the dainty brown darlings thus early in the morn." For there was nothing he loved better than to look upon a tripping herd of deer, even when he could not tickle their ribs with a clothyard shaft. Accordingly, quitting the path, he went peeping this way and that through the underbrush, spying now here and now there, with all the wiles of a master of woodcraft, and of one who had more than once donned a doublet of Lincoln green.

Now as Little John stepped blithely along, thinking of nothing but of such things as the sweetness of the hawthorn buds that bedecked the hedgerows, or gazing upward at the lark, that, springing from the dewy grass, hung aloft on quivering wings in the yellow sunlight, pouring forth its song that fell like a falling star from the sky, his luck led him away from the highway, not far from the spot where Arthur a Bland was peeping this way and that through the leaves of the thickets. Hearing a rustling of the branches, Little John stopped and presently caught sight of the brown cowhide cap of the Tanner moving among the bushes.

"I do much wonder," quoth Little John to himself, "what yon knave is after, that he should go thus peeping and peering about. I verily believe that yon scurvy varlet is no better than a thief, and cometh here after our own and the good King's dun deer." For by much roving in the forest, Little John had come to look upon all the deer in Sherwood as belonging to Robin Hood and his band as much as to good King Harry. "Nay," quoth he again, after a time, "this matter must e'en be looked into." So, quitting the highroad, he also entered the thickets, and began spying around after stout Arthur a Bland.

So for a long time they both of them went hunting about, Little John after the Tanner, and the Tanner after the deer. At last Little John trod upon a stick, which snapped under his foot, whereupon, hearing the noise, the Tanner turned quickly and caught sight of the yeoman. Seeing that the Tanner had spied him out, Little John put a bold face upon the matter.

"Hilloa," quoth he, "what art thou doing here, thou naughty fellow? Who art thou that comest ranging Sherwood's paths? In very sooth thou hast an evil cast of countenance, and I do think, truly, that thou art no better than a thief, and comest after our good King's deer."

"Nay," quoth the Tanner boldly—for, though taken by surprise, he was not a man to be frightened by big words —"thou liest in thy teeth. I am no thief, but an honest craftsman. As for my countenance, it is what it is; and, for the matter of that, thine own is none too pretty, thou saucy fellow."

"Ha!" quoth Little John in a great loud voice, "wouldst thou give me backtalk? Now I have a great part of a mind to crack thy pate for thee. I would have thee know, fellow, that I am, as it were, one of the King's foresters. Leastwise," muttered he to himself, "I and my friends do take good care of our good sovereign's deer."

"I care not who thou art," answered the bold Tanner,

"and unless thou hast many more of thy kind by thee, thou canst never make Arthur a Bland cry 'A mercy.' "

"Is it so?" cried Little John in a rage. "Now, by my faith, thou saucy rogue, thy tongue hath led thee into a pit thou wilt have a sorry time getting out of; for I will give thee such a drubbing as ne'er hast thou had in all thy life before. Take thy staff in thy hand, fellow, for I will not smite an unarmed man."

"Marry come up with a murrain!" cried the Tanner, for he, too, had talked himself into a fume. "Big words ne'er killed so much as a mouse. Who art thou that talkest so freely of cracking the head of Arthur a Bland? If I do not tan thy hide this day as ne'er I tanned a calf's hide in all my life before, split my staff into skewers for lamb's flesh and call me no more brave man! Now look to thyself, fellow!"

"Stay!" said Little John. "Let us first measure our cudgels. I do reckon my staff longer than thine, and I would not take vantage of thee by even so much as an inch."

"Nay, I pass not for length," answered the Tanner. "My staff is long enough to knock down a calf; so look to thyself, fellow, I say again."

So, without more ado, each gripped his staff in the middle, and, with fell and angry looks, they came slowly together.

Now news had been brought to Robin Hood how that Little John, instead of doing his bidding, had passed by duty for pleasure, and so had stopped overnight with merry company at the Blue Boar Inn, instead of going straight to Ancaster. So, being vexed to his heart by this, he set forth at dawn of day to seek Little John at the Blue Boar, or at least to meet the yeoman on the way, and ease his heart of what he thought of the matter. As thus he strode along in anger, putting together the words he

would use to chide Little John, he heard, of a sudden, loud and angry voices, as of men in a rage, passing fell words back and forth from one to the other. At this, Robin Hood stopped and listened. "Surely," quoth he to himself, "that is Little John's voice, and he is talking in anger also. Methinks the other is strange to my ears. Now Heaven forfend that my good trusty Little John should have fallen into the hands of the King's rangers. I must see to this matter, and that quickly."

Thus spoke Robin Hood to himself, all his anger passing away like a breath from the windowpane, at the thought that perhaps his trusty right-hand man was in some danger of his life. So cautiously he made his way through the thickets whence the voices came, and, pushing aside the leaves, peeped into the little open space where the two men, staff in hand, were coming slowly together.

"Ha!" quoth Robin to himself, "here is merry sport afoot. Now I would give three golden angels from my own pocket if yon stout fellow would give Little John a right sound drubbing! It would please me to see him well thumped for having failed in my bidding. I fear me, though, there is but poor chance of my seeing such a pleasant sight." So saying, he stretched himself at length upon the ground, that he might not only see the sport the better, but that he might enjoy the merry sight at his ease.

As you may have seen two dogs that think to fight, walking slowly round and round each other, neither cur wishing to begin the combat, so those two stout yeomen moved slowly around, each watching for a chance to take the other unaware, and so get in the first blow. At last Little John struck like a flash, and—"rap!"—the Tanner met the blow and turned it aside, and then smote back at Little John, who also turned the blow; and so this mighty battle began. Then up and down and back and forth

they trod, the blows falling so thick and fast that, at a distance, one would have thought that half a score of men were fighting. Thus they fought for nigh a half an hour, until the ground was all plowed up with the digging of their heels, and their breathing grew labored like the ox in the furrow. But Little John suffered the most, for he had become unused to such stiff labor, and his joints were not as supple as they had been before he went to dwell with the Sheriff.

All this time Robin Hood lay beneath the bush, rejoicing at such a comely bout of quarterstaff. "By my faith!" quoth he to himself, "never had I thought to see Little John so evenly matched in all my life. Belike, though, he would have overcome yon fellow before this had he been in his former trim."

At last Little John saw his chance, and, throwing all the strength he felt going from him into one blow that might have felled an ox, he struck at the Tanner with might and main. And now did the Tanner's cowhide cap stand him in good stead, and but for it he might never have held staff in hand again. As it was, the blow he caught beside the head was so shrewd that it sent him staggering across the little glade, so that, if Little John had had the strength to follow up his vantage, it would have been ill for stout Arthur. But he regained himself quickly and, at arm's length, struck back a blow at Little John, and this time the stroke reached its mark, and down went Little John at full length, his cudgel flying from his hand as he fell. Then, raising his staff, stout Arthur dealt him another blow upon the ribs.

"Hold!" roared Little John. "Wouldst thou strike a man when he is down?"

"Ay, marry would I," quoth the Tanner, giving him another thwack with his staff.

"Stop!" roared Little John. "Help! Hold, I say! I yield me! I yield me, I say, good fellow!"

"Hast thou had enough?" asked the Tanner grimly, holding his staff aloft.

"Ay, marry, and more than enough."

"And thou dost own that I am the better man of the two?"

"Yea, truly, and a murrain seize thee!" said Little John, the first aloud and the last to his beard.

"Then thou mayst go thy ways; and thank thy patron saint that I am a merciful man," said the Tanner.

"A plague o' such mercy as thine!" said Little John, sitting up and feeling his ribs where the Tanner had cudgeled him. "I make my vow, my ribs feel as though every one of them were broken in twain. I tell thee, good fellow, I did think there was never a man in all Nottinghamshire could do to me what thou hast done this day."

"And so thought I, also," cried Robin Hood, bursting out of the thicket and shouting with laughter till the tears ran down his cheeks. "O man, man!" said he, as well as he could for his mirth, " 'a didst go over like a bottle knocked from a wall. I did see the whole merry bout, and never did I think to see thee yield thyself so, hand and foot, to any man in all merry England. I was seeking thee, to chide thee for leaving my bidding undone; but thou hast been paid all I owed thee, full measure, pressed down and overflowing, by this good fellow. Marry, 'a did reach out his arm full length while thou stood gaping at him, and, with a pretty rap, tumbled thee over as never have I seen one tumbled before." So spoke bold Robin, and all the time Little John sat upon the ground, looking as though he had sour curds in his mouth. "What may be thy name, good fellow?" said Robin, next, turning to the Tanner.

"Men do call me Arthur a Bland," spoke up the Tanner boldly, "and now what may be thy name?"

"Ha, Arthur a Bland!" quoth Robin, "I have heard thy name before, good fellow. Thou didst break the crown

of a friend of mine at the fair at Ely last October. The folk there call him Jock o' Nottingham; we call him Will Scathelock. This poor fellow whom thou hast so belabored is counted the best hand at the quarterstaff in all merry England. His name is Little John, and mine Robin Hood."

"How!" cried the Tanner, "art thou indeed the great Robin Hood, and is this the famous Little John? Marry, had I known who thou art, I would never have been so bold as to lift my hand against thee. Let me help thee to thy feet, good Master Little John, and let me brush the dust from off thy coat."

"Nay," quoth Little John testily, at the same time rising carefully, as though his bones had been made of glass, "I can help myself, good fellow, without thy aid; and let me tell thee, had it not been for that vile cowskin cap of thine, it would have been ill for thee this day."

At this Robin laughed again, and, turning to the Tanner, he said, "Wilt thou join my band, good Arthur? For I make my vow thou art one of the stoutest men that ever mine eyes beheld."

"Will I join thy band?" cried the Tanner joyfully. "Ay, marry, will I! Hey for a merry life!" cried he, leaping aloft and snapping his fingers, "and hey for the life I love! Away with tanbark and filthy vats and foul cowhides! I will follow thee to the ends of the earth, good master, and not a herd of dun deer in all the forest but shall know the sound of the twang of my bowstring."

"As for thee, Little John," said Robin, turning to him and laughing, "thou wilt start once more for Ancaster, and we will go part way with thee, for I will not have thee turn again to either the right hand or the left till thou hast fairly gotten away from Sherwood. There are other inns that thou knowest yet, hereabouts." Thereupon, leaving the thickets, they took once more to the highway and departed upon their business.

Robin Hood and Will Scarlet

Thus they traveled along the sunny road, three stout fellows such as you could hardly match anywhere else in all merry England. Many stopped to gaze after them as they strode along, so broad were their shoulders and so sturdy their gait.

Quoth Robin Hood to Little John, "Why didst thou not go straight to Ancaster, yesterday, as I told thee? Thou hadst not gotten thyself into such a coil hadst thou done as I ordered."

"I feared the rain that threatened," said Little John in a sullen tone, for he was vexed at being so chaffed by Robin with what had happened to him.

"The rain!" cried Robin, stopping of a sudden in the middle of the road, and looking at Little John in wonder. "Why, thou great oaf! not a drop of rain has fallen these three days, neither has any threatened, nor hath there been a sign of foul weather in earth or sky or water."

"Nevertheless," growled Little John, "the holy Saint Swithin holdeth the waters of the heavens in his pewter pot, and he could have poured them out, had he chosen,

even from a clear sky; and wouldst thou have had me wet to the skin?"

At this Robin Hood burst into a roar of laughter. "O Little John!" said he, "what butter wits has thou in that head of thine! Who could hold anger against such a one as thou art?"

So saying, they all stepped out once more, with the right foot foremost, as the saying is.

After they had traveled some distance, the day being warm and the road dusty, Robin Hood waxed thirsty; so, there being a fountain of water as cold as ice, just behind the hedgerow, they crossed the stile and came to where the water bubbled up from beneath a mossy stone. Here, kneeling and making cups of the palms of their hands, they drank their fill, and then, the spot being cool and shady, they stretched their limbs and rested them for a space.

In front of them, over beyond the hedge, the dusty road stretched away across the plain; behind them the meadow lands and bright green fields of tender young corn lay broadly in the sun, and overhead spread the shade of the cool, rustling leaves of the beechen tree. Pleasantly to their nostrils came the tender fragrance of the purple violets and wild thyme that grew within the dewy moisture of the edge of the little fountain, and pleasantly came the soft gurgle of the water. All was so pleasant and so full of the gentle joy of the bright Maytime, that for a long time no one of the three cared to speak, but each lay on his back, gazing up through the trembling leaves of the trees to the bright sky overhead. At last, Robin, whose thoughts were not quite so busy woolgathering as those of the others, and who had been gazing around him now and then, broke the silence.

"Heyday!" quoth he, "yon is a gaily feathered bird, I take my vow."

The others looked and saw a young man walking

slowly down the highway. Gay was he, indeed, as Robin had said, and a fine figure he cut, for his doublet was of scarlet silk and his stockings also; a handsome sword hung by his side, the embossed leathern scabbard being picked out with fine threads of gold; his cap was of scarlet velvet, and a broad feather hung down behind and back of one ear. His hair was long and yellow and curled upon his shoulders, and in his hand he bore an early rose, which he smelled at daintily now and then.

"By my life!" quoth Robin Hood, laughing, "saw ye e'er such a pretty, mincing fellow?"

"Truly, his clothes have overmuch prettiness for my taste," quoth Arthur a Bland, "but, ne'ertheless, his shoulders are broad and his loins are narrow, and seest thou, good master, how that his arms hang from his body? They dangle not down like spindles, but hang stiff and bend at the elbow. I take my vow, there be no bread and milk limbs in those fine clothes, but stiff joints and tough thews."

"Methinks thou art right, friend Arthur," said Little John. "I do verily think that yon is no such roseleaf and whipped-cream gallant as he would have one take him to be."

"Pah!" quoth Robin Hood, "the sight of such a fellow doth put a nasty taste into my mouth! Look how he doth hold that fair flower betwixt his thumb and finger, as he would say, 'Good rose, I like thee not so ill but I can bear thy odor for a little while.' I take it ye are both wrong, and verily believe that were a furious mouse to run across his path, he would cry, 'La!' or 'Alack-a-day!' and fall straightway into a swoon. I wonder who he may be."

"Some great baron's son, I doubt not," answered Little John, "with good and true men's money lining his purse."

"Ay, marry, that is true, I make no doubt," quoth Robin. "What a pity that such men as he, that have no

thought but to go abroad in gay clothes, should have good fellows, whose shoes they are not fit to tie, dancing at their bidding. By Saint Dunstan, Saint Alfred, Saint Withold, and all the good men in the Saxon calendar, it doth make me mad to see such gay lordlings from over the sea go stepping on the necks of good Saxons who owned this land before ever their greatgrandsires chewed rind of brawn! By the bright bow of Heaven, I will have their ill-gotten gains from them, even though I hang for it as high as e'er a forest tree in Sherwood!"

"Why, how now, master," quoth Little John, "what heat is this? Thou dost set thy pot a-boiling, and mayhap no bacon to cook! Methinks yon fellow's hair is over-light for Norman locks. He may be a good man and true for aught thou knowest."

"Nay," said Robin, "my head against a leaden farthing, he is what I say. So, lie ye both here, I say, till I show you how I drub this fellow." So saying, Robin Hood stepped forth from the shade of the beech tree, crossed the stile, and stood in the middle of the road, with his hands on his hips, in the stranger's path.

Meantime the stranger, who had been walking so slowly that all this talk was held before he came opposite the place where they were, neither quickened his pace nor seemed to see that such a man as Robin Hood was in the world. So Robin stood in the middle of the road, waiting while the other walked slowly forward, smelling his rose, and looking this way and that, and everywhere except at Robin.

"Hold!" cried Robin, when at last the other had come close to him. "Hold! Stand where thou art!"

"Wherefore should I hold, good fellow?" said the stranger in soft and gentle voice. "And wherefore should I stand where I am? Ne'ertheless, as thou dost desire that I should stay, I will abide for a short time, that I may hear what thou mayst have to say to me."

"Then," quoth Robin, "as thou dost so fairly do as I tell thee, and dost give me such soft speech, I will also treat thee with all due courtesy. I would have thee know, fair friend, that I am, as it were, a votary at the shrine of Saint Wilfred, who, thou mayst know, took, willy-nilly, all their gold from the heathen, and melted it up into candlesticks. Wherefore, upon such as come hereabouts, I levy a certain toll, which I use for a better purpose, I hope, than to make candlesticks withal. Therefore, sweet chuck, I would have thee deliver to me thy purse, that I may look into it, and judge, to the best of my poor powers, whether thou hast more wealth about thee than our law allows. For, as our good Gaffer Swanthold sayeth, 'He who is fat from overliving must needs lose blood.'"

All this time the youth had been sniffing at the rose that he held betwixt his thumb and finger. "Nay," said he with a gentle smile, when Robin Hood had done, "I do love to hear thee talk, thou pretty fellow, and if, haply, thou are not yet done, finish, I beseech thee. I have yet some little time to stay."

"I have said all," quoth Robin, "and now, if thou wilt give me thy purse, I will let thee go thy way without let or hindrance so soon as I shall see what it may hold. I will take none from thee if thou hast but little."

"Alas! It doth grieve me much," said the other, "that I cannot do as thou dost wish. I have nothing to give thee. Let me go my way, I prythee. I have done thee no harm."

"Nay, thou goest not," quoth Robin, "till thou hast shown me thy purse."

"Good friend," said the other gently, "I have business elsewhere. I have given thee much time and have heard thee patiently. Prythee, let me depart in peace."

"I have spoken to thee, friend," said Robin sternly, "and I now tell thee again, that thou goest not one step forward till thou hast done as I bid thee." So saying, he

raised his quarterstaff above his head in a threatening way.

"Alas!" said the stranger sadly, "it doth grieve me that this thing must be. I fear much that I must slay thee, thou poor fellow!" So saying, he drew his sword.

"Put by thy weapon," quoth Robin. "I would take no vantage of thee. Thy sword cannot stand against an oaken staff such as mine. I could snap it like a barley straw. Yonder is a good oaken thicket by the roadside; take thee a cudgel thence and defend thyself fairly, if thou hast a taste for a sound drubbing."

First the stranger measured Robin with his eye, and then he measured the oaken staff. "Thou art right, good fellow," said he presently, "truly, my sword is no match for that cudgel of thine. Bide thee awhile till I get me a staff." So saying, he threw aside the rose that he had been holding all this time, thrust his sword back into the scabbard, and, with a more hasty step than he had yet used, stepped to the roadside where grew the little clump of ground oaks Robin had spoken of. Choosing among them, he presently found a sapling to his liking. He did not cut it, but, rolling up his sleeves a little way, he laid hold of it, placed his heel against the ground, and, with one mighty pull, plucked the young tree up by the roots from out the very earth. Then he came back, trimming away the roots and tender stems with his sword as quietly as if he had done nought to speak of.

Little John and the Tanner had been watching all that passed, but when they saw the stranger drag the sapling up from the earth, and heard the rending and snapping of its roots, the Tanner pursed his lips together, drawing his breath between them in a long inward whistle.

"By the breath of my body!" said Little John, as soon as he could gather his wits from their wonder, "sawest thou that, Arthur? Marry, I think our poor master will stand but an ill chance with yon fellow. By Our Lady, he

*"Alas!" said the stranger sadly. "I fear much that
I must slay thee."*

plucked up yon green tree as it were a barley straw."

Whatever Robin Hood thought, he stood his ground, and now he and the stranger in scarlet stood face to face.

Well did Robin Hood hold his own that day as a mid-country yeoman. This way and that they fought, and back and forth, Robin's skill against the stranger's strength. The dust of the highway rose up around them like a cloud, so that at times Little John and the Tanner could see nothing, but only hear the rattle of the staves against one another. Thrice Robin Hood struck the stranger; once upon the arm and twice upon the ribs, and yet had he warded all the other's blows, only one of which, had it met its mark, would have laid stout Robin lower in the dust than he had ever gone before. At last the stranger struck Robin's cudgel so fairly in the middle that he could hardly hold his staff in his hand; again he struck, and Robin bent beneath the blow; a third time he struck, and now not only fairly beat down Robin's guard, but gave him such a rap, also, that down he tumbled into the dusty road.

"Hold!" cried Robin Hood, when he saw the stranger raising his staff once more. "I yield me!"

"Hold!" cried Little John, bursting from his cover, with the Tanner at his heels. "Hold! give over, I say!"

"Nay," answered the stranger quietly, "if there be two more of you, and each as stout as this good fellow, I am like to have my hands full. Nevertheless, come on, and I will strive my best to serve you all."

"Stop!" cried Robin Hood, "we will fight no more. I take my vow, this is an ill day for thee and me, Little John. I do verily believe that my wrist, and eke my arm, are palsied by the jar of the blow that this stranger struck me."

Then Little John turned to Robin Hood. "Why, how now, good master," said he. "Alas! Thou art in an ill

plight. Marry, thy jerkin is all befouled with the dust of the road. Let me help thee to arise."

"A plague on thy aid!" cried Robin angrily. "I can get to my feet without thy help, good fellow."

"Nay, but let me at least dust thy coat for thee. I fear thy poor bones are mightily sore," quoth Little John soberly, but with a sly twinkle in his eyes.

"Give over, I say!" quoth Robin in a fume. "My coat hath been dusted enough already, without aid of thine." Then, turning to the stranger, he said, "What may be thy name, good fellow?"

"My name is Gamwell," answered the other.

"Ha!" cried Robin, "is it even so? I have near kin of that name. Whence camest thou, fair friend?"

"From Maxfield Town I come," answered the stranger. "There was I born and bred, and thence I come to seek my mother's young brother, whom men call Robin Hood. So, if perchance thou mayst direct me—"

"Ha! Will Gamwell!" cried Robin, placing both hands upon the other's shoulders and holding him off at arm's length. "Surely, it can be none other! I might have known thee by that pretty maiden air of thine—that dainty, finicking manner of gait. Dost thou not know me, lad? Look upon me well."

"Now, by the breath of my body!" cried the other, "I do believe from my heart that thou art mine own Uncle Robin. Nay, certain it is so!" And each flung his arms around the other, kissing him upon the cheek.

Then once more Robin held his kinsman off at arm's length and scanned him keenly from top to toe. "Why, how now," quoth he, "what change is here? Verily, some eight or ten years ago I left thee a stripling lad, with great joints and ill-hung limbs, and lo! here thou art, as tight a fellow as e'er I set mine eyes upon. Dost thou not remember, lad, how I showed thee the proper way to nip the goose feather betwixt thy fingers and throw out thy bow

arm steadily? Thou gavest great promise of being a keen archer. And dost thou not mind how I taught thee to fend and parry with the cudgel?"

"Yea," said young Gamwell, "and I did so look up to thee, and thought thee so above all other men that, I make my vow, had I known who thou wert, I would never have dared to lift hand against thee this day. I trust I did thee no great harm."

"No, no," quoth Robin hastily, and looking sideways at Little John, "thou didst not harm me. But say no more of that, I prythee. Yet I will say, lad, that I hope I may never feel again such a blow as thou didst give me. By'r Lady, my arm doth tingle yet from fingernail to elbow. Truly, I thought that I was palsied for life. I tell thee, coz, that thou art the strongest man that ever I laid mine eyes upon. I take my vow, I felt my stomach quake when I beheld thee pluck up yon green tree as thou didst. But tell me, how camest thou to leave Sir Edward and thy mother?"

"Alas!" answered young Gamwell, "it is an ill story, uncle, that I have to tell thee. My father's steward, who came to us after old Giles Crookleg died, was ever a saucy varlet, and I know not why my father kept him, saving that he did oversee with great judgment. It used to gall me to hear him speak up so boldly to my father, who, thou knowest, was ever a patient man to those about him, and slow to anger and harsh words. Well, one day—and an ill day it was for that saucy fellow—he sought to berate my father, I standing by. I could stand it no longer, good uncle, so, stepping forth, I gave him a box o' the ear, and—wouldst thou believe it?—the fellow straightway died o't. I think they said I broke his neck, or something o' the like. So off they packed me to seek thee and escape the law. I was on my way when thou sawest me, and here I am."

"Well, by the faith of my heart," quoth Robin Hood,

"for anyone escaping the law, thou wast taking it the most easily that ever I beheld in all my life. Whenever did anyone in all the world see one who had slain a man, and was escaping because of it, tripping along the highway like a dainty court damsel, sniffing at a rose the while?"

"Nay, uncle," answered Will Gamwell, "overhaste never churned good butter, as the old saying hath it. Moreover, I do verily believe that this overstrength of my body hath taken the nimbleness out of my heels. Why, thou didst but just now rap me thrice, and I thee never a once, save by overbearing thee by my strength."

"Nay," quoth Robin, "let us say no more on that score. I am right glad to see thee, Will, and thou wilt add great honor and credit to my band of merry fellows. But thou must change thy name, for warrants will be out presently against thee; so, because of thy gay clothes, thou shalt henceforth and for aye be called Will Scarlet."

"Will Scarlet," quoth Little John, stepping forward and reaching out his great palm, which the other took, "Will Scarlet, the name fitteth thee well. Right glad am I to welcome thee among us. I am called Little John; and this is a new member who has just joined us, a stout tanner named Arthur a Bland. Thou art like to achieve fame, Will, let me tell thee, for there will be many a merry ballad sung about the country, and many a merry story told in Sherwood of how Robin Hood taught Little John and Arthur a Bland the proper way to use the quarterstaff; likewise, as it were, how our good master bit off so large a piece of cake that he choked on it."

"Nay, good Little John," quoth Robin gently, for he liked ill to have such a jest told of him. Why should we speak of this little matter? Prythee, let us keep this day's doings among ourselves."

"With all my heart," quoth Little John. "But, good master, I thought that thou didst love a merry story, because thou hast so often made a jest about a certain

increase of fatness on my joints, of flesh gathered by my abiding with the Sheriff of—"

"Nay, good Little John," said Robin hastily, "I do bethink me I have said full enough on that score."

"It is well," quoth Little John, "for in truth I myself have tired of it somewhat. But now I bethink me, thou didst also seem minded to make a jest of the rain that threatened last night; so—"

"Nay, then," said Robin Hood testily, "I was mistaken. I remember me now it did seem to threaten rain."

"Truly, I did think so myself," quoth Little John, "therefore, no doubt, thou dost think it was wise of me to abide all night at the Blue Boar Inn, instead of venturing forth in such stormy weather; dost thou not?"

"A plague of thee and thy doings!" cried Robin Hood. "If thou wilt have it so, thou wert right to abide wherever thou didst choose."

"Once more, it is well," quoth Little John. "As for myself, I have been blind this day. I did not see thee drubbed; I did not see thee tumbled heels over head in the dust; and if any man says that thou wert, I can with a clear conscience rattle his lying tongue betwixt his teeth."

"Come," cried Robin, biting his nether lip, while the others could not forbear laughing. "We will go no farther today, but will return to Sherwood, and thou shalt go to Ancaster another time, Little John."

So said Robin, for now that his bones were sore, he felt as though a long journey would be an ill thing for him. So, turning their backs, they retraced their steps whence they came.

The Adventure with Midge, the Miller's Son

WHEN THE four yeomen had traveled for a long time toward Sherwood again, high noontide being past, they began to wax hungry. Quoth Robin Hood, "I would that I had somewhat to eat. Methinks a good loaf of white bread, with a piece of snow-white cheese, washed down with a draught of humming ale, were a feast for a king."

"Since thou speakest of it," said Will Scarlet, "methinks it would not be amiss myself. There is that within me crieth out, 'Victuals, good friend, victuals!'"

"I know a house near by," said Arthur a Bland, "and, had I but the money, I would bring ye that ye speak of; to wit, a sweet loaf of bread, a fair cheese, and a skin of brown ale."

"For the matter of that, thou knowest I have money by me, good master," quoth Little John.

"Why, so thou hast, Little John," said Robin. "How much money will it take, good Arthur, to buy us meat and drink?"

"I think that six broad pennies will buy food enow for a dozen men," said the Tanner.

"Then give him six pennies, Little John," quoth Robin, "for methinks food for three men will about fit my need. Now get thee gone, Arthur, with the money, and bring the food here, for there is a sweet shade in that thicket yonder, beside the road, and there will we eat our meal."

So Little John gave Arthur the money, and the others stepped to the thicket, there to await the return of the Tanner.

After a time he came back, bearing with him a great brown loaf of bread, and a fair, round cheese, and a goatskin full of stout March beer, slung over his shoulders. Then Will Scarlet took his sword and divided the loaf and the cheese into four fair portions, and each man helped himself. Then Robin Hood took a deep pull at the beer. "Aha!" said he, drawing in his breath, "never have I tasted sweeter drink than this."

After this no man spake more, but each munched away at his bread and cheese lustily, with ever and anon a pull at the beer.

At last Will Scarlet looked at a small piece of bread he still held in his hand, and quoth he, "Methinks I will give this to the sparrows." So, throwing it from him, he brushed the crumbs from his jerkin.

"I, too," quoth Robin, "have had enough, I think." As for Little John and the Tanner, they had by this time eaten every crumb of their bread and cheese.

"Now," quoth Robin, "I do feel myself another man, and would fain enjoy something pleasant before going farther upon our journey. I do bethink me, Will, that thou didst use to have a pretty voice, and one that tuned sweetly upon a song. Prythee, give us one ere we journey farther."

"Truly, I do not mind turning a tune," answered Will Scarlet, "but I would not sing alone."

"Nay, others will follow. Strike up, lad," quoth Robin.

"In that case, 'tis well," said Will Scarlet. "I do call to mind a song that a certain minstrel used to sing in my father's hall, upon occasion. I know no name for it and so can give you none; but thus it is." Then, clearing his throat, he sang:

"In the merry blossom time,
When love longings flood the breast,
When the flower is on the lime,
When the small fowl builds her nest,
Sweetly sings the nightingale
And the throstle cock so bold;
Cuckoo in the dewy dale,
And the turtle in the wold.
But the robin I love dear,
For he singeth through the year.
Robin! Robin!
Merry Robin!
So I'd have my true love be:
Not to fly
At the nigh
Sign of cold adversity.

"When the spring brings sweet delights,
When aloft the lark doth rise,
Lovers woo o' mellow nights,
And youths peep in maidens' eyes,
That time blooms the eglantine,
Daisies pied upon the hill,
Cowslips fair and columbine,
Dusky violets by the rill.
But the ivy green doth grow
When the north wind bringeth snow.
Ivy! Ivy!
Stanch and true!
Thus I'd have her love to be:
Not to die
At the nigh
Breath of cold adversity."

" 'Tis well sung," quoth Robin, "but, cousin, I tell thee plain, I would rather hear a stout fellow like thee sing some lusty ballad than a finicking song of flowers and birds, and what not. Yet, thou didst sing it fair, and 'tis none so bad a snatch of a song, for the matter of that. Now, Tanner, it is thy turn."

"I know not," quoth Arthur, smiling, with his head on one side, like a budding lass that is asked to dance, "I know not that I can match our sweet friend's song; moreover, I do verily think that I have caught a cold and have a certain tickling and huskiness in the windpipe."

"Nay, sing up, friend," quoth Little John, who sat next to him, patting him upon the shoulder. "Thou hast a fair, round, mellow voice; let us have a touch of it."

"Nay, an ye will ha' a poor thing," said Arthur, "I will do my best. Have ye ever heard of the wooing of Sir Keith, the stout young Cornish knight, in good King Arthur's time?"

"Methinks I have heard somewhat of it," said Robin; "but ne'ertheless strike up thy ditty and let us hear it, for, as I do remember me, it is a gallant song; so out with it, good fellow."

Thereupon, clearing his throat, the Tanner, without more ado, began to sing:

THE WOOING OF SIR KEITH

"King Arthur sat in his royal hall,
*   And about on either hand*
Was many a noble lordling tall,
*   The greatest in the land.*

"Sat Lancelot with raven locks,
*   Gawaine with golden hair,*
Sir Tristram, Kay who kept the locks,
*   And many another there.*

"And through the stainèd windows bright,
*   From o'er the red-tiled eaves,*
The sunlight blazed with colored light
*   On golden helms and greaves.*

"But suddenly a silence came
*   About the Table Round,*
For up the hall there walked a dame
*   Bent nigh unto the ground.*

"Her nose was hooked, her eyes were bleared,
　　Her locks were lank and white;
Upon her chin there grew a beard;
　　She was a gruesome sight.

"And so with crawling step she came
　　And kneeled at Arthur's feet;
Quoth Kay, 'She is the foulest dame
　　That e'er my sight did greet.'

" 'O mighty King! of thee I crave
　　A boon on bended knee';
'Twas thus she spoke. 'What wouldst thou have,'
　　Quoth Arthur, King, 'of me?'

"Quoth she, 'I have a foul disease
　　Doth gnaw my very heart,
And but one thing can bring me ease
　　Or cure my bitter smart.

" 'There is no rest, no ease for me
　　North, east, or west, or south,
Till Christian knight will willingly
　　Thrice kiss me on the mouth.

" 'Nor wedded may this childe have been
　　That giveth ease to me;
Nor may he be constrained, I ween,
　　But kiss me willingly.

" 'So is there here one Christian knight
　　Of such a noble strain
That he will give a tortured wight
　　Sweet ease of mortal pain?'

" 'A wedded man,' quoth Arthur, King,
　　'A wedded man I be,
Else would I deem it noble thing
　　To kiss thee willingly.

" 'Now, Lancelot, in all men's sight
    Thou art the head and chief
Of chivalry. Come, noble knight,
    And give her quick relief.'

"But Lancelot he turned aside
    And looked upon the ground,
For it did sting his haughty pride
    To hear them laugh around.

" 'Come thou, Sir Tristram,' quoth the King.
    Quoth he, 'It cannot be,
For ne'er can I my stomach bring
    To do it willingly.'

" 'Wilt thou, Sir Kay, thou scornful wight?'
    Quoth Kay, 'Nay, by my troth!
What noble dame would kiss a knight
    That kissed so foul a mouth?'

" 'Wilt thou, Gawaine?'   'I cannot, King.'
    'Sir Geraint?'   'Nay, not I;
My kisses no relief could bring,
    For sooner would I die.'

"Then up and spake the youngest man
    Of all about the board,
'Now such relief as Christian can
    I'll give to her, my lord.'

"It was Sir Keith, a youthful knight,
    Yet strong of limb and bold,
With beard upon his chin as light
    As finest threads of gold.

"Quoth Kay, 'He hath no mistress yet
    That he may call his own,
But here is one that's quick to get,
    As she herself has shown.'

"He kissed her once, he kissed her twice,
He kissed her three times o'er,
A wondrous change came in a trice,
And she was foul no more.

"Her cheeks grew red as any rose,
Her brow as white as lawn,
Her bosom like the winter snows,
Her eyes like those of fawn.

"Her breath grew sweet as summer breeze
That blows the meadows o'er;
Her voice grew soft as rustling trees,
And cracked and harsh no more.

"Her hair grew glittering like the gold,
Her hands as white as milk;
Her filthy rags, so foul and old,
Were changed to robes of silk.

"In great amaze the knights did stare.
Quoth Kay, 'I make my vow
If it will please thee, lady fair,
I'll gladly kiss thee now.'

"But young Sir Keith kneeled on one knee
And kissed her robes so fair.
'O let me be thy slave,' said he,
'For none to thee compare.'

"She bent her down, she kissed his brow,
She kissed his lips and eyes.
Quoth she, 'Thou art my master now,
My lord, my love, arise!

" 'And all the wealth that is mine own,
My lands, I give to thee,
For never knight hath lady shown
Such noble courtesy.

" 'Bewitched was I, in bitter pain,
But thou hast set me free,
So now I am myself again,
I give myself to thee.' "

"Yea, truly," quoth Robin Hood, when the Tanner had made an end of singing, "it is as I remember it, a fair ditty, and a ballad with a pleasing tune of a song."

"It hath oftentimes seemed to me," said Will Scarlet, "that it hath a certain motive in it, e'en such as this: That a duty which seemeth to us sometimes ugly and harsh, when we do kiss it fairly upon the mouth, so to speak, is no such foul thing after all."

"Methinks thou art right," quoth Robin, "and, contrariwise, that when we kiss a pleasure that appeareth gay it turneth foul to us; is it not so, Little John? Truly such a thing hath brought thee sore thumps this day. Nay, man, never look down in the mouth. Clear thy pipes and sing us a ditty."

"Nay," said Little John, "I have none as fair as that merry Arthur has trolled. They are all poor things that I know. Moreover, my voice is not in tune today, and I would not spoil even a tolerable song by ill singing."

Upon this all pressed Little John to sing, so that when he had denied them a proper length of time, such as is seemly in one that is asked to sing, he presently yielded. Quoth he, "Well, an ye will ha' it so, I will give you what I can. Like to fair Will, I have no title to my ditty, but thus it runs:

"O Lady mine, the spring is here,
With a hey nonny nonny;
The sweet love season of the year,
With a ninny ninny nonny;
Now lad and lass
Lie in the grass
That groweth green
With flowers between.

The buck doth rest,
The leaves do start,
The cock doth crow,
The breeze doth blow,
And all things laugh in—"

"Who may yon fellow be coming along the road?" said Robin, breaking into the song.

"I know not," quoth Little John in a surly voice. "But this I do know, that it is an ill thing to do to check the flow of a good song."

"Nay, Little John," said Robin, "be not vexed, I prythee; but I have been watching him coming along, bent beneath that great bag over his shoulder, ever since thou didst begin thy song. Look, Little John, I pray, and see if thou knowest him."

Little John looked whither Robin Hood pointed.

"Truly," quoth he, after a time, "I think yon fellow is a certain young miller I have seen now and then around the edge of Sherwood; a poor wight, methinks, to spoil a good song about."

"Now thou speakest of him," quoth Robin Hood, "methinks I myself have seen him now and then. Hath he not a mill over beyond Nottingham Town, nigh to the Salisbury road?"

"Thou art right; that is the man," said Little John.

"A good stout fellow," quoth Robin. "I saw him crack Ned o' Bradford's crown about a fortnight since, and never saw I hair lifted more neatly in all my life before."

By this time the young miller had come so near that they could see him clearly. His clothes were dusted with flour, and over his back he carried a great sack of meal, bending so as to bring the whole weight upon his shoulders, and across the sack was a thick quarterstaff. His limbs were stout and strong, and he strode along the dusty road right sturdily with the heavy sack across his shoulders. His cheeks were ruddy as a winter hip, his hair was

flaxen in color, and on his chin was a downy growth of flaxen beard.

"A good honest fellow," quoth Robin Hood, "and such an one as is a credit to English yeomanrie. Now let us have a merry jest with him. We will forth as though we were common thieves and pretend to rob him of his honest gains. Then will we take him into the forest and give him a feast such as his stomach never held in all his life before. We will flood his throat with good canary and send him home with crowns in his purse for every penny he hath. What say ye, lads?"

"Truly, it is a merry thought," said Will Scarlet.

"It is well planned," quoth Little John, "but all the saints preserve us from any more drubbings this day! Marry, my poor bones ache so that I—"

"Prythee peace, Little John," quoth Robin. "Thy foolish tongue will get us both well laughed at yet."

"My foolish tongue, forsooth," growled Little John to Arthur a Bland. "I would it could keep our master from getting us into another coil this day."

But now the Miller, plodding along the road, had come opposite to where the yeomen lay hidden, whereupon all four of them ran at him and surrounded him.

"Hold, friend!" cried Robin to the Miller; whereupon he turned slowly, with the weight of the bag upon his shoulder, and looked at each in turn all bewildered, for though a good stout man his wits did not skip like roasting chestnuts.

"Who bids me stay?" said the Miller in a voice deep and gruff, like the growl of a great dog.

"Marry, that do I," quoth Robin; "and let me tell thee, friend, thou hadst best mind my bidding."

"And who art thou, good friend?" said the Miller, throwing the great sack of meal from his shoulder to the ground, "and who are those with thee?"

"We be four good Christian men," quoth Robin, "and

would fain help thee by carrying part of thy heavy load."

"I give you all thanks," said the Miller, "but my bag is none that heavy that I cannot carry it e'en by myself."

"Nay, thou dost mistake," quoth Robin, "I meant that thou mightest perhaps have some heavy farthings or pence about thee, not to speak of silver and gold. Our good Gaffer Swanthold sayeth that gold is an overheavy burden for a two-legged ass to carry; so we would e'en lift some of this load from thee."

"Alas!" cried the Miller, "what would ye do to me? I have not about me so much as a clipped groat. Do me no harm, I pray you, but let me depart in peace. Moreover, let me tell you that ye are upon Robin Hood's ground, and should he find you seeking to rob an honest craftsman, he will clip your ears to your heads and scourge you even to the walls of Nottingham."

"In truth I fear Robin Hood no more than I do myself," quoth jolly Robin. "Thou must this day give up to me every penny thou hast about thee. Nay, if thou dost budge an inch I will rattle this staff about thine ears."

"Nay, smite me not!" cried the Miller, throwing up his elbow as though he feared the blow. "Thou mayst search me if thou wilt, but thou wilt find nothing upon me, pouch, pocket, or skin."

"Is it so?" quoth Robin Hood, looking keenly upon him. "Now I believe that what thou tellest is no true tale. If I am not much mistook thou hast somewhat in the bottom of that fat sack of meal. Good Arthur, empty the bag upon the ground; I warrant thou wilt find a shilling or two in the flour."

"Alas!" cried the Miller, falling upon his knees, "spoil not all my good meal! It can better you not, and will ruin me. Spare it, and I will give up the money in the bag."

"Ha!" quoth Robin, nudging Will Scarlet. "Is it so? And have I found where thy money lies? Marry, I have a wondrous nose for the blessed image of good King Harry.

I thought that I smelled gold and silver beneath the barley meal. Bring it straight forth, Miller."

Then slowly the Miller arose to his feet, and slowly and unwillingly he untied the mouth of the bag, and slowly thrust his hands into the meal and began fumbling about with his arms buried to the elbows in the barley flour. The others gathered round him, their heads together, looking and wondering what he would bring forth.

So they stood, all with their heads close together gazing down into the sack. But while he pretended to be searching for the money, the Miller gathered two great handfuls of meal. "Ha," quoth he, "here they are, the beauties." Then, as the others leaned still more forward to see what he had, he suddenly cast the meal into their faces, filling their eyes and noses and mouths with the flour, blinding and half choking them. Arthur a Bland was worse off than any, for his mouth was open, agape with wonder of what was to come, so that a great cloud of flour flew down his throat, setting him a-coughing till he could scarcely stand.

Then, while all four stumbled about, roaring with the smart of the meal in their eyeballs, and while they rubbed their eyes till the tears made great channels on their faces through the meal, the Miller seized another handful of flour and another and another, throwing it in their faces, so that even had they had a glimmering of light before they were now as blind as ever a beggar in Nottinghamshire, while their hair and clothes were white as snow.

Then catching up his great crabstaff, the Miller began laying about him as though he were clean gone mad. This way and that skipped the four, like peas on a drumhead, but they could see neither to defend themselves nor to run away. Thwack! thwack! went the Miller's cudgel across their backs, and at every blow great white clouds of flour rose in the air from their jackets and went drifting down the breeze.

"Stop!" roared Robin at last. "Give over, good friend, I am Robin Hood!"

"Thou liest, thou knave," cried the Miller, giving him a rap on the ribs that sent up a great cloud of flour like a puff of smoke. "Stout Robin never robbed an honest tradesman. Ha! thou wouldst have my money, wouldst thou?" And he gave him another blow. "Nay, thou art not getting thy share, thou long-legged knave. Share and share alike." And he smote Little John across the shoulders so that he sent him skipping half across the road. "Nay, fear not, it is thy turn now, black beard." And he gave the Tanner a crack that made him roar for all his coughing. "How now, red coat, let me brush the dust from thee!" cried he, smiting Will Scarlet. And so he gave them merry words and blows until they could scarcely stand, and whenever he saw one like to clear his eyes he threw more flour in his face. At last Robin Hood found his horn and clapping it to his lips, blew three loud blasts upon it.

Now it chanced that Will Stutely and a party of Robin's men were in the glade not far from where this merry sport was going forward. Hearing the hubbub of voices, and blows that sounded like the noise of a flail in the barn in wintertime, they stopped, listening and wondering what was toward. Quoth Will Stutely, "Now if I mistake not there is some stout battle with cudgels going forward not far hence. I would fain see this pretty sight." So saying, he and the whole party turned their steps whence the noise came. When they had come near where all the tumult sounded they heard the three blasts of Robin's bugle horn.

"Quick!" cried young David of Doncaster. "Our master is in sore need!" So, without stopping a moment, they dashed forward with might and main and burst forth from the covert into the highroad.

But what a sight was that which they saw! The road

was all white with meal, and five men stood there also white with meal from top to toe, for much of the barley flour had fallen back upon the Miller.

"What is thy need, master?" cried Will Stutely. "And what doth all this mean?"

"Why," quoth Robin in a mighty passion, "yon traitor fellow hath come as nigh slaying me as e'er a man in all the world. Hadst thou not come quickly, good Stutely, thy master had been dead."

Hereupon, while he and the three others rubbed the meal from their eyes, and Will Stutely and his men brushed their clothes clean, he told them all; how that he had meant to pass a jest upon the Miller, which same had turned so grievously upon them.

"Quick, men, seize the vile Miller!" cried Stutely, who was nigh choking with laughter as were the rest; whereupon several ran upon the stout fellow and seizing him, bound his arms behind his back with bowstrings.

"Ha!" cried Robin, when they brought the trembling Miller to him. "Thou wouldst murder me, wouldst thou? By my faith"—Here he stopped and stood glaring upon the Miller grimly. But Robin's anger could not hold, so first his eyes twinkled, and then in spite of all he broke into a laugh.

Now when they saw their master laugh, the yeomen who stood around could contain themselves no longer, and a mighty shout of laughter went up from all. Many could not stand, but rolled upon the ground from pure merriment.

"What is thy name, good fellow?" said Robin at last to the Miller, who stood gaping and as though he were in amaze.

"Alas, sir, I am Midge, the Miller's son," said he in a frightened voice.

"I make my vow," quoth merry Robin, smiting him upon the shoulder, "thou art the mightiest Midge that e'er

mine eyes beheld. Now wilt thou leave thy dusty mill and come and join my band? By my faith, thou art too stout a man to spend thy days betwixt the hopper and the till."

"Then truly, if thou dost forgive me for the blows I struck, not knowing who thou wast, I will join with thee right merrily," said the Miller.

"Then have I gained this day," quoth Robin, "the three stoutest yeomen in all Nottinghamshire. We will get us away to the greenwood tree, and there hold a merry feast in honor of our new friends, and mayhap a cup or two of good sack and canary may mellow the soreness of my poor joints and bones, though I warrant it will be many a day before I am again the man I was." So saying, he turned and led the way, the rest following, and so they entered the forest once more and were lost to sight.

So that night all was ablaze with crackling fires in the woodlands, for though Robin and those others spoken of, only excepting Midge, the Miller's son, had many a sore bump and bruise here and there on their bodies, they were still not so sore in the joints that they could not enjoy a jolly feast given all in welcome to the new members of the band. Thus with songs and jesting and laughter that echoed through the deeper and more silent nooks of the forest, the night passed quickly along, as such merry times are wont to do, until at last each man sought his couch and silence fell on all things and all things seemed to sleep.

But Little John's tongue was ever one that was not easy of guidance, so that, inch by inch, the whole story of his fight with the Tanner and Robin's fight with Will Scarlet leaked out. And so I have told it that you may laugh at the merry tale along with me.

Robin Hood and Allan a Dale

I͟T HAS just been told how three unlucky adventures fell upon Robin Hood and Little John all in one day, bringing them sore ribs and aching bones. So next we will tell how they made up for those ill happenings by a good action that came about not without some small pain to Robin.

Two days had passed by, and somewhat of the soreness had passed away from Robin Hood's joints, yet still, when he moved of a sudden and without thinking, pain here and there would, as it were, jog him, crying, "Thou hast had a drubbing, good fellow."

The day was bright and jocund, and the morning dew still lay upon the grass. Under the greenwood tree sat Robin Hood; on one side was Will Scarlet, lying at full length upon his back, gazing up into the clear sky, with hands clasped behind his head; upon the other side sat Little John, fashioning a cudgel out of a stout crab-tree limb; elsewhere upon the grass sat or lay many others of the band.

"By the faith of my heart," quoth merry Robin, "I do bethink me that we have had no one to dine with us for

this long time. Our money groweth low in the purse, for no one hath come to pay a reckoning for many a day. Now busk thee, good Stutely, and choose thee six men, and get thee gone to Fosse Way or thereabouts, and see that thou bringest someone to eat with us this evening. Meantime we will prepare a grand feast to do whosoever may come the greater honor. And stay, good Stutely. I would have thee take Will Scarlet with thee, for it is meet that he should become acquaint with the ways of the forest."

"Now do I thank thee, good master," quoth Stutely, springing to his feet, "that thou hast chosen me for this adventure. Truly, my limbs do grow slack through abiding idly here. As for two of my six, I will choose Midge the Miller and Arthur a Bland, for, as well thou knowest, good master, they are stout fists at the quarterstaff. Is it not so, Little John?"

At this all laughed but Little John and Robin, who twisted up his face. "I can speak for Midge," said he, "and likewise for my cousin Scarlet. This very blessed morn I looked at my ribs and found them as many colors as a beggar's cloak."

So, having chosen four more stout fellows, Will Stutely and his band set forth to Fosse Way, to find whether they might not come across some rich guest to feast that day in Sherwood with Robin and his band.

For all the livelong day they abided near this highway. Each man had brought with him a good store of cold meat and a bottle of stout March beer to stay his stomach till the homecoming. So when high noontide had come they sat them down upon the soft grass, beneath a green and wide-spreading hawthorn bush, and held a hearty and jovial feast. After this, one kept watch while the others napped, for it was a still and sultry day.

Thus they passed the time pleasantly enow, but no guest such as they desired showed his face in all the time

that they lay hidden there.   Many passed along the dusty road in the glare of the sun: now it was a bevy of chattering damsels merrily tripping along; now it was a plodding tinker; now a merry shepherd lad; now a sturdy farmer; all gazing ahead along the road, unconscious of the seven stout fellows that lay hidden so near them.   Such were the travelers along the way; but fat abbot, rich esquire, or money-laden usurer came there none.

At last the sun began to sink low in the heavens; the light grew red and the shadows long.   The air grew full of silence, the birds twittered sleepily, and from afar came, faint and clear, the musical song of the milkmaid calling the kine home to the milking.

Then Stutely arose from where he was lying. "A plague of such ill luck!" quoth he.   "Here have we abided all day, and no bird worth the shooting, so to speak, hath come within reach of our bolt.   Had I gone forth on an innocent errand, I had met a dozen stout priests or a score of pursy moneylenders.   But it is ever thus: the dun deer are never so scarce as when one has a gray goose feather nipped betwixt the fingers.   Come, lads, let us pack up and home again, say I."

Accordingly, the others arose, and, coming forth from out the thicket, they all turned their toes back again to Sherwood.   After they had gone some distance, Will Stutely, who headed the party, suddenly stopped. "Hist!" quoth he, for his ears were as sharp as those of a five-year-old fox.   "Hark, lads!   Methinks I hear a sound."   At this all stopped and listened with bated breath, albeit for a time they could hear nothing, their ears being duller than Stutely's.   At length they heard a faint and melancholy sound, like someone in lamentation.

"Ha!" quoth Will Scarlet, "this must be looked into. There is someone in distress nigh to us here."

"I know not," quoth Will Stutely, shaking his head

doubtfully, "our master is ever rash about thrusting his finger into a boiling pot; but, for my part, I see no use in getting ourselves into mischievous coils. Yon is a man's voice, if I mistake not, and a man should be always ready to get himself out from his own pothers."

Then out spake Will Scarlet boldly. "Now out upon thee, to talk in that manner, Stutely! Stay, if thou dost list. I go to see what may be the trouble of this poor creature."

"Nay," quoth Stutely, "thou dost leap so quickly, thou'lt tumble into the ditch. Who said I would not go? Come along, say I." Thus saying, he led the way, the others following, till, after they had gone a short distance, they came to a little opening in the woodland, whence a brook, after gurgling out from under the tangle of over-hanging bushes, spread out into a broad and glassy-pebbled pool. By the side of this pool, and beneath the branches of a willow, lay a youth upon his face, weeping aloud, the sound of which had first caught the quick ears of Stutely. His golden locks were tangled, his clothes were all awry, and everything about him betokened sorrow and woe. Over his head, from the branches of the osier, hung a beautiful harp of polished wood inlaid with gold and silver in fantastic devices. Beside him lay a stout ashen bow and half a score of fair, smooth arrows.

"Halloa!" shouted Will Stutely, when they had come out from the forest into the little open spot. "Who art thou, fellow, that liest there killing all the green grass with salt water?"

Hearing the voice, the stranger sprang to his feet and, snatching up his bow and fitting a shaft, held himself in readiness for whatever ill might befall him.

"Truly," said one of the yeomen, when they had seen the young stranger's face, "I do know that lad right well. He is a certain minstrel that I have seen hereabouts more

than once. It was only a week ago I saw him skipping across the hill like a yearling doe. A fine sight he was then, with a flower at his ear and a cock's plume stuck in his cap; but now, methinks, our cockerel is shorn of his gay feathers."

"Pah!" cried Will Stutely, coming up to the stranger, "wipe thine eyes, man! I do hate to see a tall, stout fellow so sniveling like a girl of fourteen over a dead tomtit. Put down thy bow, man! We mean thee no harm."

But Will Scarlet, seeing how the stranger, who had a young and boyish look, was stung by the words that Stutely had spoken, came to him and put his hand upon the youth's shoulder. "Nay, thou art in trouble, poor boy!" said he kindly. "Mind not what these fellows have said. They are rough, but they mean thee well. Mayhap they do not understand a lad like thee. Thou shalt come with us, and perchance we may find a certain one that can aid thee in thy perplexities, whatsoever they may be."

"Yea, truly, come along," said Will Stutely gruffly. "I meant thee no harm, and may mean thee some good. Take down thy singing tool from off this fair tree, and away with us."

The youth did as he was bidden and, with bowed head and sorrowful step, accompanied the others, walking beside Will Scarlet. So they wended their way through the forest. The bright light faded from the sky and a glimmering gray fell over all things. From the deeper recesses of the forest the strange whispering sounds of nighttime came to the ear; all else was silent, saving only for the rattling of their footsteps amid the crisp, dry leaves of the last winter. At last a ruddy glow shone before them here and there through the trees; a little farther and they came to the open glade, now bathed in the pale moonlight. In the center of the open crackled a great fire, throwing a red glow on all around. At the fire were

roasting juicy steaks of venison, pheasants, capons, and fresh fish from the river. All the air was filled with the sweet smell of good things cooking.

The little band made its way across the glade, many yeomen turning with curious looks and gazing after them, but none speaking or questioning them. So, with Will Scarlet upon one side and Will Stutely upon the other, the stranger came to where Robin Hood sat on a seat of moss under the greenwood tree, with Little John standing beside him.

"Good even, fair friend," said Robin Hood, rising as the other drew near. "And hast thou come to feast with me this day?"

"Alas! I know not," said the lad, looking around him with dazed eyes, for he was bewildered with all that he saw. "Truly, I know not whether I be in a dream," said he to himself in a low voice.

"Nay, marry," quoth Robin, laughing, "thou art awake, as thou wilt presently find, for a fine feast is a-cooking for thee. Thou art our honored guest this day."

Still the young stranger looked about him, as though in a dream. Presently he turned to Robin. "Methinks," said he, "I know now where I am and what hath befallen me. Art not thou the great Robin Hood?"

"Thou hast hit the bull's eye," quoth Robin, clapping him upon the shoulder. "Men hereabouts do call me by that name. Sin' thou knowest me, thou knowest also that he who feasteth with me must pay his reckoning. I trust thou hast a full purse with thee, fair stranger."

"Alas!" said the stranger, "I have no purse nor no money either, saving only the half of a sixpence, the other half of which mine own dear love doth carry in her bosom, hung about her neck by a strand of silken thread."

At this speech a great shout of laughter went up from

those around, whereat the poor boy looked as he would die of shame; but Robin Hood turned sharply to Will Stutely. "Why, how now," quoth he, "is this the guest that thou hast brought us to fill our purse? Methinks thou hast brought but a lean cock to the market."

"Nay, good master," answered Will Stutely, grinning, "he is no guest of mine; it was Will Scarlet that brought him thither."

Then up spoke Will Scarlet, and told how they had found the lad in sorrow, and how he had brought him to Robin, thinking that he might perchance aid him in his trouble. Then Robin Hood turned to the youth, and, placing his hand upon the other's shoulder, held him off at arm's length, scanning his face closely.

"A young face," quoth he in a low voice, half to himself, "a kind face, a good face. 'Tis like a maiden's for purity, and, withal, the fairest that e'er mine eyes did see; but, if I may judge fairly by thy looks, grief cometh to young as well as to old." At these words, spoken so kindly, the poor lad's eyes brimmed up with tears. "Nay, nay," said Robin hastily, "cheer up, lad; I warrant thy case is not so bad that it cannot be mended. What may be thy name?"

"Allan a Dale is my name, good master."

"Allan a Dale," repeated Robin, musing. "Allan a Dale. It doth seem to me that the name is not altogether strange to mine ears. Yea, surely thou art the minstrel of whom we have been hearing lately, whose voice so charmeth all men. Dost thou not come from the Dale of Rotherstream, over beyond Stavely?"

"Yea, truly," answered Allan, "I do come thence."

"How old art thou, Allan?" said Robin.

"I am but twenty years of age."

"Methinks thou art overyoung to be perplexed with trouble," quoth Robin kindly; then, turning to the others, he cried, "Come, lads, busk ye and get our feast ready;

only thou, Will Scarlet, and thou, Little John, stay here with me."

Then, when the others had gone, each man about his business, Robin turned once more to the youth. "Now, lad," said he, "tell us thy troubles, and speak freely. A flow of words doth ever ease the heart of sorrows; it is like opening the waste weir when the mill dam is overfull. Come, sit thou here beside me, and speak at thine ease."

Then straightway the youth told the three yeomen all that was in his heart; at first in broken words and phrases, then freely and with greater ease when he saw that all listened closely to what he said. So he told them how he had come from York to the sweet vale of Rother, traveling the country through as a minstrel, stopping now at castle, now at hall, and now at farmhouse; how he had spent one sweet evening in a certain broad, low farmhouse, where he sang before a stout franklin and a maiden as pure and lovely as the first snowdrop of spring; how he had played and sung to her, and how sweet Ellen o' the Dale had listened to him and had loved him. Then, in a low, sweet voice, scarcely louder than a whisper, he told how he had watched for her and met her now and then when she went abroad, but was all too afraid in her sweet presence to speak to her, until at last, beside the banks of Rother, he had spoken of his love, and she had whispered that which had made his heartstrings quiver for joy. Then they broke a sixpence between them, and vowed to be true to one another forever.

Next he told how her father had discovered what was a-doing, and had taken her away from him so that he never saw her again, and his heart was sometimes like to break; how this morn, only one short month and a half from the time that he had seen her last, he had heard and knew it to be so, that she was to marry old Sir Stephen of Trent, two days hence, for Ellen's father thought it would be a grand thing to have his daughter marry so high,

albeit she wished it not; nor was it wonder that a knight should wish to marry his own sweet love, who was the most beautiful maiden in all the world.

To all this the yeomen listened in silence, the clatter of many voices, jesting and laughing, sounding around them, and the red light of the fire shining on their faces and in their eyes. So simple were the poor boy's words, and so deep his sorrow, that even Little John felt a certain knotty lump rise in his throat.

"I wonder not," said Robin, after a moment's silence, "that thy true love loved thee, for thou hast surely a silver cross beneath thy tongue, even like good Saint Francis, that could charm the birds of the air by his speech."

"By the breath of my body," burst forth Little John, seeking to cover his feelings with angry words, "I have a great part of a mind to go straightway and cudgel the nasty life out of the body of that same vile Sir Stephen. Marry, come up, say I—what a plague—does an old weazen think that tender lasses are to be bought like pullets o' a market day? Out upon him!—I—but no matter, only let him look to himself."

Then up spoke Will Scarlet. "Methinks it seemeth but ill done of the lass that she should so quickly change at others' bidding, more especially when it cometh to the marrying of a man as old as this same Sir Stephen. I like it not in her, Allan."

"Nay," said Allan hotly, "thou dost wrong her. She is as soft and gentle as a stockdove. I know her better than anyone in all the world. She may do her father's bidding, but if she marries Sir Stephen, her heart will break and she will die. My own sweet dear, I—" He stopped and shook his head, for he could say nothing further.

While the others were speaking, Robin Hood had been sunk in thought. "Methinks I have a plan might fit thy case, Allan," said he. "But tell me first, thinkest thou, lad, that thy true love hath spirit enough to marry thee

were ye together in church, the banns published, and the priest found, even were her father to say her nay?"

"Ay, marry would she," cried Allan eagerly.

"Then, if her father be the man that I take him to be, I will undertake that he shall give you both his blessing as wedded man and wife, in the place of old Sir Stephen, and upon his wedding morn. But stay, now I bethink me, there is one thing reckoned not upon—the priest. Truly, those of the cloth do not love me overmuch, and when it comes to doing as I desire in such a matter, they are as like as not to prove stiff-necked. As to the lesser clergy, they fear to do me a favor because of abbot or bishop."

"Nay," quoth Will Scarlet, laughing, "so far as that goeth, I know of a certain friar that, couldst thou but get on the soft side of him, would do thy business even though Pope Joan herself stood forth to ban him. He is known as the Curtal Friar of Fountain Abbey, and dwelleth in Fountain Dale."

"But," quoth Robin, "Fountain Abbey is a good hundred miles from here. An we would help this lad, we have no time to go thither and back before his true love will be married. Nought is to be gained there, coz."

"Yea," quoth Will Scarlet, laughing again, "but this Fountain Abbey is not so far away as the one of which thou speakest, uncle. The Fountain Abbey of which I speak is no such rich and proud place as the other, but a simple little cell; yet, withal, as cosy a spot as ever stout anchorite dwelled within. I know the place well, and can guide thee thither, for, though it is a goodly distance, yet methinks a stout pair of legs could carry a man there and back in one day."

"Then give me thy hand, Allan," cried Robin, "and let me tell thee, I swear by the bright hair of Saint Ælfrida that this time two days hence Ellen a Dale shall be thy wife. I will seek this same Friar of Fountain Abbey to-

morrow day, and I warrant I will get upon the soft side of him, even if I have to drub one soft."

At this Will Scarlet laughed again. "Be not too sure of that, good uncle," quoth he, "nevertheless, from what I know of him, I think this Curtal Friar will gladly join two such fair lovers, more especially if there be good eating and drinking afoot thereafter."

But now one of the band came to say that the feast was spread upon the grass; so, Robin leading the way, the others followed to where the goodly feast was spread. Merry was the meal. Jest and story passed freely, and all laughed till the forest rang again. Allan laughed with the rest, for his cheeks were flushed with the hope that Robin Hood had given him.

At last the feast was done, and Robin Hood turned to Allan, who sat beside him. "Now, Allan," quoth he, "so much has been said of thy singing that we would fain have a taste of thy skill ourselves. Canst thou not give us something?"

"Surely," answered Allan readily; for he was no third-rate songster that must be asked again and again, but said "yes" or "no" at the first bidding; so, taking up his harp, he ran his fingers lightly over the sweetly sounding strings, and all was hushed about the cloth. Then, backing his voice with sweet music on his harp, he sang:

MAY ELLEN'S WEDDING
(Giving an account of how she was beloved by a fairy prince, who took her to his own home.)

> "May Ellen sat beneath a thorn,
>   And in a shower around
> The blossoms fell at every breeze
>   Like snow upon the ground,
> And in a lime tree near was heard
> The sweet song of a strange, wild bird.

"O sweet, sweet, sweet, O piercing sweet,
   O lingering sweet the strain!
May Ellen's heart within her breast
   Stood still with blissful pain:
And so, with listening, upturned face,
She sat as dead in that fair place.

" 'Come down from out the blossoms, bird!
   Come down from out the tree,
And on my heart I'll let thee lie,
   And love thee tenderly!'
Thus cried May Ellen, soft and low,
From where the hawthorn shed its snow.

"Down dropped the bird on quivering wing,
   From out the blossoming tree,
And nestled in her snowy breast.
   'My love! my love!' cried she;
Then straightway home, 'mid sun and flower,
She bore him to her own sweet bower.

"The day hath passed to mellow night,
   The moon floats o'er the lea,
And in its solemn, pallid light
   A youth stands silently:
A youth of beauty strange and rare,
Within May Ellen's bower there.

"He stood where o'er the pavement cold
   The glimmering moonbeams lay.
May Ellen gazed with wide, scared eyes,
   Nor could she turn away,
For, as in mystic dreams we see
A spirit, stood he silently.

"All in a low and breathless voice,
   'Whence comest thou?' said she;
'Art thou the creature of a dream,
   Or a vision that I see?'

Then soft spake he, as night winds shiver
Through straining reeds beside the river.

" 'I came, a bird on feathered wing,
 From distant Faeryland
Where murmuring waters softly sing
 Upon the golden strand,
Where sweet trees are forever green;
And there my mother is the queen.'

"No more May Ellen leaves her bower
 To grace the blossoms fair;
But in the hushed and midnight hour
 They hear her talking there,
Or, when the moon is shining white,
They hear her singing through the night.

" 'Oh, don thy silks and jewels fine,'
 May Ellen's mother said,
'For hither comes the Lord of Lyne
 And thou this lord must wed.'
May Ellen said, 'It may not be.
He ne'er shall find his wife in me.'

"Up spoke her brother, dark and grim:
 'Now by the bright blue sky,
E'er yet a day hath gone for him
 Thy wicked bird shall die!
For he hath wrought thee bitter harm,
By some strange art or cunning charm.'

"Then, with a sad and mournful song,
 Away the bird did fly,
And o'er the castle eaves, and through
 The gray and windy sky.
'Come forth!' then cried the brother grim,
'Why dost thou gaze so after him?'

"It is May Ellen's wedding day,
 The sky is blue and fair,

And many a lord and lady gay
In church are gathered there.
The bridegroom was Sir Hugh the Bold,
All clad in silk and cloth of gold.

"In came the bride in samite white,
With a white wreath on her head;
Her eyes were fixed with a glassy look,
Her face was as the dead,
And when she stood among the throng,
She sang a wild and wonderous song.

"Then came a strange and rushing sound
Like the coming wind doth bring,
And in the open windows shot
Nine swans on whistling wing,
And high above the heads they flew,
In gleaming flight the darkness through.

"Around May Ellen's head they flew
In wide and windy flight,
And three times round the circle drew.
The guests shrank in affright,
And the priest beside the altar there,
Did cross himself with muttered prayer.

"But the third time they flew around,
Fair Ellen straight was gone,
And in her place, upon the ground,
There stood a snow-white swan.
Then, with a wild and lovely song,
It joined the swift and wingèd throng.

"There's ancient men at weddings been,
For sixty years and more,
But such a wondrous wedding day,
They never saw before.
But none could check and none could stay,
The swans that bore the bride away."

Not a sound broke the stillness when Allan a Dale had done, but all sat gazing at the handsome singer, for so sweet was his voice and the music that each man sat with bated breath, lest one drop more should come and he should lose it.

"By my faith and my troth," quoth Robin at last, drawing a deep breath, "lad, thou art— Thou must not leave our company, Allan! Wilt thou not stay with us here in the sweet green forest? Truly, I do feel my heart go out toward thee with great love."

Then Allan took Robin's hand and kissed it. "I will stay with thee always, dear master," said he, "for never have I known such kindness as thou hast shown me this day."

Then Will Scarlet stretched forth his hand and shook Allan's in token of fellowship, as did Little John likewise. And thus the famous Allan a Dale became one of Robin Hood's band.

Robin Hood
Seeks the Curtal Friar

HE STOUT YEOMEN of Sherwood Forest were ever
early risers of a morn, more especially when the summertime had come, for then in the freshness of the dawn the
dew was always the brightest, and the song of the small
birds the sweetest.

Quoth Robin, "Now will I go to seek this same Friar of
Fountain Abbey of whom we spake yesternight, and I will
take with me four of my good men, and these four shall be
Little John, Will Scarlet, David of Doncaster, and Arthur
a Bland. Bide the rest of you here, and Will Stutely shall
be your chief while I am gone." Then straightway Robin
Hood donned a fine steel coat of chain mail, over which
he put on a light jacket of Lincoln green. Upon his head
he clapped a steel cap, and this he covered by one of soft
white leather, in which stood a nodding cock's plume.
By his side he hung a good broadsword of tempered steel,
the bluish blade marked all over with strange figures of
dragons, winged women, and what not. A gallant sight
was Robin so arrayed, I wot, the glint of steel showing
here and there as the sunlight caught brightly the links of
polished mail that showed beneath his green coat.

So, having arrayed himself, he and the four yeomen set forth upon their way, Will Scarlet taking the lead, for he knew better than the others whither to go. Thus, mile after mile, they strode along, now across a brawling stream, now along a sunlit road, now adown some sweet forest path, over which the trees met in green and rustling canopy, and at the end of which a herd of startled deer dashed away, with rattle of leaves and crackle of branches. Onward they walked with song and jest and laughter till noontide was passed, when at last they came to the banks of a wide, glassy, and lily-padded stream. Here a broad, beaten path stretched along beside the banks, on which path labored the horses that tugged at the slow-moving barges, laden with barley meal or what not, from the countryside to the many-towered town. But now, in the hot silence of the midday, no horse was seen nor any man besides themselves. Behind them and before them stretched the river, its placid bosom ruffled here and there by the purple dusk of a small breeze.

"Now, good uncle," quoth Will Scarlet at last, when they had walked for a long time beside this sweet, bright river, "just beyond yon bend ahead of us is a shallow ford which in no place is deeper than thy mid-thigh, and upon the other side of the stream is a certain little hermitage hidden amidst the bosky tangle of the thickets wherein dwelleth the Friar of Fountain Dale. Thither will I lead thee, for I know the way; albeit it is not overhard to find."

"Nay," quoth jolly Robin, stopping suddenly, "had I thought that I should have had to wade water, even were it so crystal a stream as this, I had donned other clothes than I have upon me. But no matter now, for after all a wetting will not wash the skin away, and what must be, must. But bide ye here, lads, for I would enjoy this merry adventure alone. Nevertheless, listen well, and if ye hear me sound upon my bugle horn, come quickly."

So saying, he turned and left them, striding onward alone.

Robin had walked no farther than where the bend of the road hid his good men from his view, when he stopped suddenly, for he thought that he heard voices. He stood still and listened, and presently heard words passed back and forth betwixt what seemed to be two men, and yet the two voices were wondrously alike. The sound came from over behind the bank, that here was steep and high, dropping from the edge of the road a half a score of feet to the sedgy verge of the river.

" 'Tis strange," muttered Robin to himself after a space, when the voices had ceased their talking, "surely there be two people that spoke the one to the other, and yet methinks their voices are mightily alike. I make my vow that never have I heard the like in all my life before. Truly, if this twain are to be judged by their voices, no two peas were ever more alike. I will look into this matter." So saying, he came softly to the river bank and laying him down upon the grass, peered over the edge and down below.

All was cool and shady beneath the bank. A stout osier grew, not straight upward, but leaning across the water, shadowing the spot with its soft foliage. All around grew a mass of feathery ferns such as hide and nestle in cool places, and up to Robin's nostrils came the tender odor of the wild thyme, that loves the moist verges of running streams. Here, with his broad back against the rugged trunk of the willow tree, and half hidden by the soft ferns around him, sat a stout, brawny fellow, but no other man was there. His head was as round as a ball, and covered with a mat of close-clipped, curly black hair that grew low down on his forehead. But his crown was shorn as smooth as the palm of one's hand, which, together with his loose robe, cowl, and string of beads, showed that which his looks never would have done, that

he was a friar. His cheeks were as red and shining as a winter crab, albeit they were nearly covered over with a close curly black beard, as were his chin and upper lip likewise. His neck was thick like that of a north country bull, and his round head closely set upon shoulders e'en a match for those of Little John himself. Beneath his bushy black brows danced a pair of little gray eyes that could not stand still for very drollery of humor. No man could look into his face and not feel his heartstrings tickled by the merriment of their look. By his side lay a steel cap, which he had laid off for the sake of the coolness to his crown. His legs were stretched wide apart, and betwixt his knees he held a great pasty compounded of juicy meats of divers kinds made savory with tender young onions, both meat and onions being mingled with a good rich gravy. In his right fist he held a great piece of brown crust at which he munched sturdily, and every now and then he thrust his left hand into the pie and drew it forth full of meat; anon he would take a mighty pull at a great bottle of Malmsey that lay beside him.

"By my faith," quoth Robin to himself, "I do verily believe that this is the merriest feast, the merriest wight, the merriest place, and the merriest sight in all merry England. Methought there was another here, but it must have been this holy man talking to himself."

So Robin lay watching the Friar, and the Friar, all unknowing that he was so overlooked, ate his meal placidly. At last he was done, and, having first wiped his greasy hands upon the ferns and wild thyme (and sweeter napkin ne'er had king in all the world), he took up his flask and began talking to himself as though he were another man, and answering himself as though he were somebody else.

"Dear lad, thou art the sweetest fellow in all the world, I do love thee as a lover loveth his lass. La, thou dost

make me shamed to speak so to me in this solitary place, no one being by, and yet if thou wilt have me say so, I do love thee as thou lovest me. Nay then, wilt thou not take a drink of good Malmsey? After thee, lad, after thee. Nay, I beseech thee, sweeten the draught with thy lips (here he passed the flask from his right hand to his left). An thou wilt force it on me so, I must needs do thy bidding, yet with the more pleasure do I so as I drink thy very great health (here he took a long, deep draught). And now, sweet lad, 'tis thy turn next (here he passed the bottle from his left hand back again to his right). I take it, sweet chuck, and here's wishing thee as much good as thou wishest me." Saying this, he took another draught, and truly he drank enough for two.

All this time merry Robin lay upon the bank and listened, while his stomach so quaked with laughter that he was forced to press his palm across his mouth to keep it from bursting forth; for, truly, he would not have spoiled such a goodly jest for the half of Nottinghamshire.

Having gotten his breath from his last draught, the Friar began talking again in this wise: "Now, sweet lad, canst thou not sing me a song? La, I know not, I am but in an ill voice this day; prythee ask me not; dost thou not hear how I croak like a frog? Nay, nay, thy voice is as sweet as any bullfinch; come, sing, I prythee, I would rather hear thee sing than eat a fair feast. Alas, I would fain not sing before one that can pipe so well and hath heard so many goodly songs and ballads, ne'ertheless, an thou wilt have it so, I will do my best. But now methinks that thou and I might sing some fair song together; dost thou not know a certain dainty little catch called 'The Loving Youth and the Scornful Maid'? Why, truly, methinks I have heard it ere now. Then dost thou not think that thou couldst take the lass's part gif I take the lad's? I know not but I will try; begin thou with the lad and I will follow with the lass."

Then, singing first with a voice deep and gruff, and anon in one high and squeaking, he blithely trolled the merry catch of

THE LOVING YOUTH AND THE SCORNFUL MAID

HE

"Ah, it's wilt thou come with me, my love?
And it's wilt thou, love, be mine?
For I will give unto thee, my love,
Gay knots and ribbons so fine.
I'll woo thee, love, on my bended knee,
And I'll pipe sweet songs to none but thee.
Then it's hark! hark! hark!
To the wingèd lark,
And it's hark to the cooing dove!
And the bright daffodil
Groweth down by the rill,
So come thou and be my love.

SHE

"Now get thee away, young man so fine;
Now get thee away, I say;
For my true love shall never be thine,
And so thou hadst better not stay.
Thou art not a fine enough lad for me,
So I'll wait till a better young man I see.
For it's hark! hark! hark!
To the wingèd lark,
And it's hark to the cooing dove!
And the bright daffodil
Groweth down by the rill,
Yet never I'll be thy love.

HE

"Then straight will I seek for another fair she,
For many a maid can be found,
And as thou wilt never have aught of me,
By thee will I never be bound.
For never is a blossom in the field so rare,
But others are found that are just as fair.

So it's hark! hark! hark!
To the joyous lark,
And it's hark to the cooing dove!
And the bright daffodil
Groweth down by the rill,
And I'll seek me another dear love.

SHE
"Young man, turn not so very quick away
Another fair lass to find.
Methinks I have spoken in haste today,
Nor have I made up my mind,
And if thou only wilt stay with me,
I'll love no other, sweet lad, but thee."

Here Robin could contain himself no longer but burst forth into a mighty roar of laughter; then, the holy Friar keeping on with the song, he joined in the chorus, and together they sang, or, as one might say, bellowed:

"So it's hark! hark! hark!
To the joyous lark,
And it's hark to the cooing dove!
For the bright daffodil
Groweth down by the rill,
And I'll be thine own true love."

So they sang together, for the stout Friar did not seem to have heard Robin's laughter, neither did he seem to know that the yeoman had joined in with the song, but, with eyes half closed, looking straight before him and wagging his round head from side to side in time to the music, he kept on bravely to the end, he and Robin finishing up with a mighty roar that might have been heard a mile. But no sooner had the last word been sung than the holy man seized his steel cap, clapped it on his head, and springing to his feet, cried in a great voice, "What spy have we here? Come forth, thou limb of evil, and I will carve thee into as fine pudding meat as e'er a wife in Yorkshire cooked of a Sunday." Hereupon he

drew from beneath his robes a great broadsword full as
stout as was Robin's.

"Nay, put up thy pinking iron, friend," quoth Robin,
standing up with the tears of laughter still on his cheeks.
"Folk who have sung so sweetly together should not fight
thereafter." Hereupon he leaped down the bank to
where the other stood. "I tell thee, friend," said he, "my
throat is as parched with that song as e'er a barley stubble
in October. Hast thou haply any Malmsey left in that
stout pottle?"

"Truly," said the Friar in a glum voice, "thou dost ask
thyself freely where thou art not bidden. Yet I trust I am
too good a Christian to refuse any man drink that is
athirst. Such as there is o't thou art welcome to a drink
of the same." And he held the pottle out to Robin.

Robin took it without more ado and putting it to his
lips, tilted his head back, while that which was within said
"glug! glug! glug!" for more than three winks, I wot. The
stout Friar watched Robin anxiously the while, and when
he was done took the pottle quickly. He shook it, held it
betwixt his eyes and the light, looked reproachfully at the
yeoman, and straightway placed it at his own lips. When
it came away again there was nought within it.

"Dost thou know the country hereabouts, thou good
and holy man?" asked Robin, laughing.

"Yea, somewhat," answered the other dryly.

"And dost thou know of a certain spot called Fountain
Abbey?"

"Yea, somewhat."

"Then perchance thou knowest also of a certain one
by the name of the Curtal Friar of Fountain Abbey."

"Yea, somewhat."

"Well then, good fellow, holy father, or whatever thou
art," quoth Robin, "I would know whether this same
Friar is to be found upon this side of the river or the
other."

"That," quoth the Friar, "is a practical question upon which the cunning rules appertaining to logic touch not. I do advise thee to find that out by the aid of thine own five senses; sight, feeling, and what not."

"I do wish much," quoth Robin, looking thoughtfully at the stout priest, "to cross yon ford and strive to find this same good Friar."

"Truly," said the other piously, "it is a goodly wish on the part of one so young. Far be it from me to check thee in so holy a quest. Friend, the river is free to all."

"Yea, good father," said Robin, "but thou seest that my clothes are of the finest and I fain would not get them wet. Methinks thy shoulders are stout and broad; couldst thou not find it in thy heart to carry me across?"

"Now, by the white hand of the holy Lady of the Fountain!" burst forth the Friar in a mighty rage, "dost thou, thou poor puny stripling, thou kiss-my-lady-la pop-penjay; thou—thou— What shall I call thee? Dost thou ask me, the holy Tuck, to carry thee? Now I swear—" Here he paused suddenly, then slowly the anger passed from his face, and his little eyes twinkled once more. "But why should I not?" quoth he piously. "Did not the holy Saint Christopher ever carry the stranger across the river? And should I, poor sinner that I am, be ashamed to do likewise? Come with me, stranger, and I will do thy bidding in an humble frame of mind." So saying, he clambered up the bank, closely followed by Robin, and led the way to the shallow pebbly ford, chuckling to himself the while as though he were enjoying some goodly jest within himself.

Having come to the ford, he girded up his robes about his loins, tucked his good broadsword beneath his arm, and stooped his back to take Robin upon it. Suddenly he straightened up. "Methinks," quoth he, "thou'lt get thy weapon wet. Let me tuck it beneath mine arm along with mine own."

"Nay, good father," said Robin, "I would not burden thee with aught of mine but myself."

"Dost thou think," said the Friar mildly, "that the good Saint Christopher would ha' sought his own ease so? Nay, give me thy tool as I bid thee, for I would carry it as a penance to my pride."

Upon this, without more ado, Robin Hood unbuckled his sword from his side and handed it to the other, who thrust it with his own beneath his arm. Then once more the Friar bent his back, and, Robin having mounted upon it, he stepped sturdily into the water and so strode onward, splashing in the shoal, and breaking all the smooth surface into ever-widening rings. At last he reached the other side and Robin leaped lightly from his back.

"Many thanks, good father," quoth he. "Thou art indeed a good and holy man. Prythee give me my sword and let me away, for I am in haste."

At this the stout Friar looked upon Robin for a long time, his head on one side, and with a most waggish twist to his face; then he slowly winked his right eye. "Nay, good youth," said he gently, "I doubt not that thou art in haste with thine affairs, yet thou dost think nothing of mine. Thine are of a carnal nature; mine are of a spiritual nature, a holy work, so to speak; moreover, mine affairs do lie upon the other side of this stream. I see by thy quest of this same holy recluse that thou art a good young man and most reverent to the cloth. I did get wet coming hither, and am sadly afraid that should I wade the water again I might get certain cricks and pains i' the joints that would mar my devotions for many a day to come. I know that since I have so humbly done thy bidding thou wilt carry me back again. Thou seest how Saint Godrick, that holy hermit whose natal day this is, hath placed in my hands two swords and in thine never a one. Therefore be persuaded, good youth, and carry me back again."

Robin Hood looked up and he looked down, biting his nether lip. Quoth he, "Thou cunning Friar, thou hast me fair and fast enow. Let me tell thee that not one of thy cloth hath so hoodwinked me in all my life before. I might have known from thy looks that thou wert no such holy man as thou didst pretend to be."

"Nay," interrupted the Friar, "I bid thee speak not so scurrilously neither, lest thou mayst perchance feel the prick of an inch or so of blue steel."

"Tut, tut," said Robin, "speak not so, Friar; the loser hath ever the right to use his tongue as he doth list. Give me my sword; I do promise to carry thee back straightway. Nay, I will not lift the weapon against thee."

"Marry, come up," quoth the Friar, "I fear thee not, fellow. Here is thy skewer; and get thyself presently ready, for I would hasten back."

So Robin took his sword again and buckled it at his side; then he bent his stout back and took the Friar upon it.

Now I wot Robin Hood had a heavier load to carry in the Friar than the Friar had in him. Moreover he did not know the ford, so he went stumbling among the stones, now stepping into a deep hole, and now nearly tripping over a boulder, while the sweat ran down his face in beads from the hardness of his journey and the heaviness of his load. Meantime, the Friar kept digging his heels into Robin's sides and bidding him hasten, calling him many ill names the while. To all this Robin answered never a word, but, having softly felt around till he found the buckle of the belt that held the Friar's sword, he worked slyly at the fastenings, seeking to loosen them. Thus it came about that, by the time he had reached the other bank with his load, the Friar's sword belt was loose albeit he knew it not; so when Robin stood on dry land and the Friar leaped from his back, the yeoman gripped hold of the sword so that blade, sheath, and strap

*The Friar kept digging his heels into Robin's sides
and bidding him hasten.*

came away from the holy man, leaving him without a weapon.

"Now then," quoth merry Robin, panting as he spake and wiping the sweat from his brow, "I have thee, fellow. This time that same saint of whom thou didst speak but now hath delivered two swords into my hand and hath stripped thine away from thee. Now if thou dost not carry me back, and that speedily, I swear I will prick thy skin till it is as full of holes as a slashed doublet."

The good Friar said not a word for a while, but he looked at Robin with a grim look. "Now," said he at last, "I did think that thy wits were of the heavy sort and knew not that thou wert so cunning. Truly, thou hast me upon the hip. Give me my sword, and I promise not to draw it against thee save in self-defense; also, I promise to do thy bidding and take thee upon my back and carry thee."

So jolly Robin gave him his sword again, which the Friar buckled to his side, and this time looked to it that it was more secure in its fastenings; then tucking up his robes once more, he took Robin Hood upon his back and without a word stepped into the water, and so waded on in silence while Robin sat laughing upon his back. At last he reached the middle of the ford where the water was deepest. Here he stopped for a moment, and then, with a sudden lift of his hand and heave of his shoulders, fairly shot Robin over his head as though he were a sack of grain.

Down went Robin into the water with a mighty splash. "There," quoth the holy man, calmly turning back again to the shore, "let that cool thy hot spirit, if it may."

Meantime, after much splashing, Robin had gotten to his feet and stood gazing about him all bewildered, the water running from him in pretty little rills. At last he shot the water out of his ears and spat some out of his mouth, and, gathering his scattered wits together, saw the stout Friar standing on the bank and laughing. Then, I

wot, was Robin Hood a mad man. "Stay, thou villain!" roared he, "I am after thee straight, and if I do not carve thy brawn for thee this day, may I never lift finger again!" So saying, he dashed, splashing, to the bank.

"Thou needst not hasten thyself unduly," quoth the stout Friar. "Fear not; I will abide here, and if thou dost not cry 'Alack-a-day' ere long time is gone, may I never more peep through the brake at a fallow deer."

And now Robin, having reached the bank, began, without more ado, to roll up his sleeves above his wrists. The Friar, also, tucked his robes more about him, showing a great, stout arm on which the muscles stood out like humps of an aged tree. Then Robin saw, what he had not wotted of before, that the Friar had also a coat of chain mail beneath his gown.

"Look to thyself," cried Robin, drawing his sword.

"Ay, marry," quoth the Friar, who held his already in his hand. So, without more ado, they came together, and thereupon began a fierce and mighty battle. Right and left, and up and down and back and forth they fought. The swords flashed in the sun and then met with a clash that sounded far and near. I wot this was no playful bout at quarterstaff, but a grim and serious fight of real earnest. Thus they strove for an hour or more, pausing every now and then to rest, at which times each looked at the other with wonder, and thought that never had he seen so stout a fellow; then once again they would go at it more fiercely than ever. Yet in all this time neither had harmed the other nor caused his blood to flow. At last merry Robin cried, "Hold thy hand, good friend!" whereupon both lowered their swords.

"Now I crave a boon ere we begin again," quoth Robin, wiping the sweat from his brow; for they had striven so long that he began to think that it would be an ill-done thing either to be smitten himself or to smite so stout and brave a fellow.

"What wouldst thou have of me?" asked the Friar.

"Only this," quoth Robin; "that thou wilt let me blow thrice upon my bugle horn."

The Friar bent his brows and looked shrewdly at Robin Hood. "Now I do verily think that thou hast some cunning trick in this," quoth he. "Ne'ertheless, I fear thee not, and will let thee have thy wish, providing thou wilt also let me blow thrice upon this little whistle."

"With all my heart," quoth Robin, "so, here goes for one." So saying, he raised his silver horn to his lips and blew thrice upon it, clear and high.

Meantime, the Friar stood watching keenly for what might come to pass, holding in his fingers the while a pretty silver whistle, such as knights use for calling their hawks back to their wrists, which whistle always hung at his girdle along with his rosary.

Scarcely had the echo of the last note of Robin's bugle come winding back from across the river, when four tall men in Lincoln green came running around the bend of the road, each with a bow in his hand and an arrow ready nocked upon the string.

"Ha! Is it thus, thou traitor knave!" cried the Friar. "Then, marry, look to thyself!" So saying, he straightway clapped the hawk's whistle to his lips and blew a blast that was both loud and shrill. And now there came a crackling of the bushes that lined the other side of the road, and presently forth from the covert burst four great, shaggy hounds. "At 'em, Sweet Lips! At 'em, Bell Throat! At 'em, Beauty! At 'em, Fangs!" cried the Friar, pointing at Robin.

And now it was well for that yeoman that a tree stood nigh him beside the road, else had he had an ill chance of it. Ere one could say "Gaffer Downthedale" the hounds were upon him, and he had only time to drop his sword and leap lightly into the tree, around which the hounds gathered, looking up at him as though he were a cat on

the eaves. But the Friar quickly called off his dogs. "At 'em!" cried he, pointing down the road to where the yeomen were standing stock still with wonder of what they saw. As the hawk darts down upon its quarry, so sped the four dogs at the yeomen; but when the four men saw the hounds so coming, all with one accord, saving only Will Scarlet, drew each man his goose feather to his ear and let fly his shaft.

And now the old ballad telleth of a wondrous thing that happened, for thus it says, that each dog so shot at leaped lightly aside, and as the arrow passed him whistling, caught it in his mouth and bit it in twain. Now it would have been an ill day for these four good fellows had not Will Scarlet stepped before the the others and met the hounds as they came rushing. "Why, how now, Fangs!" cried he sternly. "Down, Beauty! Down, sirrah! What means this?"

At the sound of his voice each dog shrank back quickly and then straightway came to him and licked his hands and fawned upon him, as is the wont of dogs that meet one they know. Then the four yeomen came forward, the hounds leaping around Will Scarlet joyously. "Why, how now!" cried the stout Friar, "what means this? Art thou wizard to turn those wolves into lambs? Ha!" cried he, when they had come still nearer, "can I trust mine eyes? What means it that I see young Master William Gamwell in such company?"

"Nay, Tuck," said the young man, as the four came forward to where Robin was now clambering down from the tree in which he had been roosting, he having seen that all danger was over for the time; "nay, Tuck, my name is no longer Will Gamwell, but Will Scarlet; and this is my good uncle, Robin Hood, with whom I am abiding just now."

"Truly, good master," said the Friar, looking somewhat abashed and reaching out his great palm to Robin,

"I ha' oft heard thy name both sung and spoken of, but I never thought to meet thee in battle. I crave thy forgiveness, and do wonder not that I found so stout a man against me."

"Truly, most holy father," said Little John, "I am more thankful than e'er I was in all my life before that our good friend Scarlet knew thee and thy dogs. I tell thee seriously that I felt my heart crumble away from me when I saw my shaft so miss its aim, and those great beasts of thine coming straight at me."

"Thou mayst indeed be thankful, friend," said the Friar gravely. "But, Master Will, how cometh it that thou dost now abide in Sherwood?"

"Why, Tuck, dost thou not know of my ill happening with my father's steward?" answered Scarlet.

"Yea, truly, yet I knew not that thou wert in hiding because of it. Marry, the times are all awry when a gentleman must lie hidden for so small a thing."

"But we are losing time," quoth Robin, "and I have yet to find that same Curtal Friar."

"Why, uncle, thou hast not far to go," said Will Scarlet, pointing to the Friar, "for there he stands beside thee."

"How?" quoth Robin, "art thou the man that I have been at such pains to seek all day, and have got such a ducking for?"

"Why, truly," said the Friar demurely, "some do call me the Curtal Friar of Fountain Dale; others again call me in jest the Abbot of Fountain Abbey; others still again call me simple Friar Tuck."

"I like the last name best," quoth Robin, "for it doth slip more glibly off the tongue. But why didst thou not tell me thou wert he I sought, instead of sending me searching for black moonbeams?"

"Why, truly, thou didst not ask me, good master," quoth stout Tuck; "but what didst thou desire of me?"

"Nay," quoth Robin, "the day groweth late, and we

cannot stand longer talking here. Come back with us to Sherwood, and I will unfold all to thee as we travel along."

So, without tarrying longer, they all departed, with the stout dogs at their heels, and wended their way back to Sherwood again; but it was long past nightfall ere they reached the greenwood tree.

Now listen, for next I will tell how Robin Hood compassed the happiness of two young lovers, aided by the merry Friar Tuck of Fountain Dale.

Robin Hood Compasses a Marriage

$\mathfrak{A}$ND NOW had come the morning when fair Ellen was to be married, and on which merry Robin had sworn that Allan a Dale should, as it were, eat out of the platter that had been filled for Sir Stephen of Trent. Up rose Robin Hood, blithe and gay, up rose his merry men one and all, and up rose last of all stout Friar Tuck, winking the smart of sleep from out his eyes. Then, while the air seemed to brim over with the song of many birds, all blended together and all joying in the misty morn, each man laved face and hands in the leaping brook, and so the day began.

"Now," quoth Robin, when they had broken their fast, and each man had eaten his fill, "it is time for us to set forth upon the undertaking that we have in hand for today. I will choose me one score of my good men to go with me, for I may need aid; and thou, Will Scarlet, wilt abide here and be the chief while I am gone." Then searching through all the band, each man of whom crowded forward eager to be chosen, Robin called such as

he wished by name, until he had a score of stout fellows, the very flower of his yeomanrie. Besides Little John and Will Stutely were nigh all those famous lads of whom I have already told you. Then, while those so chosen ran leaping, full of joy, to arm themselves with bow and shaft and broadsword, Robin Hood stepped aside into the covert, and there donned a gay, beribboned coat such as might have been worn by some strolling minstrel, and slung a harp across his shoulder, the better to carry out that part.

All the band stared and many laughed, for never had they seen their master in such a fantastic guise before.

"Truly," quoth Robin, holding up his arms and looking down at himself, "I do think it be somewhat of a gay, gaudy, grasshopper dress; but it is a pretty thing for all that, and doth not ill befit the turn of my looks, albeit I wear it but for the nonce. But stay, Little John, here are two bags that I would have thee carry in thy pouch for the sake of safekeeping. I can ill care for them myself beneath this motley."

"Why, master," quoth Little John, taking the bags and weighing them in his hand, "here is the chink of gold."

"Well, what an there be," said Robin, "it is mine own coin and the band is none the worse for what is there. Come, busk ye, lads," and he turned quickly away. "Get ye ready straightway." Then gathering the score together in a close rank, in the midst of which were Allan a Dale and Friar Tuck, he led them forth upon their way from the forest shades.

So they walked on for a long time till they had come out of Sherwood and to the vale of Rotherstream. Here were different sights from what one saw in the forest; hedgerows, broad fields of barley corn, pasture lands rolling upward till they met the sky and all dotted over with flocks of white sheep, hayfields whence came the odor of new-mown hay that lay in smooth swathes over

which skimmed the swifts in rapid flight; such they saw, and different was it, I wot, from the tangled depths of the sweet woodlands, but full as fair. Thus Robin led his band, walking blithely with chest thrown out and head thrown back, snuffing the odors of the gentle breeze that came drifting from over the hayfields.

"Truly," quoth he, "the dear world is as fair here as in the woodland shades. Who calls it a vale of tears? Methinks it is but the darkness in our minds that bringeth gloom to the world. For what sayeth that merry song thou singest, Little John? Is it not thus?

> *"For when my love's eyes do shine, do shine,*
> *And when her lips smile so rare,*
> *The day it is jocund and fine, so fine,*
> *Though let it be wet or be fair,*
> *And when the stout ale is all flowing so fast,*
> *Our sorrows and troubles are things of the past."*

"Nay," said Friar Tuck piously, "ye do think of profane things and of nought else; yet, truly, there be better safeguards against care and woe than ale drinking and bright eyes, to wit, fasting and meditation. Look upon me, have I the likeness of a sorrowful man?"

At this a great shout of laughter went up from all around, for the night before the stout Friar had emptied twice as many canakins of ale as any one of all the merry men.

"Truly," quoth Robin, when he could speak for laughter, "I should say that thy sorrows were about equal to thy goodliness."

So they stepped along, talking, singing, jesting, and laughing, until they had come to a certain little church that belonged to the great estates owned by the rich Priory of Emmet. Here it was that fair Ellen was to be married on that morn, and here was the spot toward which the yeomen had pointed their toes. On the other

side of the road from where the church stood with waving fields of barley around, ran a stone wall along the roadside. Over the wall from the highway was a fringe of young trees and bushes, and here and there the wall itself was covered by a mass of blossoming woodbine that filled all the warm air far and near with its sweet summer odor. Then straightway the yeomen leaped over the wall, alighting on the tall soft grass upon the other side, frightening a flock of sheep that lay there in the shade so that they scampered away in all directions. Here was a sweet cool shadow both from the wall and from the fair young trees and bushes, and here sat the yeomen down, and glad enough they were to rest after their long tramp of the morning.

"Now," quoth Robin, "I would have one of you watch and tell me when he sees anyone coming to the church, and the one I choose shall be young David of Doncaster. So get thee upon the wall, David, and hide beneath the woodbine so as to keep watch."

Accordingly young David did as he was bidden, the others stretching themselves at length upon the grass, some talking together and others sleeping. Then all was quiet save only for the low voices of those that talked together, and for Allan's restless footsteps pacing up and down, for his soul was so full of disturbance that he could not stand still, and saving, also, for the mellow snoring of Friar Tuck, who enjoyed his sleep with a noise as of one sawing soft wood very slowly. Robin lay upon his back and gazed aloft into the leaves of the trees, his thought leagues away, and so a long time passed.

Then up spoke Robin, "Now tell us, young David of Doncaster, what dost thou see?"

Then David answered, "I see the white clouds floating and I feel the wind a-blowing and three black crows are flying over the wold; but nought else do I see, good master."

So silence fell again and another time passed, broken only as I have said, till Robin, growing impatient, spake again. "Now tell me, young David, what dost thou see by this?"

And David answered, "I see the windmills swinging and three tall poplar trees swaying against the sky, and a flock of fieldfares are flying over the hill; but nought else do I see, good master."

So another time passed, till at last Robin asked young David once more what he saw; and David said, "I hear the cuckoo singing, and I see how the wind makes waves in the barley field; and now over the hill to the church cometh an old friar, and in his hands he carries a great bunch of keys; and lo! Now he cometh to the church door."

Then up rose Robin Hood and shook Friar Tuck by the shoulder. "Come, rouse thee, holy man!" cried he; whereupon, with much grunting, the stout Tuck got to his feet. "Marry, bestir thyself," quoth Robin, "for yonder, in the church door, is one of thy cloth. Go thou and talk to him, and so get thyself into the church, that thou mayst be there when thou art wanted; meantime, Little John, Will Stutely, and I will follow thee anon."

So Friar Tuck clambered over the wall, crossed the road, and came to the church, where the old friar was still laboring with the great key, the lock being somewhat rusty and he somewhat old and feeble.

"Hilloa, brother," quoth Tuck, "let me aid thee." So saying, he took the key from the other's hand and quickly opened the door with a turn of it.

"Who art thou, good brother?" asked the old friar, in a high, wheezing voice. "Whence comest thou, and whither art thou going?" And he winked and blinked at stout Friar Tuck like an owl at the sun.

"Thus do I answer thy questions, brother," said the other. "My name is Tuck, and I go no farther than this

spot, if thou wilt haply but let me stay while this same wedding is going forward. I come from Fountain Dale and, in truth, am a certain poor hermit, as one may say, for I live in a cell beside the fountain blessed by that holy Saint Ethelrada. But, if I understand aught, there is to be a gay wedding here today; so, if thou mindest not, I would fain rest me in the cool shade within, for I would like to see this fine sight."

"Truly, thou art welcome, brother," said the old man, leading the way within. Meantime, Robin Hood, in his guise of harper, together with Little John and Will Stutely, had come to the church. Robin sat him down on a bench beside the door, but Little John, carrying the two bags of gold, went within, as did Will Stutely.

So Robin sat by the door, looking up the road and down the road to see who might come, till, after a time, he saw six horsemen come riding sedately and slowly, as became them, for they were churchmen in high orders. Then, when they had come nearer, Robin saw who they were, and knew them. The first was the Bishop of Hereford, and a fine figure he cut, I wot. His vestments were of the richest silk, and around his neck was a fair chain of beaten gold. The cap that hid his tonsure was of black velvet, and around the edges of it were rows of jewels that flashed in the sunlight, each stone being set in gold. His hose were of flame-colored silk, and his shoes of black velvet, the long, pointed toes being turned up and fastened to his knees, and on either instep was embroidered a cross in gold thread. Beside the Bishop rode the Prior of Emmet upon a mincing palfrey. Rich were his clothes also, but not so gay as the stout Bishop's. Behind these were two of the higher brethren of Emmet, and behind these again two retainers belonging to the Bishop; for the Lord Bishop of Hereford strove to be as like the great barons as was in the power of one in holy orders.

When Robin saw this train drawing near, with flash of jewels and silk and jingle of silver bells on the trappings of the nags, he looked sourly upon them. Quoth he to himself, "Yon Bishop is overgaudy for a holy man. I do wonder whether his patron, who, methinks, was Saint Thomas, was given to wearing golden chains about his neck, silk clothing upon his body, and pointed shoes upon his feet; the money for all of which, God wot, hath been wrung from the sweat of poor tenants. Bishop, Bishop, thy pride may have a fall ere thou wottest of it."

So the holy men came to the church; the Bishop and the Prior jesting and laughing between themselves about certain fair dames, their words more befitting the lips of laymen, methinks, than holy clerks. Then they dismounted, and the Bishop, looking around, presently caught sight of Robin standing in the doorway. "Hilloa, good fellow," quoth he in a jovial voice, "who art thou that struttest in such gay feathers?"

"A harper am I from the north country," quoth Robin, "and I can touch the strings, I wot, as never another man in all merry England can do. Truly, good Lord Bishop, many a knight and burgher, clerk and layman, have danced to my music, willy-nilly, and most times greatly against their will; such is the magic of my harping. Now this day, my Lord Bishop, if I may play at this wedding, I do promise that I will cause the fair bride to love the man she marries with a love that shall last as long as that twain shall live."

"Ha! is it so?" cried the Bishop. "Meanest thou this in sooth?" And he looked keenly at Robin, who gazed boldly back again into his eyes. "Now, if thou wilt cause this maiden (who hath verily bewitched my poor cousin Stephen) thus to love the man she is to marry, as thou sayst thou canst, I will give thee whatsoever thou wilt ask me in due measure. Let me have a taste of thy skill, fellow."

"Nay," quoth Robin, "my music cometh not without I choose, even at a lord bishop's bidding. In sooth, I will not play until the bride and bridegroom come."

"Now, thou art a saucy varlet to speak so to my crest," quoth the Bishop, frowning on Robin. "Yet, I must needs bear with thee. Look, Prior, hither cometh our cousin Sir Stephen, and his ladylove."

And now, around the bend of the highroad, came others, riding upon horses. The first of all was a tall, thin man, of knightly bearing, dressed all in black silk, with a black velvet cap upon his head, turned up with scarlet. Robin looked, and had no doubt that this was Sir Stephen, both because of his knightly carriage and of his gray hairs. Beside him rode a stout Saxon franklin, Ellen's father, Edward of Deirwold; behind those two came a litter borne by two horses, and therein was a maiden whom Robin knew must be Ellen. Behind this litter rode six men-at-arms, the sunlight flashing on their steel caps as they came jingling up the dusty road.

So these also came to the church, and there Sir Stephen leaped from his horse and, coming to the litter, handed fair Ellen out therefrom. Then Robin Hood looked at her, and could wonder no longer how it came about that so proud a knight as Sir Stephen of Trent wished to marry a common franklin's daughter; nor did he wonder that no ado was made about the matter, for she was the fairest maiden that ever he had beheld. Now, however, she was all pale and drooping, like a fair white lily snapped at the stem; and so, with bent head and sorrowful look, she went within the church, Sir Stephen leading her by the hand.

"Why dost thou not play, fellow?" quoth the Bishop, looking sternly at Robin.

"Marry," said Robin calmly, "I will play in greater wise than Your Lordship thinks; but not till the right time hath come."

Said the Bishop to himself, while he looked grimly at

Robin, "When this wedding is gone by I will have this fellow well whipped for his saucy tongue and bold speech."

And now fair Ellen and Sir Stephen stood before the altar, and the Bishop himself came in his robes and opened his book, whereat fair Ellen looked up and about her in bitter despair, like the fawn that finds the hounds on her haunch. Then, in all his fluttering tags and ribbons of red and yellow, Robin Hood strode forward. Three steps he took from the pillar whereby he leaned, and stood between the bride and bridegroom.

"Let me look upon this lass," he said in a loud voice. "Why, how now! What have we here? Here be lilies in the cheeks, and not roses such as befit a bonny bride. This is no fit wedding. Thou, Sir Knight, so old, and she so young, and thou thinkest to make her thy wife? I tell thee it may not be, for thou art not her own true love."

At this all stood amazed, and knew not where to look nor what to think or say, for they were all bewildered with the happening; so, while everyone looked at Robin as though they had been changed to stone, he clapped his bugle horn to his lips and blew three blasts so loud and clear, they echoed from floor to rafter as though they were sounded by the trump of doom. Then straightway Little John and Will Stutely came leaping and stood upon either side of Robin Hood, and quickly drew their broadswords, the while a mighty voice rolled over the heads of all, "Here be I, good master, when thou wantest me"; for it was Friar Tuck that so called from the organ loft.

And now all was hubbub and noise. Stout Edward strode forward raging, and would have seized his daughter to drag her away, but Little John stepped between and thrust him back. "Stand back, old man," said he, "thou art a hobbled horse this day."

"Down with the villains!" cried Sir Stephen, and felt

for his sword, but it hung not beside him on his wedding day.

Then the men-at-arms drew their swords, and it seemed like that blood would wet the stones; but suddenly came a bustle at the door and loud voices, steel flashed in the light, and the crash of blows sounded. The men-at-arms fell back, and up the aisle came leaping eighteen stout yeomen all clad in Lincoln green, with Allan a Dale at their head. In his hand he bore Robin Hood's good stout trusty bow of yew, and this he gave to him, kneeling the while upon one knee.

Then up spake Edward of Deirwold in a deep voice of anger, "Is it thou, Allan a Dale, that hath bred all this coil in a church?"

"Nay," quoth merry Robin, "that have I done, and I care not who knoweth it, for my name is Robin Hood."

At this name a sudden silence fell. The Prior of Emmet and those that belonged to him gathered together like a flock of frightened sheep when the scent of the wolf is nigh, while the Bishop of Hereford, laying aside his book, crossed himself devoutly. "Now Heaven keep us this day," said he, "from that evil man!"

"Nay," quoth Robin, "I mean you no harm; but here is fair Ellen's betrothed husband, and she shall marry him or pain will be bred to some of you."

Then up spake stout Edward in a loud and angry voice, "Now I say nay! I am her father, and she shall marry Sir Stephen and none other."

Now all this time, while everything was in turmoil about him, Sir Stephen had been standing in proud and scornful silence. "Nay, fellow," said he coldly, "thou mayst take thy daughter back again; I would not marry her after this day's doings could I gain all merry England thereby. I tell thee plainly, I loved thy daughter, old as I am, and would have taken her up like a jewel from the sty, yet, truly, I knew not that she did love this fellow, and

was beloved by him. Maiden, if thou dost rather choose a beggarly minstrel than a high-born knight, take thy choice. I do feel shame that I should thus stand talking amid this herd, and so I will leave you." Thus saying, he turned and, gathering his men about him, walked proudly down the aisle. Then all the yeomen were silenced by the scorn of his words. Only Friar Tuck leaned over the edge of the choir loft and called out to him ere he had gone, "Good den, Sir Knight. Thou wottest old bones must alway make room for young blood." Sir Stephen neither answered nor looked up, but passed out from the church as though he had heard nought, his men following him.

Then the Bishop of Hereford spoke hastily, "I, too, have no business here, and so will depart." And he made as though he would go. But Robin Hood laid hold of his clothes and held him. "Stay, my Lord Bishop," said he, "I have yet somewhat to say to thee." The Bishop's face fell, but he stayed as Robin bade him, for he saw he could not go.

Then Robin Hood turned to stout Edward of Deirwold, and said he, "Give thy blessing on thy daughter's marriage to this yeoman, and all will be well. Little John, give me the bags of gold. Look, farmer. Here are two hundred bright golden angels; give thy blessing, as I say, and I will count them out to thee as thy daughter's dower. Give not thy blessing, and she shall be married all the same, but not so much as a cracked farthing shall cross thy palm. Choose."

Then Edward looked upon the ground with bent brows, turning the matter over and over in his mind; but he was a shrewd man and one, withal, that made the best use of a cracked pipkin; so at last he looked up and said, but in no joyous tone, "If the wench will go her own gait, let her go. I had thought to make a lady of her; yet if she chooses to be what she is like to be, I have nought to do

with her henceforth. Ne'ertheless I will give her my blessing when she is duly wedded."

"It may not be," spake up one of those of Emmet. "The banns have not been duly published, neither is there any priest here to marry them."

"How sayst thou?" roared Tuck from the choir loft. "No priest? Marry, here stands as holy a man as thou art, any day of the week, a clerk in orders, I would have thee know. As for the question of banns, stumble not over that straw, brother, for I will publish them." So saying, he called the banns; and, says the old ballad, lest three times should not be enough, he published them nine times o'er. Then straightway he came down from the loft and forthwith performed the marriage service; and so Allan and Ellen were duly wedded.

And now Robin counted out two hundred golden angels to Edward of Deirwold, and he, upon his part, gave his blessing, yet not, I wot, as though he meant it with overmuch good will. Then the stout yeomen crowded around and grasped Allan's palm, and he, holding Ellen's hand within his own, looked about him all dizzy with his happiness.

Then at last jolly Robin turned to the Bishop of Hereford, who had been looking on at all that passed with a grim look. "My Lord Bishop," quoth he, "thou mayst bring to thy mind that thou didst promise me that did I play in such wise as to cause this fair lass to love her husband, thou wouldst give me whatsoever I asked in reason. I have played my play, and she loveth her husband, which she would not have done but for me; so now fulfill thy promise. Thou hast upon thee that which, methinks, thou wouldst be the better without; therefore, I prythee, give me that golden chain that hangeth about thy neck as a wedding present for this fair bride."

The the Bishop's cheeks grew red with rage and his eyes flashed. He looked at Robin with a fell look, but

saw that in the yeoman's face which bade him pause. Then slowly he took the chain from about his neck and handed it to Robin, who flung it over Ellen's head so that it hung glittering about her shoulders. Then said merry Robin, "I thank thee, on the bride's part, for thy handsome gift, and truly thou thyself art more seemly without it. Now, shouldst thou ever come nigh to Sherwood I much hope that I shall give thee there such a feast as thou hast ne'er had in all thy life before."

"May Heaven forfend!" cried the Bishop earnestly; for he knew right well what manner of feast it was that Robin Hood gave his guests in Sherwood Forest.

But now Robin Hood gathered his men together, and, with Allan and his young bride in their midst, they all turned their footsteps toward the woodlands. On the way thither Friar Tuck came close to Robin and plucked him by the sleeve. "Thou dost lead a merry life, good master," quoth he, "But dost thou not think that it would be for the welfare of all your souls to have a good stout chaplain, such as I, to oversee holy matters? Truly, I do love this life mightily." At this merry Robin Hood laughed amain, and bade him stay and become one of their band if he wished.

That night there was such a feast held in the greenwood as Nottinghamshire never saw before. To that feast you and I were not bidden, and pity it is that we were not; so, lest we should both feel the matter the more keenly, I will say no more about it.

Robin Hood Aids
a Sorrowful Knight

So PASSED the gentle springtime away in budding beauty; its silver showers and sunshine, its green meadows and its flowers. So, likewise, passed the summer with its yellow sunlight, its quivering heat and deep, bosky foliage, its long twilights and its mellow nights, through which the frogs croaked and fairy folk were said to be out on the hillsides. All this had passed and the time of fall had come, bringing with it its own pleasures and joyousness; for now, when the harvest was gathered home, merry bands of gleaners roamed the country about, singing along the roads in the daytime, and sleeping beneath the hedgerows and the hay-ricks at night. Now the hips burned red in the tangled thickets and the haws waxed black in the hedgerows, the stubble lay all crisp and naked to the sky, and the green leaves were fast turning russet and brown. Also, at this merry season, good things of the year are gathered in in great store. Brown ale lies ripening in the cellar, hams and bacon hang in the smoke-shed, and crabs are stowed away in the straw for roasting in the wintertime, when the north wind piles the snow in drifts around the gables and the fire crackles warm upon the hearth.

So passed the seasons then, so they pass now, and so they will pass in time to come, while we come and go like leaves of the tree that fall and are soon forgotten.

Quoth Robin Hood, snuffing the air, "Here is a fair day, Little John, and one that we can ill waste in idleness.

Choose such men as thou dost need, and go thou east while I will wend to the west, and see that each of us bringeth back some goodly guest to dine this day beneath the greenwood tree."

"Marry," cried Little John, clapping his palms together for joy, "thy bidding fitteth my liking like haft to blade. I'll bring thee back a guest this day, or come not back mine own self."

Then they each chose such of the band as they wished, and so went forth by different paths from the forest.

Now, you and I cannot go two ways at the same time while we join in these merry doings; so we will e'en let Little John follow his own path while we tuck up our skirts and trudge after Robin Hood. And here is good company, too; Robin Hood, Will Scarlet, Allan a Dale, Will Scathelock, Midge, the Miller's son, and others. A score or more of stout fellows had abided in the forest, with Friar Tuck, to make ready for the homecoming, but all the rest were gone either with Robin Hood or Little John.

They traveled onward, Robin following his fancy and the others following Robin. Now they wended their way through an open dale with cottage and farm lying therein, and now again they entered woodlands once more. Passing by fair Mansfield Town, with its towers and battlements and spires all smiling in the sun, they came at last out of the forest lands. Onward they journeyed, through highway and byway, through villages where goodwives and merry lasses peeped through the casements at the fine show of young men, until at last they came over beyond Alverton in Derbyshire. By this time high noontide had come, yet they had met no guest such as was worth their while to take back to Sherwood; so, coming at last to a certain spot where a shrine stood at the crossing of two roads, Robin called upon them to stop, for here on either side was shelter of high hedgerows, behind which was

good hiding, whence they could watch the roads at their ease, while they ate their midday meal. Quoth merry Robin, "Here, methinks, is good lodging, where peaceful folk, such as we be, can eat in quietness; therefore we will rest here, and see what may, perchance, fall into our luck-pot." So they crossed a stile and came behind a hedgerow where the mellow sunlight was bright and warm, and where the grass was soft, and there sat them down. Then each man drew from the pouch that hung beside him that which he had brought to eat, for a merry walk such as this had been sharpens the appetite till it is as keen as a March wind. So no more words were spoken, but each man saved his teeth for better use—munching at brown crust and cold meat right lustily.

In front of them, one of the highroads crawled up the steep hill and then dipped suddenly over its crest, sharp-cut with hedgerow and shaggy grass against the sky. Over the top of the windy hill peeped the eaves of a few houses of the village that fell back into the valley behind; there, also, showed the top of a windmill, the sails slowly rising and dipping from behind the hill against the clear blue sky, as the light wind moved them with creaking and labored swing.

So the yeomen lay behind the hedge and finished their midday meal; but still the time slipped along and no one came. At last, a man came slowly riding over the hill and down the stony road toward the spot where Robin and his band lay hidden. He was a good stout knight, but sorrowful of face and downcast of mien. His clothes were plain and rich, but no chain of gold, such as folk of his stand in life wore at most times, hung around his neck, and no jewel was about him; yet no one could mistake him for aught but one of proud and noble blood. His head was bowed upon his breast and his hands drooped limp on either side; and so he came slowly riding, as

though sunk in sad thoughts, while even his good horse, the reins loose upon his neck, walked with hanging head, as though he shared his master's grief.

Quoth Robin Hood, "Yon is verily a sorry-looking gallant, and doth seem to have donned ill-content with his jerkin this morning; nevertheless, I will out and talk with him, for there may be some pickings here for a hungry daw. Methinks his dress is rich, though he himself is so downcast. Bide ye here till I look into this matter." So saying, he arose and left them, crossed the road to the shrine, and there stood, waiting for the sorrowful knight to come near him. So, presently, when the knight came riding slowly along, jolly Robin stepped forward and laid his hand upon the bridle rein. "Hold, Sir Knight," quoth he. "I prythee tarry for a short time, for I have a few words to say to thee."

"What art thou, friend, who dost stop a traveler in this manner upon his most gracious Majesty's highway?" said the Knight.

"Marry," quoth Robin, "that is a question hard to answer. One man calleth me kind, another calleth me cruel; this one calleth me good honest fellow, and that one, vile thief. Truly, the world hath as many eyes to look upon a man withal as there are spots on a toad; so, with what pair of eyes thou regardest me lieth entirely with thine own self. My name is Robin Hood."

"Truly, good Robin," said the Knight, a smile twitching at the corners of his mouth, "thou hast a quaint conceit. As for the pair of eyes with which I regard thee, I would say that they are as favorable as may be, for I hear much good of thee and little ill. What is thy will of me?"

"Now, I make my vow, Sir Knight," quoth Robin, "thou hast surely learned thy wisdom of good Gaffer Swanthold, for he sayeth, 'Fair words are as easy spoke as foul, and bring good will in the stead of blows.' Now I

will show thee the truth of this saying; for, if thou wilt go with me this day to Sherwood Forest, I will give thee as merry a feast as ever thou hadst in all thy life."

"Thou art indeed kind," said the Knight, "but methinks thou will find me but an ill-seeming and sorrowful guest. Thou hadst best let me pass on my way in peace."

"Nay," quoth Robin, "thou mightst go thine own way but for one thing, and that I will tell thee. We keep an inn, as it were, in the very depths of Sherwood, but so far from highroads and beaten paths that guests do not often come nigh us; so I and my friends set off merrily and seek them when we grow dull of ourselves. Thus the matter stands, Sir Knight; yet I will furthermore tell thee that we count upon our guests paying a reckoning."

"I take thy meaning, friend," said the Knight gravely, "but I am not thy man, for I have no money by me."

"Is it sooth?" said Robin, looking at the Knight keenly. "I can scarce choose but believe thee; yet, Sir Knight, there be those of thy order whose word is not to be trusted as much as they would have others believe. Thou wilt think no ill if I look for myself in this matter." Then, still holding the horse by the bridle rein, he put his fingers to his lips and blew a shrill whistle, whereupon fourscore yeomen came leaping over the stile and ran to where the Knight and Robin stood. "These," said Robin, looking upon them proudly, "are some of my merry men. They share and share alike with me all joys and troubles, gains and losses. Sir Knight, I prythee tell me what money thou hast about thee."

For a time the Knight said not a word, but a slow red arose into his cheeks; at last he looked Robin in the face and said, "I know not why I should be ashamed, for it should be no shame to me; but, friend, I tell thee the truth, when I say that in my purse are ten shillings, and that that is every groat that Sir Richard of the Lea hath in all the wide world."

When Sir Richard ended a silence fell, until at last Robin said, "And dost thou pledge me thy knightly word that this is all thou has with thee?"

"Yea," answered Sir Richard, "I do pledge thee my most solemn word, as a true knight, that it is all the money I have in the world. Nay, here is my purse, ye may find for yourselves the truth of what I say." And he held his purse out to Robin.

"Put up thy purse, Sir Richard," quoth Robin. "Far be it from me to doubt the word of so gentle a knight. The proud I strive to bring low, but those that walk in sorrow I would aid if I could. Come, Sir Richard, cheer up thy heart and go with us into the greenwood. Even I may perchance aid thee, for thou surely knowest how the good Athelstane was saved by the little blind mole that digged a trench over which he that sought the king's life stumbled."

"Truly, friend," said Sir Richard, "methinks thou meanest kindness in thine own way; nevertheless my troubles are such that it is not likely that thou canst cure them. But I will go with thee this day into Sherwood." Hereupon he turned his horse's head, and they all wended their way to the woodlands, Robin walking on one side of the Knight and Will Scarlet on the other, while the rest of the band trudged behind.

After they had traveled thus for a time Robin Hood spake. "Sir Knight," said he, "I would not trouble thee with idle questions; but dost thou find it in thy heart to tell me thy sorrows?"

"Truly, Robin," quoth the Knight, "I see no reason why I should not do so. Thus it is: My castle and my lands are in pawn for a debt that I owe. Three days hence the money must be paid or else all mine estate is lost forever, for then it falls into the hands of the Priory of Emmet, and what they swallow they never give forth again."

Quoth Robin, "I understand not why those of thy kind live in such a manner that all their wealth passeth from them like snow beneath the springtide sun."

"Thou wrongest me, Robin," said the Knight, "for listen: I have a son but twenty winters old, nevertheless he has won his spurs as knight. Last year, on a certain evil day, the jousts were held at Chester, and thither my son went, as did I and my lady wife. I wot it was a proud time for us, for he unhorsed each knight that he tilted against. At last he ran a course with a certain great knight, Sir Walter of Lancaster, yet, though my son was so youthful, he kept his seat, albeit both spears were shivered to the haft; but it happened that a splinter of my boy's lance ran through the visor of Sir Walter's helmet and pierced through his eye into his brain, so that he died ere his esquire could unlace his helm. Now, Robin, Sir Walter had great friends at court, therefore his kinsmen stirred up things against my son so that, to save him from prison, I had to pay a ransom of six hundred pounds in gold. All might have gone well even yet, only that, by ins and outs and crookedness of laws, I was shorn like a sheep that is clipped to the quick. So it came that I had to pawn my lands to the Priory of Emmet for more money, and a hard bargain they drove with me in my hour of need. Yet I would have thee understand I grieve so for my lands only because of my dear lady wife."

"But where is thy son now?" asked Robin, who had listened closely to all the Knight had said.

"In Palestine," said Sir Richard, "battling like a brave Christian soldier for the cross and the holy sepulcher. Truly, England was an ill place for him because of Sir Walter's death and the hate of the Lancastrian's kinsmen."

"Truly," said Robin, much moved, "thine is a hard lot. But tell me, what is owing to Emmet for thine estates?"

"Only four hundred pounds," said Sir Richard.

At this, Robin smote his thigh in anger. "O the blood-suckers!" cried he. "A noble estate to be forfeit for four hundred pounds! But what will befall thee if thou dost lose thy lands, Sir Richard?"

"It is not mine own lot that doth trouble me in that case," said the Knight, "but my dear lady's; for should I lose my land she will have to betake herself to some kinsman and there abide in charity, which, methinks, would break her proud heart. As for me, I will over the salt sea, and so to Palestine to join my son in fight for the holy sepulcher."

Then up spake Will Scarlet. "But has thou no friend that will help thee in thy dire need?"

"Never a man," said Sir Richard. "While I was rich enow at home, and had friends, they blew great boasts of how they loved me. But when the oak falls in the forest the swine run from beneath it lest they should be smitten down also. So my friends have left me; for not only am I poor but I have great enemies."

Then Robin said, "Thou sayst thou hast no friends, Sir Richard. I make no boast, but many have found Robin Hood a friend in their troubles. Cheer up, Sir Knight, I may help thee yet."

The Knight shook his head with a faint smile, but for all that, Robin's words made him more blithe of heart, for in truth hope, be it never so faint, bringeth a gleam into darkness, like a little rushlight that costeth but a groat.

The day was well-nigh gone when they came near to the greenwood tree. Even at a distance they saw by the number of men that Little John had come back with some guest, but when they came near enough, whom should they find but the Lord Bishop of Hereford! The good Bishop was in a fine stew, I wot. Up and down he walked beneath the tree like a fox caught in a hencoop. Behind him were three Black Friars standing close together in a

frightened group, like three black sheep in a tempest. Hitched to the branches of the trees close at hand were six horses, one of them a barb with gay trappings upon which the Bishop was wont to ride, and the others laden with packs of divers shapes and kinds, one of which made Robin's eyes glisten, for it was a box not overlarge, but heavily bound with bands and ribs of iron.

When the Bishop saw Robin and those with him come into the open he made as though he would have run toward the yeoman, but the fellow that guarded the Bishop and the three friars thrust his quarterstaff in front, so that his lordship was fain to stand back, though with frowning brow and angry speech.

"Stay, my Lord Bishop," cried jolly Robin in a loud voice, when he saw what had passed, "I will come to thee with all speed, for I would rather see thee than any man in merry England." So saying, he quickened his steps and soon came to where the Bishop stood fuming.

"How now," quoth the Bishop in a loud and angry voice, when Robin had so come to him, "is this the way that thou and thy band treat one so high in the church as I am? I and these brethren were passing peacefully along the highroad with our pack horses, and a half score of men to guard them, when up comes a great strapping fellow full seven feet high, with fourscore or more men back of him, and calls upon me to stop—me, the Lord Bishop of Hereford, mark thou! Whereupon my armed guards—beshrew them for cowards!—straight ran away. But look ye; not only did this fellow stop me, but he threatened me, saying that Robin Hood would strip me as bare as a winter hedge. Then, besides all this, he called me such vile names as 'fat priest,' 'man-eating bishop,' 'money-gorging usurer,' and what not, as though I were no more than a strolling beggar or tinker."

At this, the Bishop glared like an angry cat, while even Sir Richard laughed; only Robin kept a grave face.

"Alas! my lord," said he, "that thou hast been so ill-treated by my band! I tell thee truly that we greatly reverence thy cloth. Little John, stand forth straightway."

At these words Little John came forward, twisting his face into a whimsical look, as though he would say, "Ha' mercy upon me, good master." Then Robin turned to the Bishop of Hereford and said, "Was this the man who spake so boldly to Your Lordship?"

"Ay, truly it was the same," said the Bishop, "a naughty fellow, I wot."

"And didst thou, Little John," said Robin in a sad voice, "call his lordship a fat priest?"

"Ay," said Little John sorrowfully.

"And a man-eating bishop?"

"Ay," said Little John, more sorrowfully than before.

"And a money-gorging usurer?"

"Ay," said Little John in so sorrowful a voice that it might have drawn tears from the Dragon of Wentley.

"Alas, that these things should be!" said jolly Robin, turning to the Bishop, "for I have ever found Little John a truthful man."

At this, a roar of laughter went up, whereat the blood rushed into the Bishop's face till it was cherry red from crown to chin; but he said nothing and only swallowed his words, though they well-nigh choked him.

"Nay, my Lord Bishop," said Robin, "we are rough fellows, but I trust not such ill men as thou thinkest, after all. There is not a man here that would harm a hair of thy reverence's head. I know thou art galled by our jesting, but we are all equal here in the greenwood, for there are no bishops nor barons nor earls among us, but only men, so thou must share our life with us while thou dost abide here. Come, busk ye, my merry men, and get the feast ready. Meantime, we will show our guests our woodland sports."

So, while some went to kindle the fires for roasting meats, others ran leaping to get their cudgels and long-bows. Then Robin brought forward Sir Richard of the Lea. "My Lord Bishop," said he, "here is another guest that we have with us this day. I wish that thou mightest know him better, for I and all my men will strive to honor you both at this merrymaking."

"Sir Richard," said the Bishop in a reproachful tone, "methinks thou and I are companions and fellow sufferers in this den of—" He was about to say "thieves," but he stopped suddenly and looked askance at Robin Hood.

"Speak out, Bishop," quoth Robin, laughing. "We of Sherwood check not an easy flow of words. 'Den of thieves' thou wast about to say."

Quoth the Bishop, "Mayhap that was what I meant to say, Sir Richard; but this I will say, that I saw thee just now laugh at the scurrilous jests of these fellows. It would have been more becoming of thee, methinks, to have checked them with frowns instead of spurring them on by laughter."

"I meant no harm to thee," said Sir Richard, "but a merry jest is a merry jest, and I may truly say I would have laughed at it had it been against mine own self."

But now Robin Hood called upon certain ones of his band who spread soft moss upon the ground and laid deerskins thereon. Then Robin bade his guests be seated, and so they all three sat down, some of the chief men, such as Little John, Will Scarlet, Allan a Dale, and others, stretching themselves upon the ground near and thereat the bowmen shot, and such shooting was done that day as it would have made one's heart leap to see. And all the while Robin talked so quaintly to the Bishop and the Knight that, the one forgetting his vexation and the other his troubles, they both laughed aloud again and again.

Then Allan a Dale came forth and tuned his harp, and all was hushed around, and he sang in his wondrous voice

songs of love, of war, of glory, and of sadness, and all listened without a movement or a sound. So Allan sang till the great round silver moon gleamed with its clear white light amid the upper tangle of the mazy branches of the trees. At last two fellows came to say that the feast was ready spread, so Robin, leading his guests with either hand, brought them to where great smoking dishes that sent savory smells far and near stood along the white linen cloth spread on the grass. All around was a glare of torches that lit everything up with a red light. Then, straightway sitting down, all fell to with noise and hubbub, the rattling of platters blending with the sound of loud talking and laughter. A long time the feast lasted, but at last all was over, and the bright wine and humming ale passed briskly. Then Robin Hood called aloud for silence, and all was hushed till he spoke.

"I have a story to tell you all, so listen to what I have to say," quoth he; whereupon, without more ado, he told them all about Sir Richard, and how his lands were in pawn. But, as he went on, the Bishop's face, that had erst been smiling and ruddy with merriment, waxed serious, and he put aside the horn of wine he held in his hand, for he knew the story of Sir Richard, and his heart sank within him with grim forebodings. Then, when Robin Hood had done, he turned to the Bishop of Hereford. "Now, my Lord Bishop," said he, "dost thou not think this is ill done of anyone, much more of a churchman, who should live in humbleness and charity?"

To this the Bishop answered not a word but looked upon the ground with moody eyes.

Quoth Robin, "Now, thou art the richest bishop in all England; canst thou not help this needy brother?" But still the Bishop answered not a word.

Then Robin turned to Little John, and quoth he, "Go thou and Will Stutely and bring forth those five pack horses yonder." Whereupon the two yeomen did as they

were bidden, those about the cloth making room on the green, where the light was brightest, for the five horses which Little John and Will Stutely presently led forward.

"Who hath the score of the goods?" asked Robin Hood, looking at the Black Friars.

Then up spake the smallest of all, in a trembling voice —an old man he was, with a gentle, wrinkled face. "That have I; but, I pray thee, harm me not."

"Nay," quoth Robin, "I have never harmed harmless man yet; but give it to me, good father." So the old man did as he was bidden, and handed Robin the tablet on which was marked down the account of the various packages upon the horses. This Robin handed to Will Scarlet, bidding him to read the same. So Will Scarlet, lifting his voice that all might hear, began:

"Three bales of silk to Quentin, the mercer at Ancaster."

"That we touch not," quoth Robin, "for this Quentin is an honest fellow, who hath risen by his own thrift." So the bales of silk were laid aside unopened.

"One bale of silk velvet for the Abbey of Beaumont."

"What do these priests want of silk velvet?" quoth Robin. "Nevertheless, though they need it not, I will not take all from them. Measure it off into three lots, one to be sold for charity, one for us, and one for the abbey." So this, too, was done as Robin Hood bade.

"Twoscore of great wax candles for the chapel of Saint Thomas."

"That belongeth fairly to the chapel," quoth Robin, "so lay it to one side. Far be it from us to take from the blessed Saint Thomas that which belongeth to him." So this, also, was done according to Robin's bidding, and the candles were laid to one side, along with honest Quentin's unopened bales of silk. So the list was gone through with, and the goods adjudged according to what Robin thought most fit. Some things were laid aside untouched,

and many were opened and divided into three equal parts, for charity, for themselves, and for the owners. And now all the ground in the torchlight was covered over with silks and velvets and cloths of gold and cases of rich wines, and so they came to the last line upon the tablet—"A box belonging to the Lord Bishop of Hereford."

At these words the Bishop shook as with a chill, and the box was set upon the ground.

"My Lord Bishop, hast thou the key of this box?" asked Robin.

The Bishop shook his head.

"Go, Will Scarlet," said Robin, "thou art the strongest man here—bring a sword straightway, and cut this box open, if thou canst." Then up rose Will Scarlet and left them, coming back in a short time, bearing a great two-handed sword. Thrice he smote that strong, ironbound box, and at the third blow it burst open and a great heap of gold came rolling forth, gleaming red in the light of the torches. At this sight a murmur went all around among the band, like the sound of the wind in distant trees; but no man came forward nor touched the money.

Quoth Robin, "Thou, Will Scarlet, thou, Allan a Dale, and thou, Little John, count it over."

A long time it took to count all the money, and when it had been duly scored up, Will Scarlet called out that there were fifteen hundred golden pounds in all. But in among the gold they found a paper, and this Will Scarlet read in a loud voice, and all heard that this money was the rental and fines and forfeits from certain estates belonging to the Bishopric of Hereford.

"My Lord Bishop," said Robin Hood, "I will not strip thee, as Little John said, like a winter hedge, for thou shalt take back one third of thy money. One third of it thou canst well spare to us for thy entertainment and that of thy train, for thou art very rich; one third of it thou canst better spare for charity, for, Bishop, I hear that

thou art a hard master to those beneath thee and a close hoarder of gains that thou couldst better and with more credit to thyself give to charity than spend upon thy own likings."

At this the Bishop looked up, but he could say never a word; yet he was thankful to keep some of his wealth.

Then Robin turned to Sir Richard of the Lea, and quoth he, "Now, Sir Richard, the church seemed like to despoil thee, therefore some of the overplus of church gains may well be used in aiding thee. Thou shalt take that five hundred pounds laid aside for people more in need than the Bishop is, and shalt pay thy debts to Emmet therewith."

Sir Richard looked at Robin until something arose in his eyes that made all the lights and the faces blur together. At last he said, "I thank thee, friend, from my heart, for what thou doest for me; yet, think not ill if I cannot take thy gift freely. But this I will do: I will take the money and pay my debts, and in a year and a day hence will return it safe either to thee or to the Lord Bishop of Hereford. For this I pledge my most solemn knightly word. I feel free to borrow, for I know no man that should be more bound to aid me than one so high in that church that hath driven such a hard bargain."

"Truly, Sir Knight," quoth Robin, "I do not understand those fine scruples that weigh with those of thy kind; but, nevertheless, it shall all be as thou dost wish. But thou hadst best bring the money to me at the end of the year, for mayhap I may make better use of it than the Bishop." Thereupon, turning to those near him, he gave his orders, and five hundred pounds were counted out and tied up in a leathern bag for Sir Richard. The rest of the treasure was divided, and part taken to the treasurehouse of the band, and part put by with the other things for the Bishop.

Then Sir Richard arose. "I cannot stay later, good

friends," said he, "for my lady will wax anxious if I come not home; so I crave leave to depart."

Then Robin Hood and all his merry men arose, and Robin said, "We cannot let thee go hence unattended, Sir Richard."

Then up spake Little John, "Good master, let me choose a score of stout fellows from the band, and let us arm ourselves in a seemly manner and so serve as retainers to Sir Richard till he can get others in our stead."

"Thou hast spoken well, Little John, and it shall be done," said Robin.

Then up spake Will Scarlet, "Let us give him a golden chain to hang about his neck, such as befits one of his blood, and also golden spurs to wear at his heels."

Then Robin Hood said, "Thou hast spoken well, Will Scarlet, and it shall be done."

Then up spake Will Stutely, "Let us give him yon bale of rich velvet and yon roll of cloth of gold to take home to his noble lady wife as a present from Robin Hood and his merry men all."

At this all clapped their hands for joy, and Robin said: "Thou hast well spoken, Will Stutely, and it shall be done."

Then Sir Richard of the Lea looked all around and strove to speak, but could scarcely do so for the feelings that choked him; at last he said in a husky, trembling voice, "Ye shall all see, good friends, that Sir Richard o' the Lea will ever remember your kindness this day. And if ye be at any time in dire need or trouble, come to me and my lady, and the walls of Castle Lea shall be battered down ere harm shall befall you. I—" He could say nothing further, but turned hastily away.

But now Little John and nineteen stout fellows whom he had chosen for his band, came forth all ready for the journey. Each man wore upon his breast a coat of linked mail, and on his head a cap of steel, and at his side a good stout sword. A gallant show they made as they stood all

in a row. Then Robin came and threw a chain of gold about Sir Richard's neck, and Will Scarlet knelt and buckled the golden spurs upon his heel; and now Little John led forward Sir Richard's horse, and the Knight mounted. He looked down at Robin for a little time, then of a sudden stooped and kissed his cheek. All the forest glades rang with the shout that went up as the Kinght and the yeomen marched off through the woodland with glare of torches and gleam of steel, and so were gone.

Then up spake the Bishop of Hereford in a mournful voice, "I, too, must be jogging, good fellow, for the night waxes late."

But Robin laid his hand upon the Bishop's arm and stayed him. "Be not so hasty, Lord Bishop," said he. "Three days hence Sir Richard must pay his debts to Emmet; until that time thou must be content to abide with me lest thou breed trouble for the Knight. I promise thee that thou shalt have great sport, for I know that thou art fond of hunting the dun deer. Lay by thy mantle of melancholy, and strive to lead a joyous yeoman life for three stout days. I promise thee thou shalt be sorry to go when the time has come."

So the Bishop and his train abided with Robin for three days, and much sport his lordship had in that time, so that, as Robin had said, when the time had come for him to go he was sorry to leave the greenwood. At the end of three days Robin set him free, and sent him forth from the forest with a guard of yeomen to keep freebooters from taking what was left of the packs and bundles.

But, as the Bishop rode away, he vowed within himself that he would sometime make Robin rue the day that he stopped him in Sherwood.

But now we shall follow Sir Richard; so listen, and you shall hear what befell him, and how he paid his debts at Emmet Priory, and likewise in due season to Robin Hood.

How Sir Richard
of the Lea Paid His Debts

THE LONG HIGHWAY stretched straight on, gray and dusty in the sun. On either side were dikes full of water bordered by osiers, and far away in the distance stood the towers of Emmet Priory with tall poplar trees around.

Along the causeway rode a knight with a score of stout men-at-arms behind him. The Knight was clad in a plain, long robe of gray serge, gathered in at the waist with a broad leathern belt, from which hung a long dagger and a stout sword. But though he was so plainly dressed himself, the horse he rode was a noble barb, and its trappings were rich with silk and silver bells.

So thus the band journeyed along the causeway between the dikes, till at last they reached the great gate of Emmet Priory. There the Knight called to one of his men and bade him knock at the porter's lodge with the haft of his sword.

The porter was drowsing on his bench within the lodge, but at the knock he roused himself and, opening the wicket, came hobbling forth and greeted the Knight, while a tame starling that hung in a wicker cage within

piped out, *"In cælo quies! In cælo quies!"* such being the words that the poor old lame porter had taught him to speak.

"Where is thy prior?" asked the Knight of the old porter.

"He is at meat, good knight, and he looketh for thy coming," quoth the porter, "for, if I mistake not, thou art Sir Richard of the Lea."

"I am Sir Richard of the Lea; then I will go seek him forthwith," said the Knight.

"But shall I not send thy horse to stable?" said the porter. "By Our Lady, it is the noblest nag, and the best harnessed, that e'er I saw in all my life before." And he stroked the horse's flank with his palm.

"Nay," quoth Sir Richard, "the stables of this place are not for me, so make way, I prythee." So saying, he pushed forward, and, the gates being opened, he entered the stony courtyard of the Priory, his men behind him. In they came with rattle of steel and clashing of swords, and ring of horses' feet on cobblestones, whereat a flock of pigeons that strutted in the sun flew with flapping wings to the high eaves of the round towers.

While the Knight was riding along the causeway to Emmet, a merry feast was toward in the refectory there. The afternoon sun streamed in through the great arched windows and lay in broad squares of light upon the stone floor and across the board covered with a snowy linen cloth, whereon was spread a princely feast. At the head of the table sat Prior Vincent of Emmet all clad in soft robes of fine cloth and silk; on his head was a black velvet cap picked out with gold, and around his neck hung a heavy chain of gold, with a great locket pendant therefrom. Beside him, on the arm of his great chair, roosted his favorite falcon, for the Prior was fond of the gentle craft of hawking. On his right hand sat the Sheriff of

Nottingham in rich robes of purple all trimmed about with fur, and on his left a famous doctor of law in dark and sober garb. Below these sat the high cellarer of Emmet, and others chief among the brethren.

Jest and laughter passed around, and all was as merry as merry could be. The wizened face of the man of law was twisted into a wrinkled smile, for in his pouch were fourscore golden angels that the Prior had paid him in fee for the case betwixt him and Sir Richard of the Lea. The learned doctor had been paid beforehand, for he had not overmuch trust in the holy Vincent of Emmet.

Quoth the Sheriff of Nottingham, "But art thou sure, Sir Prior, that thou hast the lands so safe?"

"Ay, marry," said Prior Vincent, smacking his lips after a deep draught of wine, "I have kept a close watch upon him, albeit he was unawares of the same, and I know right well that he hath no money to pay me."

"Ay, true," said the man of law in a dry, husky voice, "his land is surely forfeit if he cometh not to pay; but, Sir Prior, thou must get a release beneath his sign manual, or else thou canst not hope to hold the land without trouble from him."

"Yea," said the Prior, "so thou hast told me ere now, but I know that this knight is so poor that he will gladly sign away his lands for two hundred pounds of hard money."

Then up spake the high cellarer, "Methinks it is a shame to so drive a misfortunate knight to the ditch. I think it sorrow that the noblest estate in Derbyshire should so pass away from him for a paltry five hundred pounds. Truly, I—"

"How now," broke in the Prior in a quivering voice, his eyes glistening and his cheeks red with anger, "dost thou prate to my very beard, sirrah? By Saint Hubert, thou hadst best save thy breath to cool thy pottage, else it may scald thy mouth."

"Nay," said the man of law smoothly, "I dare swear this same knight will never come to settlement this day, but will prove recreant. Nevertheless, we will seek some means to gain his lands from him, so never fear."

But even as the doctor spoke, there came a sudden clatter of horses' hoofs and a jingle of iron mail in the courtyard below. Then up spake the Prior and called upon one of the brethren that sat below the salt, and bade him look out of the window and see who was below, albeit he knew right well it could be none but Sir Richard.

So the brother arose and went and looked, and he said, "I see below a score of stout men-at-arms and a knight just dismounting from his horse. He is dressed in long robes of gray which, methinks, are of poor seeming; but the horse he rideth upon hath the richest coursing that ever I saw. The Knight dismounts and they come this way, and are even now below in the great hall."

"Lo, see ye there now," quoth Prior Vincent. "Here ye have a knight with so lean a purse as scarce to buy him a crust of bread to munch, yet he keeps a band of retainers and puts rich trappings upon his horse's hide, while his own back goeth bare. Is it not well that such men should be brought low?"

"But art thou sure," said the little doctor tremulously, "that this knight will do us no harm? Such as he are fierce when crossed, and he hath a band of naughty men at his heels. Mayhap thou hadst better give an extension of his debt." Thus he spake, for he was afraid Sir Richard might do him a harm.

"Thou needst not fear," said the Prior, looking down at the little man beside him. "This knight is gentle and would as soon think of harming an old woman as thee."

As the Prior finished, a door at the lower end of the refectory swung open, and in came Sir Richard, with folded hands and head bowed upon his breast. Thus

humbly he walked slowly up the hall, while his men-at-arms stood about the door. When he had come to where the Prior sat, he knelt upon one knee. "Save and keep thee, Sir Prior," said he, "I am come to keep my day."

Then the first word that the Prior said to him was "Hast thou brought my money?"

"Alas! I have not so much as one penny upon my body," said the Knight; whereat the Prior's eyes sparkled.

"Now, thou art a shrewd debtor, I wot," said he. Then, "Sir Sheriff, I drink to thee."

But still the Knight kneeled upon the hard stones, so the Prior turned to him again. "What wouldst thou have?" quoth he sharply.

At these words, a slow red mounted into the Knight's cheeks; but still he knelt. "I would crave thy mercy," said he. "As thou hopest for Heaven's mercy, show mercy to me. Strip me not of my lands and so reduce a true knight to poverty."

"Thy day is broken and thy lands forfeit," said the man of law, plucking up his spirits at the Knight's humble speech.

Quoth Sir Richard, "Thou man of law, wilt thou not befriend me in mine hour of need?"

"Nay," said the other, "I hold with this holy Prior, who hath paid me my fees in hard gold, so that I am bounden to him."

"Wilt thou not be my friend, Sir Sheriff?" said Sir Richard.

"Nay, 'fore Heaven," quoth the Sheriff of Nottingham, "this is no business of mine, yet I will do what I may," and he nudged the Prior beneath the cloth with his knee. "Wilt thou not ease him of some of his debts, Sir Prior?"

At this the Prior smiled grimly. "Pay me three hun-

dred pounds, Sir Richard," said he, "and I will give thee
quittance of thy debt."

"Thou knowest, Sir Prior, that it is as easy for me to
pay four hundred pounds as three hundred," said Sir
Richard. "But wilt thou not give me another twelvemonth to pay my debt?"

"Not another day," said the Prior sternly.

"And is this all thou wilt do for me?" asked the
Knight.

"Now, out upon thee, false knight!" cried the Prior,
bursting forth in anger. "Either pay thy debt as I have
said, or release thy land and get thee gone from out my
hall."

Then Sir Richard arose to his feet. "Thou false, lying
priest!" said he in so stern a voice that the man of law
shrunk affrighted, "I am no false knight, as thou knowest
full well, but have even held my place in the press and the
tourney. Hast thou so little courtesy that thou wouldst
see a true knight kneel for all this time, or see him come
into thy hall and never offer him meat or drink?"

Then quoth the man of law in a trembling voice, "This
is surely an ill way to talk of matters appertaining to
business; let us be mild in speech. What wilt thou pay
this knight, Sir Prior, to give thee release of his land?"

"I would have given him two hundred pounds," quoth
the Prior, "but since he hath spoken so vilely to my teeth,
not one groat over one hundred pounds will he get."

"Hadst thou offered me a thousand pounds, false
prior," said the Knight, "thou wouldst not have got an
inch of my land." Then turning to where his men-at-
arms stood near the door, he called, "Come hither," and
beckoned with his finger; whereupon the tallest of them
all came forward and handed him a long leathern bag.
Sir Richard took the bag and shot from it upon the table a
glittering stream of golden money. "Bear in mind, Sir
Prior," said he, "that thou hast promised me quittance for

three hundred pounds. Not one farthing above that shalt thou get." So saying, he counted out three hundred pounds and pushed it toward the Prior.

But now the Prior's hands dropped at his sides and the Prior's head hung upon his shoulder, for not only had he lost all hopes of the land, but he had forgiven the Knight one hundred pounds of his debt and had needlessly paid the man of law fourscore angels. To him he turned, and quoth he, "Give me back my money that thou hast."

"Nay," cried the other shrilly, "it is but my fee that thou didst pay me, and thou gettest it not back again." And he hugged his gown about him.

"Now, Sir Prior," quoth Sir Richard, "I have held my day and paid all the dues demanded of me; so, as there is no more betwixt us, I leave this vile place straightway." So saying, he turned upon his heel and strode away.

All this time the Sheriff had been staring with wide-open eyes and mouth agape at the tall man-at-arms, who stood as though carved out of stone. At last he gasped out, "Reynold Greenleaf!"

At this, the tall man-at-arms, who was no other than Little John, turned, grinning, to the Sheriff. "I give thee good den, fair gossip," quoth he. "I would say, sweet Sheriff, that I have heard all thy pretty talk this day, and it shall be duly told unto Robin Hood. So, farewell for the nonce, till we meet again in Sherwood Forest." Then he, also, turned and followed Sir Richard down the hall, leaving the Sheriff, all pale and amazed, shrunk together upon his chair.

A merry feast it was to which Sir Richard came, but a sorry lot he left behind him, and little hunger had they for the princely food spread before them. Only the learned doctor was happy, for he had his fee.

Now a twelvemonth and a day passed since Prior Vincent of Emmet sat at feast, and once more the mellow fall

of another year had come. But the year had brought great change, I wot, to the lands of Sir Richard of the Lea; for, where before shaggy wild grasses grew upon the meadow lands, now all stretch away in golden stubble, betokening that a rich and plentiful crop had been gathered therefrom. A year had made a great change in the castle, also, for, where were empty moats and the crumbling of neglect, all was now orderly and well kept.

Bright shone the sun on battlement and tower, and in the blue air overhead a flock of clattering jackdaws flew around the gilded weather vane and spire. Then, in the brightness of the morning, the drawbridge fell across the moat with a rattle and clank of chains, the gate of the castle swung slowly open, and a goodly array of steel-clad men-at-arms, with a knight all clothed in chain mail, as white as frost on brier and thorn of a winter morning, came flashing out from the castle courtyard. In his hand the Knight held a great spear, from the point of which fluttered a blood-red pennant as broad as the palm of one's hand. So this troop came forth from the castle, and in the midst of them walked three pack horses laden with parcels of divers shapes and kinds.

Thus rode forth good Sir Richard of the Lea to pay his debt to Robin Hood this bright and merry morn. Along the highway they wended their way, with measured tramp of feet and rattle and jingle of sword and harness. Onward they marched till they came nigh to Denby, where, from the top of a hill, they saw, over beyond the town, many gay flags and streamers floating in the bright air. Then Sir Richard turned to the man-at-arms nearest to him. "What is toward yonder at Denby today?" quoth he.

"Please Your Worship," answered the man-at-arms, "a merry fair is held there today, and a great wrestling match, to which many folk have come, for a prize hath been offered of a pipe of red wine, a fair golden ring, and

a pair of gloves, all of which go to the best wrestler."

"Now, by my faith," quoth Sir Richard, who loved good manly sports right well, "this will be a goodly thing to see. Methinks we have to stay a little while on our journey, and see this merry sport." So he turned his horse's head aside toward Denby and the fair, and thither he and his men made their way.

There they found a great hubbub of merriment. Flags and streamers were floating, tumblers were tumbling on the green, bagpipes were playing, and lads and lasses were dancing to the music. But the crowd were gathered most of all around a ring where the wrestling was going forward, and thither Sir Richard and his men turned their steps.

Now when the judges of the wrestling saw Sir Richard coming and knew who he was, the chief of them came down from the bench where he and the others sat, and went to the Knight and took him by the hand, beseeching him to come and sit with them and judge the sport. So Sir Richard got down from his horse and went with the others to the bench raised beside the ring.

Now there had been great doings that morning, for a certain yeoman named Egbert, who came from Stoke over in Staffordshire, had thrown with ease all those that came against him; but a man of Denby, well known through all the countryside as William of the Scar, had been biding his time with the Stoke man; so, when Egbert had thrown everyone else, stout William leaped into the ring. Then a tough bout followed, and at last he threw Egbert heavily, whereat there was a great shouting and shaking of hands, for all the Denby men were proud of their wrestler.

When Sir Richard came, he found stout William, puffed up by the shouts of his friends, walking up and down the ring, daring anyone to come and try a throw with him. "Come one, come all!" quoth he. "Here

stand I, William of the Scar, against any man. If there is none in Derbyshire to come against me, come all who will, from Nottingham, Stafford, or York, and if I do not make them one and all root the ground with their noses like swine in the forests, call me no more brave William the wrestler."

At this all laughed; but above all the laughter a loud voice was heard to cry out, "Sin' thou talkest so big, here cometh one from Nottinghamshire to try a fall with thee, fellow"; and straighway a tall youth with a tough quarterstaff in his hand came pushing his way through the crowd and at last leaped lightly over the rope into the ring. He was not as heavy as stout William, but he was taller and broader in the shoulders, and all his joints were well knit. Sir Richard looked upon him keenly, then, turning to one of the judges, he said, "Knowest thou who this youth is? Methinks I have seen him before."

"Nay," said the judge, "he is a stranger to me."

Meantime, without a word, the young man, laying aside his quarterstaff, began to take off his jerkin and body clothing until he presently stood with naked arms and body; and a comely sight he was when so bared to the view, for his muscles were cut round and smooth and sharp like swift-running water.

And now each man spat upon his hands and, clapping them upon his knees, squatted down, watching the other keenly, so as to take the vantage of him in the grip. Then like a flash they leaped together, and a great shout went up, for William had gotten the better hold of the two. For a short time they strained and struggled and writhed, and then stout William gave his most cunning trip and throw, but the stranger met it with greater skill than his, and so the trip came to nought. Then, of a sudden, with a twist and a wrench, the stranger loosed himself, and he of the scar found himself locked in a pair of arms that fairly made his ribs crack. So, with heavy, hot breath-

ing, they stood for a while straining, their bodies all glistening with sweat, and great drops of sweat trickling down their faces. But the stranger's hug was so close that at last stout William's muscles softened under his grip, and he gave a sob. Then the youth put forth all his strength and gave a sudden trip with his heel and a cast over his right hip, and down stout William went, with a sickening thud, and lay as though he would never move hand nor foot again.

But now no shout went up for the stranger, but an angry murmur was heard among the crowd, so easily had he won the match. Then one of the judges, a kinsman to William of the Scar, rose with trembling lip and baleful look. Quoth he, "If thou hath slain that man it will go ill with thee, let me tell thee, fellow." But the stranger answered boldly, "He took his chance with me as I took mine with him. No law can touch me to harm me, even if I slew him, so that it was fairly done in the wrestling ring."

"That we shall see," said the judge, scowling upon the youth, while once more an angry murmur ran around the crowd; for, as I have said, the men of Denby were proud of stout William of the Scar.

Then up spoke Sir Richard gently. "Nay," said he, "the youth is right; if the other dieth, he dieth in the wrestling ring, where he took his chance, and was cast fairly enow."

But in the meantime three men had come forward and lifted stout William from the ground and found that he was not dead, though badly shaken by his heavy fall. Then the chief judge rose and said, "Young man, the prize is duly thine. Here is the red-gold ring, and here the gloves, and yonder stands the pipe of wine to do with whatsoever thou dost list."

At this, the youth, who had donned his clothes and taken up his staff again, bowed without a word, then,

taking the gloves and the ring, and thrusting the one into his girdle and slipping the other upon his thumb, he turned and, leaping lightly over the ropes again, made his way through the crowd, and was gone.

"Now, I wonder who yon youth may be," said the judge, turning to Sir Richard, "he seemeth like a stout Saxon from his red cheeks and fair hair. This William of ours is a stout man, too, and never have I seen him cast in the ring before, albeit he hath not yet striven with such great wrestlers as Thomas of Cornwall, Diccon of York, and young David of Doncaster. Hath he not a firm foot in the ring, thinkest thou, Sir Richard?"

"Ay, truly, and yet this youth threw him fairly, and with wondrous ease. I much wonder who he can be." Thus said Sir Richard in a thoughtful voice.

For a time the Knight stood talking to those about him, but at last he arose and made ready to depart, so he called his men about him and, tightening the girths of his saddle, he mounted his horse once more.

Meanwhile the young stranger had made his way through the crowd, but, as he passed, he heard all around him such words muttered as "Look at the cockerel!" "Behold how he plumeth himself!" "I dare swear he cast good William unfairly!" "Yea, truly, saw ye not birdlime upon his hands?" "It would be well to cut his cock's comb!" To all this the stranger paid no heed, but strode proudly about as though he heard it not. So he walked slowly across the green to where the booth stood wherein was dancing, and standing at the door he looked in on the sport. As he stood thus, a stone struck his arm of a sudden with a sharp jar, and, turning, he saw that an angry crowd of men had followed him from the wrestling ring. Then, when they saw him turn so, a great hooting and yelling arose from all, so that the folk came running out from the dancing booth to see what was to do. At last a tall, broad-shouldered, burly

blacksmith strode forward from the crowd swinging a mighty blackthorn club in his hand.

"Wouldst thou come here to our fair town of Denby, thou Jack in the Box, to overcome a good honest lad with vile, juggling tricks?" growled he in a deep voice like the bellow of an angry bull. "Take that, then!" And of a sudden he struck a blow at the youth that might have felled an ox. But the other turned the blow deftly aside, and gave back another so terrible that the Denby man went down with a groan, as though he had been smitten by lightning. When they saw their leader fall, the crowd gave another angry shout; but the stranger placed his back against the tent near which he stood, swinging his terrible staff, and so fell had been the blow that he struck the stout smith that none dared to come within the measure of his cudgel, so the press crowded back, like a pack of dogs from a bear at bay. But now some coward hand from behind threw a sharp jagged stone that smote the stranger on the crown, so that he staggered back, and the red blood gushed from the cut and ran down his face and over his jerkin. Then, seeing him dazed with this vile blow, the crowd rushed upon him, so that they overbore him and he fell beneath their feet.

Now it might have gone ill with the youth, even to the losing of his young life, had not Sir Richard come to this fair; for of a sudden, shouts were heard, and steel flashed in the air, and blows were given with the flat of swords, while through the midst of the crowd Sir Richard of the Lea came spurring on his white horse. Then the crowd, seeing the steel-clad knight and the armed men, melted away like snow on the warm hearth, leaving the young man all bloody and dusty upon the ground.

Finding himself free, the youth arose and, wiping the blood from his face, looked up. Quoth he, "Sir Richard of the Lea, mayhap thou hast saved my life this day."

"Who art thou that knowest Sir Richard of the Lea so

well?" quoth the Knight. "Methinks I have seen thy face before, young man."

"Yea, thou hast," said the youth, "for men call me David of Doncaster."

"Ha!" said Sir Richard, "I wonder that I knew thee not, David; but thy beard hath grown longer, and thou thyself art more set in manhood since this day twelvemonth. Come hither into the tent, David, and wash the blood from thy face. And thou, Ralph, bring him straightway a clean jerkin. Now I am sorry for thee, yet I am right glad that I have had a chance to pay a part of my debt of kindness to thy good master Robin Hood, for it might have gone ill with thee had I not come, young man."

So saying, the Knight led David into the tent, and there the youth washed the blood from his face and put on the clean jerkin.

In the meantime a whisper had gone around from those that stood nearest that this was none other than the great David of Doncaster, the best wrestler in all the mid-country, who only last spring had cast stout Adam o' Lincoln in the ring at Selby, in Yorkshire, and now held the mid-country champion belt. Thus it happened that when young David came forth from the tent along with Sir Richard, the blood all washed from his face, and his soiled jerkin changed for a clean one, no sounds of anger were heard, but all pressed forward to see the young man, feeling proud that one of the great wrestlers of England should have entered the ring at Denby fair. For thus fickle is a mass of men.

Then Sir Richard called aloud, "Friends, this is David of Doncaster; so think it no shame that your Denby man was cast by such a wrestler. He beareth you no ill will for what hath passed, but let it be a warning to you how ye treat strangers henceforth. Had ye slain him it would have been an ill day for you, for Robin Hood would have harried your town as the kestrel harries the dovecote. I

have bought the pipe of wine from him, and now I give it freely to you to drink as ye list. But never hereafterward fall upon a man for being a stout yeoman."

At this all shouted amain; but in truth they thought more of the wine than of the Knight's words. Then Sir Richard, with David beside him and his men-at-arms around, turned about and left the fair.

But in after days, when the men that saw that wrestling bout were bent with age, they would shake their heads when they heard of any stalwart game, and say, "Ay, ay; but thou shouldst have seen the great David of Doncaster cast stout William of the Scar at Denby fair."

Robin Hood stood in the merry greenwood with Little John and most of his stout yeomen around him, awaiting Sir Richard's coming. At last a glint of steel was seen through the brown forest leaves, and forth from the covert into the open rode Sir Richard at the head of his men. He came straight forward to Robin Hood and leaping from off his horse, clasped the yeoman in his arms.

"Why, how now," said Robin, after a time, holding Sir Richard off and looking at him from top to toe, "methinks thou art a gayer bird than when I saw thee last."

"Yes, thanks to thee, Robin," said the Knight, laying his hand upon the yeoman's shoulder. "But for thee I would have been wandering in misery in a far country by this time. But I have kept my word, Robin, and have brought back the money that thou didst lend me, and which I have doubled four times over again, and so become rich one more. Along with this money I have brought a little gift to thee and thy brave men from my dear lady and myself." Then, turning to his men, he called aloud, "Bring forth the pack horses."

But Robin stopped him. "Nay, Sir Richard," said he, "think it not bold of me to cross thy bidding, but we of Sherwood do no business till after we have eaten and

drunk." Whereupon, taking Sir Richard by the hand, he led him to the seat beneath the greenwood tree, while others of the chief men of the band came and seated themselves around. Then quoth Robin, "How cometh it that I saw young David of Doncaster with thee and thy men, Sir Knight?"

Then straightway the Knight told all about his stay at Denby and of the happening at the fair, and how it was like to go hard with young David; so he told his tale, and quoth he, "It was this, good Robin, that kept me so late on the way, otherwise I would have been here an hour agone."

Then, when he had done speaking, Robin stretched out his hand and grasped the Knight's palm. Quoth he in a trembling voice, "I owe thee a debt I can never hope to repay, Sir Richard, for let me tell thee, I would rather lose my right hand than have such ill befall young David of Doncaster as seemed like to come upon him at Denby."

So they talked until after a while one came forward to say that the feast was spread; whereupon all arose and went thereto. When at last it was done, the Knight called upon his men to bring the pack horses forward, which they did according to his bidding. Then one of the men brought the Knight a strongbox, which he opened and took from it a bag and counted out five hundred pounds, the sum he had gotten from Robin.

"Sir Richard," quoth Robin, "thou wilt pleasure us all if thou wilt keep that money as a gift from us of Sherwood. It is not so, my lads?"

Then all shouted "Ay" with a mighty voice.

"I thank you all deeply," said the Knight earnestly, "but think it not ill of me if I cannot take it. Gladly have I borrowed it from you, but it may not be that I can take it as a gift."

Then Robin Hood said no more but gave the money to Little John to put away in the treasury, for he had

shrewdness enough to know that nought breeds ill will and heart bitterness like gifts forced upon one that cannot choose but take them.

Then Sir Richard had the packs laid upon the ground and opened, whereupon a great shout went up that made the forest ring again, for lo, there were tenscore bows of finest Spanish yew, all burnished till they shone again, and each bow inlaid with fanciful figures in silver, yet not inlaid so as to mar their strength. Beside these were tenscore quivers of leather embroidered with golden thread, and in each quiver were a score of shafts with burnished heads that shone like silver; each shaft was feathered with peacock's plumes, innocked with silver.

Sir Richard gave to each yeoman a bow and a quiver of arrows, but to Robin he gave a stout bow inlaid with the cunningest workmanship in gold, while each arrow in his quiver was innocked with gold.

Then all shouted again for joy of the fair gift, and all swore among themselves that they would die if need be for Sir Richard and his lady.

At last the time came when Sir Richard must go, whereupon Robin Hood called his band around him, and each man of the yeomen took a torch in his hand to light the way through the woodlands. So they came to the edge of Sherwood, and there the Knight kissed Robin upon the cheeks and left him and was gone.

Thus Robin Hood helped a noble knight out his dire misfortunes, that else would have smothered the happiness from his life.

Little John Turns Barefoot Friar

COLD WINTER had passed and spring had come. No leafy thickness had yet clad the woodlands, but the budding leaves hung like a tender mist about the trees. In the open country the meadow lands lay a sheeny green, the cornfields a dark velvety color, for they were thick and soft with the growing blades. The plowboy shouted in the sun, and in the purple new-turned furrows flocks of birds hunted for fat worms. All the broad moist earth smiled in the warm light, and each little green hill clapped its hand for joy.

On a deer's hide, stretched on the ground in the open in front of the greenwood tree, sat Robin Hood basking in the sun like an old dog fox. Leaning back with his hands clasped about his knees, he lazily watched Little John rolling a stout bowstring from long strands of hempen thread, wetting the palms of his hands ever and anon, and rolling the cord upon his thigh. Near by sat Allan a Dale fitting a new string to his harp.

Quoth Robin at last, "Methinks I would rather roam this forest in the gentle springtime than be King of all merry England. What palace in the broad world is as fair as this sweet woodland just now, and what king in all the world hath such appetite for plover's eggs and lampreys as I for juicy venison and sparkling ale? Gaffer Swanthold speaks truly when he saith, 'Better a crust with content than honey with a sour heart.'"

"Yea," quoth Little John, as he rubbed his new-made bowstring with yellow beeswax, "the life we lead is the life for me. Thou speakest of the springtime, but methinks even the winter hath its own joys. Thou and I, good master, have had more than one merry day, this winter past, at the Blue Boar. Dost thou not remember that night thou and Will Stutely and Friar Tuck and I passed at that same hostelry with the two beggars and the strolling friar?"

"Yea," quoth merry Robin, laughing, "that was the night that Will Stutely must needs snatch a kiss from the stout hostess, and got a canakin of ale emptied over his head for his pains."

"Truly, it was the same," said Little John, laughing also. "Methinks that was a goodly song that the strolling friar sang. Friar Tuck, thou hast a quick ear for a tune, dost thou not remember it?"

"I did have the catch of it one time," said Tuck. "Let me see," and he touched his forefinger to his forehead in thought, humming to himself, and stopping ever and anon to fit what he had got to what he searched for in his mind. At last he found it all and clearing his throat, sang merrily:

> *"In the blossoming hedge the robin cock sings,*
> *For the sun it is merry and bright,*
> *And he joyfully hops and he flutters his wings,*
> *For his heart is all full of delight.*
> *For the May bloometh fair,*
> *And there's little of care,*
> *And plenty to eat in the Maytime rare.*
> *When the flowers all die,*
> *Then off he will fly,*
> *To keep himself warm*
> *In some jolly old barn*
> *Where the snow and the wind neither chill him nor*
> *harm.*

"And such is the life of the strolling friar,
With aplenty to eat and to drink;
For the goodwife will keep him a seat by the fire,
And the pretty girls smile at his wink.
Then he lustily trolls,
As he onward strolls,
A rollicking song for the saving of souls.
When the wind doth blow,
With the coming of snow,
There's a place by the fire
For the fatherly friar,
And a crab in the bowl for his heart's desire."

Thus Friar Tuck sang in a rich and mellow voice, rolling his head from side to side in time with the music, and when he had done, all clapped their hands and shouted with laughter, for the song fitted him well.

"In very sooth," quoth Little John, "it is a goodly song, and, were I not a yeoman of Sherwood Forest, I had rather be a strolling friar than aught else in the world."

"Yea, it is a goodly song," said Robin Hood, "but methought those two burly beggars told the merrier tales and led the merrier life. Dost thou not remember what that great black-bearded fellow told of his begging at the fair in York?"

"Yea," said Little John, "but what told the friar of the harvest home in Kentshire? I hold that he led a merrier life than the other two."

"Truly, for the honor of the cloth," quoth Friar Tuck, "I hold with my good gossip, Little John."

"Now," quoth Robin, "I hold to mine own mind. But what sayst thou, Little John, to a merry adventure this fair day? Take thou a friar's gown from our chest of strange garments, and don the same, and I will stop the first beggar I meet and change clothes with him. Then let us wander the country about, this sweet day, and see what befalls each of us."

"That fitteth my mind," quoth Little John, "so let us forth, say I."

Thereupon Little John and Friar Tuck went to the storehouse of the band, and there chose for the yeoman the robe of a Gray Friar. Then they came forth again, and a mighty roar of laughter went up, for not only had the band never seen Little John in such guise before, but the robe was too short for him by a good palm's-breadth. But Little John's hands were folded in his loose sleeves, and Little John's eyes were cast upon the ground, and at his girdle hung a great, long string of beads.

And now Little John took up his stout staff, at the end of which hung a chubby little leathern pottle, such as palmers carry at the tips of their staves; but in it was something, I wot, more like good Malmsey than cold spring water, such as godly pilgrims carry. Then up rose Robin and took his stout staff in his hand, likewise, and slipped ten golden angels into his pouch; for no beggar's garb was among the stores of the band, so he was fain to run his chance of meeting a beggar and buying his clothes of him.

So, all being made ready, the two yeomen set forth on their way, striding lustily along all in the misty morning. Thus they walked down the forest path until they came to the highway, and then along the highway till it split in twain, leading on one hand to Blyth and on the other to Gainsborough. Here the yeomen stopped.

Quoth jolly Robin, "Take thou the road to Gainsborough, and I will take that to Blyth. So, fare thee well, holy father, and mayst thou not ha' cause to count thy beads in earnest ere we meet again."

"Good den, good beggar that is to be," quoth Little John, "and mayst thou have no cause to beg for mercy ere I see thee next."

So each stepped sturdily upon his way until a green hill rose between them, and the one was hid from the sight of the other.

*The robe was too short for Little John by
a good palm's breadth.*

Little John walked along, whistling, for no one was nigh upon all the road. In the budding hedges the little birds twittered merrily, and on either hand the green hills swept up to the sky, the great white clouds of springtime sailing slowly over their crowns in lazy flight. Up hill and down dale walked Little John, the fresh wind blowing in his face and his robes fluttering behind him, and so at last he came to a crossroad that led to Tuxford. Here he met three pretty lasses, each bearing a basket of eggs to market. Quoth he, "Whither away, fair maids?" And he stood in their path, holding his staff in front of them, to stop them.

Then they huddled together and nudged one another, and one presently spake up and said, "We are going to the Tuxford market, holy friar, to sell our eggs."

"Now out upon it!" quoth Little John, looking upon them with his head on one side. "Surely, it is a pity that such fair lasses should be forced to carry eggs to market. Let me tell you, an I had the shaping of things in this world, ye should all three have been clothed in the finest silks, and ride upon milk-white horses, with pages at your side, and feed upon nothing but whipped cream and strawberries; for such a life would surely befit your looks."

At this speech all three of the pretty maids looked down, blushing and simpering. One said, "La!" another, "Marry, a' maketh sport of us!" and the third, "Listen, now, to the holy man!" But at the same time they looked at Little John from out the corners of their eyes.

"Now, look you," said Little John, "I cannot see such dainty damsels as ye are carrying baskets along a highroad. Let me take them mine own self, and one of you, if ye will, may carry my staff for me."

"Nay," said one of the lasses, "but thou canst not carry three baskets all at one time."

"Yea, but I can," said Little John, "and that I will

show you presently. I thank the good Saint Wilfred that he hath given me a pretty wit. Look ye, now. Here I take this great basket, so; here I tie my rosary around the handle, thus; and here I slip the rosary over my head and sling the basket upon my back, in this wise." And Little John did according to his words, the basket hanging down behind him like a peddler's pack; then, giving his staff to one of the maids, and taking a basket upon either arm, he turned his face toward Tuxford Town and stepped forth merrily, a laughing maid on either side, and one walking ahead, carrying the staff. In this wise they journeyed along, and everyone they met stopped and looked after them, laughing, for never had anybody seen such a merry sight as this tall, strapping Gray Friar, with robes all too short for him, laden with eggs, and tramping the road with three pretty lasses. For this Little John cared not a whit, but when such folks gave jesting words to him he answered back as merrily, speech for speech.

So they stepped along toward Tuxford, chatting and laughing, until they came nigh to the town. Here Little John stopped and set down the baskets, for he did not care to go into the town lest he should, perchance, meet some of the Sheriff's men. "Alas! sweet chucks," quoth he, "here I must leave you. I had not thought to come this way, but I am glad that I did so. Now, ere we part, we must drink sweet friendship." So saying, he unslung the leathern pottle from the end of his staff, and, drawing the stopper therefrom, he handed it to the lass who had carried his staff, first wiping the mouth of the pottle upon his sleeve. Then each lass took a fair drink of what was within, and when it had passed all around, Little John finished what was left, so that not another drop could be squeezed from it. Then, kissing each lass sweetly, he wished them all good den, and left them. But the maids stood looking after him as he walked away whistling.

"What a pity," quoth one, "that such a stout, lusty lad should be in holy orders."

"Marry," quoth Little John to himself, as he strode along, "yon was no such ill happening; Saint Dunstan send me more of the like."

After he had trudged along for a time he began to wax thirsty again in the warmth of the day. He shook his leathern pottle beside his ear, but not a sound came therefrom. Then he placed it to his lips and tilted it high aloft, but not a drop was there. "Little John! Little John!" said he sadly to himself, shaking his head the while, "woman will be thy ruin yet, if thou dost not take better care of thyself."

But at last he reached the crest of a certain hill, and saw below a sweet little thatched inn lying snugly in the dale beneath him, toward which the road dipped sharply. At the sight of this, a voice within him cried aloud, "I give thee joy, good friend, for yonder is thy heart's delight, to wit, a sweet rest and a cup of brown beer." So he quickened his pace down the hill and so came to the little inn, from which hung a sign with a stag's head painted upon it. In front of the door a clucking hen was scratching in the dust with a brood of chickens about her heels, the sparrows were chattering of household affairs under the eaves, and all was so sweet and peaceful that Little John's heart laughed within him. Beside the door stood two stout cobs with broad soft-padded saddles, well fitted for easy traveling, and speaking of rich guests in the parlor. In front of the door three merry fellows, a tinker, a peddler, and a beggar, were seated on a bench in the sun quaffing stout ale.

"I give you good den, sweet friends," quoth Little John, striding up to where they sat.

"Give thee good den, holy father," quoth the merry Beggar with a grin. "But look thee, thy gown is too short. Thou hadst best cut a piece off the top and tack it

to the bottom, so that it may be long enough. But come, sit beside us here and take a taste of ale, if thy vows forbid thee not."

"Nay," quoth Little John, also grinning, "the blessed Saint Dunstan hath given me a free dispensation for all indulgence in that line." And he thrust his hand into his pouch for money to pay his score.

"Truly," quoth the Tinker, "without thy looks belie thee, holy friar, the good Saint Dunstan was wise, for without such dispensation his votary is like to ha' many a penance to make. Nay, take thy hand from out thy pouch, brother, for thou shalt not pay this shot. Ho, landlord, a pot of ale!"

So the ale was brought and given to Little John. Then, blowing the froth a little way to make room for his lips, he tilted the bottom of the pot higher and higher, till it pointed to the sky, and he had to shut his eyes to keep the dazzle of the sunshine out of them. Then he took the pot away, for there was nothing in it, and heaved a full deep sigh, looking at the others with moist eyes and shaking his head solemnly.

"Ho, landlord!" cried the Peddler, "bring this good fellow another pot of ale, for truly it is a credit to us all to have one among us who can empty a canakin so lustily."

So they talked among themselves merrily, until after a while quoth Little John, "Who rideth those two nags yonder?"

"Two holy men like thee, brother," quoth the Beggar. "They are now having a goodly feast within, for I smelled the steam of a boiled pullet just now. The landlady sayeth they come from Fountain Abbey, in Yorkshire, and go to Lincoln on matters of business."

"They are a merry couple," said the Tinker, "for one is as lean as an old wife's spindle, and the other as fat as a suet pudding."

"Talking of fatness," said the Peddler, "thou thyself lookest none too ill-fed, holy friar."

"Nay, truly," said Little John, "thou seest in me what the holy Saint Dunstan can do for them that serve him upon a handful of parched peas and a trickle of cold water."

At this a great shout of laughter went up. "Truly, it is a wondrous thing," quoth the Beggar, "I would have made my vow, to see the masterly manner in which thou didst tuck away yon pot of ale, that thou hadst not tasted clear water for a brace of months. Has not this same holy Saint Dunstan taught thee a goodly song or two?"

"Why, as for that," quoth Little John, grinning, "mayhap he hath lent me aid to learn a ditty or so."

"Then, prythee, let us hear how he hath taught thee," quoth the Tinker.

At this Little John cleared his throat and, after a word or two about a certain hoarseness that troubled him, sang thus:

> *"Ah, pretty, pretty maid, whither dost thou go?*
> *I prythee, prythee, wait for thy lover also,*
> > *And we'll gather the rose*
> > *As it sweetly blows,*
> *For the merry, merry winds are blo-o-o-wing."*

Now it seemed as though Little John's songs were never to get sung, for he had got no farther than this when the door of the inn open and out came the two brothers of Fountain Abbey, the landlord following them, and, as the saying is, washing his hands with humble soap. But when the brothers of Fountain Abbey saw who it was that sang, and how he was clad in the robes of a Gray Friar, they stopped suddenly, the fat little Brother drawing his heavy eyebrows together in a mighty frown, and the thin Brother twisting up his face as though he had sour beer in his mouth. Then, as Little John gathered his breath for a

new verse, "How, now," roared forth the fat Brother, his voice coming from him like loud thunder from a little cloud, "thou naughty fellow, is this a fit place for one in thy garb to tipple and sing profane songs?"

"Nay," quoth Little John, "sin' I cannot tipple and sing, like Your Worship's reverence, in such a goodly place as Fountain Abbey, I must e'en tipple and sing where I can."

"Now, out upon thee," cried the tall lean Brother in a harsh voice, "now, out upon thee, that thou shouldst so disgrace thy cloth by this talk and bearing."

"Marry, come up!" quoth Little John. "Disgrace, sayest thou? Methinks it is more disgrace for one of our garb to wring hard-earned farthings out of the gripe of poor lean peasants. It is not so, brother?"

At this the Tinker and the Peddler and the Beggar nudged one another, and all grinned, and the friars scowled blackly at Little John; but they could think of nothing further to say, so they turned to their horses. Then Little John arose of a sudden from the bench where he sat, and ran to where the brothers of Fountain Abbey were mounting. Quoth he, "Let me hold your horses' bridles for you. Truly, your words have smitten my sinful heart, so that I will abide no longer in this den of evil, but will go forward with you. No vile temptation, I wot, will fall upon me in such holy company."

"Nay, fellow," said the lean Brother harshly, for he saw that Little John made sport of them, "we want none of thy company, so get thee gone."

"Alas," quoth Little John, "I am truly sorry that ye like me not nor my company, but as for leaving you, it may not be, for my heart is so moved, that, willy-nilly, I must go with you for the sake of your holy company."

Now, at this talk all the good fellows on the bench grinned till their teeth glistened, and even the landlord could not forbear to smile. As for the friars, they looked

at one another with a puzzled look, and knew not what to do in the matter. They were so proud that it made them feel sick with shame to think of riding along the highroad with a strolling friar, in robes all too short for him, running beside them, but yet they could not make Little John stay against his will, for they knew he could crack the bones of both of them in a twinkling were he so minded. Then up spake the fat Brother more mildly than he had done before. "Nay, good brother," said he, "we will ride fast, and thou wilt tire to death at the pace."

"Truly, I am grateful to thee for the thought of me," quoth Little John, "but have no fear, brother; my limbs are stout, and I could run like a hare from here to Gainsborough."

At these words a sound of laughing came from the bench, whereat the lean Brother's wrath boiled over, like water into the fire, with great fuss and noise. "Now, out upon thee, thou naughty fellow!" he cried. "Art thou not ashamed to bring disgrace so upon our cloth? Bide thee here, thou sot, with these porkers. Thou art no fit company for us."

"La, ye there now!" quoth Little John. "Thou hearest, landlord; thou art not fit company for these holy men; go back to thine alehouse. Nay, if these most holy brothers of mine do but give me the word, I'll beat thy head with this stout staff till it is as soft as whipped eggs."

At these words a great shout of laughter went up from those on the bench, and the landlord's face grew red as a cherry from smothering his laugh in his stomach; but he kept his merriment down, for he wished not to bring the ill-will of the brothers of Fountain Abbey upon him by unseemly mirth. So the two brethren, as they could do nought else, having mounted their nags, turned their noses toward Lincoln and rode away.

"I cannot stay longer, sweet friends," quoth Little John, as he pushed in betwixt the two cobs, "therefore I

wish you good den. Off we go, we three." So saying, he swung his stout staff over his shoulder and trudged off, measuring his pace with that of the two nags.

The two brothers glowered at Little John when he so pushed himself betwixt them, then they drew as far away from him as they could, so that the yeoman walked in the middle of the road, while they rode on the footpath on either side of the way. As they so went away, the Tinker, the Peddler, and the Beggar ran skipping out into the middle of the highway, each with a pot in his hand, and looked after them laughing.

While they were in sight of those at the inn, the brothers walked their horses soberly, not caring to make ill matters worse by seeming to run away from Little John, for they could not but think how it would sound in folks' ears when they heard how the brethren of Fountain Abbey scampered away from a strolling friar, like the Ugly One, when the blessed Saint Dunstan loosed his nose from the red-hot tongs where he had held it fast; but when they had crossed the crest of the hill and the inn was lost to sight, quoth the fat Brother to the thin Brother, "Brother Ambrose, had we not better mend our pace?"

"Why truly, gossip," spoke up Little John, "methinks it would be well to boil our pot a little faster, for the day is passing on. So it will not jolt thy fat too much, onward, say I."

At this the two friars said nothing, but they glared again on Little John with baleful looks; then, without another word, they clucked to their horses, and both broke into a canter. So they galloped for a mile and more, and Little John ran betwixt them as lightly as a stag and never turned a hair with the running. At last the fat Brother drew his horse's rein with a groan, for he could stand the shaking no longer. "Alas," said Little John, with not so much as a catch in his breath, "I did sadly fear that this pace would shake thy poor old fat paunch."

To this the fat Friar said never a word, but he stared straight before him, and he gnawed his nether lip. And now they traveled forward more quietly, Little John in the middle of the road whistling merrily to himself, and the two friars in the footpath on either side saying never a word.

Then presently they met three merry minstrels, all clad in red, who stared amain to see a Gray Friar with such short robes walking in the middle of the road, and two brothers, with heads bowed with shame, riding upon richly caparisoned cobs on the footpaths. When they had come near to the minstrels, Little John waved his staff like an usher clearing the way. "Make way!" he cried in a loud voice. "Make way! make way! For here we go, we three!" Then how the minstrels stared, and how they laughed! But the fat Friar shook as with an ague, and the lean Friar bowed his head over his horse's neck.

Then next they met two noble knights in rich array, with hawk on wrist, and likewise two fair ladies clad in silks and velvets, all a-riding on noble steeds. These all made room, staring, as Little John and the two friars came along the road. To them Little John bowed humbly. "Give you greetings, lords and ladies," said he. "But here we go, we three."

Then all laughed, and one of the fair ladies cried out, "what three meanest thou, merry friend?"

Little John looked over his shoulder, for they had now passed each other, and he called back, "Big Jack, lean Jack, and fat Jack-pudding."

At this the fat Friar gave a groan and seemed as if he were like to fall from his saddle for shame; the other brother said nothing, but he looked before him with a grim and stony look.

Just ahead of them the road took a sudden turn around a high hedge, and some twoscore paces beyond the bend another road crossed the one they were riding upon.

When they had come to the crossroad and were well away from those they had left, the lean Friar drew rein suddenly. "Look ye, fellow," quoth he in a voice quivering with rage, "we have had enough of thy vile company, and care no longer to be made sport of. Go thy way, and let us go ours in peace."

"La there, now!" quoth Little John. "Methought we were such a merry company, and here thou dost blaze up like fat in the pan. But truly, I ha' had enow of you today, though I can ill spare your company. I know ye will miss me, but gin ye want me again, whisper to Goodman Wind, and he will bring news thereof to me. But ye see I am a poor man and ye are rich. I pray you give me a penny or two to buy me bread and cheese at the next inn."

"We have no money, fellow," said the lean Friar harshly. "Come, Brother Thomas, let us forward."

But Little John caught the horses by the bridle reins, one in either hand. "Ha' ye in truth no money about you whatsoever?" said he. "Now, I pray you, brothers, for charity's sake, give me somewhat to buy a crust of bread, e'en though it be only a penny."

"I tell thee, fellow, we have no money," thundered the fat little Friar with the great voice.

"Ha' ye, in holy truth, no money?" asked Little John.

"Not a farthing," said the lean Friar sourly.

"Not a groat," said the fat Friar loudly.

"Nay," quoth Little John, "this must not be. Far be it from me to see such holy men as ye are depart from me with no money. Get both of you down straightway from off your horses, and we will kneel here in the middle of the crossroads and pray the blessed Saint Dunstan to send us some money to carry us on our journey."

"What sayest thou, thou limb of evil!" cried the lean Friar, fairly gnashing his teeth with rage. "Dost thou bid me, the high cellarer of Fountain Abbey, to get down

from my horse and kneel in the dirty road to pray to some beggarly Saxon saint?"

"Now," quoth Little John, "I ha' a great part of a mind to crack thy head for thee for speaking thus of the good Saint Dunstan! But get down straightway, for my patience will not last much longer, and I may forget that ye are both in holy orders." So saying, he twirled his stout staff till it whistled again.

At this speech both friars grew as pale as dough. Down slipped the fat Brother from off his horse on one side, and down slipped the lean Brother on the other.

"Now, brothers, down on your knees and pray," said Little John; thereupon, putting his heavy hands upon the shoulder of each, he forced them to their knees, he kneeling also. Then Little John began to beseech Saint Dunstan for money, which he did in a great loud voice. After he had so besought the Saint for a time, he bade the friars feel in their pouches and see if the Saint had sent them anything; so each put his hand slowly in the pouch that hung beside him, but brought nothing thence.

"Ha!" quoth Little John, "have your prayers so little virtue? Then let us at it again." Then straightway he began calling on Saint Dunstan again, somewhat in this wise: "O gracious Saint Dunstan! Send some money straightway to these poor folk, lest the fat one waste away and grow as lean as the lean one, and the lean one waste away to nothing at all, ere they get to Lincoln Town; but send them only ten shillings apiece, lest they grow puffed up with pride. Any more than that that thou sendest, send to me.

"Now," quoth he, rising, "let us see what each man hath." Then he thrust his hand into his pouch and drew thence four golden angels. "What have ye, brothers?" said he.

Then once again each friar slowly thrust his hand into

his pouch, and once again brought it out with nothing in it.

"Have ye nothing?" quoth Little John. "Nay, I warrant there is somewhat that hath crept into the seams of your pouches, and so ye ha' missed it. Let me look."

So he went first to the lean Friar, and, thrusting his hand into the pouch, he drew forth a leathern bag and counted therefrom one hundred and ten pounds of golden money. "I thought," quoth Little John, "that thou hadst missed, in some odd corner of thy pouch, the money that the blessed Saint had sent thee. And now let me see whether thou hast not some, also, brother."

Thereupon he thrust his hand into the pouch of the fat Friar and drew thence a bag like the other and counted out from it threescore and ten pounds. "Look ye now," quoth he, "I knew the good Saint had sent thee some pittance that thou, also, hadst missed."

Then, giving them one pound between them, he slipped the rest of the money into his own pouch, saying, "Ye pledged me your holy word that ye had no money. Being holy men, I trust that ye would not belie your word so pledged, therefore I know the good Saint Dunstan hath sent this in answer to my prayers. But as I only prayed for ten shillings to be sent to each of you, all over and above that belongeth by rights to me, and so I take it. I give you good den, brothers, and may ye have a pleasant journey henceforth." So saying, he turned and left them, striding away. The friars looked at one another with a woeful look, and slowly and sadly they mounted their horses again and rode away with never a word.

But Little John turned his footsteps back again to Sherwood Forest, and merrily he whistled as he strode along.

And now we will see what befell Robin Hood in his venture as beggar.

Robin Hood Turns Beggar

⟨A⟩FTER JOLLY ROBIN had left Little John at the forking of the roads, he walked merrily onward in the mellow sunshine that shone about him. Ever and anon he would skip and leap or sing a snatch of song, for pure joyousness of the day; for, because of the sweetness of the springtide, his heart was as lusty within him as that of a colt newly turned out to grass. Sometimes he would walk a long distance, gazing aloft at the great white swelling clouds that moved slowly across the deep blue sky; anon he would stop and drink in the fullness of life of all things, for the hedgerows were budding tenderly and the grass of the meadows was waxing long and green; again he would stand still and listen to the pretty song of the little birds in the thickets or hearken to the clear crow of the cock daring the sky to rain, whereat he would laugh, for it took but little to tickle Robin's heart into merriment. So he trudged manfully along, ever willing to stop for this reason or for that, and ever ready to chat with such merry lasses as he met now and then. So the morning slipped along, but yet he met no beggar with whom he could change clothes. Quoth he, "If I do not change my luck in haste, I am like to have an empty day of it, for it is well nigh half gone already, and, although I have had a merry walk through the countryside, I know nought of a beggar's life."

Then, after a while, he began to grow hungry, whereupon his mind turned from thoughts of springtime and

flowers and birds and dwelled upon boiled capons, Malmsey, white bread, and the like, with great tenderness. Quoth he to himself, "I would I had Willie Wynkin's wishing coat; I know right well what I should wish for, and this it should be." Here he marked upon the fingers of his left hand with the forefinger of his right hand those things which he wished for. "Firstly, I would have a sweet brown pie of tender larks; mark ye, not dry cooked, but with a good sop of gravy to moisten it withal. Next, I would have a pretty pullet, fairly boiled, with tender pigeons' eggs, cunningly sliced, garnishing the platter around. With these I would have a long, slim loaf of wheaten bread that hath been baked upon the hearth; it should be warm from the fire, with glossy brown crust, the color of the hair of mine own Maid Marian, and this same crust should be as crisp and brittle as the thin white ice that lies across the furrows in the early winter's morning. These will do for the more solid things; but with these I must have three pottles, fat and round, one full of Malmsey, one of Canary, and one brimming full of mine own dear lusty sack." Thus spoke Robin to himself, his mouth growing moist at the corners with the thoughts of the good things he had raised in his own mind.

So, talking to himself, he came to where the dusty road turned sharply around the hedge, all tender with the green of the coming leaf, and there he saw before him a stout fellow sitting upon a stile, swinging his legs in idleness. All about this lusty rogue dangled divers pouches and bags of different sizes and kinds, a dozen or more, with great, wide, gaping mouths, like a brood of hungry daws. His coat was gathered in at his waist, and was patched with as many colors as there are stripes upon a Maypole in the springtide. On his head he wore a great tall leathern cap, and across his knees rested a stout quarterstaff of blackthorn, full as long and heavy as Robin's. As jolly a beggar was he as ever trod the lanes and byways

of Nottinghamshire, for his eyes were as gray as slate, and snapped and twinkled and danced with merriment, and his black hair curled close all over his head in little rings of kinkiness.

"Halloa, good fellow," quoth Robin, when he had come nigh to the other, "what art thou doing here this merry day, when the flowers are peeping and the buds are swelling?"

Then the other winked one eye and straightway trolled forth in a merry voice:

> *"I sit upon the stile,*
> *And I sing a little while*
> *As I wait for my own true dear, O,*
> *For the sun is shining bright,*
> *And the leaves are dancing light,*
> *And the little fowl sings she is near, O.*

"And so it is with me, bully boy, saving that my doxy cometh not."

"Now that is a right sweet song," quoth Robin, "and, were I in the right mind to listen to thee, I could bear well to hear more; but I have two things of seriousness to ask of thee; so listen, I prythee."

At this the jolly Beggar cocked his head on one side, like a rogue of a magpie. Quoth he, "I am an ill jug to pour heavy things into, good friend, and, if I mistake not, thou hast few serious words to spare at any time."

"Nay," quoth jolly Robin, "what I would say first is the most serious of all thoughts to me, to wit, 'Where shall I get somewhat to eat and drink?'"

"Sayst thou so?" quoth the Beggar. "Marry, I make no such serious thoughts upon the matter. I eat when I can get it, and munch my crust when I can get no crumb; likewise, when there is no ale to be had I wash the dust from out my throat with a trickle of cold water. I was sitting here, as thou camest upon me, bethinking myself

whether I should break my fast or no. I do love to let my hunger grow mightily keen ere I eat, for then a dry crust is as good to me as a venison pasty with suet and raisins is to stout King Harry. I have a sharp hunger upon me now, but methinks in a short while it will ripen to a right mellow appetite."

"Now, in good sooth," quoth merry Robin, laughing, "thou hast a quaint tongue betwixt thy teeth. But hast thou truly nought but a dry crust about thee? Methinks thy bags and pouches are fat and lusty for such thin fare."

"Why, mayhap there is some other cold fare therein," said the Beggar slyly.

"And hast thou nought to drink but cold water?" said Robin.

"Never so much as a drop," quoth the Beggar. "Over beyond yon clump of trees is as sweet a little inn as ever thou hast lifted eyelid upon; but I go not thither, for they have a nasty way with me. Once, when the good Prior of Emmet was dining there, the landlady set a dear little tart of stewed crabs and barley sugar upon the window sill to cool, and, seeing it there, and fearing it might be lost, I took it with me till that I could find the owner thereof. Ever since then they have acted very ill toward me; yet truth bids me say that they have the best ale there that ever rolled over my tongue."

At this Robin laughed aloud. "Marry," quoth he, "they did ill toward thee for thy kindness. But tell me truly, what hast thou in thy pouches?"

"Why," quoth the Beggar, peeping into the mouths of his bags, "I find here a goodly piece of pigeon pie, warpped in a cabbage leaf to hold the gravy. Here I behold a dainty streaked piece of brawn, and here a fair lump of white bread. Here I find four oaten cakes and a cold knuckle of ham. Ha! In sooth, 'tis strange; but here I behold six eggs that must have come by accident

from some poultry yard hereabouts. They are raw, but roasted upon the coals and spread with a piece of butter that I see—"

"Peace, good friend!" cried Robin, holding up his hand. "Thou makest my poor stomach quake with joy for what thou tellest me so sweetly. If thou wilt give me to eat, I will straightway hie me to that little inn thou didst tell of but now, and will bring a skin of ale for thy drinking and mine."

"Friend, thou hast said enough," said the beggar, getting down from the stile. "I will feast thee with the best that I have and bless Saint Cedric for thy company. But, sweet chuck, I prythee bring three quarts of ale at least, one for thy drinking and two for mine, for my thirst is such that methinks I can drink ale as the sands of the River Dee drink salt water."

So Robin straightway left the Beggar, who, upon his part, went to a budding lime bush back of the hedge, and there spread his feast upon the grass and roasted his eggs upon a little fagot fire, with a deftness gained by long labor in that line. After a while back came Robin bearing a goodly skin of ale upon his shoulder, which he laid upon the grass. Then, looking upon the feast spread upon the ground—and a fair sight it was to look upon— he slowly rubbed his hand over his stomach, for to his hungry eyes it seemed the fairest sight that he had beheld in all his life.

"Friend," said the Beggar, "let me feel the weight of that skin."

"Yea, truly," quoth Robin, "help thyself, sweet chuck, and meantime let me see whether thy pigeon pie is fresh or no."

So the one seized upon the ale and the other upon the pigeon pie, and nothing was heard for a while but the munching of food and the gurgle of ale as it left the skin.

At last, after a long time had passed thus, Robin pushed the food from him and heaved a great sigh of deep content, for he felt as though he had been made all over.

"And now, good friend," quoth he, leaning upon one elbow, "I would have at thee about that other matter of seriousness of which I spoke not long since."

"How!" said the Beggar reproachfully, "thou wouldst surely not talk of things appertaining to serious affairs upon such ale as this!"

"Nay," quoth Robin, laughing. "I would not check thy thirst, sweet friend; drink while I talk to thee. Thus it is: I would have thee know that I have taken a liking to thy craft and would fain have a taste of a beggar's life mine own self."

Said the Beggar, "I marvel not that thou hast taken a liking to my manner of life, good fellow, but 'to like' and 'to do' are two matters of different sorts. I tell thee, friend, one must serve a long apprenticeship ere one can learn to be even so much as a clapper-dudgeon, much less a crank or an Abraham-man.* I tell thee, lad, thou art too old to enter upon that which it may take thee years to catch the hang of."

"Mayhap that may be so," quoth Robin, "for I bring to mind that Gaffer Swanthold sayeth Jack Shoemaker maketh ill bread; Tom Baker maketh ill shoon. Nevertheless, I have a mind to taste a beggar's life, and need but the clothing to be as good as any."

"I tell thee, fellow," said the Beggar, "if thou wert clad as sweetly as good Saint Wynten, the patron of our craft, thou wouldst never make a beggar. Marry, the first jolly traveler that thou wouldst meet would beat thee to a pudding for thrusting thy nose into a craft that belongeth not to thee."

* Classes of traveling mendicants that infested England as late as the middle of the seventeenth century. *Vide* Dakkar's *English Villainies,* etc.

"Nevertheless," quoth Robin, "I would have a try at it; and methinks I shall change clothes with thee, for thy garb seemeth to be pretty, not to say gay. So not only will I change clothes, but I will give thee two golden angels to boot. I have brought my stout staff with me, thinking that I might have to rap some one of the brethren of thy cloth over the head by way of argument in this matter, but I love thee so much for the feast thou hast given me that I would not lift even my little finger against thee, so thou needst not have a crumb of fear."

To this the Beggar listened with his knuckles resting against his hips, and when Robin had ended he cocked his head on one side and thrust his tongue into his cheek.

"Marry, come up," quoth he at last. "Lift thy finger against me, forsooth! Art thou out of thy wits, man? My name is Riccon Hazel, and I come from Holywell, in Flintshire, over by the River Dee. I tell thee, knave, I have cracked the head of many a better man than thou art, and even now I would scald thy crown for thee but for the ale thou hast given me. Now thou shalt not have so much as one tag-rag of my coat, even could it save thee from hanging."

"Now, fellow," said Robin, "it would ill suit me to spoil thy pretty head for thee, but I tell thee plainly, that but for this feast I would do that to thee would stop thy traveling the country for many a day to come. Keep thy lips shut, lad, or thy luck will tumble out of thy mouth with thy speech!"

"Now out, and alas for thee, man, for thou hast bred thyself ill this day!" cried the Beggar, rising and taking up his staff. "Take up thy club and defend thyself, fellow, for I will not only beat thee but I will take from thee thy money and leave thee not so much as a clipped groat to buy thyself a lump of goose grease to rub thy cracked crown withal. So defend thyself, I say."

Then up leaped merry Robin and snatched up his staff

also. "Take my money, if thou canst," quoth he. "I promise freely to give thee every farthing if thou dost touch me." And he twirled his staff in his fingers till it whistled again.

Then the Beggar swung his staff also, and struck a mighty blow at Robin, which the yeoman turned. Three blows the Beggar struck, yet never one touched so much as a hair of Robin's head. Then stout Robin saw his chance, and, ere you could count three, Riccon's staff was over the hedge, and Riccon himself lay upon the green grass with no more motion than you could find in an empty pudding bag.

"How now!" quoth merry Robin, laughing. "Wilt thou have my hide or my money, sweet chuck?" But to this the other answered never a word. Then Robin, seeing his plight, and that he was stunned with the blow, ran, still laughing, and brought the skin of ale and poured some of it on the Beggar's head and some down his throat, so that presently he opened his eyes and looked around as though wondering why he lay upon his back.

Then Robin, seeing that he had somewhat gathered the wits that had just been rapped out of his head, said, "Now, good fellow, wilt thou change clothes with me, or shall I have to tap thee again? Here are two golden angels if thou wilt give me freely all thy rags and bags and thy cap and things. If thou givest them not freely, I much fear me I shall have to—" and he looked up and down his staff.

Then Riccon sat up and rubbed the bump on his crown. "Now, out upon it!" quoth he. "I did think to drub thee sweetly, fellow. I know not how it is, but I seem, as it were, to have bought more beer than I can drink. If I must give up my clothes, I must, but first promise me, by thy word as a true yeoman, that thou wilt take nought from me but my clothes."

"I promise on the word of a true yeoman," quoth

Robin, thinking that the fellow had a few pennies that he would save.

Thereupon the Beggar drew a little knife that hung at his side and, ripping up the lining of his coat, drew thence ten bright golden pounds, which he laid upon the ground beside him with a cunning wink at Robin. "Now thou mayst have my clothes and welcome," said he, "and thou mightst have had them in exchange for thine without the cost of a single farthing, far less two golden angels."

"Marry," quoth Robin, laughing, "thou art a sly fellow, and I tell thee truly, had I known thou hadst so much money by thee maybe thou mightst not have carried it away, for I warrant thou didst not come honestly by it."

Then each stripped off his clothes and put on those of the other, and as lusty a beggar was Robin Hood as e'er you could find of a summer's day. But stout Riccon of Holywell skipped and leaped and danced for joy of the fair suit of Lincoln green that he had so gotten. Quoth he, "I am a gay-feathered bird now. Truly, my dear Moll Peascod would never know me in this dress. Thou mayst keep the cold pieces of the feast, friend, for I mean to live well and lustily while my money lasts and my clothes are gay."

So he turned and left Robin and, crossing the stile, was gone, but Robin heard him singing from beyond the hedge as he strode away:

> *"For Polly is smiling and Molly is glad*
> *When the beggar comes in at the door,*
> *And Jack and Dick call him a fine lusty lad,*
> *And the hostess runs up a great score.*
>
> *Then hey, Willy Waddykin,*
> *Stay, Billy Waddykin,*
> *And let the brown ale flow free, flow free,*
> *The beggar's the man for me."*

Robin listened till the song ended in the distance, then he also crossed the stile into the road, but turned his toes away from where the Beggar had gone. The road led up a gentle hill and up the hill Robin walked, a half score or more of bags dangling about his legs. Onward he strolled for a long time, but other adventure he found not. The road was bare of all else but himself, as he went kicking up little clouds of dust at each footstep; for it was noontide, the most peaceful time of all the day, next to twilight. All the earth was silent in the restfulness of eating time; the plowhorses stood in the furrow munching, with great bags over their noses holding sweet food, the plowman sat under the hedge and the plowboy also, and they, too, were munching, each one holding a great piece of bread in one fist and a great piece of cheese in the other.

So Robin, with all the empty road to himself, strode along whistling merrily, his bags and pouches bobbing and dangling at his thighs. At last he came to where a little grass-grown path left the road and, passing through a stile and down a hill, led into a little dell and on across a rill in the valley and up the hill on the other side, till it reached a windmill that stood on the cap of the rise where the wind bent the trees in swaying motion. Robin looked at the spot and liked it, and, for no reason but that his fancy led him, he took the little path and walked down the grassy sunny slope of the open meadow, and so came to the little dingle and, ere he knew it, upon four lusty fellows that sat with legs outstretched around a goodly feast spread upon the ground.

Four merry beggars were they, and each had slung about his neck a little board that rested upon his breast. One board had written upon it, "I am blind," another, "I am deaf," another, "I am dumb," and the fourth, "Pity the lame one." But although all these troubles written upon the boards seemed so grievous, the four stout fel-

lows sat around feasting as merrily as though Cain's wife had never opened the pottle that held misfortunes and let them forth like a cloud of flies to pester us.

The deaf man was the first to hear Robin, for he said, "Hark, brothers, I hear someone coming." And the blind man was the first to see him, for he said, "He is an honest man, brothers, and one of like craft to ourselves." Then the dumb man called to him in a great voice and said, "Welcome, brother; come and sit while there is still some of the feast left and a little Malmsey in the pottle." At this, the lame man, who had taken off his wooden leg and unstrapped his own leg, and was sitting with it stretched out upon the grass so as to rest it, made room for Robin among them. "We are glad to see thee, brother," said he, holding out the flask of Malmsey.

"Marry," quoth Robin, laughing, and weighing the flask in his hands ere he drank, "methinks it is no more than seemly of you all to be glad to see me, seeing that I bring sight to the blind, speech to the dumb, hearing to the deaf, and such a lusty leg to a lame man. I drink to your happiness, brothers, as I may not drink to your health, seeing ye are already hale, wind and limb."

At this all grinned, and the Blind beggar, who was the chief man among them, and was the broadest shouldered and most lusty rascal of all, smote Robin upon the shoulder, swearing he was a right merry wag.

"Whence comest thou, lad?" asked the Dumb man.

"Why," quoth Robin, "I came this morning from sleeping overnight in Sherwood."

"Is it even so?" said the Deaf man. "I would not for all the money we four are carrying to Lincoln Town sleep one night in Sherwood. If Robin Hood caught one of our trade in his woodlands he would, methinks, clip his ears."

"Methinks he would, too," quoth Robin, laughing. "But what money is this that ye speak of?"

Then up spake the Lame man. "Our king, Peter of York," said he, "hath sent us to Lincoln with those moneys that—"

"Stay, brother Hodge," quoth the Blind man, breaking into the talk, "I would not doubt our brother here, but bear in mind we know him not. What art thou, brother? Upright-man, Jurkman, Clapper-dudgeon, Dommerer, or Abraham-man?"

At these words Robin looked from one man to the other with mouth agape. "Truly," quoth he, "I trust I am an upright man, at least, I strive to be; but I know not what thou meanest by such jargon, brother. It were much more seemly, methinks, if yon Dumb man, who hath a sweet voice, would give us a song."

At these words a silence fell on all, and after a while the Blind man spoke again. Quoth he, "Thou dost surely jest when thou sayest that thou dost not understand such words. Answer me this: Hast thou ever fibbed a chouse quarrons in the Rome pad for the loure in his bung?" *

"Now out upon it," quoth Robin Hood testily, "an ye make sport of me by pattering such gibberish, it will be ill for you all, I tell you. I have the best part of a mind to crack the heads of all four of you, and would do so, too, but for the sweet Malmsey ye have given me. Brother, pass the pottle lest it grow cold."

But all the four beggars leaped to their feet when Robin had done speaking, and the Blind man snatched up a heavy knotted cudgel that lay beside him on the grass, as did the others likewise. Then Robin, seeing that things were like to go ill with him, albeit he knew not what all the coil was about, leaped to his feet also and, catching up his trusty staff, clapped his back against the tree and stood upon his guard against them. "How, now!" cried he, twirling his staff betwixt his fingers,

* *I.e.*, in old beggar's cant, "beaten a man or gallant upon the highway for the money in his purse." Dakkar's *English Villainies.*

"would you four stout fellows set upon one man? Stand back, ye rascals, or I will score your pates till they have as many marks upon them as a pothouse door! Are ye mad? I have done you no harm."

"Thou liest!" quoth the one who pretended to be blind and who, being the lustiest villain, was the leader of the others, "thou liest! For thou hast come among us as a vile spy. But thine ears have heard too much for thy body's good, and thou goest not forth from this place unless thou goest feet foremost, for this day thou shalt die! Come, brothers, all together! Down with him!" Then, whirling up his cudgel, he rushed upon Robin as an angry bull rushes upon a red rag. But Robin was ready for any happening. "Crick! Crack!" he struck two blows as quick as a wink, and down went the Blind man, rolling over and over upon the grass.

At this the others bore back and stood at a little distance scowling upon Robin. "Come on, ye scum!" cried he merrily. "Here be cakes and ale for all. Now, who will be next served?"

To this speech the beggars answered never a word, but they looked at Robin as great Blunderbore looked upon stout Jack the slayer of giants, as though they would fain eat him, body and bones; nevertheless, they did not care to come nigher to him and his terrible staff. Then, seeing them so hesitate, Robin of a sudden leaped upon them, striking even as he leaped. Down went the Dumb man, and away flew his cudgel from his hand as he fell. At this the others ducked to avoid another blow, then, taking to their heels, scampered, the one one way and the other the other, as though they had the west wind's boots upon their feet. Robin looked after them, laughing, and thought that never had he seen so fleet a runner as the Lame man; but neither of the beggars stopped nor turned around, for each felt in his mind the wind of Robin's cudgel about his ears.

Then Robin turned to the two stout knaves lying upon the ground. Quoth he, "These fellows spake somewhat about certain moneys they were taking to Lincoln; methinks I may find it upon this stout blind fellow, who hath as keen sight as e'er a trained woodsman in Nottingham or Yorkshire. It were a pity to let sound money stay in the pockets of such thieving knaves." So saying, he stooped over the burly rascal and searched among his rags and tatters, till presently his fingers felt a leathern pouch slung around his body beneath his patched and tattered coat. This he stripped away and, weighing it in his hands, bethought himself that it was mighty heavy. "It were a sweet thing," said he to himself, "if this were filled with gold instead of copper pence." Then, sitting down upon the grass, he opened the pocket and looked into it. There he found four round rolls wrapped up in dressed sheepskin; one of these rolls he opened; then his mouth gaped and his eyes stared, I wot, as though they would never close again, for what did he see but fifty pounds of bright golden money? He opened the other pockets and found in each one the same, fifty bright new-stamped golden pounds. Quoth Robin, "I have oft heard that the Beggars' Guild was over-rich, but never did I think that they sent such sums as this to their treasury. I shall take it with me, for it will be better used for charity and the good of my merry band than in the enriching of such knaves as these." So saying, he rolled up the money in the sheepskin again, and putting it back in the purse, he thrust the pouch into his own bosom. Then taking up the flask of Malmsey, he held it toward the two fellows lying on the grass, and quoth he, "Sweet friends, I drink your health and thank you dearly for what ye have so kindly given me this day, and so I wish you good den." Then, taking up his staff, he left the spot and went merrily on his way.

But when the two stout beggars that had been rapped

upon the head roused themselves and sat up, and when the others had gotten over their fright and come back, they were as sad and woebegone as four frogs in dry weather, for two of them had cracked crowns, their Malmsey was all gone, and they had not so much as a farthing to cross their palms withal.

But after Robin left the little dell he strode along merrily, singing as he went; and so blithe was he and such a stout beggar, and, withal, so fresh and clean, that every merry lass he met had a sweet word for him and felt no fear, while the very dogs, that most times hate the sight of a beggar, snuffed at his legs in friendly wise and wagged their tails pleasantly; for dogs know an honest man by his smell, and an honest man Robin was—in his own way.

Thus he went along till at last he had come to the wayside cross nigh Ollerton, and, being somewhat tired, he sat him down to rest upon the grassy bank in front of it. "It groweth nigh time," quoth he to himself, "that I were getting back again to Sherwood; yet it would please me well to have one more merry adventure ere I go back again to my jolly band." So he looked up the road and down the road to see who might come, until at last he saw someone drawing near, riding upon a horse. When the traveler came nigh enough for him to see him well, Robin laughed, for a strange enough figure he cut. He was a thin, wizened man, and, to look upon him, you could not tell whether he was thirty years old or sixty, so dried up was he even to skin and bone. As for the nag, it was as thin as the rider, and both looked as though they had been baked in Mother Huddle's Oven, where folk are dried up so that they live forever.

But although Robin laughed at the droll sight, he knew the wayfarer to be a certain rich corn engrosser of Worksop, who more than once had bought all the grain in the countryside and held it till it reached even famine prices, thus making much money from the needs of poor people,

and for this he was hated far and near by everyone that knew aught of him.

So, after a while, the Corn Engrosser came riding up to where Robin sat; whereupon merry Robin stepped straightway forth, in all his rags and tatters, his bags and pouches dangling about him, and laid his hand upon the horse's bridle rein, calling upon the other to stop.

"Who art thou, fellow, that doth dare to stop me thus upon the King's highway?" said the lean man, in a dry, sour voice.

"Pity a poor beggar," quoth Robin. "Give me but a farthing to buy me a piece of bread."

"Now, out upon thee!" snarled the other. "Such sturdy rogues as thou art are better safe in the prisons or dancing upon nothing, with a hempen collar about the neck, than strolling the highways so freely."

"Tut," quoth Robin, "how thou talkest! Thou and I are brothers, man. Do we not both take from the poor people that which they can ill spare? Do we not make our livings by doing nought of any good? Do we not both live without touching palm to honest work? Have we either of us ever rubbed thumbs over honestly gained farthings? Go to! We are brothers, I say; only thou art rich and I am poor; wherefore, I prythee once more, give me a penny."

"Dost thou prate so to me, sirrah?" cried the Corn Engrosser in a rage. "Now I will have thee soundly whipped if ever I catch thee in any town where the law can lay hold of thee! As for giving thee a penny, I swear to thee that I have not so much as a single groat in my purse. Were Robin Hood himself to take me, he might search me from crown to heel without finding the smallest piece of money upon me. I trust I am too sly to travel so nigh to Sherwood with money in my pouch, and that thief at large in the woods."

Then merry Robin looked up and down, as if to see

that there was no one nigh, and then, coming close to the Corn Engrosser, he stood on tiptoe and spake in his ear, "Thinkest thou in sooth that I am a beggar, as I seem to be? Look upon me. There is not a grain of dirt upon my hands or my face or my body. Didst thou ever see a beggar so? I tell thee I am as honest a man as thou art. Look, friend." Here he took the purse of money from his breast and showed to the dazzled eyes of the Corn Engrosser the bright golden pieces. "Friend, these rags serve but to hide an honest rich man from the eyes of Robin Hood."

"Put up thy money, lad," cried the other quickly. "Art thou a fool, to trust to beggar's rags to shield thee from Robin Hood? If he caught thee, he would strip thee to the skin, for he hates a lusty beggar as he doth a fat priest or those of my kind."

"Is it indeed so?" quoth Robin. "Had I known this, mayhap I had not come hereabouts in this garb. But I must go forward now, as much depends upon my journeying. Where goest thou, friend?"

"I go to Grantham," said the Corn Engrosser, "but I shall lodge tonight at Newark, if I can get so far upon my way."

"Why, I myself am on the way to Newark," quoth merry Robin, "so that, as two honest men are better than one in roads beset by such a fellow as this Robin Hood, I will jog along with thee, if thou hast no dislike to my company."

"Why, as thou art an honest fellow and a rich fellow," said the Corn Engrosser, "I mind not thy company; but, in sooth, I have no great fondness for beggars."

"Then forward," quoth Robin, "for the day wanes and it will be dark ere we reach Newark." So off they went, the lean horse hobbling along as before, and Robin running beside, albeit he was so quaking with laughter within him that he could hardly stand; yet he dared not laugh

aloud, lest the Corn Engrosser should suspect something. So they traveled along till they reached a hill just on the outskirts of Sherwood. Here the lean man checked his lean horse into a walk, for the road was steep, and he wished to save his nag's strength, having far to go ere he reached Newark. Then he turned in his saddle and spake to Robin again, for the first time since they had left the cross. "Here is thy greatest danger, friend," said he, "for here we are nighest to that vile thief Robin Hood, and the place where he dwells. Beyond this we come again to the open honest country, and so are more safe in our journeying."

"Alas!" quoth Robin, "I would that I had as little money by me as thou hast, for this day I fear that Robin Hood will get every groat of my wealth."

Then the other looked at Robin and winked cunningly. Quoth he, "I tell thee, friend, that I have nigh as much by me as thou hast, but it is hidden so that never a knave in Sherwood could find it."

"Thou dost surely jest," quoth Robin. "How could one hide so much as two hundred pounds upon his person?"

"Now, as thou art so honest a fellow, and, withal, so much younger than I am, I will tell thee that which I have told to no man in all the world before, and thus thou mayst learn never again to do such a foolish thing as to trust to beggar's garb to guard thee against Robin Hood. Seest thou these clogs upon my feet?"

"Yea," quoth Robin, laughing, "truly, they are large enough for any man to see, even were his sight as foggy as that of Peter Patter, who never could see when it was time to go to work."

"Peace, friend," said the Corn Engrosser, "for this is no matter for jesting. The soles of these clogs are not what they seem to be, for each one is a sweet little box; and by twisting the second nail from the toe, the upper of

the shoe and part of the sole lifts up like a lid, and in the spaces within are fourscore and ten bright golden pounds in each shoe, all wrapped in hair, to keep them from clinking and so telling tales of themselves."

When the Corn Engrosser had told this, Robin broke into a roar of laughter and, laying his hands upon the bridle rein, stopped the sad-looking nag. "Stay, good friend," quoth he, between bursts of merriment, "thou art the slyest old fox that e'er I saw in all my life!—In the soles of his shoon, quotha!—If ever I trust a poor-seeming man again, shave my head and paint it blue! A corn factor, a horse jockey, an estate agent, and a jackdaw for cunningness, say I!" And he laughed again till he shook in his shoes with mirth.

All this time the Corn Engrosser had been staring at Robin, his mouth agape with wonder. "Art thou mad," quoth he, "to talk in this way, so loud and in such a place? Let us forward, and save thy mirth till we are safe and sound at Newark."

"Nay," quoth Robin, the tears of merriment wet on his cheeks, "on second thoughts I go no farther than here, for I have good friends hereabouts. Thou mayst go forward if thou dost list, thou sweet pretty fellow, but thou must go forward barefoot, for I am afraid that thy shoon must be left behind. Off with them, friend, for I tell thee I have taken a great fancy to them."

At these words the corn factor grew pale as a linen napkin. "Who art thou that talkest so?" said he.

Then merry Robin laughed again, and quoth he, "Men hereabouts call me Robin Hood; so, sweet friend, thou hadst best do my bidding and give me thy shoes, wherefore hasten, I prythee, or else thou wilt not get to fair Newark Town till after dark."

At the sound of the name of Robin Hood, the corn factor quaked with fear, so that he had to seize his horse by the mane to save himself from falling off its back.

Then straightway, and without more words, he stripped off his clogs and let them fall upon the road. Robin, still holding the bridle rein, stooped and picked them up. Then he said, "Sweet friend, I am used to ask those that I have dealings with to come and feast at Sherwood with me. I will not ask thee, because of our pleasant journey together; for I tell thee there be those in Sherwood that would not be so gentle with thee as I have been. The name of Corn Engrosser leaves a nasty taste upon the tongue of all honest men. Take a fool's advice of me and come no more so nigh to Sherwood, or mayhap some day thou mayst of a sudden find a clothyard shaft betwixt thy ribs. So, with this, I give thee good den." Hereupon he clapped his hand to the horse's flank and off went nag and rider. But the man's face was all bedewed with the sweat of fright, and never again, I wot, was he found so close to Sherwood Forest as he had been this day.

Robin stood and looked after him, and, when he was fairly gone, turned, laughing, and entered the forest carrying the shoes in his hand.

That night in sweet Sherwood the red fires glowed brightly in wavering light on tree and bush, and all around sat or lay the stout fellows of the band to hear Robin Hood and Little John tell their adventures. All listened closely, and again and again the woods rang with shouts of laughter.

When all was told, Friar Tuck spoke up. "Good master," said he, "thou hast had a pretty time, but still I hold to my saying, that the life of the barefoot friar is the merrier of the two."

"Nay," quoth Will Stutely, "I hold with our master, that he hath had the pleasanter doings of the two, for he hath had two stout bouts at quarterstaff this day."

So some of the band held with Robin Hood and some with Little John. As for me, I think—But I leave it with you to say for yourselves which you hold with.

Robin Hood Shoots Before Queen Eleanor

THE HIGHROAD stretched white and dusty in the hot summer afternoon sun, and the trees stood motionless along the roadside. All across the meadow lands the hot air danced and quivered, and in the limpid waters of the lowland brook, spanned by a little stone bridge, the fish hung motionless above the yellow gravel, and the dragonfly sat quite still, perched upon the sharp tip of a spike of the rushes, with its wings glistening in the sun.

Along the road a youth came riding upon a fair milk-white barb, and the folk that he passed stopped and turned and looked after him, for never had so lovely a lad or one so gaily clad been seen in Nottingham before. He could not have been more than sixteen years of age, and was as fair as any maiden. His long yellow hair flowed behind him as he rode along, all clad in silk and velvet, with jewels flashing and dagger jingling against the pommel of the saddle. Thus came the Queen's Page, young Richard Partington, from famous London Town down into Nottinghamshire, upon Her Majesty's bidding, to seek Robin Hood in Sherwood Forest.

The road was hot and dusty and his journey had been

long, for that day he had come all the way from Leicester Town, a good twenty miles and more; wherefore young Partington was right glad when he saw before him a sweet little inn, all shady and cool beneath the trees, in front of the door of which a sign hung pendant, bearing the picture of a blue boar. Here he drew rein and called loudly for a pottle of Rhenish wine to be brought him, for stout country ale was too coarse a drink for this young gentleman. Five lusty fellows sat upon the bench beneath the pleasant shade of the wide-spreading oak in front of the inn door, drinking ale and beer, and all stared amain at this fair and gallant lad. Two of the stoutest of them were clothed in Lincoln green, and a great heavy oaken staff leaned against the gnarled oak tree trunk beside each fellow.

The landlord came and brought a pottle of wine and a long narrow glass upon a salver, which he held up to the Page as he sat upon his horse. Young Partington poured forth the bright yellow wine and holding the glass aloft, cried, "Here is to the health and long happiness of my royal mistress, the noble Queen Eleanor; and may my journey and her desirings soon have end, and I find a certain stout yeoman men call Robin Hood."

At these words all stared, but presently the two stout yeomen in Lincoln green began whispering together. Then one of the two, whom Partington thought to be the tallest and stoutest fellow he had ever beheld, spoke up and said, "What seekest thou of Robin Hood, Sir Page? And what does our good Queen Eleanor wish of him? I ask this of thee, not foolishly, but with reason, for I know somewhat of this stout yeoman."

"An thou knowest aught of him, good fellow," said young Partington, "thou wilt do great service to him and great pleasure to our royal Queen by aiding me to find him."

Then up spake the other yeoman, who was a handsome

fellow with sunburned face and nut-brown, curling hair, "Thou hast an honest look, Sir Page, and our Queen is kind and true to all stout yeomen. Methinks I and my friend here might safely guide thee to Robin Hood, for we know where he may be found. Yet I tell thee plainly, we would not for all merry England have aught of harm befall him."

"Set thy mind at ease; I bring nought of ill with me," quoth Richard Partington. "I bring a kind message to him from our Queen, therefore an ye know where he is to be found, I pray you to guide me thither."

Then the two yeomen looked at one another again, and the tall man said, "Surely it were safe to do this thing, Will"; whereat the other nodded. Thereupon both arose, and the tall yeoman said, "We think thou art true, Sir Page, and meanest no harm, therefore we will guide thee to Robin Hood as thou dost wish."

Then Partington paid his score, and the yeomen coming forward, they all straightway departed upon their way.

Under the greenwood tree, in the cool shade that spread all around upon the sward, with flickering lights here and there, Robin Hood and many of his band lay upon the soft green grass, while Allan a Dale sang and played upon his sweetly sounding harp. All listened in silence, for young Allan's singing was one of the greatest joys in all the world to them; but as they so listened there came of a sudden the sound of a horse's feet, and presently Little John and Will Stutely came forth from the forest path into the open glade, young Richard Partington riding between them upon his milk-white horse. The three came toward where Robin Hood sat, all the band staring with might and main, for never had they seen so gay a sight as this young Page, nor one so richly clad in silks and velvets and gold and jewels. Then Robin arose

and stepped forth to meet him, and Partington leaped from his horse and doffing his cap of crimson velvet, met Robin as he came.

"Now, welcome!" cried Robin. "Now, welcome, fair youth, and tell me, I prythee, what bringeth one of so fair a presence and clad in such noble garb to our poor forest of Sherwood?"

Then young Partington said, "If I err not, thou art the famous Robin Hood, and these thy stout band of outlawed yeomen. To thee I bring greetings from our noble Queen Eleanor. Oft hath she heard thee spoken of and thy merry doings hereabouts, and fain would she behold thy face; therefore she bids me tell thee that if thou wilt presently come to London Town, she will do all in her power to guard thee against harm, and will send thee back safe to Sherwood Forest again. Four days hence, in Finsbury Fields, our good King Henry, of great renown, holdeth a grand shooting match, and all the most famous archers of merry England will be thereat. Our Queen would fain see thee strive with these, knowing that if thou wilt come thou wilt, with little doubt, carry off the prize. Therefore she hath sent me with this greeting, and furthermore sends thee, as a sign of great good will, this golden ring from off her own fair thumb, which I give herewith into thy hands."

Then Robin Hood bowed his head and taking the ring, kissed it right loyally, and then slipped it upon his little finger. Quoth he, "Sooner would I lose my life than this ring; and ere it departs from me, my hand shall be cold in death or stricken off at the wrist. Fair Sir Page, I will do our Queen's bidding, and will presently hie with thee to London; but, ere we go, I will feast thee here in the woodlands with the very best we have."

"It may not be," said the Page; "we have no time to tarry, therefore get thyself ready straightway; and if there be any of thy band that thou wouldst take with

thee, our Queen bids me say that she will make them right welcome likewise."

"Truly, thou art right," quoth Robin, "and we have but short time to stay; therefore I will get me ready presently. I will choose three of my men, only, to go with me, and these three shall be Little John, mine own true right-hand man, Will Scarlet, my cousin, and Allan a Dale, my minstrel. Go, lads, and get ye ready straightway, and we will presently off with all speed that we may. Thou, Will Stutely, shall be the chief of the band while I am gone."

Then Little John and Will Scarlet and Allan a Dale ran leaping, full of joy, to make themselves ready, while Robin also prepared himself for the journey. After a while they all four came forth, and a right fair sight they made, for Robin was clad in blue from head to foot, and Little John and Will Scarlet in good Lincoln green, and as for Allan a Dale, he was dressed in scarlet from the crown of his head to the toes of his pointed shoes. Each man wore beneath his cap a little head covering of burnished steel set with rivets of gold, and underneath his jerkin a coat of linked mail, as fine as carded wool, yet so tough that no arrow could pierce it. Then, seeing all were ready, young Partington mounted his horse again, and the yeomen having shaken hands all around, the five departed upon their way.

That night they took up their inn in Melton Mowbray, in Leicestershire, and the next night they lodged at Kettering, in Northamptonshire; and the next at Bedford Town; and the next at St. Albans, in Hertfordshire. This place they left not long after the middle of the night, and traveling fast through the tender dawning of the summer day, when the dews lay shining on the meadows and faint mists hung in the dales, when the birds sang their sweetest and the cobwebs beneath the hedges glimmered like fairy cloth of silver, they came at last to the towers and walls of

famous London Town, while the morn was still young and all golden toward the east.

Queen Eleanor sat in her royal bower, through the open casements of which poured the sweet yellow sunshine in great floods of golden light. All about her stood her ladies-in-waiting chatting in low voices, while she herself sat dreamily where the mild air came softly drifting into the room laden with the fresh perfumes of the sweet red roses that bloomed in the great garden beneath the wall. To her came one who said that her page, Richard Partington, and four stout yeomen waited her pleasure in the court below. Then Queen Eleanor arose joyously and bade them be straightway shown into her presence.

Thus Robin Hood and Little John and Will Scarlet and Allan a Dale came before the Queen into her own royal bower. Then Robin kneeled before the Queen with his hands folded upon his breast, saying in simple phrase, "Here am I, Robin Hood. Thou didst bid me come, and lo, I do thy bidding. I give myself to thee as thy true servant, and will do thy commanding, even if it be to the shedding of the last drop of my life's blood."

But good Queen Eleanor smiled pleasantly upon him, bidding him to arise. Then she made them all be seated to rest themselves after their long journey. Rich food was brought them and noble wines, and she had her own pages to wait upon the wants of the yeomen. At last, after they had eaten all they could, she began questioning them of their merry adventures. Then they told her all of the lusty doings herein spoken of, and among others that concerning the Bishop of Hereford and Sir Richard of the Lea, and how the Bishop had abided three days in Sherwood Forest. At this, the Queen and the ladies about her laughed again and again, for they pictured to themselves the stout Bishop abiding in the forest and

ranging the woods in lusty sport with Robin and his band. Then, when they had told all that they could bring to mind, the Queen asked Allan to sing to her, for his fame as a minstrel had reached even to the court at London Town. So straightway Allan took up his harp in his hand, and, without more asking, touched the strings lightly till they all rang sweetly, then he sang thus:

> "Gentle river, gentle river,
>   Bright thy crystal waters flow,
> Sliding where the aspens shiver,
>   Gliding where the lilies blow,

> "Singing over pebbled shallows,
>   Kissing blossoms bending low,
> Breaking 'neath the dipping swallows,
>   Purpling where the breezes blow.

> "Floating on thy breast forever
>   Down thy current I could glide;
> Grief and pain should reach me never
>   On thy bright and gentle tide.

> "So my aching heart seeks thine, love,
>   There to find its rest and peace,
> For, through loving, bliss is mine, love,
>   And my many troubles cease."

Thus Allan sang, and as he sang all eyes dwelled upon him and not a sound broke the stillness, and even after he had done the silence hung for a short space. So the time passed till the hour drew nigh for the holding of the great archery match in Finsbury Fields.

A gay sight were famous Finsbury Fields on that bright and sunny morning of lusty summertime. Along the end of the meadow stood the booths for the different bands of archers, for the King's yeomen were divided into companies of fourscore men, and each company had a captain

over it; so on the bright greensward stood ten booths of striped canvas, a booth for each band of the royal archers, and at the peak of each fluttered a flag in the mellow air, and the flag was the color that belonged to the captain of each band. From the center booth hung the yellow flag of Tepus, the famous bow bearer of the King; next to it, on one hand, was the blue flag of Gilbert of the White Hand, and on the other the blood-red pennant of stout young Clifton of Buckinghamshire. The seven other archer captains were also men of great renown; among them were Egbert of Kent and William of Southampton; but those first named were most famous of all. The noise of many voices in talk and laughter came from within the booths, and in and out ran the attendants like ants about an ant-hill. Some bore ale and beer, and some bundles of bowstrings or sheaves of arrows. On each side of the archery range were rows upon rows of seats reaching high aloft, and in the center of the north side was a raised dais for the King and Queen, shaded by canvas of gay colors, and hung about with streaming silken pennants of red and blue and green and white. As yet the King and Queen had not come, but all the other benches were full of people, rising head above head high aloft till it made the eye dizzy to look upon them. Eightscore yards distant from the mark from which the archers were to shoot stood ten fair targets, each target marked by a flag of the color belonging to the band that was to shoot thereat. So all was ready for the coming of the King and Queen.

At last a great blast of bugles sounded, and into the meadow came riding six trumpeters with silver trumpets, from which hung velvet banners heavy with rich workings of silver and gold thread. Behind these came stout King Henry upon a dapple-gray stallion, with his Queen beside him upon a milk-white palfrey. On either side of them walked the yeomen of the guard, the bright sunlight flashing from the polished blades of the steel halberds they

carried. Behind these came the Court in a great crowd, so that presently all the lawn was alive with bright colors, with silk and velvet, with waving plumes and gleaming gold, with flashing jewels and sword hilts; a gallant sight on that bright summer day.

Then all the people arose and shouted, so that their voices sounded like the storm upon the Cornish coast, when the dark waves run upon the shore and leap and break, surging amid the rocks; so, amid the roaring and the surging of the people, and the waving of scarfs and kerchiefs, the King and Queen came to their place, and, getting down from their horses, mounted the broad stairs that led to the raised platform, and there took their seats on two thrones bedecked with purple silks and cloths of silver and of gold.

When all was quiet a bugle sounded, and straightway the archers came marching in order from their tents. Fortyscore they were in all, as stalwart a band of yeomen as could be found in all the wide world. So they came in orderly fashion and stood in front of the dais where King Henry and his Queen sat. King Henry looked up and down their ranks right proudly, for his heart warmed within him at the sight of such a gallant band of yeomen. Then he bade his herald Sir Hugh de Mowbray stand forth and proclaim the rules governing the game. So Sir Hugh stepped to the edge of the platform and spoke in a loud clear voice, and thus he said:

That each man should shoot seven arrows at the target that belonged to his band, and, of the fourscore yeomen of each band, the three that shot the best should be chosen. These three should shoot three arrows apiece, and the one that shot the best should again be chosen. Then each of these should again shoot three arrows apiece, and the one that shot the best should have the first prize, the one that shot the next best should have the second, and the one that shot the next best should have

the third prize. Each of the others should have fourscore silver pennies for his shooting. The first prize was to be twoscore and ten golden pounds, a silver bugle horn inlaid with gold, and a quiver with ten white arrows tipped with gold and feathered with the white swan's-wing therein. The second prize was to be fivescore of the fattest bucks that run on Dallen Lea, to be shot when the yeoman that won them chose. The third prize was to be two turns of good Rhenish wine.

So Sir Hugh spoke, and when he had done all the archers waved their bows aloft and shouted. Then each band turned and marched in order back to its place.

And now the shooting began, the captains first taking stand and speeding their shafts and then making room for the men who shot, each in turn, after them. Two hundred and eightyscore shafts were shot in all, and so deftly were they sped that when the shooting was done each target looked like the back of a hedgehog when the farm dog snuffs at it. A long time was taken in this shooting, and when it was over the judges came forward, looked carefully at the targets, and proclaimed in a loud voice which three had shot the best from the separate bands. Then a great hubbub of voices arose, each man among the crowd that looked on calling for his favorite archer. Then ten fresh targets were brought forward, and every sound was hushed as the archers took their places once more.

This time the shooting was more speedily done, for only nine shafts were shot by each band. Not an arrow missed the targets, but in that of Gilbert of the White Hand five arrows were in the small white spot that marked the center; of these five three were sped by Gilbert. Then the judges came forward again, and looking at the targets, called aloud the names of the archer chosen as the best bowman of each band. Of these Gilbert of the White Hand led, for six of the ten arrows he had shot had lodged

in the center; but stout Tepus and young Clifton trod close upon his heels; yet the others stood a fair chance for the second or third place.

And now, amid the roaring of the crowd, those ten stout fellows that were left went back to their tents to rest for a while and change their bowstrings, for nought must fail at this next round, and no hand must tremble or eye grow dim because of weariness.

Then while the deep buzz and hum of talking sounded all around like the noise of the wind in the leafy forest, Queen Eleanor turned to the King, and quoth she, "Thinkest thou that these yeomen so chosen are the very best archers in all merry England?"

"Yea, truly," said the King, smiling, for he was well pleased with the sport that he had seen; "and I tell thee, that not only are they the best archers in all merry England, but in all the wide world beside."

"But what wouldst thou say," quoth Queen Eleanor, "if I were to find three archers to match the best three yeomen of all thy guard?"

"I would say thou hast done what I could not do," said the King, laughing, "for I tell thee there lives not in all the world three archers to match Tepus and Gilbert and Clifton of Buckinghamshire."

"Now," said the Queen, "I know of three yeomen, and in truth I have seen them not long since, that I would not fear to match against any three that thou canst choose from among all thy fortyscore archers; and, moreover, I will match them here this very day. But I will only match them with thy archers providing that thou wilt grant a free pardon to all that may come in my behalf."

At this, the King laughed loud and long. "Truly," said he, "thou art taking up with strange matters for a queen. If thou wilt bring those three fellows that thou speakest of, I will promise faithfully to give them free pardon for forty days, to come or to go wheresoever they

please, nor will I harm a hair of their heads in all that time. Moreover, if these that thou bringest shoot better than my yeomen, man for man, they shall have the prizes for themselves according to their shooting. But as thou hast so taken up of a sudden with sports of this kind, hast thou a mind for a wager?"

"Why, in sooth," said Queen Eleanor, laughing, "I know nought of such matters, but if thou hast a mind to do somewhat in that way, I will strive to pleasure thee. What wilt thou wager upon thy men?"

Then the merry King laughed again, for he dearly loved a goodly jest; so he said, amidst his laughter, "I will wager thee ten tuns of Rhenish wine, ten tuns of the stoutest ale, and tenscore bows of tempered Spanish yew, with quivers and arrows to match."

All that stood around smiled at this, for it seemed a merry wager for a king to give to a queen; but Queen Eleanor bowed her head quietly. "I will take thy wager," said she, "for I know right well where to place those things that thou hast spoken of. Now, who will be on my side in this matter?" And she looked around upon them that stood about; but no one spake or cared to wager upon the Queen's side against such archers as Tepus and Gilbert and Clifton. Then the Queen spoke again, "Now, who will back me in this wager? Wilt thou, my Lord Bishop of Hereford?"

"Nay," quoth the Bishop hastily, "it ill befits one of my cloth to deal in such matters. Moreover, there are no such archers as His Majesty's in all the world; therefore I would but lose my money."

"Methinks the thought of thy gold weigheth more heavily with thee than the wrong to thy cloth," said the Queen, smiling, and at this a ripple of laughter went around, for everyone knew how fond the Bishop was of his money. Then the Queen turned to a knight who stood near, whose name was Sir Robert Lee. "Wilt

thou back me in this manner?" said she. "Thou art surely rich enough to risk so much for the sake of a lady."

"To pleasure my Queen I will do it," said Sir Robert Lee, "but for the sake of no other in all the world would I wager a groat, for no man can stand against Tepus and Gilbert and Clifton."

Then turning to the King, Queen Eleanor said, "I want no such aid as Sir Robert giveth me; but against thy wine and beer and stout bows of yew I wager this girdle all set with jewels from around my waist; and surely that is worth more than thine."

"Now, I take thy wager," quoth the King. "Send for thy archers straightway. But here come forth the others; let them shoot, and then I will match those that win against all the world."

"So be it," said the Queen. Thereupon, beckoning to young Richard Partington, she whispered something in his ear, and straightway the Page bowed and left the place, crossing the meadow to the other side of the range, where he was presently lost in the crowd. At this, all that stood around whispered to one another, wondering what it all meant, and what three men the Queen was about to set against those famous archers of the King's guard.

And now the ten archers of the King's guard took their stand again, and all the great crowd was hushed to the stillness of death. Slowly and carefully each man shot his shafts, and so deep was the silence that you could hear every arrow rap against the target as it struck it. Then, when the last shaft had sped, a great roar went up; and the shooting, I wot, was well worthy of the sound. Once again Gilbert had lodged three arrows in the white; Tepus came second with two in the white and one in the black ring next to it; but stout Clifton had gone down and Hubert of Suffolk had taken the third place, for, while

both those two good yeomen had lodged two in the white, Clifton had lost one shot upon the fourth ring, and Hubert came in with one in the third.

All the archers around Gilbert's booth shouted for joy till their throats were hoarse, tossing their caps aloft, and shaking hands with one another.

In the midst of all the noise and hubbub five men came walking across the lawn toward the King's pavilion. The first was Richard Partington, and was known to most folk there, but the others were strange to everybody. Beside young Partington walked a yeoman clad in blue, and behind came three others, two in Lincoln green and one in Scarlet. This last yeoman carried three stout bows of yew tree, two fancifully inlaid with silver and one with gold. While these five men came walking across the meadow, a messenger came running from the King's booth and summoned Gilbert and Tepus and Hubert to go with him. And now the shouting quickly ceased, for all saw that something unwonted was toward, so the folk stood up in their places and leaned forward to see what was the ado.

When Partington and the others came before the spot where the King and Queen sat, the four yeomen bent their knees and doffed their caps unto her. King Henry leaned far forward and stared at them closely, but the Bishop of Hereford, when he saw their faces, started as though stung by a wasp. He opened his mouth as though about to speak, but, looking up, he saw the Queen gazing at him with a smile upon her lips, so he said nothing, but bit his nether lip, while his face was as red as a cherry.

Then the Queen leaned forward and spake in a clear voice. "Locksley," said she, "I have made a wager with the King that thou and two of thy men can outshoot any three that he can send against you. Wilt thou do thy best for my sake?"

"Yea," quoth Robin Hood, to whom she spake, "I will do my best for thy sake, and, if I fail, I make my vow never to finger bowstring more."

Now, although Little John had been somewhat abashed in the Queen's bower, he felt himself the sturdy fellow he was when the soles of his feet pressed green grass again; so he said boldly, "Now, blessings on thy sweet face, say I. An there lived a man that would not do his best for thee—I will say nought, only I would like to have the cracking of his knave's pate!"

"Peace, Little John!" said Robin Hood hastily, in a low voice; but good Queen Eleanor laughed aloud, and a ripple of merriment sounded all over the booth.

The Bishop of Hereford did not laugh, neither did the King, but he turned to the Queen, and quoth he, "Who are these men that thou hast brought before us?"

Then up spoke the Bishop hastily, for he could hold his peace no longer: "Your Majesty," quoth he, "yon fellow in blue is a certain outlawed thief of the mid-country, named Robin Hood; yon tall, strapping villain goeth by the name of Little John; the other fellow in green is a certain backsliding gentleman, known as Will Scarlet; the man in red is a rogue of a northern minstrel, named Allan a Dale."

At this speech the King's brows drew together blackly, and he turned to the Queen. "Is this true?" said he sternly.

"Yea," said the Queen, smiling, "the Bishop hath told the truth; and truly he should know them well, for he and two of his friars spent three days in merry sport with Robin Hood in Sherwood Forest. I did little think that the good Bishop would so betray his friends. But bear in mind that thou hast pledged thy promise for the safety of these good yeomen for forty days."

"I will keep my promise," said the King, in a deep voice that showed the anger in his heart, "but when these forty

days are gone let this outlaw look to himself, for mayhap things will not go so smoothly with him as he would like." Then he turned to his archers, who stood near the Sherwood yeomen, listening and wondering at all that passed. Quoth he, "Gilbert, and thou, Tepus, and thou, Hubert, I have pledged myself that ye shall shoot against these three fellows. If ye outshoot the knaves I will fill your caps with silver pennies; if ye fail ye shall lose your prizes that ye have won so fairly, and they go to them that shoot against you, man to man. Do your best, lads, and if ye win this bout ye shall be glad of it to the last days of your life. Go, now, and get you gone to the butts."

Then the three archers of the King turned and went back to their booths, and Robin and his men went to their places at the mark from which they were to shoot. Then they strung their bows and made themselves ready, looking over their quivers of arrows, and picking out the roundest and the best feathered.

But when the King's archers went to their tents, they told their friends all that had passed, and how that these four men were the famous Robin Hood and three of his band, to wit, Little John, Will Scarlet, and Allan a Dale. The news of this buzzed around among the archers in the booths, for there was not a man there that had not heard of these great mid-country yeomen. From the archers the news was taken up by the crowd that looked on at the shooting, so that at last everybody stood up, craning their necks to catch sight of the famous outlaws.

Six fresh targets were now set up, one for each man that was to shoot; whereupon Gilbert and Tepus and Hubert came straightway forth from the booths. Then Robin Hood and Gilbert of the White Hand tossed a farthing aloft to see who should lead in the shooting, and the lot fell to Gilbert's side; thereupon he called upon Hubert of Suffolk to lead.

Hubert took his place, planted his foot firmly, and

fitted a fair, smooth arrow; then, breathing upon his fingertips, he drew the string slowly and carefully. The arrow sped true, and lodged in the white; again he shot, and again he hit the clout; a third shaft he sped, but this time failed of the center, and but struck the black, yet not more than a finger's-breadth from the white. At this a shout went up, for it was the best shooting that Hubert had yet done that day.

Merry Robin laughed, and quoth he, "Thou wilt have an ill time bettering that round, Will, for it is thy turn next. Brace thy thews, lad, and bring not shame upon Sherwood."

Then Will Scarlet took his place; but, because of over-caution, he spoiled his target with the very first arrow that he sped, for he hit the next ring to the black, the second from the center. At this Robin bit his lips. "Lad, lad," quoth he, "hold not the string so long! Have I not often told thee what Gaffer Swanthold sayeth, that 'overcaution spilleth the milk'?" To this Will Scarlet took heed, so the next arrow he shot lodged fairly in the center ring; again he shot, and again he smote the center; but, for all that, stout Hubert had outshot him, and showed the better target. Then all those that looked on clapped their hands for joy because that Hubert had overcome the stranger.

Quoth the King grimly, to the Queen, "If thy archers shoot no better than that, thou art like to lose thy wager, lady." But Queen Eleanor smiled, for she looked for better things from Robin Hood and Little John.

And now Tepus took his place to shoot. He, also, took overheed to what he was about, and so he fell into Will Scarlet's error. The first arrow he struck into the center ring, but the second missed its mark, and smote the black; the last arrow was tipped with luck, for it smote the very center of the clout, upon the black spot that marked it. Quoth Robin Hood, "That is the sweetest shot that hath been sped this day; but, nevertheless, friend Tepus,

thy cake is burned, methinks. Little John, it is thy turn next."

So Little John took his place as bidden, and shot his three arrows quickly. He never lowered his bow arm in all the shooting, but fitted each shaft with his longbow raised; yet all three of his arrows smote the center within easy distance of the black. At this no sound of shouting was heard, for, although it was the best shooting that had been done that day, the folk of London Town did not like to see the stout Tepus overcome by a fellow from the countryside, even were he as famous as Little John.

And now stout Gilbert of the White Hand took his place and shot with the greatest care; and again, for the third time in one day, he struck all three shafts into the clout.

"Well done, Gilbert!" quoth Robin Hood, smiting him upon the shoulder. "I make my vow, thou art one of the best archers that ever mine eyes beheld. Thou shouldst be a free and merry ranger like us, lad, for thou art better fitted for the greenwood than for the cobblestones and gray walls of London Town." So saying, he took his place, and drew a fair, round arrow from his quiver, which he turned over and over ere he fitted it to his bowstring.

Then the King muttered in his beard, "Now, blessed Saint Hubert, if thou wilt but jog that rogue's elbow so as to make him smite even the second ring, I will give eight-score waxen candles three fingers'-breadth in thickness to thy chapel nigh Matching." But it may be Saint Hubert's ears were stuffed with tow, for he seemed not to hear the King's prayer this day.

Having gotten three shafts to his liking, merry Robin looked carefully to his bowstring ere he shot. "Yea," quoth he to Gilbert, who stood nigh him to watch his shooting, "thou shouldst pay us a visit at merry Sherwood." Here he drew the bowstring to his ear. "In

London"—here he loosed his shaft—"thou canst find nought to shoot at but rooks and daws; there one can tickle the ribs of the noblest stags in England." So he shot even while he talked, yet the shaft lodged not more than half an inch from the very center.

"By my soul!" cried Gilbert. "Art thou the devil in blue, to shoot in that wise?"

"Nay," quoth Robin, laughing, "not quite so ill as that, I trust." And he took up another shaft and fitted it to the string. Again he shot, and again he smote his arrow close beside the center; a third time he loosed his bowstring and dropped his arrow just betwixt the other two and into the very center, so that the feathers of all three were ruffled together, seeming from a distance to be one thick shaft.

And now a low murmur ran all among that great crowd, for never before had London seen such shooting as this; and never again would it see it after Robin Hood's day had gone. All saw that the King's archers were fairly beaten, and stout Gilbert clapped his palm to Robin's, owning that he could never hope to draw such a bowstring as Robin Hood or Little John. But the King, full of wrath, would not have it so, though he knew in his mind that his men could not stand against those fellows. "Nay!" cried he, clenching his hands upon the arms of his seat, "Gilbert is not yet beaten! Did he not strike the clout thrice? Although I have lost my wager, he hath not yet lost the first prize. They shall shoot again, and still again, till either he or that knave Robin Hood cometh off the best. Go thou, Sir Hugh, and bid them shoot another round, and another, until one or the other is overcome." Then Sir Hugh, seeing how wroth the King was, said never a word, but went straightway to do his bidding; so he came to where Robin Hood and the other stood, and told them what the King had said.

"With all my heart," quoth merry Robin, "I will shoot

from this time till tomorrow day if it can pleasure my most gracious lord and King. Take thy place, Gilbert lad, and shoot."

So Gilbert took his place once more, but this time he failed, for, a sudden little wind arising, his shaft missed the center ring, but by not more than the breadth of a barley straw.

"Thy eggs are cracked, Gilbert," quoth Robin, laughing; and straightway he loosed a shaft, and once more smote the white circle of the center.

Then the King arose from his place, and not a word said he, but he looked around with a baleful look, and it would have been an ill day for anyone that he saw with a joyous or a merry look upon his face. Then he and his Queen and all the court left the place, but the King's heart was brimming full of wrath.

After the King had gone, all the yeomen of the archer guard came crowding around Robin, and Little John, and Will, and Allan, to snatch a look at these famous fellows from the mid-country; and with them came many that had been onlookers at the sport, for the same purpose. Thus it happened presently that the yeomen, to whom Gilbert stood talking, were all surrounded by a crowd of people that formed a ring about them.

After a while the three judges that had the giving away of the prizes came forward, and the chief of them all spake to Robin and said, "According to agreement, the first prize belongeth rightly to thee; so here I give thee the silver bugle, here the quiver of ten golden arrows, and here a purse of twoscore and ten golden pounds." And as he spake he handed those things to Robin, and then turned to Little John. "To thee," he said, "belongeth the second prize, to wit, fivescore of the finest harts that run on Dallen Lea. Thou mayest shoot them whensoever thou dost list." Last of all he turned to stout Hubert. "Thou," said he, "hast held thine own against the yeomen

with whom thou didst shoot, and so thou has kept the prize duly thine, to wit, two tuns of good Rhenish wine. These shall be delivered to thee whensoever thou dost list." Then he called upon the other seven of the King's archers who had last shot, and gave each fourscore silver pennies.

Then up spake Robin, and quoth he, "This silver bugle I keep in honor of this shooting match; but thou, Gilbert, art the best archer of all the King's guard, and to thee I freely give this purse of gold. Take it, man, and would it were ten times as much, for thou art a right yeoman, good and true. Furthermore, to each of the ten that last shot I give one of these golden shafts apiece. Keep them always by you, so that ye may tell your grandchildren, an ye are ever blessed with them, that ye are the very stoutest yeomen in all the wide world."

At this all shouted aloud, for it pleased them to hear Robin speak so of them.

Then up spake Little John. "Good friend Tepus," said he, "I want not those harts of Dallen Lea that yon stout judge spoke of but now, for in truth we have enow and more than enow in our own country. Twoscore and ten I give to thee for thine own shooting, and five I give to each band for their pleasure."

At this another great shout went up, and many tossed their caps aloft, and swore among themselves that no better fellows ever walked the sod than Robin Hood and his stout yeomen.

While they so shouted with loud voices, a tall burly yeoman of the King's guard came forward and plucked Robin by the sleeve. "Good master," quoth he, "I have somewhat to tell thee in thine ear; a silly thing, God wot, for one stout yeoman to tell another; but a young peacock of a page, one Richard Partington, was seeking thee without avail in the crowd, and, not being able to find thee, told me that he bore a message to thee from a certain

lady that thou wottest of. This message he bade me tell thee privily, word for word, and thus it was. Let me see—I trust I have forgot it not—yea, thus it was: 'The lion growls. Beware thy head.' "

"Is it so?" quoth Robin, starting; for he knew right well that it was the Queen sent the message, and that she spake of the King's wrath. "Now, I thank thee, good fellow, for thou hast done me greater service than thou knowest of this day." Then he called his three yeomen together and told them privately that they had best be jogging, as it was like to be ill for them so nigh merry London Town. So, without tarrying longer, they made their way through the crowd until they had come out from the press. Then, without stopping, they left London Town and started away northward.

The Chase of Robin Hood

So ROBIN HOOD and the others left the archery range at Finsbury Fields, and, tarrying not, set forth straightway upon their homeward journey. It was well for them that they did so, for they had not gone more than three or four miles upon their way when six of the yeomen of the King's guard came bustling among the crowd that still lingered, seeking for Robin and his men, to seize upon them and make them prisoners. Truly, it was an ill-done thing in the King to break his promise, but it all came about through the Bishop of Hereford's doing, for thus it happened:

After the King left the archery ground, he went straightway to his cabinet, and with him went the Bishop of Hereford and Sir Robert Lee; but the King said never a word to these two, but sat gnawing his nether lip, for his heart was galled within him by what had happened. At last the Bishop of Hereford spoke, in a low, sorrowful voice: "It is a sad thing, Your Majesty, that this knavish outlaw should be let to escape in this wise; for, let him but get back to Sherwood Forest safe and sound, and he may snap his fingers at king and king's men."

At these words the King raised his eyes and looked grimly upon the Bishop. "Sayst thou so?" quoth he. "Now, I will show thee, in good time, how much thou dost

err, for, when the forty days are past and gone, I will seize upon this thieving outlaw, if I have to tear down all of Sherwood to find him.   Thinkest thou that the laws of the King of England are to be so evaded by one poor knave without friends or money?"

Then the Bishop spoke again, in his soft, smooth voice: "Forgive my boldness, Your Majesty, and believe that I have nought but the good of England and Your Majesty's desirings at heart; but what would it boot though my gracious lord did root up every tree of Sherwood?   Are there not other places for Robin Hood's hiding?   Cannock Chase is not far from Sherwood, and the great Forest of Arden is not far from Cannock Chase.   Beside these are many other woodlands in Nottingham and Derby, Lincoln and York, amid any of which Your Majesty might as well think to seize upon Robin Hood as to lay finger upon a rat among the dust and broken things of a garret.   Nay, my gracious lord, if he doth once plant foot in the woodland, he is lost to the law forever."

At these words the King tapped his fingertips upon the table beside him with vexation.   "What wouldst thou have me do, Bishop?" quoth he.   "Didst thou not hear me pledge my word to the Queen?   Thy talk is as barren as the wind from the bellows upon dead coals."

"Far be it from me," said the cunning Bishop, "to point the way to one so clear-sighted as Your Majesty; but, were I the King of England, I should look upon the matter in this wise: I have promised my Queen, let us say, that for forty days the cunningest rogue in all England shall have freedom to come and go; but, lo! I find this outlaw in my grasp; shall I, then, foolishly cling to a promise so hastily given?   Suppose that I had promised to do Her Majesty's bidding, whereupon she bade me to slay myself; should I, then, shut mine eyes and run blindly upon my sword?   Thus would I argue within myself.   Moreover, I would say unto myself, a woman knoweth nought of the

great things appertaining to state government; and, likewise, I know a woman is ever prone to take up a fancy, even as she would pluck a daisy from the roadside, and then throw it away when the savor is gone; therefore, though she hath taken a fancy to this outlaw, it will soon wane away and be forgotten. As for me, I have the greatest villain in all England in my grasp; shall I, then, open my hand and let him slip betwixt my fingers? Thus, Your Majesty, would I say to myself, were I the King of England." So the Bishop talked, and the King lent his ear to his evil counsel, until, after a while, he turned to Sir Robert Lee and bade him send six of the yeomen of the guard to take Robin Hood and his three men prisoners.

Now Sir Robert Lee was a gentle and noble knight, and he felt grieved to the heart to see the King so break his promise; nevertheless, he said nothing, for he saw how bitterly the King was set against Robin Hood; but he did not send the yeomen of the guard at once, but went first to the Queen, and told her all that had passed, and bade her send word to Robin of his danger. This he did not for the well-being of Robin Hood, but because he would save his lord's honor if he could. Thus it came about that when, after a while, the yeomen of the guard went to the archery field, they found not Robin and the others, and so got no cakes at that fair.

The afternoon was already well-nigh gone when Robin Hood, Little John, Will, and Allan set forth upon their homeward way, trudging along merrily through the yellow slanting light, which speedily changed to rosy red as the sun sank low in the heavens. The shadows grew long, and finally merged into the grayness of the mellow twilight. The dusty highway lay all white betwixt the dark hedgerows, and along it walked four fellows like four shadows, the pat of their feet sounding loud, and their voices, as they talked, ringing clear upon the silence of the air. The great round moon was floating breathlessly up

in the eastern sky when they saw before them the twinkling lights of Barnet Town, some ten or twelve miles from London. Down they walked through the stony streets and past the cosy houses with overhanging gables, before the doors of which sat the burghers and craftsmen in the mellow moonlight, with their families about them, and so came at last, on the other side of the hamlet, to a little inn, all shaded with roses and woodbines. Before this inn Robin Hood stopped, for the spot pleased him well. Quoth he, "Here will we take up our inn and rest for the night, for we are well away from London Town and our King's wrath. Moreover, if I mistake not, we will find sweet faring within. What say ye, lads?"

"In sooth, good master," quoth Little John, "thy bidding and my doing ever fit together like cakes and ale. Let us in, I say also."

Then up spake Will Scarlet: "I am ever ready to do what thou sayest, uncle, yet I could wish that we were farther upon our way ere we rest for the night. Nevertheless, if thou thinkest best, let us in for the night, say I also."

So in they went and called for the best that the place afforded. Then a right good feast was set before them, with two stout bottles of old sack to wash it down withal. These things were served by as plump and buxom a lass as you could find in all the land, so that Little John, who always had an eye for a fair lass, even when meat and drink were by, stuck his arms akimbo and fixed his eyes upon her, winking sweetly whenever he saw her looking toward him. Then you should have seen how the lass twittered with laughter, and how she looked at Little John out of the corners of her eyes, a dimple coming in either cheek; for the fellow had always a taking way with the womenfolk.

So the feast passed merrily, and never had that inn seen such lusty feeders as these four stout fellows; but at last

they were done their eating, though it seemed as though they never would have ended, and sat loitering over the sack. As they so sat, the landlord came in of a sudden, and said that there was one at the door, a certain young esquire, Richard Partington, of the Queen's household, who wished to see the lad in blue, and speak with him, without loss of time. So Robin arose quickly, and, bidding the landlord not to follow him, left the others gazing at one another, and wondering what was about to happen.

When Robin came out of the inn, he found young Richard Partington sitting upon his horse in the white moonlight, awaiting his coming.

"What news bearest thou, Sir Page?" said Robin. "I trust that it is not of an ill nature."

"Why," said young Partington, "for the matter of that, it is ill enow. The King hath been bitterly stirred up against thee by that vile Bishop of Hereford. He sent to arrest thee at the archery butts at Finsbury Fields, but not finding thee there, he hath gathered together his armed men, fiftyscore and more, and is sending them in haste along this very road to Sherwood, either to take thee on the way or to prevent thy getting back to the woodlands again. He hath given the Bishop of Hereford command over all these men, and thou knowest what thou hast to expect of the Bishop of Hereford—short shrift and a long rope. Two bands of horsemen are already upon the road, not far behind me, so thou hadst best get thee gone from this place straightway, for, if thou tarriest longer, thou art like to sleep this night in a cold dungeon. This word the Queen hath bidden me bring to thee."

"Now, Richard Partington," quoth Robin, "this is the second time that thou hast saved my life, and if the proper time ever cometh I will show thee that Robin Hood never forgets these things. As for that Bishop of Hereford, if I ever catch him nigh to Sherwood again, things will be like

to go ill with him.   Thou mayst tell the good Queen that I will leave this place without delay, and will let the landlord think that we are going to Saint Albans; but when we are upon the highroad again, I will go one way through the country and will send my men the other, so that if one falleth into the King's hands the others may haply escape.   We will go by devious ways, and so, I hope, will reach Sherwood in safety.   And now, Sir Page, I wish thee farewell."

"Farewell, thou bold yeoman," said young Partington, "and mayst thou reach thy hiding in safety."   So each shook the other's hand, and the lad, turning his horse's head, rode back toward London, while Robin entered the inn once more.

There he found his yeomen sitting in silence, waiting his coming; likewise the landlord was there, for he was curious to know what Master Partington had to do with the fellow in blue.   "Up, my merry men!" quoth Robin, "this is no place for us, for those are after us with whom we will stand but an ill chance an we fall into their hands. So we will go forward once more, nor will we stop this night till we reach Saint Albans."   Hereupon, taking out his purse, he paid the landlord his score, and so they left the inn.

When they had come to the highroad without the town, Robin stopped and told them all that had passed between young Partington and himself, and how that the King's men were after them with hot heels.   Then he told them that here they should part company; they three going to the eastward and he to the westward, and so, skirting the main highroads, would come by devious paths to Sherwood.   "So, be ye wily," said Robin Hood, "and keep well away from the northward roads till ye have gotten well to the eastward.   And thou, Will Scarlet, take the lead of the others, for thou hast a cunning turn to thy wits."   Then Robin kissed the three upon the cheeks,

and they kissed him, and so they parted company.

Not long after this, a score or more of the King's men came clattering up to the door of the inn at Barnet Town. Here they leaped from their horses and quickly surrounded the place, the leader of the band and four others entering the room where the yeomen had been. But they found that their birds had flown again, and that the King had been balked a second time.

"Methought that they were naughty fellows," said the host, when he heard whom the men-at-arms sought. "But I heard that blue-clad knave say that they would go straight forward to Saint Albans; so, an ye hurry forward, ye may, perchance, catch them on the highroad betwixt here and there." For this news the leader of the band thanked mine host right heartily, and, calling his men together, mounted and set forth again, galloping forward to Saint Albans upon a wild goose chase.

After Little John and Will Scarlet and Allan a Dale had left the highway near Barnet, they traveled toward the eastward, without stopping, as long as their legs could carry them, until they came to Chelmsford, in Essex. Thence they turned northward, and came through Cambridge and Lincolnshire, to the good town of Gainsborough. Then, striking to the westward and the south, they came at last to the northern borders of Sherwood Forest, without in all that time having met so much as a single band of the King's men. Eight days they journeyed thus ere they reached the woodlands in safety; but when they got to the greenwood glade, they found that Robin had not yet returned.

For Robin was not as lucky in getting back as his men had been, as you shall presently hear.

After having left the great northern road, he turned his face to the westward, and so came past Aylesbury, to fair Woodstock, in Oxfordshire. Thence he turned his footsteps northward, traveling for a great distance by way of

Warwick Town, till he came to Dudley, in Staffordshire. Seven days it took him to journey thus far, and then he thought he had gotten far enough to the north, so, turning toward the eastward, shunning the main roads, and choosing byways and grassy lanes, he went, by way of Litchfield and Ashby de la Zouch, toward Sherwood, until he came to a place called Stanton. And now Robin's heart began to laugh aloud, for he thought that his danger had gone by, and that his nostrils would soon snuff the spicy air of the woodlands once again. But there is many a slip betwixt the cup and the lip, and this Robin was to find. For thus it was:

When the King's men found themselves foiled at Saint Albans, and that Robin and his men were not to be found high nor low, they knew not what to do. Presently another band of horsemen came, and another, until all the moonlit streets were full of armed men. Betwixt midnight and dawn another band came to the town, and with them came the Bishop of Hereford. When he heard that Robin Hood had once more slipped out of the trap, he stayed not a minute, but, gathering his bands together, he pushed forward to the northward with speed, leaving orders for all the troops that came to Saint Albans to follow after him without tarrying. On the evening of the fourth day he reached Nottingham Town, and there straightway divided his men into bands of six or seven, and sent them all through the countryside, blocking every highway and byway to the eastward and the southward and the westward of Sherwood. The Sheriff of Nottingham called forth all his men likewise, and joined with the Bishop, for he saw that this was the best chance that had ever befallen of paying back his score in full to Robin Hood. Will Scarlet and Little John and Allan a Dale had just missed the King's men to the eastward, for the very next day after they had passed the line and entered Sherwood the roads through which they had traveled were

*As he stooped, drinking, something hissed past his ear
and struck the water beside him.*

blocked, so that, had they tarried in their journeying, they would surely have fallen into the Bishop's hands.

But of all this Robin knew not a whit; so he whistled merrily as he trudged along the road beyond Stanton, with his heart as free from care as the yolk of an egg is from cobwebs. At last he came to where a little stream spread across the road in a shallow sheet, tinkling and sparkling as it fretted over its bed of golden gravel. Here Robin stopped, being athirst, and, kneeling down, he made a cup of the palms of his hands, and began to drink. On either side of the road, for a long distance, stood tangled thickets of bushes and young trees, and it pleased Robin's heart to hear the little birds singing therein, for it made him think of Sherwood, and it seemed as though it had been a lifetime since he had breathed the air of the woodlands. But of a sudden, as he thus stooped, drinking, something hissed past his ear, and struck with a splash into the gravel and water beside him. Quick as a wink Robin sprang to his feet, and, at one bound, crossed the stream and the roadside, and plunged headlong into the thicket, without looking around, for he knew right well that that which had hissed so venomously beside his ear was a gray goose shaft, and that to tarry so much as a moment meant death. Even as he leaped into the thicket six more arrows rattled among the branches after him, one of which pierced his doublet, and would have struck deeply into his side but for the tough coat of steel that he wore. Then up the road came riding some of the King's men at headlong speed. They leaped from their horses and plunged straightway into the thicket after Robin. But Robin knew the ground better than they did, so crawling here, stooping there, and, anon, running across some little open, he soon left them far behind, coming out, at last, upon another road about eight hundred paces distant from the one he had left. Here he stood for a moment, listening to the distant shouts of the seven men

as they beat up and down in the thickets like hounds that had lost the scent of the quarry. Then, buckling his belt more tightly around his waist, he ran fleetly down the road toward the eastward and Sherwood.

But Robin had not gone more than three furlongs in that direction when he came suddenly to the brow of a hill, and saw beneath him another band of the King's men seated in the shade along the roadside in the valley beneath. Then he paused not a moment, but, seeing that they had not caught sight of him, he turned and ran back whence he had come, knowing that it was better to run the chance of escaping those fellows that were yet in the thickets than to rush into the arms of those in the valley. So back he ran with all speed, and had gotten safely past the thickets, when the seven men came forth into the open road. They raised a great shout when they saw him, such as the hunter gives when the deer breaks cover, but Robin was then a quarter of a mile and more away from them, coursing over the ground like a greyhound. He never slackened his pace, but ran along, mile after mile, till he had come nigh to Mackworth, over beyond the Derwent River, nigh to Derby Town. Here, seeing that he was out of present danger, he slackened in his running, and at last sat him down beneath a hedge where the grass was the longest and the shade the coolest, there to rest and catch his wind. "By my soul, Robin," quoth he to himself, "that was the narrowest miss that e'er thou hadst in all thy life. I do say most solemnly that the feather of that wicked shaft tickled mine ear as it whizzed past. This same running hath given me a most craving appetite for victuals and drink. Now I pray Saint Dunstan that he send me speedily some meat and beer."

It seemed as though Saint Dunstan was like to answer his prayer, for along the road came plodding a certain cobbler, one Quince, of Derby, who had been to take a

pair of shoes to a farmer nigh Kirk Langly, and was now coming back home again, with a fair boiled capon in his pouch and a stout pottle of beer by his side, which same the farmer had given him for joy of such a stout pair of shoon. Good Quince was an honest fellow, but his wits were somewhat of the heavy sort, like unbaked dough, so that the only thing that was in his mind was, "Three shillings sixpence ha'penny for thy shoon, good Quince—three shillings sixpence ha'penny for thy shoon," and this traveled round and round inside of his head, without another thought getting into his noddle, as a pea rolls round and round inside an empty quart pot.

"Halloa, good friend," quoth Robin, from beneath the hedge, when the other had gotten nigh enough, "whither away so merrily this bright day?"

Hearing himself so called upon, the Cobbler stopped, and, seeing a well-clad stranger in blue, he spoke to him in seemly wise. "Give ye good den, fair sir, and I would say that I come from Kirk Langly, where I ha' sold my shoon and got three shillings sixpence ha'penny for them in as sweet money as ever thou sawest, and honestly earned too, I would ha' thee know. But, an I may be so bold, thou pretty fellow, what dost thou there beneath the hedge?"

"Marry," quoth merry Robin, "I sit beneath the hedge here to drop salt on the tails of golden birds; but in sooth thou art the first chick of any worth I ha' seen this blessed day."

At these words the Cobbler's eyes opened big and wide, and his mouth grew round with wonder, like a knothole in a board fence. "Alack-a-day," quoth he, "look ye, now! I ha' never seen those same golden birds. And dost thou in sooth find them in these hedges, good fellow? Prythee, tell me, are there many of them? I would fain find them mine own self."

"Ay, truly," quoth Robin, "they are as thick here as fresh herring in Cannock Chase."

"Look ye, now!" said the Cobbler, all drowned in wonder. "And dost thou in sooth catch them by dropping salt on their pretty tails?"

"Yea," quoth Robin, "but this salt is of an odd kind, let me tell thee, for it can only be gotten by boiling down a quart of moonbeams in a wooden platter, and then one hath but a pinch. But tell me, now, thou witty man, what hast thou gotten there in that pouch by thy side and in that pottle?"

At these words the Cobbler looked down at those things of which merry Robin spoke, for the thoughts of the golden bird had driven them from his mind, and it took him some time to scrape the memory of them back again. "Why," said he at last, "in the one is good March beer, and in the other is a fat capon. Truly, Quince the Cobbler will ha' a fine feast this day an I mistake not."

"But tell me, good Quince," said Robin, "hast thou a mind to sell those things to me? For the hearing of them sounds sweet in mine ears. I will give thee these gay clothes of blue that I have upon my body and ten shillings to boot for thy clothes and thy leather apron and thy beer and thy capon. What sayst thou, bully boy?"

"Nay, thou dost jest with me," said the Cobbler, "for my clothes are coarse and patched, and thine are of fine stuff and very pretty."

"Never a jest do I speak," quoth Robin. "Come, strip thy jacket off and I will show thee, for I tell thee I like thy clothes well. Moreover, I will be kind to thee, for I will feast straightway upon the good things thou hast with thee, and thou shalt be bidden to the eating." At these words he began slipping off his doublet, and the Cobbler, seeing him so in earnest, began pulling off his clothes also, for Robin Hood's garb tickled his eye. So each put on the other fellow's clothes, and Robin gave the honest

Cobbler ten bright new shillings. Quoth merry Robin, "I ha' been a many things in my life before, but never have I been an honest cobbler. Come, friend, let us fall to and eat, for something within me cackles aloud for that good fat capon." So both sat down and began to feast right lustily, so that when they were done the bones of the capon were picked as bare as charity.

Then Robin stretched his legs out with a sweet feeling of comfort within him. Quoth he, "By the turn of thy voice, good Quince, I know that thou hast a fair song or two running loose in thy head like colts in a meadow. I prythee, turn one of them out for me."

"A song or two I ha'," quoth the Cobbler, "poor things, poor things, but such as they are thou art welcome to one of them." So, moistening his throat with a swallow of beer, he sang:

> *"Of all the joys, the best I love,*
> *   Sing hey my frisking Nan, O,*
> *And that which most my soul doth move,*
> *   It is the clinking can, O.*
>
> *"All other bliss I'd throw away,*
> *   Sing hey my frisking Nan, O,*
> *But this—"*

The stout Cobbler got no further in his song, for of a sudden six horsemen burst upon them where they sat, and seized roughly upon the honest craftsman, hauling him to his feet, and nearly plucking the clothes from him as they did so. "Ha!" roared the leader of the band in a great big voice of joy, "have we then caught thee at last, thou blue-clad knave? Now, blessed be the name of Saint Hubert, for we are fourscore pounds richer this minute than we were before, for the good Bishop of Hereford hath promised that much to the band that shall bring thee to him. Oho! thou cunning rascal! thou wouldst look so innocent, forsooth! We know thee, thou old fox. But

off thou goest with us to have thy brush clipped forthwith." At these words the poor Cobbler gazed all around
him with his great blue eyes as round as those of a dead
fish, while his mouth gaped as though he had swallowed
all his words and so lost his speech.

Robin also gaped and stared in a wondering way, just
as the Cobbler would have done in his place. "Alack-
a-daisy, me," quoth he. "I know not whether I be sitting
here or in No-man's-land! What meaneth all this stir i' th'
pot, dear good gentlemen? Surely this a sweet, honest
fellow."

" 'Honest fellow,' sayst thou, clown?" quoth one of the
men. "Why, I tell thee that this is that same rogue that
men call Robin Hood."

At this speech the Cobbler stared and gaped more than
ever, for there was such a threshing of thoughts going on
within his poor head that his wits were all befogged with
the dust and chaff thereof. Moreover, as he looked at
Robin Hood, and saw the yeoman look so like what he
knew himself to be, he began to doubt and to think that
mayhap he was the great outlaw in real sooth. Said he in
a slow, wondering voice, "Am I in very truth that fellow?—Now I had thought—but nay, Quince, thou art
mistook—yet—am I?—Nay, I must indeed be Robin
Hood! Yet, truly, I had never thought to pass from an
honest craftsman to such a great yeoman."

"Alas!" quoth Robin Hood, "look ye there, now! See
how your ill-treatment hath curdled the wits of this poor
lad and turned them all sour! I, myself, am Quince, the
Cobbler of Derby Town."

"Is it so?" said Quince. "Then, indeed, I am somebody else, and can be none other than Robin Hood.
Take me, fellows; but let me tell you that ye ha' laid hand
upon the stoutest yeoman that ever trod the woodlands."

"Thou wilt play madman, wilt thou?" said the leader of
the band. "Here, Giles, fetch a cord and bind this

knave's hands behind him. I warrant we will bring his wits back to him again when we get him safe before our Good Bishop at Tutbury Town." Thereupon they tied the Cobbler's hands behind him, and led him off with a rope, as the farmer leads off the calf he hath brought from the fair. Robin stood looking after them, and when they were gone he laughed till the tears rolled down his cheeks; for he knew that no harm would befall the honest fellow, and he pictured to himself the Bishop's face when good Quince was brought before him as Robin Hood. Then, turning his steps once more to the eastward, he stepped out right foot foremost toward Nottinghamshire and Sherwood Forest.

But Robin Hood had gone through more than he wotted of. His journey from London had been hard and long, and in a se'ennight he had traveled sevenscore and more of miles. He thought now to travel on without stopping until he had come to Sherwood, but ere he had gone a half a score of miles he felt his strength giving way beneath him like a river bank which the waters have undermined. He sat him down and rested, but he knew within himself that he could go no farther that day, for his feet felt like lumps of lead, so heavy were they with weariness. Once more he arose and went forward, but after traveling a couple of miles he was fain to give the matter up, so, coming to an inn just then, he entered and calling the landlord, bade him show him to a room, although the sun was only then just sinking in the western sky. There were but three bedrooms in the place, and to the meanest of these the landlord showed Robin Hood, but little Robin cared for the looks of the place, for he could have slept that night upon a bed of broken stones. So, stripping off his clothes without more ado, he rolled into the bed and was asleep almost ere his head touched the pillow.

Not long after Robin had so gone to his rest a great

cloud peeped blackly over the hills to the westward. Higher and higher it arose until it piled up into the night like a mountain of darkness. All around beneath it came ever and anon a dull red flash, and presently a short grim mutter of the coming thunder was heard. Then up rode four stout burghers of Nottingham Town, for this was the only inn within five miles' distance, and they did not care to be caught in such a thunderstorm as this that was coming upon them. Leaving their nags to the stable-man, they entered the best room of the inn, where fresh green rushes lay all spread upon the floor, and there called for the goodliest fare that the place afforded. After having eaten heartily they bade the landlord show them to their rooms, for they were aweary, having ridden all the way from Dronfield that day. So off they went, grumbling at having to sleep two in a bed, but their troubles on this score, as well as all others, were soon lost in the quietness of sleep.

And now came the first gust of wind, rushing past the place, clapping and banging the doors and shutters, smelling of the coming rain, and all wrapped in a cloud of dust and leaves. As though the wind had brought a guest along with it, the door opened of a sudden and in came a friar of Emmet Priory, and one in high degree, as was shown by the softness and sleekness of his robes and the richness of his rosary. He called to the landlord, and bade him first have his mule well fed and bedded in the stable, and then to bring him the very best there was in the house. So presently a savory stew of tripe and onions, with sweet little fat dumplings, was set before him, likewise a good stout pottle of Malmsey, and straightway the holy friar fell to with great courage and heartiness, so that in a short time nought was left but a little pool of gravy in the center of the platter, not large enow to keep the life in a starving mouse.

In the meantime the storm broke. Another gust of

wind went rushing by, and with it fell a few heavy drops of rain, which presently came rattling down in showers, beating against the casements like a hundred little hands. Bright flashes of lightning lit up every raindrop, and with them came cracks of thunder that went away rumbling and bumping as though Saint Swithin were busy rolling great casks of water across rough ground overhead. The womenfolks screamed, and the merry wags in the tap-room put their arms around their waists to soothe them into quietness.

At last the holy friar bade the landlord show him to his room; but when he heard that he was to bed with a cobbler, he was as ill contented a fellow as you could find in all England, nevertheless there was nothing for it, and he must sleep there or nowhere; so, taking up his candle, he went off, grumbling like the now distant thunder. When he came to the room where he was to sleep he held the light over Robin and looked at him from top to toe; then he felt better pleased, for, instead of a rough, dirty-bearded fellow, he beheld as fresh and clean a lad as one could find in a week of Sundays; so, slipping off his clothes, he also huddled into the bed, where Robin, grunting and grumbling in his sleep, made room for him. Robin was more sound asleep, I wot, than he had been for many a day, else he would never have rested so quietly with one of the friar's sort so close beside him. As for the friar, had he known who Robin Hood was, you may well believe he would almost as soon have slept with an adder as with the man he had for a bedfellow.

So the night passed comfortably enough, but at the first dawn of day Robin opened his eyes and turned his head upon the pillow. Then how he gaped and how he stared, for there beside him lay one all shaven and shorn, so that he knew that it must be a fellow in holy orders. He pinched himself sharply, but, finding he was awake, sat up in bed, while the other slumbered as peacefully as

though he were safe and sound at home in Emmet Priory. "Now," quoth Robin to himself, "I wonder how this thing hath dropped into my bed during the night." So saying, he arose softly, so as not to awaken the other, and looking about the room he espied the friar's clothes lying upon a bench near the wall. First he looked at the clothes, with his head on one side, and then he looked at the friar and slowly winked one eye. Quoth he, "Good Brother What-e'er-thy-name-may-be, as thou hast borrowed my bed so freely I'll e'en borrow thy clothes in return." So saying, he straightway donned the holy man's garb, but kindly left the cobbler's clothes in the place of it. Then he went forth into the freshness of the morning, and the stableman that was up and about the stables opened his eyes as though he saw a green mouse before him, for such men as the friars of Emmet were not wont to be early risers; but the man bottled his thoughts, and only asked Robin whether he wanted his mule brought from the stable.

"Yea, my son," quoth Robin—albeit he knew nought of the mule—"and bring it forth quickly, I prythee, for I am late and must be jogging." So presently the stableman brought forth the mule, and Robin mounted it and went on his way rejoicing.

As for the holy friar, when he arose he was in as pretty a stew as any man in all the world, for his rich, soft robes were gone, likewise his purse with ten golden pounds in it, and nought was left but patched clothes and a leathern apron. He raged and swore like any layman, but as his swearing mended nothing and the landlord could not aid him, and as, moreover, he was forced to be at Emmet Priory that very morning upon matters of business, he was fain either to don the cobbler's clothes or travel the road in nakedness. So he put on the clothes, and, still raging and swearing vengeance against all the cobblers in Derbyshire, he set forth upon his way afoot; but his ills

had not yet done with him, for he had not gone far ere he fell into the hands of the King's men, who marched him off, willy-nilly, to Tutbury Town and the Bishop of Hereford. In vain he swore he was a holy man, and showed his shaven crown; off he must go, for nothing would do but that he was Robin Hood.

Meanwhile merry Robin rode along contentedly, passing safely by two bands of the King's men, until his heart began to dance within him because of the nearness of Sherwood; so he traveled ever on to the eastward, till, of a sudden, he met a noble knight in a shady lane. Then Robin checked his mule quickly and leaped from off its back. "Now, well met, Sir Richard of the Lea," cried he, "for rather than any other man in England would I see thy good face this day!" Then he told Sir Richard all the happenings that had befallen him, and that now at last he felt himself safe, being so nigh to Sherwood again. But when Robin had done, Sir Richard shook his head sadly. "Thou art in greater danger now, Robin, than thou hast yet been," said he, "for before thee lie bands of the Sheriff's men blocking every road and letting none pass through the lines without examining them closely. I myself know this, having passed them but now. Before thee lie the Sheriff's men and behind thee the King's men, and thou canst not hope to pass either way, for by this time they will know of thy disguise and will be in waiting to seize upon thee. My castle and everything within it are thine, but nought could be gained there, for I could not hope to hold it against such a force as is now in Nottingham of the King's and the Sheriff's men." Having so spoken, Sir Richard bent his head in thought, and Robin felt his heart sink within him like that of the fox that hears the hounds at his heels and finds his den blocked with earth so that there is no hiding for him. But presently Sir Richard spoke again, saying, "One thing thou canst do, Robin, and one only. Go back to London

and throw thyself upon the mercy of our good Queen Eleanor. Come with me straightway to my castle. Doff these clothes and put on such as my retainers wear. Then I will hie me to London Town with a troop of men behind me, and thou shalt mingle with them, and thus will I bring thee to where thou mayst see and speak with the Queen. Thy only hope is to get to Sherwood, for there none can reach thee, and thou wilt never get to Sherwood but in this way."

So Robin went with Sir Richard of the Lea, and did as he said, for he saw the wisdom of that which the knight advised, and that this was his only chance of safety.

Queen Eleanor walked in her royal garden, amid the roses that bloomed sweetly, and with her walked six of her ladies-in-waiting, chattering blithely together. Of a sudden a man leaped up to the top of the wall from the other side, and then, hanging for a moment, dropped lightly upon the grass within. All the ladies-in-waiting shrieked at the suddenness of his coming, but the man ran to the Queen and kneeled at her feet, and she saw that it was Robin Hood.

"Why, how now, Robin!" cried she, "dost thou dare to come into the very jaws of the raging lion? Alas, poor fellow! Thou art lost indeed if the King finds thee here. Dost thou not know that he is seeking thee through all the land?"

"Yea," quoth Robin, "I do know right well that the King seeks me, and therefore I have come; for, surely, no ill can befall me when he hath pledged his royal word to Your Majesty for my safety. Moreover, I know Your Majesty's kindness and gentleness of heart, and so I lay my life freely in your gracious hands."

"I take thy meaning, Robin Hood," said the Queen, "and that thou dost convey reproach to me, as well thou mayst, for I know that I have not done by thee as I ought

to have done. I know right well that thou must have been hard pressed by peril to leap so boldly into one danger to escape another. Once more I promise thee mine aid, and will do all I can to send thee back in safety to Sherwood Forest. Bide thou here till I return." So saying, she left Robin in the garden of roses, and was gone a long time.

When she came back Sir Robert Lee was with her, and the Queen's cheeks were hot and the Queen's eyes were bright, as though she had been talking with high words. Then Sir Robert came straight forward to where Robin Hood stood, and he spoke to the yeoman in a cold, stern voice. Quoth he, "Our gracious Sovereign the King hath mitigated his wrath toward thee, fellow, and hath once more promised that thou shalt depart in peace and safety. Not only hath he promised this, but in three days he will send one of his pages to go with thee and see that none arrest thy journey back again. Thou mayst thank thy patron saint that thou hast such a good friend in our noble Queen, for, but for her persuasion and arguments, thou hadst been a dead man, I can tell thee. Let this peril that thou hast passed through teach thee two lessons. First, be more honest. Second, be not so bold in thy comings and goings. A man that walketh in the darkness as thou dost may escape for a time, but in the end he will surely fall into the pit. Thou hast put thy head in the angry lion's mouth, and yet thou hast escaped by a miracle. Try it not again." So saying, he turned and left Robin and was gone.

For three days Robin abided in London in the Queen's household, and at the end of that time the King's head Page, Edward Cunningham, came, and taking Robin with him, departed northward upon his way to Sherwood. Now and then they passed bands of the King's men coming back again to London, but none of those bands stopped them, and so, at last, they reached the sweet, leafy woodlands.

Robin Hood and
Guy of Gisbourne

A LONG TIME passed after the great shooting match, and during that time Robin followed one part of the advice of Sir Robert Lee, to wit, that of being less bold in his comings and his goings; for though mayhap he may not have been more honest (as most folks regard honesty), he took good care not to travel so far from Sherwood that he could not reach it both easily and quickly.

Great changes had fallen in this time; for King Henry had died and King Richard had come to the crown that fitted him so well through many hard trials, and through adventures as stirring as any that ever befell Robin Hood. But though great changes came, they did not reach to Sherwood's shades, for there Robin Hood and his men dwelled as merrily as they had ever done, with hunting and feasting and singing and blithe woodland sports; for it was little the outside striving of the world troubled them.

The dawning of a summer's day was fresh and bright, and the birds sang sweetly in a great tumult of sound. So loud was their singing that it awakened Robin Hood where he lay sleeping, so that he stirred, and turned, and

arose. Up rose Little John also, and all the merry men; then, after they had broken their fast, they set forth hither and thither upon the doings of the day.

Robin Hood and Little John walked down a forest path where all around the leaves danced and twinkled as the breeze trembled through them and the sunlight came flickering down. Quoth Robin Hood, "I make my vow, Little John, my blood tickles my veins as it flows through them this gay morn. What sayst thou to our seeking adventures, each one upon his own account?"

"With all my heart," said Little John. "We have had more than one pleasant doing in that way, good master. Here are two paths; take thou the one to the right hand, and I will take the one to the left, and then let us each walk straight ahead till he tumble into some merry doing or other."

"I like thy plan," quoth Robin, "therefore we will part here. But look thee, Little John, keep thyself out of mischief, for I would not have ill befall thee for all the world."

"Marry, come up," quoth Little John, "how thou talkest! Methinks thou art wont to get thyself into tighter coils than I am like to do."

At this Robin Hood laughed. "Why, in sooth, Little John," said he, "thou hast a blundering hard-headed way that seemeth to bring thee right side uppermost in all thy troubles; but let us see who cometh out best this day." So saying, he clapped his palm to Little John's and each departed upon his way, the trees quickly shutting the one from the other's sight.

Robin Hood strolled onward till he came to where a broad woodland road stretched before him. Overhead the branches of the trees laced together in flickering foliage, all golden where it grew thin to the sunlight; beneath his feet the ground was soft and moist from the sheltering shade. Here in this pleasant spot the sharpest adventure

that ever befell Robin Hood came upon him; for, as he walked down the woodland path thinking of nought but the songs of the birds, he came of a sudden to where a man was seated upon the mossy roots beneath the shade of a broad-spreading oak tree. Robin Hood saw that the stranger had not caught sight of him, so he stopped and stood quite still, looking at the other a long time before he came forward. And the stranger, I wot, was well worth looking at, for never had Robin seen a figure like that sitting beneath the tree. From his head to his feet he was clad in a horse's hide, dressed with the hair upon it. Upon his head was a cowl that hid his face from sight, and which was made of the horse's skin, the ears whereof stuck up like those of a rabbit. His body was clad in a jacket made of the hide, and his legs were covered with the hairy skin likewise. By his side was a heavy broadsword and a sharp, double-edged dagger. A quiver of smooth round arrows hung across his shoulders, and his stout bow of yew leaned against the tree beside him.

"Halloa, friend," cried Robin, coming forward at last, "who art thou that sittest there? And what is that that thou hast upon thy body? I make my vow I ha' never seen such a sight in all my life before. Had I done an evil thing, or did my conscience trouble me, I would be afraid of thee, thinking that thou wast someone from down below bringing a message bidding me come straightway to King Nicholas."

To this speech the other answered not a word, but he pushed the cowl back from his head and showed a knit brow, a hooked nose, and a pair of fierce, restless black eyes, which altogether made Robin think of a hawk as he looked on his face. But beside this there was something about the lines on the stranger's face, and his thin cruel mouth, and the hard glare of his eyes, that made one's flesh creep to look upon.

"Who art thou, rascal?" said he at last, in a loud, harsh voice.

"Tut, tut," quoth merry Robin, "speak not so sourly, brother. Hast thou fed upon vinegar and nettles this morning that thy speech is so stinging?"

"An thou likest not my words," said the other fiercely, "thou hadst best be jogging, for I tell thee plainly, my deeds match them."

"Nay, but I do like thy words, thou sweet, pretty thing," quoth Robin, squatting down upon the grass in front of the other. "Moreover, I tell thee thy speech is witty and gamesome as any I ever heard in all my life."

The other said not a word, but he glared upon Robin with a wicked and baleful look, such as a fierce dog bestows upon a man ere it springs at his throat. Robin returned the gaze with one of wide-eyed innocence, not a shadow of a smile twinkling in his eyes or twitching at the corners of his mouth. So they sat staring at one another for a long time, until the stranger broke the silence suddenly. "What is thy name, fellow?" said he.

"Now," quoth Robin, "I am right glad to hear thee speak, for I began to fear the sight of me had stricken thee dumb. As for my name, it may be this or it may be that; but methinks it is more meet for thee to tell me thine, seeing that thou art the greater stranger in these parts. Prythee, tell me, sweet chuck, why wearest thou that dainty garb upon thy pretty body?"

At these words the other broke into a short, harsh roar of laughter. "By the bones of the Dæmon Odin," said he, "thou art the boldest-spoken man that ever I have seen in all my life. I know not why I do not smite thee down where thou sittest, for only two days ago I skewered a man over back of Nottingham Town for saying not half so much to me as thou hast done. I wear this garb, thou fool, to keep my body warm; likewise it is near as good as

a coat of steel against a common sword-thrust. As for my name, I care not who knoweth it. It is Guy of Gisbourne, and thou mayst have heard it before. I come from the woodlands over in Herefordshire, upon the lands of the Bishop of that ilk. I am an outlaw, and get my living by hook and by crook in a manner it boots not now to tell of. Not long since the Bishop sent for me, and said that it I would do a certain thing that the Sheriff of Nottingham would ask of me, he would get me a free pardon, and give me tenscore pounds to boot. So straightway I came to Nottingham Town and found my sweet Sheriff; and what thinkest thou he wanted of me? Why, forsooth, to come here to Sherwood to hunt up one Robin Hood, also an outlaw, and to take him alive or dead. It seemeth that they have no one here to face that bold fellow, and so sent all the way to Herefordshire, and to me, for thou knowest the old saying, 'Set a thief to catch a thief.' As for the slaying of this fellow, it galleth me not a whit, for I would shed the blood of my own brother for the half of two hundred pounds."

To all this Robin listened, and as he listened his gorge rose. Well he knew of this Guy of Gisbourne, and of all the bloody and murderous deeds that he had done in Herefordshire, for his doings were famous throughout all the land. Yet, although he loathed the very presence of the man, he held his peace, for he had an end to serve. "Truly," quoth he, "I have heard of thy gentle doings. Methinks there is no one in all the world that Robin Hood would rather meet than thee."

At this Guy of Gisbourne gave another harsh laugh. "Why," quoth he, "it is a merry thing to think of one stout outlaw like Robin Hood meeting another stout outlaw like Guy of Gisbourne. Only in this case it will be an ill happening for Robin Hood, for the day he meets Guy of Gisbourne he shall die."

"But thou gentle, merry spirit," quoth Robin, "dost

thou not think that mayhap this same Robin Hood may be the better man of the two? I know him right well, and many think that he is one of the stoutest men hereabouts."

"He may be the stoutest of men hereabouts," quoth Guy of Gisbourne, "yet, I tell thee, fellow, this sty of yours is not the wide world. I lay my life upon it I am the better man of the two. He an outlaw, forsooth! Why, I hear that he hath never let blood in all his life, saving when he first came to the forest. Some call him a great archer; marry, I would not be afraid to stand against him all the days of the year with a bow in my hand."

"Why, truly, some folk do call him a great archer," said Robin Hood, "but we of Nottinghamshire are famous hands with the longbow. Even I, though but a simple hand at the craft, would not fear to try a bout with thee."

At these words Guy of Gisbourne looked upon Robin with wondering eyes, and then gave another roar of laughter till the woods rang. "Now," quoth he, "thou art a bold fellow to talk to me in this way. I like thy spirit in so speaking up to me, for few men have dared to do so. Put up a garland, lad, and I will try a bout with thee."

"Tut, tut," quoth Robin, "only babes shoot at garlands hereabouts. I will put up a good Nottingham mark for thee." So saying, he arose, and going to a hazel thicket not far off, he cut a wand about twice the thickness of a man's thumb. From this he peeled the bark, and, sharpening the point, stuck it up in the ground in front of a great oak tree. Thence he measured off fourscore paces, which brought him beside the tree where the other sat. "There," quoth he, "is the kind of mark that Nottingham yeomen shoot at. Now let me see thee split that wand if thou art an archer."

Then Guy of Gisbourne arose. "Now out upon it!" cried he. "The Devil himself could not hit such a mark as that."

"Mayhap he could and mayhap he could not," quoth merry Robin, "but that we shall never know till thou hast shot thereat."

At these words Guy of Gisbourne looked upon Robin with knit brows, but, as the yeoman still looked innocent of any ill meaning, he bottled his words and strung his bow in silence. Twice he shot, but neither time did he hit the wand, missing it the first time by a span and the second time by a good palm's-breadth. Robin laughed and laughed. "I see now," quoth he, "that the Devil himself could not hit that mark. Good fellow, if thou art no better with the broadsword than thou art with the bow and arrow, thou wilt never overcome Robin Hood."

At these words Guy of Gisbourne glared savagely upon Robin. Quoth he, "Thou hast a merry tongue, thou villain; but take care that thou makest not too free with it, or I may cut it out from thy throat for thee."

Robin Hood strung his bow and took his place with never a word, albeit his heartstrings quivered with anger and loathing. Twice he shot, the first time hitting within an inch of the wand, the second time splitting it fairly in the middle. Then, without giving the other a chance for speech, he flung his bow upon the ground. "There, thou bloody villain!" cried he fiercely, "let that show thee how little thou knowest of manly sports. And now look thy last upon the daylight, for the good earth hath been befouled long enough by thee, thou vile beast! This day, Our Lady willing, thou diest—I am Robin Hood." So saying, he flashed forth his bright sword in the sunlight.

For a time Guy of Gisbourne stared upon Robin as though bereft of wits; but his wonder quickly passed to a wild rage. "Art thou indeed Robin Hood?" cried he. "Now I am glad to meet thee, thou poor wretch! Shrive thyself, for thou wilt have no time for shriving when I am done with thee." So saying, he also drew his sword.

And now came the fiercest fight that ever Sherwood

saw; for each man knew that either he or the other must die, and that no mercy was to be had in this battle. Up and down they fought, till all the sweet green grass was crushed and ground beneath the trampling of their heels. More than once the point of Robin Hood's sword felt the softness of flesh, and presently the ground began to be sprinkled with bright red drops, albeit not one of them came from Robin's veins. At last Guy of Gisbourne made a fierce and deadly thrust at Robin Hood, from which he leaped back lightly, but in so leaping he caught his heel in a root and fell heavily upon his back. "Now, Holy Mary aid me!" muttered he, as the other leaped at him, with a grin of rage upon his face. Fiercely Guy of Gisbourne stabbed at the other with his great sword; but Robin caught the blade in his naked hand, and, though it cut his palm, he turned the point away so that it plunged deep into the ground close beside him; then, ere a blow could be struck again, he leaped to his feet, with his good sword in his hand. And now despair fell upon Guy of Gisbourne's heart in a black cloud, and he looked around him wildly, like a wounded hawk. Seeing that his strength was going from him, Robin leaped forward, and, quick as a flash, struck a back-handed blow beneath the sword arm. Down fell the sword from Guy of Gisbourne's grasp, and back he staggered at the stroke, and, ere he could regain himself, Robin's sword passed through and through his body. Round he spun upon his heel, and, flinging his hands aloft with a shrill, wild cry, fell prone upon his face upon the green sod.

Then Robin Hood wiped his sword and thrust it back into the scabbard, and, coming to where Guy of Gisbourne lay, he stood over him with folded arms, talking to himself the while. "This is the first man I have slain since I shot the King's forester in the hot days of my youth. I ofttimes think bitterly, even yet, of that first life I took, but of this I am as glad as though I had slain a wild

boar that laid waste a fair country. Since the Sheriff of Nottingham hath sent such a one as this against me, I will put on the fellow's garb and go forth to see whether I may not find his worship, and perchance pay him back some of the debt I owe him upon this score."

So saying, Robin Hood stripped the hairy garments from off the dead man, and put them on himself, all bloody as they were. Then, strapping the other's sword and dagger around his body and carrying his own in his hand, together with the two bows of yew, he drew the cowl of horse's hide over his face, so that none could tell who he was, and set forth from the forest, turning his steps toward the eastward and Nottingham Town. As he strode along the country roads, men, women, and children hid away from him, for the terror of Guy of Gisbourne's name and of his doings had spread far and near.

And now let us see what befell Little John while these things were happening.

Little John walked on his way through the forest paths until he had come to the outskirts of the woodlands, where, here and there, fields of barley, corn, or green meadow lands lay smiling in the sun. So he came to the highroad and to where a little thatched cottage stood back of a cluster of twisted crab trees, with flowers in front of it. Here he stopped of a sudden, for he thought that he heard the sound of someone in sorrow. He listened, and found that it came from the cottage; so, turning his footsteps thither, he pushed open the wicket and entered the place. There he saw a gray-haired dame sitting beside a cold hearthstone, rocking herself to and fro and weeping bitterly.

Now Little John had a tender heart for the sorrows of other folk, so, coming to the old woman and patting her kindly upon the shoulder, he spoke comforting words to her, bidding her cheer up and tell him her troubles, for

that mayhap he might do something to ease them. At all this the good dame shook her head; but all the same his kind words did soothe her somewhat, so after a while she told him all that bore upon her mind. That that morning she had three as fair, tall sons beside her as one could find in all Nottinghamshire, but that they were now taken from her, and were like to be hanged straightway; that, want having come upon them, her eldest boy had gone out, the night before, into the forest, and had slain a hind in the moonlight; that the King's rangers had followed the blood upon the grass until they had come to her cottage, and had there found the deer's meat in the cupboard; that, as neither of the younger sons would betray their brother, the foresters had taken all three away, in spite of the oldest saying that he alone had slain the deer; that, as they went, she had heard the rangers talking among themselves, saying that the Sheriff had sworn that he would put a check upon the great slaughter of deer that had been going on of late by hanging the very first rogue caught thereat upon the nearest tree, and that they would take the three youths to the King's Head Inn, near Nottingham Town, where the Sheriff was abiding that day, there to await the return of a certain fellow he had sent into Sherwood to seek for Robin Hood.

To all this Little John listened, shaking his head sadly now and then. "Alas," quoth he, when the good dame had finished her speech, "this is indeed an ill case. But who is this that goeth into Sherwood after Robin Hood, and why doth he go to seek him? But no matter for that now; only that I would that Robin Hood were here to advise us. Nevertheless, no time may be lost in sending for him at this hour, if we would save the lives of thy three sons. Tell me, hast thou any clothes hereabouts that I may put on in place of these of Lincoln green? Marry, if our stout Sheriff catcheth me without disguise, I am like to be run up more quickly than thy sons, let me tell thee."

Then the old woman told him that she had in the house some of the clothes of her good husband, who had died only two years before. These she brought to Little John, who, doffing his garb of Lincoln green, put them on in its stead. Then, making a wig and false beard of uncarded wool, he covered his own brown hair and beard, and, putting on a great, tall hat that had belonged to the old peasant, he took his staff in one hand and his bow in the other, and set forth with all speed to where the Sheriff had taken up his inn.

A mile or more from Nottingham Town, and not far from the southern borders of Sherwood Forest, stood the cosy inn bearing the sign of the King's Head. Here was a great bustle and stir on this bright morning, for the Sheriff and a score of his men had come to stop there and await Guy of Gisbourne's return from the forest. Great hiss and fuss of cooking was going on in the kitchen, and great rapping and tapping of wine kegs and beer barrels was going on in the cellar. The Sheriff sat within, feasting merrily of the best the place afforded, and the Sheriff's men sat upon the bench before the door, quaffing ale, or lay beneath the shade of the broad-spreading oak trees, talking and jesting and laughing. All around stood the horses of the band, with a great noise of stamping feet and a great switching of tails. To this inn came the King's rangers, driving the widow's three sons before them. The hands of the three youths were tied tightly behind their backs, and a cord from neck to neck fastened them all together. So they were marched to the room where the Sheriff sat at meat, and stood trembling before him as he scowled sternly upon them.

"So," quoth he, in a great, loud, angry voice, "ye have been poaching upon the King's deer, have you? Now I will make short work of you this day, for I will hang up all three of you as a farmer would hang up three crows to scare others of the kind from the field. Our fair county of

Nottingham hath been too long a breeding place for such naughty knaves as ye are. I have put up with these things for many years, but now I will stamp them out once for all, and with you I will begin."

Then one of the poor fellows opened his mouth to speak, but the Sheriff roared at him in a loud voice to be silent, and bade the rangers to take them away till he had done his eating and could attend to the matters concerning them. So the three poor youths were marched outside, where they stood with bowed heads and despairing hearts, till after a while the Sheriff came forth. Then he called his men about him, and quoth he, "These three villains shall be hanged straightway, but not here, lest they breed ill luck to this goodly inn. We will take them over yonder to that belt of woodlands, for I would fain hang them upon the very trees of Sherwood itself, to show those vile outlaws therein what they may expect of me if I ever have the good luck to lay hands upon them." So saying, he mounted his horse, as did his men-at-arms likewise, and all together they set forth for the belt of woodlands he had spoken of, the poor youths walking in their midst guarded by the rangers. So they came at last to the spot, and here nooses were fastened around the necks of the three, and the ends of the cords flung over the branch of a great oak tree that stood there. Then the three youths fell upon their knees and loudly besought mercy of the Sheriff; but the Sheriff of Nottingham laughed scornfully. "Now," quoth he, "I would that I had a priest here to shrive you; but, as none is nigh, you must e'en travel your road with all your sins packed upon your backs, and trust to Saint Peter to let you in through the gates of Paradise like three peddlers into the town."

In the meantime, while all this had been going forward, an old man had drawn near and stood leaning on his staff, looking on. His hair and beard were all curly and white, and across his back was a bow of yew that looked much

too strong for him to draw. As the Sheriff looked around ere he ordered his men to string the three youths up to the oak tree, his eyes fell upon this strange old man. Then his worship beckoned to him, saying, "Come hither, father, I have a few words to say to thee." So Little John, for it was none other than he, came forward, and the Sheriff looked upon him, thinking that there was something strangely familiar in the face before him. "How, now," said he, "methinks I have seen thee before. What may thy name be, father?"

"Please Your Worship," said Little John, in a cracked voice like that of an old man, "my name is Giles Hobble, at Your Worship's service."

"Giles Hobble, Giles Hobble," muttered the Sheriff to himself, turning over the names that he had in his mind to try to find one to fit to this. "I remember not thy name," said he at last, "but it matters not. Hast thou a mind to earn sixpence this bright morn?"

"Ay, marry," quoth Little John, "for money is not so plenty with me that I should cast sixpence away an I could earn it by an honest turn. What is it Your Worship would have me do?"

"Why, this," said the Sheriff. "Here are three men that need hanging as badly as any e'er I saw. If thou wilt string them up I will pay thee twopence apiece for them. I like not that my men-at-arms should turn hangmen. Wilt thou try thy hand?"

"In sooth," said Little John, still in the old man's voice, "I ha' never done such a thing before; but an a sixpence is to be earned so easily I might as well ha' it as anybody. But, Your Worship, are these naughty fellows shrived?"

"Nay," said the Sheriff, laughing, "never a whit; but thou mayst turn thy hand to that also if thou art so minded. But hasten, I prythee, for I would get back to mine inn betimes."

So Little John came to where the three youths stood

trembling, and, putting his face to the first fellow's cheek as though he were listening to him, he whispered softly into his ear, "Stand still, brother, when thou feelest thy bonds cut, but when thou seest me throw my woolen wig and beard from my head and face, cast the noose from thy neck and run for the woodlands." Then he slyly cut the cord that bound the youth's hands; who, upon his part, stood still as though he were yet bound. Then he went to the second fellow, and spoke to him in the same way, and also cut his bonds. This he did to the third likewise, but all so slyly that the Sheriff, who sat upon his horse laughing, wotted not what was being done, nor his men either.

Then Little John turned to the Sheriff. "Please Your Worship," said he, "will you give me leave to string my bow? For I would fain help these fellows along the way, when they are swinging, with an arrow beneath the ribs."

"With all my heart," said the Sheriff, "only, as I said before, make thou haste in thy doings."

Little John put the tip of his bow to his instep, and strung the weapon so deftly that all wondered to see an old man so strong. Next he drew a good smooth arrow from his quiver and fitted it to the string; then, looking all around to see that the way was clear behind him, he suddenly cast away the wool from his head and face, shouting in a mighty voice, "Run!" Quick as a flash the three youths flung the nooses from their necks and sped across the open to the woodlands as the arrow speeds from the bow. Little John also flew toward the covert like a greyhound, while the Sheriff and his men gazed after him all bewildered with the sudden doing. But ere the yeoman had gone far the Sheriff roused himself. "After him!" he roared in a mighty voice; for he knew now who it was with whom he had been talking, and wondered that he had not known him before.

Little John heard the Sheriff's words, and seeing that he could not hope to reach the woodlands before they

would be upon him, he stopped and turned suddenly, holding his bow as though he were about to shoot. "Stand back!" cried he fiercely. "The first man that cometh a foot forward, or toucheth finger to bowstring, dieth!"

At these words the Sheriff's men stood as still as stocks, for they knew right well that Little John would be as good as his word, and that to disobey him meant death. In vain the Sheriff roared at them, calling them cowards, and urging them forward in a body; they would not budge an inch, but stood and watched Little John as he moved slowly away toward the forest, keeping his gaze fixed upon them. But when the Sheriff saw his enemy thus slipping betwixt his fingers he grew mad with his rage, so that his head swam and he knew not what he did. Then of a sudden he turned his horse's head, and plunging his spurs into its sides he gave a great shout, and, rising in his stirrups, came down upon Little John like the wind. Then Little John raised his deadly bow and drew the gray goose feather to his cheek. But alas for him! For, ere he could loose the shaft, the good bow that had served him so long, split in his hands, and the arrow fell harmless at his feet. Seeing what had happened, the Sheriff's men raised a shout, and, following their master, came rushing down upon Little John. But the Sheriff was ahead of the others, and so caught up with the yeoman before he reached the shelter of the woodlands, then leaning forward he struck a might blow. Little John ducked and the Sheriff's sword turned in his hand, but the flat of the blade struck the other upon the head and smote him down, stunned and senseless.

"Now, I am right glad," said the Sheriff, when the men came up and found that Little John was not dead, "that I have not slain this man in my haste! I would rather lose five hundred pounds than have him die thus instead of hanging, as such a vile thief should do. Go, get some

water from yonder fountain, William, and pour it over his head."

The man did as he was bidden, and presently Little John opened his eyes and looked around him, all dazed and bewildered with the stun of the blow. Then they tied his hands behind him, and lifting him up set him upon the back of one of the horses, with his face to its tail and his feet strapped beneath its belly. So they took him back to the King's Head Inn, laughing and rejoicing as they went along. But in the meantime the widow's three sons had gotten safely away, and were hidden in the woodlands.

Once more the Sheriff of Nottingham sat within the King's Head Inn. His heart rejoiced within him, for he had at last done that which he had sought to do for years, taken Little John prisoner. Quoth he to himself, "This time tomorrow the rogue shall hang upon the gallows tree in front of the great gate of Nottingham Town, and thus shall I make my long score with him even." So saying, he took a deep draught of Canary. But it seemed as if the Sheriff had swallowed a thought with his wine, for he shook his head and put the cup down hastily. "Now," he muttered to himself, "I would not for a thousand pounds have this fellow slip through my fingers; yet, should his master escape that foul Guy of Gisbourne, there is no knowing what he may do, for he is the cunningest knave in all the world—this same Robin Hood. Belike I had better not wait until tomorrow to hang the fellow." So saying, he pushed his chair back hastily, and going forth from the inn called his men together. Quoth he, "I will wait no longer for the hanging of this rogue, but it shall be done forthwith, and that from the very tree whence he saved those three young villains by stepping betwixt them and the law. So get ye ready straightway."

Then once more they sat Little John upon the horse, with his face to the tail, and so, one leading the horse whereon he sat and the others riding around him, they

went forward to that tree from the branches of which they had thought to hang the poachers. On they went, rattling and jingling along the road till they came to the tree. Here one of the men spake to the Sheriff of a sudden. "Your Worship," cried he, "is not yon fellow coming along toward us that same Guy of Gisbourne whom thou didst send into the forest to seek Robin Hood?"

At these words the Sheriff shaded his eyes and looked eagerly. "Why, certes," quoth he, "yon fellow is the same. Now, Heaven send that he hath slain the master thief, as we will presently slay the man!"

When Little John heard this speech he looked up, and straightway his heart crumbled away within him, for not only were the man's garments all covered with blood, but he wore Robin Hood's bugle horn and carried his bow and broadsword.

"How now!" cried the Sheriff, when Robin Hood, in Guy of Gisbourne's clothes, had come nigh to them. "What luck hath befallen thee in the forest? Why, man, thy clothes are all over blood!"

"An thou likest not my clothes," said Robin in a harsh voice like that of Guy of Gisbourne, "thou mayst shut thine eyes. Marry, the blood upon me is that of the vilest outlaw that ever trod the woodlands, and one whom I have slain this day, albeit not without wound to myself."

Then out spake Little John, for the first time since he had fallen into the Sheriff's hands. "O thou vile, bloody wretch! I know thee, Guy of Gisbourne, for who is there that hath not heard of thee and cursed thee for thy vile deeds of blood and rapine? Is it by such a hand as thine that the gentlest heart that ever beat is stilled in death? Truly, thou art a fit tool for this coward Sheriff of Nottingham. Now I die joyfully, nor do I care how I die, for life is nought to me!" So spake Little John, the salt tears rolling down his brown cheeks.

But the Sheriff of Nottingham clapped his hands for joy. "Now, Guy of Gisbourne," cried he, "if what thou tellest me is true, it will be the best day's doings for thee that ever thou hast done in all thy life."

"What I have told thee is sooth, and I lie not," said Robin, still in Guy of Gisbourne's voice. "Look, is not this Robin Hood's sword, and is not this his good bow of yew, and is not this his bugle horn? Thinkest thou he would have given them to Guy of Gisbourne of his own free will?"

Then the Sheriff laughed aloud for joy. "This is a good day!" cried he. "The great outlaw dead and his right-hand man in my hands! Ask what thou wilt of me, Guy of Gisbourne, and it is thine!"

"Then this I ask of thee," said Robin. "As I have slain the master I would now kill the man. Give this fellow's life into my hands, Sir Sheriff."

"Now thou art a fool!" cried the Sheriff. "Thou mightst have had money enough for a knight's ransom if thou hadst asked for it. I like ill to let this fellow pass from my hands, but as I have promised, thou shalt have him."

"I thank thee right heartily for thy gift," cried Robin. "Take the rogue down from the horse, men, and lean him against yonder tree, while I show you how we stick a porker whence I come!"

At these words some of the Sheriff's men shook their heads; for, though they cared not a whit whether Little John were hanged or not, they hated to see him butchered in cold blood. But the Sheriff called to them in a loud voice, ordering them to take the yeoman down from the horse and lean him against the tree, as the other bade.

While they were doing this Robin Hood strung both his bow and that of Guy of Gisbourne, albeit none of them took notice of his doing so. Then, when Little John stood against the tree, he drew Guy of Gisbourne's sharp,

double-edged dagger. "Fall back! fall back!" cried he. "Would ye crowd so on my pleasure, ye unmannerly knaves? Back, I say! Farther yet!" So they crowded back, as he ordered, many of them turning their faces away, that they might not see what was about to happen.

"Come!" cried Little John. "Here is my breast. It is meet that the same hand that slew my dear master should butcher me also! I know thee, Guy of Gisbourne!"

"Peace, Little John!" said Robin in a low voice. "Twice thou hast said thou knowest me, and yet thou knowest me not at all. Couldst thou not tell me beneath this wild beast's hide? Yonder, just in front of thee, lie my bow and arrows, likewise my broadsword. Take them when I cut thy bonds. Now! Get them quickly!" So saying, he cut the bonds, and Little John, quick as a wink, leaped forward and caught up the bow and arrows and the broadsword. At the same time Robin Hood threw back the cowl of horse's hide from his face and bent Guy of Gisbourne's bow, with a keen, barbed arrow fitted to the string. "Stand back!" cried he sternly. "The first man that toucheth finger to bowstring dieth! I have slain thy man, Sheriff; take heed that it is not thy turn next." Then, seeing that Little John had armed himself, he clapped his bugle horn to his lips and blew three blasts both loud and shrill.

Now when the Sheriff of Nottingham saw whose face it was beneath Guy of Gisbourne's hood, and when he heard those bugle notes ring in his ear, he felt as if his hour had come. "Robin Hood!" roared he, and without another word he wheeled his horse in the road and went off in a cloud of dust. The Sheriff's men, seeing their master thus fleeing for his life, thought that it was not their business to tarry longer, so, clapping spurs to their horses, they also dashed away after him. But though the Sheriff of Nottingham went fast, he could not outstrip a clothyard arrow. Little John twanged his bowstring with

a shout, and when the Sheriff dashed in through the gates of Nottingham Town at full speed, a gray goose shaft stuck out behind him like a moulting sparrow with one feather in its tail. For a month afterward the poor Sheriff could sit upon nought but the softest cushions that could be gotten for him.

Thus the Sheriff and a score of men ran away from Robin Hood and Little John; so that when Will Stutely and a dozen or more of stout yeomen burst from out the covert, they saw nought of their master's enemies, for the Sheriff and his men were scurrying away in the distance, hidden within a cloud of dust like a little thunderstorm.

Then they all went back into the forest once more, where they found the widow's three sons, who ran to Little John and kissed his hands. But it would not do for them to roam the forest at large any more; so they promised that, after they had gone and told their mother of their escape, they would come that night to the greenwood tree, and thenceforth become men of the band.

King Richard
Comes to Sherwood Forest

N OT MORE than two months had passed and gone since these stirring adventures befell Robin Hood and Little John, when all Nottinghamshire was a mighty stir and tumult, for King Richard of the Lion's Heart was making a royal progress through merry England, and everyone expected him to come to Nottingham Town in his journeying. Messengers went riding back and forth between the Sheriff and the King, until at last the time was fixed upon when His Majesty was to stop in Nottingham, as the guest of his worship.

And now came more bustle than ever; a great running hither and thither, a rapping of hammers and a babble of voices sounded everywhere through the place, for the folk were building great arches across the streets, beneath which the King was to pass, and were draping these arches with silken banners and streamers of many colors. Great hubbub was going on in the Guild Hall of the town, also, for here a grand banquet was to be given to the King and the nobles of his train, and the best master carpenters were busy building a throne where the King and the Sheriff were to sit at the head of the table, side by side.

It seemed to many of the good folk of the place as if the day that should bring the King into the town would never come; but all the same it did come in its own season, and bright shone the sun down into the stony streets, which were all alive with a restless sea of people. On either side of the way great crowds of town and country folk stood packed as close together as dried herring in a box, so that the Sheriff's men, halberds in hands, could hardly press them back to leave space for the King's riding.

"Take care whom thou pushest against!" cried a great, burly friar to one of these men. "Wouldst thou dig thine elbows into me, sirrah? By'r Lady of the Fountain, an thou dost not treat me with more deference I will crack thy knave's pate for thee, even though thou be one of the mighty Sheriff's men."

At this a great shout of laughter arose from a number of tall yeomen in Lincoln green that were scattered through the crowd thereabouts; but one that seemed of more authority than the others nudged the holy man with his elbow. "Peace, Tuck," said he, "didst thou not promise me, ere thou camest here, that thou wouldst put a check upon thy tongue?"

"Ay, marry," grumbled the other, "but 'a did not think to have a hard-footed knave trample all over my poor toes as though they were no more than so many acorns in the forest."

But of a sudden all this bickering ceased, for a clear sound of many bugle horns came winding down the street. Then all the people craned their necks and gazed in the direction whence the sound came, and the crowding and the pushing and the swaying grew greater than ever. And now a gallant array of men came gleaming into sight, and the cheering of the people ran down the crowd as the fire runs in dry grass.

Eight and twenty heralds in velvet and cloth of gold came riding forward. Over their heads fluttered a cloud

of snow-white feathers, and each herald bore in his hand a long silver trumpet, which he blew musically. From each trumpet hung a heavy banner of velvet and cloth of gold, with the royal arms of England emblazoned thereon. After these came riding fivescore noble knights, two by two, all fully armed, saving that their heads were uncovered. In their hands they bore tall lances, from the tops of which fluttered pennons of many colors and devices. By the side of each knight walked a page clad in rich clothes of silk and velvet, and each page bore in his hands his master's helmet, from which waved long, floating plumes of feathers. Never had Nottingham seen a fairer sight than those fivescore noble knights, from whose armor the sun blazed in dazzling light as they came riding on their great war horses, with clashing of arms and jingling of chains. Behind the knights came the barons and the nobles of the mid-country, in robes of silk and cloth of gold, with golden chains about their necks and jewels at their girdles. Behind these again came a great array of men-at-arms, with spears and halberds in their hands, and, in the midst of these, two riders side by side. One of the horsemen was the Sheriff of Nottingham in his robes of office. The other, who was a head taller than the Sheriff, was clad in a rich but simple garb, with a broad, heavy chain about his neck. His hair and beard were like threads of gold, and his eyes were as blue as the summer sky. As he rode along he bowed to the right hand and the left, and a mighty roar of voices followed him as he passed; for this was King Richard.

Then, above all the tumult and the shouting a great voice was heard roaring, "Heaven, its saints bless thee, our gracious King Richard! and likewise Our Lady of the Fountain, bless thee!" Then King Richard, looking toward the spot whence the sound came, saw a tall, burly, strapping priest standing in front of all the crowd with his legs wide apart as he backed against those behind.

"By my soul, Sheriff," said the King, laughing, "ye have the tallest priests in Nottinghamshire that e'er I saw in all my life. If Heaven never answered prayers because of deafness, methinks I would nevertheless have blessings bestowed upon me, for that man yonder would make the great stone image of Saint Peter rub its ears and hearken unto him. I would that I had an army of such as he."

To this the Sheriff answered never a word, but all the blood left his cheeks, and he caught at the pommel of his saddle to keep himself from falling; for he also saw the fellow that so shouted, and knew him to be Friar Tuck; and, moreover, behind Friar Tuck he saw the faces of Robin Hood and Little John and Will Scarlet and Will Stutely and Allan a Dale and others of the band.

"How now," said the King hastily, "art thou ill, Sheriff, that thou growest so white?"

"Nay, Your Majesty," said the Sheriff, "it was nought but a sudden pain that will soon pass by." Thus he spake, for he was ashamed that the King should know that Robin Hood feared him so little that he thus dared to come within the very gates of Nottingham Town.

Thus rode the King into Nottingham Town on that bright afternoon in the early fall season; and none rejoiced more than Robin Hood and his merry men to see him come so royally unto his own.

Eventide had come; the great feast in the Guild Hall at Nottingham Town was done, and the wine passed freely. A thousand waxen lights gleamed along the board, at which sat lord and noble and knight and squire in goodly array. At the head of the table, upon a throne all hung with cloth of gold, sat King Richard with the Sheriff of Nottingham beside him.

Quoth the King to the Sheriff, laughing as he spoke, "I have heard much spoken concerning the doings of certain fellows hereabouts, one Robin Hood and his band, who

are outlaws and abide in Sherwood Forest. Canst thou not tell me somewhat of them, Sir Sheriff? For I hear that thou hast had dealings with them more than once."

At these words the Sheriff of Nottingham looked down gloomily, and the Bishop of Hereford, who was present, gnawed his nether lip. Quoth the Sheriff, "I can tell Your Majesty but little concerning the doings of those naughty fellows, saving that they are the boldest lawbreakers in all the land."

Then up spake young Sir Henry of the Lea, a great favorite with the King, under whom he had fought in Palestine. "May it please Your Majesty," said he, "when I was away in Palestine I heard ofttimes from my father, and in most cases I heard of this very fellow, Robin Hood. If Your Majesty would like I will tell you a certain adventure of this outlaw."

Then the King laughingly bade him tell his tale, whereupon he told how Robin Hood had aided Sir Richard of the Lea with money that he had borrowed from the Bishop of Hereford. Again and again the King and those present roared with laughter, while the poor Bishop waxed cherry red in the face with vexation, for the matter was a sore thing with him. When Sir Henry of the Lea was done, others of those present, seeing how the King enjoyed this merry tale, told other tales concerning Robin and his merry men.

"By the hilt of my sword," said stout King Richard, "this is as bold and merry a knave as ever I heard tell of. Marry, I must take this matter in hand and do what thou couldst not do, Sheriff, to wit, clear the forest of him and his band."

That night the King sat in the place that was set apart for his lodging while in Nottingham Town. With him were young Sir Henry of the Lea and two other knights and three barons of Nottinghamshire; but the King's mind still dwelled upon Robin Hood. "Now," quoth he, "I

would freely give a hundred pounds to meet this roguish fellow, Robin Hood, and to see somewhat of his doings in Sherwood Forest."

Then up spake Sir Hubert of Bingham, laughing: "If Your Majesty hath such a desire upon you it is not so hard to satisfy. If Your Majesty is willing to lose one hundred pounds, I will engage to cause you not only to meet this fellow, but to feast with him in Sherwood."

"Marry, Sir Hubert," quoth the King, "this pleaseth me well. But how wilt thou cause me to meet Robin Hood?"

"Why, thus," said Sir Hubert, "let Your Majesty and us here present put on the robes of seven of the Order of Black Friars, and let Your Majesty hang a purse of one hundred pounds beneath your gown; then let us undertake to ride from here to Mansfield Town tomorrow, and, without I am much mistaken, we will both meet with Robin Hood and dine with him before the day be passed."

"I like thy plan, Sir Hubert," quoth the King merrily, "and tomorrow we will try it and see whether there be virtue in it."

So it happened that when early the next morning the Sheriff came to where his liege lord was abiding, to pay his duty to him, the King told him what they had talked of the night before, and what merry adventure they were set upon undertaking that morning. But when the Sheriff heard this he smote his forehead with his fist. "Alas!" said he, "what evil counsel is this that hath been given thee! O my gracious lord and King, you know not what you do! This villain that you thus go to seek hath no reverence either for king or king's laws."

"But did I not hear aright when I was told that this Robin Hood hath shed no blood since he was outlawed, saving only that of that vile Guy of Gisbourne, for whose death all honest men should thank him?"

"Yea, Your Majesty," said the Sheriff, "you have heard aright. Nevertheless—"

"Then," quoth the King, breaking in on the Sheriff's speech, "what have I to fear in meeting him, having done him no harm? Truly, there is no danger in this. But mayhap thou wilt go with us, Sir Sheriff."

"Nay," quoth the Sheriff hastily, "Heaven forbid!"

But now seven habits such as Black Friars wear were brought, and the King and those about him having clad themselves therein, and His Majesty having hung a purse with a hundred golden pounds in it beneath his robes, they all went forth and mounted the mules that had been brought to the door for them. Then the King bade the Sheriff be silent as to their doings, and so they set forth upon their way. Onward they traveled, laughing and jesting, until they passed through the open country; between bare harvest fields whence the harvest had been gathered home; through scattered glades that began to thicken as they went farther along, till they came within the heavy shade of the forest itself. They traveled in the forest for several miles without meeting anyone such as they sought, until they had come to that part of the road that lay nearest to Newstead Abbey.

"By the holy Saint Martin," quoth the King, "I would that I had a better head for remembering things of great need. Here have we come away and brought never so much as a drop of anything to drink with us. Now I would give half a hundred pounds for somewhat to quench my thirst withal."

No sooner had the King so spoken, than out from the covert at the roadside stepped a tall fellow with yellow beard and hair and a pair of merry blue eyes. "Truly, holy brother," said he, laying his hand upon the King's bridle rein, "it were an unchristian thing to not give fitting answer to so fair a bargain. We keep an inn hereabouts, and for fifty pounds we will not only give thee a good

draught of wine, but will give thee as noble a feast as ever thou didst tickle thy gullet withal." So saying, he put his fingers to his lips and blew a shrill whistle. Then straightway the bushes and branches on either side of the road swayed and crackled, and threescore broad-shouldered yeomen in Lincoln green burst out of the covert.

"How now, fellow," quoth the King, "who art thou, thou naughty rogue? Hast thou no regard for such holy men as we are?"

"Not a whit," quoth merry Robin Hood, for the fellow was he, "for in sooth all the holiness belonging to rich friars, such as ye are, one could drop into a thimble and the goodwife would never feel it with the tip of her finger. As for my name, it is Robin Hood, and thou mayst have heard it before."

"Now out upon thee!" quoth King Richard. "Thou art a bold and naughty fellow and a lawless one withal, as I have often heard tell. Now, prythee, let me, and these brethren of mine, travel forward in peace and quietness."

"It may not be," said Robin, "for it would look but ill of us to let such holy men travel onward with empty stomachs. But I doubt not that thou hast a fat purse to pay thy score at our inn since thou offerest freely so much for a poor draught of wine. Show me thy purse, reverend brother, or I may perchance have to strip thy robes from thee to search for it myself."

"Nay, use no force," said the King sternly. "Here is my purse, but lay not thy lawless hands upon our person."

"Hut, tut," quoth merry Robin, "what proud words are these? Art thou the King of England, to talk so to me? Here, Will, take this purse and see what there is within."

Will Scarlet took the purse and counted out the money. Then Robin bade him keep fifty pounds for themselves,

and put fifty back into the purse. This he handed to the King. "Here, brother," quoth he, "take this half of thy money, and thank Saint Martin, on whom thou didst call before, that thou hast fallen into the hands of such gentle rogues that they will not strip thee bare, as they might do. But wilt thou not put back thy cowl? For I would fain see thy face."

"Nay," said the King, drawing back, "I may not put back my cowl, for we seven have vowed that we will not show our faces for four and twenty hours."

"Then keep them covered in peace," said Robin, "and far be it from me to make you break your vows."

So he called seven of his yeomen and bade them each one take a mule by the bridle; then, turning their faces toward the depths of the woodlands, they journeyed onward until they came to the open glade and the greenwood tree.

Little John, with threescore yeomen at his heels, had also gone forth that morning to wait along the roads and bring a rich guest to Sherwood glade, if such might be his luck, for many with fat purses must travel the roads at this time, when such great doings were going on in Nottinghamshire; but though Little John and so many others were gone, Friar Tuck and twoscore or more stout yeomen were seated or lying around beneath the great tree, and when Robin and the others came they leaped to their feet to meet him.

"By my soul," quoth merry King Richard, when he had gotten down from his mule and stood looking about him, "thou hast in very truth a fine lot of young men about thee, Robin. Methinks King Richard himself would be glad of such a bodyguard."

"These are not all of my fellows," said Robin proudly, "for threescore more of them are away on business with my good right-hand man, Little John. But, as for King Richard, I tell thee, brother, there is not a man of us all

but would pour out our blood like water for him. Ye churchmen cannot rightly understand our King; but we yeomen love him right loyally for the sake of his brave doings which are so like our own."

But now Friar Tuck came bustling up. "Gi' ye good den, brothers," said he. "I am right glad to welcome some of my cloth in this naughty place. Truly, methinks these rogues of outlaws would stand but an ill chance were it not for the prayers of Holy Tuck, who laboreth so hard for their well-being." Here he winked one eye slyly and stuck his tongue into his cheek.

"Who art thou, mad priest?" said the King in a serious voice, albeit he smiled beneath his cowl.

At this Friar Tuck looked all around with a slow gaze. "Look you now," quoth he, "never let me hear you say again that I am no patient man. Here is a knave of a friar calleth me a mad priest, and yet I smite him not. My name is Friar Tuck, fellow—the holy Friar Tuck."

"There, Tuck," said Robin, "thou hast said enow. Prythee, cease thy talk and bring some wine. These reverend men are athirst, and sin' they have paid so richly for their score they must e'en have the best."

Friar Tuck bridled at being so checked in his speech, nevertheless he went straightway to do Robin's bidding; so presently a great crock was brought, and wine was poured out for all the guests and for Robin Hood. Then Robin held his cup aloft. "Stay!" cried he. "Tarry in your drinking till I give you a pledge. Here is to good King Richard of great renown, and may all enemies to him be confounded."

Then all drank the King's health, even the King himself. "Methinks, good fellow," said he, "thou hast drunk to thine own confusion."

"Never a whit," quoth merry Robin, "for I tell thee that we of Sherwood are more loyal to our lord the King than those of thine order. We would give up our lives for his

benefiting, while ye are content to lie snug in your abbeys and priories let reign who will."

At this the King laughed. Quoth he, "Perhaps King Richard's welfare is more to me than thou wottest of, fellow. But enough of that matter. We have paid well for our fare, so canst thou not show us some merry entertainment? I have oft heard that ye are wondrous archers; wilt thou not show us somewhat of your skill?"

"With all my heart," said Robin, "we are always pleased to show our guests all the sport that is to be seen. As Gaffer Swanthold sayeth, ' 'Tis a hard heart that will not give a caged starling of the best'; and caged starlings ye are with us. Ho, lads! Set up a garland at the end of the glade."

Then, as the yeomen ran to do their master's bidding, Tuck turned to one of the mock friars. "Hearest thou our master?" quoth he, with a sly wink. "Whenever he cometh across some poor piece of wit he straightway layeth it on the shoulders of this Gaffer Swanthold— whoever he may be—so that the poor goodman goeth traveling about with all the odds and ends and tags and rags of our master's brain packed on his back." Thus spake Friar Tuck, but in a low voice so that Robin could not hear him, for he felt somewhat nettled at Robin's cutting his talk so short.

In the meantime the mark at which they were to shoot was set up at sixscore paces distance. It was a garland of leaves and flowers two spans in width, which same was hung upon a stake in front of a broad tree trunk. "There," quoth Robin, "yon is a fair mark, lads. Each of you shoot three arrows thereat; and if any fellow misseth by so much as one arrow, he shall have a buffet of Will Scarlet's fist."

"Hearken to him!" quoth Friar Tuck. "Why, master, thou dost bestow buffets from thy strapping nephew as though they were love taps from some bouncing lass. I

warrant thou art safe to hit the garland thyself, or thou wouldst not be so free of his cuffing."

First David of Doncaster shot, and lodged all three of his arrows within the garland. "Well done, David!" cried Robin, "thou hast saved thine ears from a warming this day." Next Midge, the Miller, shot, and he, also, lodged his arrows in the garland. Then followed Wat, the Tinker, but alas for him! For one of his shafts missed the mark by the breadth of two fingers.

"Come hither, fellow," said Will Scarlet, in his soft, gentle voice, "I owe thee somewhat that I would pay forthwith." Then Wat, the Tinker, came forward and stood in front of Will Scarlet, screwing up his face and shutting his eyes tightly, as though he already felt his ears ringing with the buffet. Will Scarlet rolled up his sleeve, and, standing on tiptoe to give the greater swing to his arm, he struck with might and main. *"Whoof!"* came his palm against the Tinker's head, and down went stout Wat to the grass, heels over head, as the wooden image at the fair goes down when the skillful player throws a cudgel at it. Then, as the Tinker sat up upon the grass, rubbing his ear and winking and blinking at the bright stars that danced before his eyes, the yeomen roared with mirth till the forest rang. As for King Richard, he laughed till the tears ran down his cheeks. Thus the band shot, each in turn, some getting off scot free, and some winning a buffet that always sent them to the grass. And now, last of all, Robin took his place, and all was hushed as he shot. The first shaft he shot split a piece from the stake on which the garland was hung; the second lodged within an inch of the other. "By my halidom," said King Richard to himself, "I would give a thousand pounds for this fellow to be one of my guard!" And now, for the third time Robin shot; but, alas for him! The arrow was ill-feathered, and, wavering to one side, it smote an inch outside the garland.

At this a great roar went up, those of the yeomen who

sat upon the grass rolling over and over and shouting with laughter, for never before had they seen their master so miss his mark; but Robin flung his bow upon the ground with vexation. "Now, out upon it!" cried he. "That shaft had an ill feather to it, for I felt it as it left my fingers. Give me a clean arrow, and I will engage to split the wand with it."

At these words the yeomen laughed louder than ever. "Nay, good uncle," said Will Scarlet in his soft, sweet voice, "thou hast had thy fair chance and hast missed thine aim out and out. I swear the arrow was as good as any that hath been loosed this day. Come hither; I owe thee somewhat, and would fain pay it."

"Go, good master," roared Friar Tuck, "and may my blessing go with thee. Thou hast bestowed these love taps of Will Scarlet's with great freedom. It were pity an thou gottest not thine own share."

"It may not be," said merry Robin. "I am king here, and no subject may raise hand against the king. But even our great King Richard may yield to the holy Pope without shame, and even take a tap from him by way of penance; therefore I will yield myself to this holy friar, who seemeth to be one in authority, and will take my punishment for him." Thus saying, he turned to the King, "I prythee, brother, wilt thou take my punishing into thy holy hands?"

"With all my heart," quoth merry King Richard, rising from where he was sitting. "I owe thee somewhat for having lifted a heavy weight of fifty pounds from my purse. So make room for him on the green, lads."

"An thou makest me tumble," quoth Robin, "I will freely give thee back thy fifty pounds; but I tell thee, brother, if thou makest me not feel grass all along my back, I will take every farthing thou hast for thy boastful speech."

"So be it," said the King, "I am willing to venture it."

Thereupon he rolled up his sleeve and showed an arm that made the yeomen stare. But Robin, with his feet wide apart, stood firmly planted, waiting the other, smiling. Then the King swung back his arm, and, balancing himself a moment, he delivered a buffet at Robin that fell like a thunderbolt. Down went Robin headlong upon the grass, for the stroke would have felled a stone wall. Then how the yeomen shouted with laughter till their sides ached, for never had they seen such a buffet given in all their lives. As for Robin, he presently sat up and looked all around him, as though he had dropped from a cloud and had lit in a place he had never seen before. After a while, still gazing about him at his laughing yeomen, he put his fingertips softly to his ear and felt all around it tenderly. "Will Scarlet," said he, "count this fellow out his fifty pounds; I want nothing more either of his money or of him. A murrain seize him and his buffeting! I would that I had taken my dues from thee, for I verily believe he hath deafened mine ear from ever hearing again."

Then, while gusts of laughter still broke from the band, Will Scarlet counted out the fifty pounds, and the King dropped it back into his purse again. "I give thee thanks, fellow," said he, "and if ever thou shouldst wish for another box of the ear to match the one thou hast, come to me and I will fit thee with it for nought."

So spake the merry King; but, even as he ended, there came suddenly the sound of many voices, and out from the covert burst Little John and threescore men, with Sir Richard of the Lea in the midst. Across the glade they came running, and, as they came, Sir Richard shouted to Robin: "Make haste, dear friend, gather thy band together and come with me! King Richard left Nottingham Town this very morning, and cometh to seek thee in the woodlands. I know not how he cometh, for it was but a rumor of this that reached me; nevertheless, I know that it

The King delivered a buffet at Robin that fell like a thunderbolt.

is the truth. Therefore hasten with all thy men, and come
to Castle Lea, for there thou mayst lie hidden till thy
present danger passeth. Who are these strangers that
thou hast with thee?"

"Why," quoth merry Robin, rising from the grass,
"these are certain gentle guests that came with us from the
highroad over by Newstead Abbey. I know not their
names, but I have become right well acquaint with this
lusty rogue's palm this morning. Marry, the pleasure of
this acquaintance hath cost me a deaf ear and fifty pounds
to boot!"

Sir Richard looked keenly at the tall friar, who, drawing himself up to his full height, looked fixedly back at the
knight. Then of a sudden Sir Richard's cheeks grew
pale, for he knew who it was that he looked upon.
Quickly he leaped from off his horse's back and flung
himself upon his knees before the other. At this, the
King, seeing that Sir Richard knew him, threw back his
cowl, and all the yeomen saw his face and knew him also,
for there was not one of them but had been in the crowd
in the good town of Nottingham, and had seen him riding
side by side with the Sheriff. Down they fell upon their
knees, nor could they say a word. Then the King looked
all around right grimly, and, last of all, his glance came
back and rested again upon Sir Richard of the Lea.

"How is this, Sir Richard?" said he sternly. "How
darest thou step between me and these fellows? And
how darest thou offer thy knightly Castle of the Lea for a
refuge to them? Wilt thou make it a hiding place for the
most renowned outlaws in England?"

Then Sir Richard of the Lea raised his eyes to the
King's face. "Far be it from me, " said he, "to do aught
that could bring Your Majesty's anger upon me. Yet,
sooner would I face Your Majesty's wrath than suffer
aught of harm that I could stay to fall upon Robin Hood
and his band; for to them I owe life, honor, everything.

Should I, then, desert him in his hour of need?"

Ere the knight had done speaking, one of the mock friars that stood near the King came forward and knelt beside Sir Richard, and throwing back his cowl showed the face of young Sir Henry of the Lea. Then Sir Henry grasped his father's hand and said, "Here kneels one who hath served thee well, King Richard, and, as thou knowest, hath stepped between thee and death in Palestine; yet do I abide by my dear father, and here I say also, that I would freely give shelter to this noble outlaw, Robin Hood, even though it brought thy wrath upon me, for my father's honor and my father's welfare are as dear to me as mine own."

King Richard looked from one to the other of the kneeling knights, and at last the frown faded from his brow and a smile twitched at the corners of his lips. "Marry, Sir Richard," quoth the King, "thou art a bold-spoken knight, and thy freedom of speech weigheth not heavily against thee with me. This young son of thine taketh after his sire both in boldness of speech and of deed, for, as he sayeth, he stepped one time betwixt me and death; wherefore I would pardon thee for his sake even if thou hadst done more than thou hast. Rise all of you, for ye shall suffer no harm through me this day, for it were pity that a merry time should end in a manner as to mar its joyousness."

Then all arose and the King beckoned Robin Hood to come to him. "How now," quoth he, "is thine ear still too deaf to hear me speak?"

"Mine ears would be deafened in death ere they would cease to hear Your Majesty's voice," said Robin. "As for the blow that Your Majesty struck me, I would say that though my sins are haply many, methinks they have been paid up in full thereby."

"Thinkest thou so?" said the King with somewhat of sternness in his voice. "Now I tell thee that but for three

things, to wit, my mercifulness, my love for a stout woodsman, and the loyalty thou hast avowed for me, thine ears, mayhap, might have been more tightly closed than ever a buffet from me could have shut them. Talk not lightly of thy sins, good Robin. But come, look up. Thy danger is past, for hereby I give thee and all thy band free pardon. But, in sooth, I cannot let you roam the forest as ye have done in the past; therefore I will take thee at thy word, when thou didst say thou wouldst give thy service to me, and thou shalt go back to London with me. We will take that bold knave Little John also, and likewise thy cousin, Will Scarlet, and thy minstrel Allan a Dale. As for the rest of thy band, we will take their names and have them duly recorded as royal rangers; for methinks it were wiser to have them changed to law-abiding caretakers of our deer in Sherwood than to leave them to run at large as outlawed slayers thereof. But now get a feast ready; I would see how ye live in the woodlands."

So Robin bade his men make ready a grand feast. Straightway great fires were kindled and burned brightly, at which savory things roasted sweetly. While this was going forward, the King bade Robin call Allan a Dale, for he would hear him sing. So word was passed for Allan, and presently he came, bringing his harp.

"Marry," said King Richard, "if thy singing match thy looks it is fair enough. Prythee, strike up a ditty and let us have a taste of thy skill."

Then Allan touched his harp lightly, and all words were hushed while he sang thus:

> " 'Oh, where hast thou been, my daughter?
> Oh, where hast thou been this day,
> Daughter, my daughter?'
> 'Oh, I have been to the river's side,
> Where the waters lie all gray and wide,
> And the gray sky broods o'er the leaden tied,
> And the shrill wind sighs a straining.'

" 'What sawest thou there, my daughter?
What sawest thou there this day,
Daughter, my daughter?'
'Oh, I saw a boat come drifting nigh,
Where the quivering rushes hiss and sigh,
And the water soughs as it gurgles by,
And the shrill wind sighs a straining.'

" 'What sailed in the boat, my daughter?
What sailed in the boat this day,
Daughter, my daughter?'
'Oh, there was one all clad in white,
And about his face hung a pallid light,
And his eyes gleamed sharp like the stars at night,
And the shrill wind sighed a straining.'

" 'And what said he, my daughter?
What said he to thee this day,
Daughter, my daughter?'
'Oh, said he nought, but did he this:
Thrice on my lips did he press a kiss,
And my heartstrings shrunk with an awful bliss,
And the shrill wind sighed a straining.'

" 'Why growest thou so cold, my daughter?
Why growest thou so cold and white,
Daughter, my daughter?'
Oh, never a word the daughter said,
But she sat all straight with a drooping head,
For her heart was stilled and her face was dead:
And the shrill wind sighed a straining."

All listened in silence; and when Allan a Dale had done
King Richard heaved a sigh. "By the breath of my body,
Allan," quoth he, "thou hast such a wondrous sweet voice
that it strangely moves my heart. But what doleful ditty
is this for the lips of a stout yeoman? I would rather hear
thee sing a song of love and battle than a sad thing like

that. Moreover, I understand it not; what meanest thou by the words?"

"I know not, Your Majesty," said Allan, shaking his head, "for ofttimes I sing that which I do not clearly understand mine own self."

"Well, well," quoth the King, "let it pass; only I tell thee this, Allan, thou shouldst turn thy songs to such matters as I spoke of, to wit, love or war; for in sooth thou hast a sweeter voice than Blondell, and methought he was the best minstrel that ever I heard."

But now one came forward and said that the feast was ready; so Robin Hood brought King Richard and those with him to where it lay all spread out on fair white linen cloths which lay upon the soft green grass. Then King Richard sat him down and feasted and drank, and when he was done he swore roundly that he had never sat at such a lusty repast in all his life before.

That night he lay in Sherwood Forest upon a bed of sweet green leaves, and early the next morning he set forth from the woodlands for Nottingham Town, Robin Hood and all of his band going with him. You may guess what a stir there was in the good town when all these famous outlaws came marching into the streets. As for the Sheriff, he knew not what to say nor where to look when he saw Robin Hood in such high favor with the King, while all his heart was filled with gall because of the vexation that lay upon him.

The next day the King took leave of Nottingham Town; so Robin Hood and Little John and Will Scarlet and Allan a Dale shook hands with all the rest of the band, kissing the cheeks of each man, and swearing that they would often come to Sherwood and see them. Then each mounted his horse and rode away in the train of the King.

Epilogue

THUS END the Merry Adventures of Robin Hood; for, in spite of his promise, it was many a year ere he saw Sherwood again.

After a year or two at court Little John came back to Nottinghamshire, where he lived in an orderly way, though within sight of Sherwood, and where he achieved great fame as the champion of all England with the quarterstaff. Will Scarlet after a time came back to his own home, whence he had been driven by his unlucky killing of his father's steward. The rest of the band did their duty as royal rangers right well. But Robin Hood and Allan a Dale did not come again to Sherwood so quickly, for thus it was:

Robin, through his great fame as an archer, became a favorite with the King, so that he speedily rose in rank to be the chief of all the yeomen. At last the King, seeing how faithful and how loyal he was, created him Earl of Huntingdon; so Robin followed the King to the wars, and found his time so full that he had no chance to come back to Sherwood for even so much as a day. As for Allan a Dale and his wife, the fair Ellen, they followed Robin Hood and shared in all his ups and downs of life.

And now, dear friend, you who have journeyed with me in all these merry doings, I will not bid you follow me further, but will drop your hand here with a "good den," if you wish it; for that which cometh hereafter speaks of the breaking up of things, and shows how joys and pleasures that are dead and gone can never be set upon their feet to walk again. I will not dwell upon the matter overlong, but will tell as speedily as may be of how that stout fellow, Robin Hood, died as he had lived, not at court as Earl of Huntingdon, but with bow in hand, his heart in the greenwood, and he himself a right yeoman.

King Richard died upon the battlefield, in such a way as properly became a lion-hearted king, as you yourself, no doubt, know; so, after a time, the Earl of Huntingdon —or Robin Hood, as we still call him as of old—finding nothing for his doing abroad, came back to merry England again. With him came Allan a Dale and his wife, the fair Ellen, for these two had been chief of Robin's household ever since he had left Sherwood Forest.

It was in the springtime when they landed once more on the shores of England. The leaves were green and the small birds sang blithely, just as they used to do in fair Sherwood when Robin Hood roamed the woodland shades with a free heart and a light heel. All the sweetness of the time and the joyousness of everything brought back to Robin's mind his forest life, so that a great longing came upon him to behold the woodlands once more. So he went straightway to King John and besought leave of him to visit Nottingham for a short season. The King gave him leave to come and to go, but bade him not stay longer than three days at Sherwood. So Robin Hood and Allan a Dale set forth without delay to Nottinghamshire and Sherwood Forest.

The first night they took up their inn at Nottingham Town, yet they did not go to pay their duty to the Sheriff, for his worship bore many a bitter grudge against Robin

Hood, which grudges had not been lessened by Robin's rise in the world. The next day at an early hour they mounted their horses and set forth for the woodlands. As they passed along the road it seemed to Robin that he knew every stick and stone that his eyes looked upon. Yonder was a path that he had ofttimes trod of a mellow evening, with Little John beside him; here was one, now nigh choked with brambles, along which he and a little band had walked when they went forth to seek a certain curtal friar.

Thus they rode slowly onward, talking about these old, familiar things; old and yet new, for they found more in them than they had ever thought of before. Thus at last they came to the open glade, and the broad, wide-spreading greenwood tree which was their home for so many years. Neither of the two spoke when they stood beneath that tree. Robin looked all about him at the well-known things, so like what they used to be and yet so different; for, where once was the bustle of many busy fellows was now the quietness of solitude; and, as he looked, the woodlands, the greensward, and the sky all blurred together in his sight through salt tears, for such a great yearning came upon him as he looked on these things (as well known to him as the fingers of his right hand) that he could not keep back the water from his eyes.

That morning he had slung his good old bugle horn over his shoulder, and now, with the yearning, came a great longing to sound his bugle once more. He raised it to his lips; he blew a blast. "Tirila, lirila," the sweet, clear notes went winding down the forest paths, coming back again from the more distant bosky shades in faint echoes of sound, "Tirila, lirila, tirila, lirila," until it faded away and was lost.

Now it chanced that on that very morn Little John was walking through a spur of the forest upon certain matters

of business, and as he paced along, sunk in meditation, the faint, clear notes of a distant bugle horn came to his ear. As leaps the stag when it feels the arrow at its heart, so leaped Little John when that distant sound met his ear. All the blood in his body seemed to rush like a flame into his cheeks as he bent his head and listened. Again came the bugle note, thin and clear, and yet again it sounded. Then Little John gave a great, wild cry of yearning, of joy, and yet of grief, and, putting down his head, he dashed into the thicket. Onward he plunged, crackling and rending, as the wild boar rushes through the underbrush. Little recked he of thorns and briers that scratched his flesh and tore his clothing, for all he thought of was to get, by the shortest way, to the greenwood glade whence he knew the sound of the bugle horn came. Out he burst from the covert, at last, a shower of little broken twigs falling about him, and, without pausing a moment, rushed forward and flung himself at Robin's feet. Then he clasped his arms around the master's knees, and all his body was shaken with great sobs; neither could Robin nor Allan a Dale speak, but stood looking down at Little John, the tears rolling down their cheeks.

While they thus stood, seven royal rangers rushed into the open glade and raised a great shout of joy at the sight of Robin; and at their head was Will Stutely. Then, after a while, came four more, panting with their running, and two of these four were Will Scathelock and Midge, the Miller; for all of these had heard the sound of Robin Hood's horn. All these ran to Robin and kissed his hands and his clothing, with great sound of weeping.

After a while Robin looked around him with tear-dimmed eyes and said, in a husky voice, "Now, I swear that never again will I leave these dear woodlands. I have been away from them and from you too long. Now do I lay by the name of Robert, Earl of Huntingdon, and take upon me once again that nobler title, Robin Hood, the

Yeoman." At this a great shout went up, and all the yeomen shook one another's hands for joy.

The news that Robin Hood had come back again to dwell in Sherwood as of old spread like wildfire all over the countryside, so that ere a se'ennight had passed nearly all of his old yeomen had gathered about him again. But when the news of all this reached the ears of King John, he swore both loud and deep, and took a solemn vow that he would not rest until he had Robin Hood in his power, dead or alive. Now there was present at court a certain knight, Sir William Dale, as gallant a soldier as ever donned harness. Sir William Dale was well acquainted with Sherwood Forest, for he was head keeper over that part of it that lay nigh to good Mansfield Town; so to him the King turned, and bade him take an army of men and go straightway to seek Robin Hood. Likewise the King gave Sir William his signet ring to show to the Sheriff, that he might raise all his armed men to aid the others in their chase of Robin. So Sir William and the Sheriff set forth to do the King's bidding and to search for Robin Hood; and for seven days they hunted up and down, yet found him not.

Now, had Robin Hood been as peaceful as of old, everything might have ended in smoke, as other such ventures had always done before; but he had fought for years under King Richard, and was changed from what he used to be. It galled his pride to thus flee away before those sent against him, as a chased fox flees from the hounds; so thus it came about, at last, that Robin Hood and his yeomen met Sir William and the Sheriff and their men in the forest, and a bloody fight followed. The first man slain in that fight was the Sheriff of Nottingham, for he fell from his horse with an arrow in his brain ere half a score of shafts had been sped. Many a better man than the Sheriff kissed the sod that day, but at last, Sir William Dale being wounded and most of his men slain, he with-

drew, beaten, and left the forest. But scores of good fellows were left behind him, stretched out all stiff beneath the sweet green boughs.

But though Robin Hood had beaten off this enemies in fair fight, all this lay heavily upon his mind, so that he brooded over it until a fever seized upon him. For three days it held him, and though he strove to fight it off, he was forced to yield at last. Thus it came that, on the morning of the fourth day, he called Little John to him, and told him that he could not shake the fever from him, and that he would go to his cousin, the prioress of the nunnery near Kirklees, in Yorkshire, who was a skillful leech, and he would have her open a vein in his arm and take a little blood from him, for the bettering of his health. Then he bade Little John make ready to go also, for he might perchance need aid in his journeying. So Little John and he took their leave of the others, and Robin Hood bade Will Stutely be the captain of the band until they should come back. Thus they came by easy stages and slow journeying until they reached the Nunnery of Kirklees.

Now Robin had done much to aid this cousin of his; for it was through King Richard's love of him that she had been made prioress of the place. But there is nought in the world so easily forgot as gratitude; so, when the Prioress of Kirklees had heard how her cousin, the Earl of Huntingdon, had thrown away his earldom and gone back again to Sherwood, she was vexed to the soul, and feared lest her cousinship with him should bring the King's wrath upon her also. Thus it happened that when Robin came to her and told her how he wished her services as leech, she began plotting ill against him in her mind, thinking that by doing evil to him she might find favor with his enemies. Nevertheless, she kept this well to herself and received Robin with seeming kindness. She led him up the winding stone stair to a room which

was just beneath the eaves of a high, round tower; but she would not let Little John come with him.

So the poor yeoman turned his feet away from the door of the nunnery, and left his master in the hands of the women. But, though he did not come in, neither did he go far away; for he laid him down in a little glade near by, where he could watch the place that Robin abided, like some great, faithful dog turned away from the door where his master has entered.

After the women had gotten Robin Hood to the room beneath the eaves, the Prioress sent all of the others away; then, taking a little cord, she tied it tightly about Robin's arm, as though she were about to bleed him. And so she did bleed him, but the vein she opened was not one of those that lie close and blue beneath the skin; deeper she cut than that for she opened one of those veins through which the bright red blood runs leaping from the heart. Of this Robin knew not; for, though he saw the blood flow, it did not come fast enough to make him think that there was anything ill in it.

Having done this vile deed, the Prioress turned and left her cousin, locking the door behind her. All that livelong day the blood ran from Robin Hood's arm, nor could he check it, though he strove in every way to do so. Again and again he called for help, but no help came, for his cousin had betrayed him, and Little John was too far away to hear his voice. So he bled and bled until he felt his strength slipping away from him. Then he arose, tottering, and bearing himself up by the palms of his hands against the wall, he reached his bugle horn at last. Thrice he sounded it, but weakly and faintly, for his breath was fluttering through sickness and loss of strength; nevertheless, Little John heard it where he lay in the glade, and, with a heart all sick with dread, he came running and leaping toward the nunnery. Loudly he knocked at the door, and in a loud voice shouted for

them to let him in; but the door was of massive oak, strongly barred, and studded with spikes, so they felt safe, and bade Little John begone.

Then Little John's heart was mad with grief and fear for his master's life. Wildly he looked about him, and his sight fell upon a heavy stone mortar, such as three men could not lift nowadays. Little John took three steps forward, and, bending his back, heaved the stone mortar up from where it stood deeply rooted. Staggering under its weight, he came forward and hurled it crashing against the door. In burst the door, and away fled the frightened nuns, shrieking, at his coming. Then Little John strode in, and never a word said he, but up the winding stone steps he ran till he reached the room wherein his master was. Here he found the door locked also, but, putting his shoulder against it, he burst the locks as though they were made of brittle ice.

There he saw his own dear master leaning against the gray stone wall, his face all white and drawn, and his head swaying to and fro with weakness. Then, with a great, wild cry of love and grief and pity, Little John leaped forward and caught Robin Hood in his arms. Up he lifted him as a mother lifts her child, and carrying him to the bed, laid him tenderly thereon.

And now the Prioress came in hastily, for she was frightened at what she had done, and dreaded the vengeance of Little John and the others of the band; then she stanched the blood by cunning bandages, so that it flowed no more. All the while Little John stood grimly by, and after she had done he sternly bade her to begone, and she obeyed, pale and trembling. Then, after she had departed, Little John spake cheering words, laughing loudly, and saying that all this was a child's fright, and that no stout yeoman would die at the loss of a few drops of blood. "Why," quoth he, "give thee a se'ennight and thou wilt be roaming the woodlands as boldly as ever."

But Robin shook his head and smiled faintly where he lay. "Mine own dear Little John," whispered he, "Heaven bless thy kind, rough heart. But, dear friend, we will never roam the woodlands together again."

"Ay, but we will!" quoth Little John loudly. "I say again, ay—out upon it—who dares say that any more harm shall come upon thee? Am I not by? Let me see who dares touch"—Here he stopped of a sudden, for his words choked him. At last he said, in a deep, husky voice, "Now, if aught of harm befalls thee because of this day's doings, I swear by Saint George that the red cock shall crow over the rooftree of this house, for the hot flames shall lick every crack and cranny thereof. As for these women"—here he ground his teeth—"it will be an ill day for them!"

But Robin Hood took Little John's rough, brown fist in his white hands, and chid him softly in his low, weak voice, asking him since what time Little John had thought of doing harm to women, even in vengeance. Thus he talked till, at last, the other promised, in a choking voice, that no ill should fall upon the place, no matter what happened. Then a silence fell, and Little John sat with Robin Hood's hand in his, gazing out of the open window, ever and anon swallowing a great lump that came in his throat. Meantime the sun dropped slowly to the west, till all the sky was ablaze with a red glory. Then Robin Hood, in a weak, faltering voice, bade Little John raise him, that he might look out once more upon the woodlands; so the yeoman lifted him in his arms, as he bade, and Robin Hood's head lay on his friend's shoulder. Long he gazed, with a wide, lingering look, while the other sat with bowed head, the hot tears rolling one after another from his eyes, and dripping upon his bosom, for he felt that the time of parting was near at hand. Then, presently, Robin Hood bade him string his stout bow for him, and choose a smooth fair arrow from his quiver.

This Little John did, though without disturbing his master or rising from where he sat. Robin Hood's fingers wrapped lovingly around his good bow, and he smiled faintly when he felt it in his grasp; then he nocked the arrow on that part of the string that the tips of his fingers knew so well. "Little John," said he, "Little John, mine own dear friend, and him I love better than all others in the world, mark, I prythee, where this arrow lodges, and there let my grave be digged. Lay me with my face toward the East, Little John, and see that my resting place be kept green, and that my weary bones be not disturbed."

As he finished speaking, he raised himself of a sudden and sat upright. His old strength seemed to come back to him, and, drawing the bowstring to his ear, he sped the arrow out of the open casement. As the shaft flew, his hand sank slowly with the bow till it lay across his knees, and his body likewise sank back again into Little John's loving arms; but something had sped from that body, even as the winged arrow sped from the bow.

For some minutes Little John sat motionless, but presently he laid that which he held gently down, then, folding the hands upon the breast and covering up the face, he turned upon his heel and left the room without a word or a sound.

Upon the steep stairway he met the Prioress and some of the chief among the sisters. To them he spoke in a deep, quivering voice, and said he, "An ye go within a score of feet of yonder room, I will tear down your rookery over your heads so that not one stone shall be left upon another. Bear my words well in mind, for I mean them." So saying, he turned and left them, and they presently saw him running rapidly across the open, through the falling of the dusk, until he was swallowed up by the forest.

The early gray of the coming morn was just beginning

to lighten the black sky toward the eastward when Little John and six more of the band came rapidly across the open toward the nunnery. They saw no one, for the sisters were all hidden away from sight, having been frightened by Little John's words. Up the stone stair they ran, and a great sound of weeping was presently heard. After a while this ceased, and then came the scuffling and shuffling of men's feet as they carried a heavy weight down the steep and winding stairs. So they went forth from the nunnery, and, as they passed through the doors thereof, a great, loud sound of wailing arose from the glade that lay all dark in the dawning, as though many men, hidden in the shadows, had lifted up their voices in sorrow.

Thus died Robin Hood, at Kirklees Nunnery, in fair Yorkshire, with mercy in his heart toward those that had been his undoing; for thus he showed mercy for the erring and pity for the weak through all the time of his living.

His yeomen were scattered henceforth, but no great ill befell them thereafter, for a more merciful sheriff and one who knew them not so well succeeding the one that had gone, and they being separated here and there throughout the countryside, they abided in peace and quietness, so that many lived to hand down these tales to their children and their children's children.

A certain one sayeth that upon a stone at Kirklees is an old inscription. This I give in the ancient English in which it was written, and thus it runs:

> HEAR UNDERNEAD DIS LAITL STEAN
> LAIS ROBERT EARL OF HUNTINGTUN
> NEA ARCIR VER AS HIE SAE GEUD
> AN PIPL KAULD IM ROBIN HEUD
> SICK UTLAWS AS HI AN IS MEN
> VIL ENGLAND NIDIR SI AGEN.
>
> OBIIT 24 KAL. DEKEMBRIS 1247.

And now, dear friend, we also must part, for our merry journeyings have ended, and here, at the grave of Robin Hood, we turn, each going his own way.